"Balto's Nose"

a novel of the

Monuments Men and Women

Thomas Thibeault

"Endurance · Fidelity · Intelligence"

Ridgetop Press
P.O. Box 1522
Swainsboro
Georgia
USA
30401

The Library of Congress has catalogued Balto's Nose as follows:

LCCN 2011913418

Thibeault, Thomas.
Balto's Nose/Thomas Thibeault

ISBN 978-0-9836618-0-1

1 World War II - fiction. 2. Art History - fiction.
3. Art Looting - fiction 4. New York - fiction.

For Anna

Chapter 1

Pilgrimage

She was so perfect. She sat secure in her own beauty, defying all to ignore her. Maturer than a girl, younger than the man sitting beside her, she could have stepped straight out of the cover of a glamour magazine. She was perfect, so Michael hated her.

Michael sat behind her, glimpsing her profile as she spoke to the older man beside her. His contempt bubbled into a sneer, and he thought she had all the beauty money could buy. She was no different from the paintings lining the auction room walls, the Trophy Wife bought by the rich old man. Michael had not yet crossed the shadow line into middle age, so he could afford such indignation. His grandfather had insisted they spend the morning at Sotheby's Auction Rooms, "just like when you were a kid," and out of love and duty, Michael had agreed to tag along with Granddad Glenn.

Glenn sat beside Michael, savoring the atmosphere like a perfect Martini. He loved the decorous bustle of the auction, for Sotheby's had always been his Aladdin's Cave, a shrine to his love. The building's eleven stories of geometric steel and glass snuggled into 72nd Street and York Avenue like a cathedral or a Mecca, and Glenn smiled at the quaint conceit of "Auction Rooms." He imagined paintings flying around the Empire State Building looking for somewhere to roost and statues strolling through Times Square. New York was Glenn's home, but Sotheby's brought the whole world home to him.

Glenn gazed at the backs of the heads of the couple sitting before him. The man had arrived at that choice between spreading baldness or expensive replacements and looked like he could afford either option. The younger woman clutching his arm let her hair sweep over square shoulders and ripple into a brown cascade. He didn't have to ask Michael's opinion of the couple because he had long accepted his grandson's resentment of the wealthy. Glenn had learned to enjoy the differences between people, but it had taken most of his eighty-two years, like interest mounting in a long forgotten account.

The chairs were always arranged like neat pews, and they sat in their usual seats, second row from the back to better scrutinize the bidders. Glenn had raised his grandson for three of Michael's almost four decades and could read his every mood. But such things would be put aside on this trip. Glenn swung his right leg over his left knee, wedged his left elbow onto the back of the chair, and propped up his cheek over a balled fist. He always settled into this pose so he could see everything and listen to the war stories of his memory.

The auction hall was two stories high with the stage and the auctioneer's podium front and center. Glenn's eyes wandered to the left aisle and blinked at attendants carrying the paintings, statues, and any object that would sell, from the adjoining rooms to the stage. For most of his adult life, Glenn had witnessed the procession of masterpieces, childhood treasures, and just plain junk parade down the aisle to the auction block. His head swiveled to the right so he could inspect a choir of twenty not too pretty and not too old women sitting along a tier of tables running from the front to the back of the hall. They sat before computers wearing shell-like earphones, poised to process the whispers of "absent bidders." Glenn remembered the days when those girls grabbed at a rainbow of telephones, a different color for each continent, but now the computers ruled the tables.

From London to Paris to New York, Sotheby's auctioned everything valuable because just selling through Sotheby's made anything valuable. It was a money machine more precise than the mint, and much faster. The company supplied cash to bankrupts and class to billionaires, with a thirty percent commission on every transaction. Under the auctioneers' gavels, Sotheby's was the master of the art of the profitable.

Glenn had seen the fruits of genius stand before hushed worshippers as the price mounted to unbelievable heights on the electronic board to the right of the auctioneer. At one auction, a framed set of the Duke of Windsor's briefs fetched $10,000, and Glenn had mused, "he must have been in such a hurry to 'marry the woman he loved' that he left his underpants behind." When Van Gogh's *Portrait of Dr. Gachet* was sold, the machine ran out of numbers and the auctioneer's voice cracked at "eighty million dollars." Glenn had sat stunned with the rest of the pilgrims. When he could finally comprehend the money changing hands, his humor erupted. He could not stop giggling because he remembered that Dr. Gachet had treated Van Gogh for insanity and had almost died of shock when his patient committed suicide. This money madness probably would have killed both Gachet and Van Gogh.

Michael squirmed and turned to Glenn to demand, "Did we have to come here today?" Glenn feigned a spasm of rheumatism to cover his impish smile.

"These trips can be very profitable."

"You know I hate these places, Anda."

"Anda" was Michael's pet name for Glenn. When Michael was still trying to get his mouth around speech, he couldn't pronounce "granddad," so the smiling face peering through the bars of Michael's crib would be forever "Anda." Michael would roll "Anda" around his mouth in times of trouble, and the taste of his grandfather's pet-name never failed to heal both childish hurts and the searing disappointments of manhood. There had been plenty of both. "Well, if it's that important to you, I suppose one wasted morning is Okay," Michael conceded.

Michael habitually dismissed the sellers from the process and gave up any interest in their possessions. The owners were not important to Michael. They were the past, but the sale was all about the future and the spiraling profits which these objects would generate.

"You know this has nothing to do with art. It's all just business," Michael grunted.

"Of course it is," said Glenn, "but it's still a good show... and we don't even have to buy tickets."

The owners fascinated Glenn. He enjoyed speculating about why they were selling their most prized possessions. He would make up the personal problems that had forced them to part with such treasures. Maybe they had children to put through college, so the sale was to ensure a brighter future. Maybe they had terrible diseases and selling a painting that had been in the family for generations was the only way to pay medical bills and have any future at all. For Glenn, the sale was the place where the familiar past met the uncertain future in the desperate present.

The front rows were an expectant wobble of the wealthiest bidders, but the seats at the back formed a little huddle where the merely curious always sat. Michael looked over the rows of art work waiting to be auctioned and ran a desultory thumb over the edge of the catalogue. He had just enough experience to know that the catalogue was both an advertisement and a souvenir. They were just pages waiting for cheap frames and had no bearing on what was really happening. It was like an old-time slave sale; nobody cared about the mulattos, quadroons or octoroons shuffling to the block. All that was necessary was to judge the future profits generated by the sale and the ownership. The hubbub in the hall mumbled itself into a hushed thrill, as a very little man approached the podium. Glenn winked and said, "Ah, today we have The Leprechaun."

Michael smiled at their private joke and remembered the tale Anda told him one St. Patrick's Day. The leprechauns were such nasty little creatures that The Shining Ones had grown weary of the leprechauns' crude jokes and childish pranks, so they decided to punish the little pests. The Shining Ones commanded the leprechauns to guard the pot of gold at the end of the rainbow. The leprechauns were so grateful for this honor that they wept for joy as they danced over the rainbow and disappeared into the clouds. The Shining Ones were so amazed by the leprechauns' greed and stupidity they never told the leprechauns that guarding the gold at the end of the rainbow was a punishment. The diminutive auctioneer beamed his pride as guard of the gold and took such pleasure in every resounding thump of his gavel that Anda and Michael had named him their Leprechaun. Whenever he appeared at the podium, Michael would always hum "Over the Rainbow," but they never shared their joke with the auctioneer, for that would have been cruel.

They sat watching the stream of exquisite objects parade past them and they listened to the audience's gasps at each crack of the gavel. Glenn was amused, once again, that greed was so much more satisfying than lust, for the sheer number of one afternoon's sales would have exhausted any Casanova. He had long ago come to the conclusion that, in the world of art sales, money was more important than sex. You had to recuperate after sex, but money feeds the appetite with each deposit. A man may spend himself between the sheets, but there was no limit to the spending and getting for people who had enough money to make even more money, by multiplying what they already had. He was sure that each successful bidder had to smoke or drink or meditate until the trembling of increased bank accounts finally settled itself into the desire for more.

Michael had no such thoughts. He knew and appreciated Anda's view of what they were doing, for he had grown up surrounded by the reproduction paintings in Anda's Brooklyn apartment. The Saturdays of his childhood had been spent playing with Anda. They started with a breakfast of soup in the kitchen. Michael loved the canned noodle soup just because Anda had cooked it especially for him, and there were hot dogs in Central Park for dessert. Anda's apartment was close to the college, so it was a weekly adventure to walk the cracked streets to his office, pick up his students' papers, and then wander the neighborhood. Those walks were a treasure hunt to discover adventures in every store window, see webs of diamonds spraying from corner fire hydrants, and hear tales of woe or longing or triumph from each of Anda's students. The students all were little mysteries wrapped up in whatever clothes were fashionable at the time. Michael could remember each decade by the cut of one's pant legs, from rolled up straight leg jeans to bell-bottomed booby traps to the carefree accordion of chinos. The calendar was a slow motion fashion show teased by the zephyrs of taste, his little way of remembering his days and years without actually having to count them.

Michael was indifferent to the auctions because he judged them as predictable as a football game. The outcome was always the same: someone bought what someone sold and the thing changed hands and that was about it. Sometimes it was fun to look at the people and wile away the time until Anda jerked his head and they could have a hot dog.

But Glenn never tired of the ceremony of the auction, as regular as a Mass and as varied as the needs of each supplicant. Today's worshippers were no different. There was the expectant old lady who had found a retirement supplement in a cobwebbed suitcase. The sprinkling of art school students affecting boredom and signing their superiority to anyone who caught their rolling eyes. The lawyers and bankers seeking culture for office walls. Glenn had imagined them all in a thousand and one lives.

To Michael, the professionals with pencils poised over catalogues and notebooks wouldn't be out of place at the dog track, where they would probably get a higher return on their investments. The paintings should be lined up against a wall with windows for "Win," "Place," or "Show." It was all the same thing, give or take a couple centuries of dust. The man in front of Michael was the usual collection of credit cards with his store-bought wife. Michael cast a cold eye over the expensive hairdo and gauged her just old enough to offer experience and expectation in equal proportions. She was definitely in control of the older man because she was exactly what he had ordered.

Glenn smiled indulgently at Michael out of the corner of his eye, for he knew his grandson was working up to his usual rant against the wealthy. Michael had money problems and resented the rich because he thought they had no such problems. Glenn appreciated that there was a touch of the revolutionary in Michael, calling it envy and blaming himself for his grandson's intolerance. Glenn thought he had told baby Michael just one too many bed-time stories of Robin Hood and the tales had grown legs and green tights as the boy became a man. Still, it was better to be wrong for the right reasons than right for all the wrong reasons. They were together and it was enough for Glenn that they were having another Saturday morning in town.

The procession over the auctioneer's podium continued with the regularity of a train schedule. With every sale, the prices and the excitement mounted, until the congregation could hardly recover from the shock of the previous purchase before the next one was announced. Michael was bored. He fidgeted for the hot dog reward in the park. Glenn lounged patiently behind his impish smile, waiting for the surprise.

The Leprechaun introduced the last painting as if he were the Master of Ceremonies at a state banquet. Two grinning assistants carried in a painting and delicately placed it on an easel. The Leprechaun gestured grandly toward it and announced, "Sotheby's is proud to offer for your consideration one of the truly great jokes of the art world, the *Head of Christ* by Han van Meegeren." Michael's mouth gaped into a strangled question.

Michael stared at the painting from Anda's apartment. The *Head of Christ* had hung amidst the clutter of framed prints scissored from outdated calendars, reproductions scotch taped to the wall, canvases from mediocre students, and photos of his father, his mother, and himself. Michael remembered the living room walls as four jumbles of rectangles huddling so closely together that he couldn't tell the actual color of the walls. The amazing kaleidoscope of Anda's apartment was his whole childhood, where every frame was a story and every story was a time when he loved his Anda more than the story could tell. He stared; there was something so jolting about seeing the Jesus Head in the auction hall that it took time to understand the painting was really being sold. He had never realized it was something other people would ever want, having taken it for granted all his life. Seeing that painting at Sotheby's was like running into an old friend at an emergency room. "How did?" he whispered, but Anda's "sh" silenced him with a librarian's commanding hiss.

The Leprechaun chortled to the hall, "You will all immediately recognize that this is one of the world's outstanding forgeries." He launched into his little lecture explaining how, in 1937, Han van Meegeren secretly painted copies of the Dutch Masters. Glenn recounted the tale in his own mind, for he had pieced together every scrap of van Meegeren's fraud for some of his more enterprising students. Van Meegeren's talent had been dismissed by the rulers of the art world as that of a "mere society painter." The rejection had consumed van Meegeren, until he discovered his most delicious revenge. He would paint a canvas in the style of Jan Vermeer of Delft and pass it off as an original.

The Leprechaun dazzled them with more details of van Meegeren's criminal comedy. "For over five years, he experimented to reproduce in the 20th century the masterpieces of the 17th century. Van Meegeren's mastery of technique and his obsession with the art market earned him a rather large fortune in fakes. He would trick the art critics into judging a van Meegeren as a long lost Vermeer and show them up for the fools they were. Indeed, the experts all verified the authenticity of van Meegeren's daubs as the work of the 17th century master Jan Vermeer. By rescuing these "lost" Vermeers, the critics who rejected van Meegeren became his victims. *Head of Christ* is one of his most successful and profitable experiments."

Glenn knew van Meegeren had succeeded beyond his wildest dreams. Van Meegeren's fake Vermeers were a master forger's sleight-of-hand and his critic-victims never knew he had turned their expertise and arrogance against them. The more they praised themselves for their discoveries, the louder van Meegeren cackled to the bank. He produced copies not just of Vermeer, but also of Rembrandt and Rubens, and set them adrift through Holland's auction rooms and private collections. The Dutch State Museum even bought one of the most obvious fakes, *The Supper at Emmaus*, paying the highest price for any painting in their collection. The newly unearthed Vermeers were a cultural and financial miracle, and a mirage.

Glenn understood van Meegeren's desire for revenge and was fascinated that he got away with it for as long as he did. The more Glenn researched the fraud, the more he appreciated van Meegeren's problem. Even though van Meegeren had completely fooled his enemies, he had to savor his revenge in silence. Trouble was, he could never tell anybody, for that would be the end of the scam. If he continued to produce more fakes, he would become wealthy beyond even his almost limitless appetites for women, the high life, and morphine. Glenn knew that van Meegeren could not perpetrate such a fraud on his own. The more Glenn delved into the story, the more he discovered that van Meegeren had used a web of crooked art dealers and ignorant collectors as his middlemen. His accomplices knew nothing of each other, so the secret was as secure as the money was safe. Van Meegeren bragged to himself that he needed a net income to support his gross habits, so he chose the cash over the public humiliation of his tormentors. He kept his mouth shut and his wallet open and spent World War II moving from one of his mansions to another. The audience thrilled to the twists in the tale. Glenn thought the whole thing luscious.

The Leprechaun lowered his voice to raise the suspense and confided to the hall, "Van Meegeren's forgery was so successful that Herman Goering purchased it, thinking that he had finally acquired the work of Vermeer, the most coveted addition to his collection. Van Meegeren was delighted with the sale until he discovered that Goering had paid for the fake painting with counterfeit money."

The room erupted in knowing laughter, but Glenn knew this was one of the art world's little fantasies. Goering had not bought a forgery with forged money. He had traded 137 "decadent" paintings by Monet, Van Gogh, and Pissarro for van Meegeren's Vermeer. Goering had bought one fake with a truck-load of masterpieces because he couldn't tell the difference between the fraud and the real thing. That was what so amused Glenn: a monster such as Goering could acquire anything he wanted, but he didn't know what was in front of his face. Goering buying a van Meegeren with Monets was an even greater joke than van Meegeren's revenge on the art world.

Michael listened to every wheezy chortle but felt a part of his childhood was being taken away. He hadn't looked at the painting in years - it was just so much wallpaper - but he felt that he somehow owned it. This sale was turning into a robbery, but of what he couldn't actually tell. He was jolted out of his indignation by the first bid of "one hundred thousand dollars."

The Leprechaun held a round disc of hardwood between his thumb and forefinger and gestured to the bidders with his pinky, "Do I hear two, two hundred thousand," and the little finger surprisingly launched at the man with the trophy wife. The Leprechaun's arm spiraled to the far right of the room. "Do I hear three?"

Glenn saw the bidding was so quick that Michael couldn't keep up with the soaring sums. "He was never good at arithmetic," Glenn thought.

The bidding danced between the floor and the line of laptops. Heads nodded from the hall and the women shot glances over their computers firing bids to the podium. Nobody knew who was bidding through the internet, or even if the computers were connected, but it didn't matter. They all believed that every bid was as real as a banker's check and the belief fed the frenzy. Glenn's head followed the rhythm of the bids, casually swaying from the hall to the computers, as if he were at a tennis match. Pulses quickened when the bids spurted from a walk to a trot and the auction became a melee of credit cards and check books.

The man with the trophy wife seemed to be in charge. About every five bids, he would add a few more thousand dollars to the pile, and the audience would applaud his nonchalant confidence. The atmosphere took on a quality somewhere between a cattle auction and a casino, but there was no doubting that this was a classy affair. Nobody shouted. Everyone was civil and their excitement was all the more intense because it was so restrained.

The Leprechaun's finger arched to the back of the room, and Michael whispered to Glenn, "One million?" Glenn nodded. Michael's eyes slammed into the *Head of Christ* as if watching a car crash in slow motion. There was nothing slow about this wreck. The bids crumpled into each other, each more hopefully victorious than the last. The bidders couldn't bear to look. They could only listen. They heard "one million, three hundred thousand." Trembling voices fumbled "four," coughed "five," whispered "six." The trophy man simply called "two." There was a pause as the audience thought he had started to count backwards, and then an explosion of admiring gasps when the Leprechaun confirmed that "the bid is two million."

Michael's mind flew into moneyed vertigo as the bidding resumed. His ears registered the antiphony of voices between the audience and the wall, but he just couldn't understand the sums through his mind. All he could see was a green tornado billowing around the *Head of Christ*.

Glenn sat as composed as a mourner at the funeral of a hated relative and just waited for the end. There were three taps of the gavel and the auctioneer delayed the gratification just long enough for silence to descend. They waited for the benediction until the auctioneer breathed a cracked whisper, "sold for three million and seven-hundred thousand dollars."

The bidders uncurled themselves into a standing ovation for one of the computer girls. They applauded her stamina and she stood to take her bow. She had stayed the course and her client was now the proud owner of a real fake.

The audience paraded from their seats to the reception rooms and the bars. Glenn stood for an old man's seventh inning stretch, but Michael was unable to stand. He looked up at Anda, waggled his head, and breathed "How?" Glenn smiled down at Michael to say, "Well. That's a two hot dog story."

Glenn gently lifted Michael by the elbow and guided him through the crowd. They wove their way through a gaggle of bidders clutching glasses in commiseration or congratulation. Michael did not see the large man raising a Martini glass to Glenn as they passed the bar. The woman turned her face to Glenn and threw a smile over her left shoulder. Glenn's eye was caught by the sparkle and her smile cascaded over rose madder lips. But it was the glow of her pearl earring that glazed her picture. Glenn liked to mix the colors of people in his mind. Michael was deaf to the excited hubbub and ignored the man with the Martini and the expensive wife as Glenn led him out the main door into the cold blasts of the plaza.

Glenn walked Michael up York Avenue and turned left on 79th Street. They played hop scotch with the jammed cars on 2nd Avenue and slowly marched to Park Avenue. By the time Glenn had walked his grandson to the corner of 5th Avenue, Michael's mind was just starting to decode three point seven million dollars.

They waited for the green light to cross 5th Avenue into Central Park. Michael fixed his gaze on the steam rising from the hot dog wagon huddled up against the iron railings. Glenn stamped his feet and buried his chin deeper into his collar, turned up against the first blasts of a New York winter. Glenn saw the couple from the auction walk past them to the subway entrance. The woman looked directly at Glenn. She was so perfect, mature beauty masking a depth of understanding of her world. Her face was liquid merriment and Glenn loved her for the gift. Michael didn't notice them at all. He stood rooted to the sidewalk facing the hot dog stand across the avenue and didn't see the couple disappear down the subway entrance. Michael's cold breath mumbled to Glenn, "Do we really have three million, seven hundred thousand dollars for that picture?"

"Yup," chirped Glenn, "minus the commission and the taxes."

Michael wanted answers, but Glenn just said, "You'll have to pay for the hot dogs. I'm fresh out of cash."

Chapter 2

Memorials

Central Park gave Glenn and Michael a welcome and familiar silence. The farther they walked from angry horns, the closer they came to childish squeals, and as the sirens faded into distant missions, the birds massaged their ears. There was no need to speak. As always, they had finished their ceremonial lunch on the benches at the 79th Street entrance and started their wander along friendly paths.

For Glenn, the Park had its own understated uniqueness. Everybody thought it was natural because it had a few trees strategically placed to give the illusion of rustic walks from long ago. But Glenn knew that everything about the park was completely artificial, even the earth they walked on. It was a huge rectangle, a canvas where the city had painted its life for a century and a half. Central Park had first been a cemetery and a shanty town, but then the civic-minded millionaires cleared out the living and the dead to make a space for "refreshing airs and the recreation of the populace." It was to be a place of rest in the midst of frantic work and, for most of its life and many New Yorkers, it had fulfilled its promises. The park had served generations and Glenn had drunk in his fair share of its invigorating airs.

Over eight decades, Glenn had become friends with the park. He had probed its little mysteries and, because he could love its beauty, the park had revealed its secrets to him. Glenn had come to see the magic of the park change from season to season. The first flowers of Spring washed the slushy terraces in pastels to blossom into the deeper watercolors of Summer. The Fall scattered leaves and the park rioted in the vibrant mellowness of landcapes in oil. But Winter brought out the starkness of life. The first snow etched the bare branches with silver sparkles and then the park would hibernate for three months in the deep, engraved lines of midwinter.

It was always Winter when Glenn faced his choices. He would hide in the park, but the place forced him to face his decisions. The park in Winter was etched with his own choices, so he found it peculiarly fitting that, with the first dusting of snow, the park showed Glenn the engraving of his own life. When he stood back to consider the park over the years, he could see his reflection in its changing textures. In his forties, he had chuckled to himself that all that time the park had been talking to him, but he hadn't been listening. Since then, he had grown eyes and opened his ears to understand the tales the park was telling of himself.

He had even attempted to share this seasonal artistry on a field trip with one of his Introduction to Art classes from the college, but they only appreciated the shopping and each other. His lecture on the symmetry of the ponds bored them, and they were most indifferent to the ten million cartloads of soil that had been imported from New Jersey because the trees wouldn't grow in the stoney soil of Manhattan. Glenn had no answers to the students' persistent questions about the "park fairies" and the "junkies," so he let them follow their dreams to a shopping mall, the subway, and home. After that fruitless day of wandering through their ignorance, Glenn had vowed never to leave a classroom again, not with students, and, true to his promise, spent the next thirty years teaching from text books and colored slides.

Michael thought of the park as his own because Anda had opened his ears. Now he could savor the assurances whispered to him around every corner. The Children's Zoo was his time to remember the bears and the cat. When he was six years old, Anda had taken him to the zoo to see the animals displayed in their own fairy-tale houses. The Three Little Pigs were housed in structures of wood, straw, and brick, and The Three Bears had forsaken the plaster cave for their very own cozy residence complete with waiting bowls of porridge nailed to a picnic table. Goldilocks was nowhere to be seen, but the three cubs looked like they had stepped out of an illustration in a Little Golden Book.

Michael had dragged Anda's sleeve to the edge of the enclosure, when a cat jumped into the bears' pit. Glenn was desperate to divert Michael's attention back to the Three Little Pigs because he didn't want his grandson to witness the cat being torn to pieces, but Michael would not move. After a few seconds, Glenn too was immobile in amazement. The cat had jumped over the safety moat and sat within reach of the cub. It launched itself into the cub's lap, but the bear only swayed back and forth on its haunches in delight and licked the cat. The cub bellowed laughter when the cat dug its claws into the thick black fur, and soon the cat was coated with saliva.

Glenn and Michael watched this performance three times. Each time, the cat would wander a few feet away from the disappointed cub and three times it would race back to the warm nest of fur to receive its licking. Soon the bear slid onto its back and the cat nestled into a snooze on the bear's tummy. The bear was as gentle as a nursing mother and the cat thoroughly enjoyed its cleaning.

Glenn was so fascinated that he asked one of the zookeepers about the scene. The keeper explained that this happened every afternoon, just before closing time. The cat threaded its way through the legs of visitors, scrunched through the bars of the palings, and jumped the moat into the bears' den. When it left on soggy paws, "that cat rules the whole neighborhood for ten blocks 'cause every dog thinks someone let loose the bears on them." After that, Glenn usually let Michael stop to savor the wonders each day presented and didn't worry about "what may be bad for the child to see."

The park was also the only place where Glenn didn't balk at the memory of his only daughter's death. Somewhere between the pond and the statues, he allowed himself to meet her again. Jessica had been killed in a car crash in 1985 along with her husband George. The new fangled air bags had been useless in a head-on with both cars going 85 on the Brooklyn-Queens Expressway just over Flushing Avenue.

*****

Glenn knew it had been quick because the policeman told him there were no tire tracks leading up to the crater of the two cars. “You must understand, Sir, they knew nothing because they didn’t have time for the split second it takes to hit the brakes.” Glenn loved the policeman for his soft words and tough kindness. He could have mouthed some platitude about “didn’t know what hit them,” but the policeman could see that Glenn needed something more. He needed the truth. The policeman didn’t shy away from his duty to comfort, but he took care not to add to Glenn's pain. He gave just the right amount of detail to reassure Glenn, but not enough to leave him with nightmares. Glenn needed facts to quiet his pain, proof to make him believe his daughter hadn’t suffered, and the policeman supplied it. The angel was in the details.

The other driver wasn’t the usual drunk who walks away without a scratch. He was a confused old man who had somehow gotten on the wrong side of the road. It was the middle of the night and the traffic was too light for him to notice, so he hit the gas and the time it took him to get up to speed was the last ten seconds of three lives.

Months later, the policeman called Glenn and asked to come ’round to the apartment, “at any time which would be convenient for you, Mr. Carnehan.” The policeman brought one black and white photograph that looked like something Weegee would place in the Evening News. Fearful that the policeman was going to show him bits of Jessica scattered over the road, Glenn looked away from the photo. “It’s OK, Sir, this is just a picture of road repairs.” Glenn looked into the rectangle and saw two concrete crash barriers on the freeway. They did not join and were separated by about six feet. “The other car went through this hole in the cement wall. There was construction on the road that night, and somebody forgot to connect the wall separating the two lanes of traffic. The old man simply took a wrong turn in a place where there should have been no turn and gunned the engine to get away from all the construction. He thought he was on the right side of the road, but he was going the wrong way."

Glenn and Ellen sat stunned with their forefingers and thumbs holding up the white edges of the photo, as if he were hanging laundry out to dry. A simple mistake had torn a whole generation out of their lives. One wrong turn and grandparents had become parents to their own grandson. And it all happened in seconds, and nobody was really to blame.

Glenn offered the photo to the policeman, but he waved away Glenn's hand. "Naw, dat's awright. I made another print for you, so's you'd know what really happened." The angel in a rumpled sports coat and an uncomfortable tie had given Glenn the proof his mind demanded and had left him with the evidence to quell future doubts. There was something so considerate about this man that Glenn imagined a halo circling the policeman's head, but it was just late afternoon peeking through the window blinds.

*****

They marched down the Mall and walked by the carousel. As they had thirty years ago, they ignored the gaudy promises of a merry-go-round. Michael had sat for hours on one of its lead encrusted mounts, oblivious to the brass ring. Glenn had been lost to find something which would interest the child and resented the whirling circle's claim that "everyone loves the ride." The carousel's circle of lackadaisical light whirled in Glenn's memory and became the beach toy in their hall closet.

*****

After the funeral, Glenn had found the plastic ring they always took to Coney Island. Jessica was over-protective and would not allow Michael anywhere near the water without his "life preserver." There was always the little ceremony where Glenn would spread the blanket and raise the umbrella, while Jessica took her time blowing up the rubber ring which she was convinced would save her child from drowning and imagined shark attacks. Michael would hop with impatience and protest that he was too big for the ring, but Jessica ignored his whining and wriggling, pulled the ring over his head, and gave it a secure yank up to his armpits. Michael would escape and run to the sea and, if the ring did not fit snugly enough to allay her fears, Jessica would drag Michael back to the blanket and force more air into the tube until it held in place. After their last trip to the water, Jessie had tossed the ring into the hall closet because she was late and they had a long drive home down the freeway.

There were still grains of sand clinging to the heat welded seams of this life saver, pregnant with memory and pain. Glenn clutched the ring holding the last breath of his daughter and carefully placed it on the top shelf of the closet over the shoe boxes of family photos and souvenirs away from the inquisitive fingers of a ten-year-old.

The ring had nestled there for two years and would not give up its treasure. Glenn had waited for an afternoon when both he and Ellen, his wife, were both home with nothing planned for the evening. They sat on the couch in the living room talking of Jessica and looking over the pictures of her childhood and the family portrait of Jessica, George and Michael. They both knew what had to be done and had waited the two years it took to muster the courage they needed.

Ellen kept the apartment spotless and chided Glenn for his messiness, but together they knew where each of their possessions was placed and such domestic order helped them to heal their torn lives. When Glenn asked where the can opener was, Ellen could say, "It lives in the top left drawer near the sink." If a health inspector wandered into the apartment, he would probably write up a report saying that it was too clean.

Glenn retrieved the rubber ring from the hall shelf and brought it into the living room. Glenn and Ellen sat together and cuddled the circle on their laps. Glenn's firm fingers pinched the valve that held the last of their daughter and his aching heart opened the stopper to feel Jess's farewell kiss on his cheek. Jessie's scent filled Ellen's nose and for a moment Ellen was gazing down at her newborn. Parents should not outlive their children. They drank in Jessie's breath knowing it would be her last caress.

They sat watching the day sink beneath the living room window and draped the deflated ring over their arms. Ellen smoothed out its creases and folded it into a slice of rainbow. Glenn slowly slid it into a brown manilla envelope and they locked it into a shoe box reliquary on the top shelf of the hall closet for some distant finder to ask what it was and wonder "Why do old people keep all this junk?"

*****

Glenn and Michael continued their saunter through the park, ignoring the statues of a Polish king with crossed swords, Columbus planting a flag, and the trio of Alice, the Mad Hatter, and the March Hare. They rounded the pond, and Michael looked down the corridor of his life to see Anda teaching him how to skate.

*****

Anda and Nanna Ellen had cushioned the loss of his parents as best they could, but they were powerless to stop the voices in his head and the bullies of the fourth grade screaming "orphan." Subway rides and trips to the city were better than toys because he could spend his time with Anda rather than with the latest gadget designed to separate children from their parents' money. Nanna had considered the movies as a diversion but had refused to take Michael to *Cocoon,* about old people almost dying or *Prizzi's*

Honor, featuring yet another Mafia murder. They were too disgusting for Michael. The local flea pit had become a house of horrors. They just didn't make movies fit for children any more.

Anda had tried to interest Michael in building something, so the apartment became a Lego construction site. That lasted about three days and left them tripping over the debris of half-finished houses, derelict barns, and something that looked like a raccoon. Then there was the set of felt pens which were guaranteed to be "as washable as they were indestructible," but Michael had proven both claims false in a day. It was late October before Glenn discovered the skates calling to him from a window near the Flatbush subway station.

He bought them both a pair of skates and decided the pond at Central Park was the perfect location to get some fresh air. Anda didn't know how to skate well, but at least he could stand up. Michael would squat on the skates and Glenn would pull him a few feet with his rump leaving a snowy trail behind him. The object was to stretch Michael into a standing position without too much injury. The skates always gouged themselves into an abrupt halt, sending Michael sprawling forward into Anda's waiting arms. It took some time for Michael to realize that, if he kept the skates parallel, he could go forward, but if he let his toes bend into each other, they tripped his face into Anda's jacket or all the way down into an ice ridge. For weeks, the subway ride into Manhattan was the prelude to their shared prat-falls until they could hold hands, slalom from leg to leg in a generally forward motion and keep from cracking their skulls on the ice. Michael loved their horizontal failures, which made their vertical achievements all the more triumphant. They would always have the moment when they learned to stand tall on the ice.

Now, they could break out of their sloppy figure-eights and let their clutching hands and shaky legs guide them to the farthest shore of the pond. Michael tried to pick up some speed, forgot about the angle of the skates, and slid under Anda's legs to pile them both in a bruised heap. Somewhere in the cracked ridges and spiraled gouges of the ice, Michael's cold breath burped out a giggle. Glenn lay prostrate beside him and they laughed away their sorrows until they were surprised by their own joy.

*****

Without breaking step, they turned left off the Mall into East Drive. They walked with the easy stride of going to meet an old friend waiting for them just around the corner. As they rounded the curve, they saw a dog standing on top of a rocky mound to their right. The dog ignored them and gazed into the distant mist. The plaque on the mound showed a dog team rushing through snow drifts and proclaimed that the statue was the memorial to "Balto."

> "Dedicated to the indomitable spirit of the sled dogs that relayed antitoxins 660 miles over rough ice, across treacherous waters, through Arctic blizzards from Nenana to the relief of stricken Nome in the winter of 1925."

Purists would argue about whether Balto was an Alaskan malamute or a Siberian husky, and the question was hotly debated by patriotic kennel clubs during the Cold War. To Glenn and Michael, Balto was just "one hell of a dog."

*****

After their triumph on the ice, Glenn had introduced Michael to Balto. Michael was fascinated by the statue of the doggie with his head held high and "the sniffly nose." Glenn started to explain what Balto had done and made the mistake of telling Michael that Balto had been a "bad sled dog." Michael asked if Balto was a bad dog because he bit people, so Glenn made up a story of how Balto just liked to play and was always jumping up on people, always running after deer and leaving his driver in a drift. This was better than a cartoon and Glenn saw that Michael was really interested in the adventures of Balto. Glenn's finger traced the snowstorm molded onto the bronze plaque and told Michael, "when Balto raced into that blizzard, everybody thought the bad dog would turn over the sled, scatter the medicines, and hurt hundreds of people waiting for their vaccines."

Michael had been tuckered out by their skating and asked, "What's a vaccine?" Glenn said, "It's a special sort of medicine." He saw the curiosity light up Michael's eyes. "They didn't have trains, or airplanes, or even cars because they lived in Alaska near the North Pole where Santa lives. So, they had to have the special medicine taken to them by a man on a sled that was pulled by a team of dogs. Balto was the leader of the dogs and it was their job to deliver the medicine, but people were afraid Balto would just run off to play in the snow." Michael stared at the statue, and Glenn could see that Balto was running through Michael's mind. He kept the tale to the pitch of a ten-year-old's interest and let the dog do the talking. He whispered, "If Balto went to play, the people wouldn't get their medicine."

Michael was hungry for more, so Glenn added the details that would round out the story. "There was a fifty-mile stretch of really dangerous ice and open water. In that blizzard, the driver couldn't see his mittens in front of his face. All he could do was hold tight onto to the handles of the sled and trust to Balto's nose. It was in that moment the bad dog became a hero, for he never wavered, never broke his concentration. Balto kept to the track and led his team into Nome with the medicine."

Glenn waited for the images to dance in Michael's mind. When he saw Michael's eyes glint in admiration, he gave the meaning of the fable. "Balto probably didn't know what he had done, but he did it anyway. That's what courage is; when you don't know, but you do it just the same. Balto had no idea what was going to happen to him; he just knew he had to stay on the track which only he could smell. People have really bad noses, so Balto just kept on going, even though he didn't have any idea where he was going. Call it dumb or call it smart, I don't know what to call it, but I like to think that Balto knew he was doing something important. I hope he just sensed that keeping the track and running beyond the limits of his strength gave him something even his driver didn't have and didn't really know about. Dogs are funny that way. One moment they're off chasing rabbits and the next they're jumping through burning windows with a live baby in their mouths. I don't know why they do those things, but I like to think they know why. I just wish people were the same."

Glenn and Michael stood before their furry hero. Glenn took Michael's arm to help him up the slope. Their legs ached from the skating and their feet were a bit unsure, so every step was as carefully placed as a mountain explorer's. They climbed up the mound to Balto's side and rested with both hands on his metal back. Glenn clasped Michael's hand in his and they shuffled along Balto's hard fur to his head. Like thousands of other children before him, Michael stretched forth his hand to pet Balto. Tenderly, Glenn spread Michael's fingers over the statue's nose and caressed some of Balto's sprit into their own lives.

The metal on his muzzle had been rubbed to a gleaming beacon that would have made Rudolph jealous. What Michael liked best was that Balto had been a real, live dog. Rudolph was just a made-up Santa story. Rudolph would fly away into the clouds when children outgrew Santa Claus, but Balto would stand scanning the distance in Central Park forever. Delivering medicine was way better than delivering presents.

*****

There is no time to put away childish things when those things help us to live a life less anguished. The dog had brought relief to Alaskan children in the same year Glenn was born, and his memory would bring the same gifts of faith, hope, and courage to his grandson's life. Glenn listened to the echo of himself telling Michael, "Truth be told, when people complain that it's a dog's life, they've never met Balto."

Chapter 3

Album

The aftertaste of mustard, meat, and memory lingered through Michael's Saturday trip into the city and the subway ride home to Anda's Brooklyn apartment. Even before he had moved his family out to the country, Michael had long taken for granted the three stories of Anda's world. The building had weathered the assaults of time and survived the more brutal ravages of its tenants. The wood floors of its "select apartments" were first gouged by the Fox-trotting heels of Jazz Age flappers. They then absorbed the worried pacing of World War II, when they and their inhabitants longed for better days. The '50s filled every space with the pitter patter of baby booming veterans who soon escaped in their station wagons to the suburbs. Slumlords let the building slide into their rent-controlled '60s squalor until the tabloids cursed it as a "drug-riddled health hazard." Its Phoenix season dawned with savvy developers and signs proclaiming it a "restored historic site." So the building rose again on its third mortgage through clouds of brick dust and plaster powder.

Glenn saw the humor in the advertisements claiming that his home was "highly desirable" because he never wanted to live anywhere else. The apartment was Glenn and Ellen's honeymoon suite from the moment he carried her, wobbling over the threshold in 1947. They settled into the second-floor apartment and never left. The four rooms became their nest, an oasis that shrugged off everything the outside world threw at them. Houses, factories, stores and questionable warehouses rose and fell around them, but their home remained, a solitary witness to survival.

The design was so typical of Brooklyn that Glenn had come to love both its decorous symmetry and its functional convenience. The front door opened into the living room flooded with light from the bay windows stretched across the whole west wall. Two bedrooms punctuated the hall, which led from the front room to the back parlor, where the kitchen opened onto the yard and the world of alleys beyond. Glenn had studied the architect's original blueprint and was delighted to see the parlor was a suntrap for the morning light while the living room was a theatre for sunset. He loved the fact that he could start and end his day in sunlight, but Ellen was impressed by how the arrangement of the apartment would cut down on the electricity bills. They were both right.

Michael sat on the living room sofa staring at the blank rectangle where the *Head of Christ* used to grimace and pondered another sort of bill. The shock of three point seven million dollars stunned him, for he just couldn't fathom that Anda had all that money just hanging there with its mouth open all that time. "When did you paint the wall blue?" he asked Anda, and Glenn replied from the hall closet, "Nineteen fifty-two."

Glenn carried a small trunk into the living room and laid it on the floor beside Michael's feet. He sat beside Michael on the sofa and puffed, "You've never seen this stuff." Glenn delayed opening the box just long enough to capture Michael's interest. "I forget all that's in here, but let's have a look."

He popped the clasps and creaked open the lid to reveal an old uniform, folders of papers, and a photo album. He placed the album unopened on the coffee table.

"You look first," Glenn almost ordered.

Michael sensed that with the turn of each page he would gain knowledge he could never forget. That was how it always was when Anda would sit him on his knee and guide Little Michael through one of the big books of big pictures. These Adam and Eve moments were always annoying and made him a bit nervous, but his curiosity always won out. He slowly opened the album. Each page revealed old photographs held firmly at the corners by bright metal triangles. The pages were as black as the day they were bound into the old Woolworth's album because they'd never seen much daylight. The photos were all of soldiers during World War II. Michael thought they looked like those he'd seen in textbooks or documentaries about the "Greatest Generation." Glenn clearly remembered what would emerge with each opening, but he let Michael turn the pages, and waited for his reaction.

Glenn spoke almost in a whisper, pleading with his memory and conjuring up his youth. Michael needed a little reminding of his grandfather's time in the army. It was so long ago. Anda was one of the only people in his life who had never disappointed him. Anda, Nanna, rest her soul, and Michael's wife Anne added up to the quality of his life. The men in the photos gazed back at Michael and demanded "And what of us? We were once young and loved our families too." Michael's eyes were pulled closer to one photo and he blurted out, "There's you." Glenn swelled with the pride of Michael's recognition, "Yup. All twenty years of me. Full of piss and vinegar and the occasional beer."

Young Glenn's head twisted over his shoulder at the camera. The photographer had caught him in the act of drinking from his canteen as his helmet fell off the back of his head. Glenn recalled, "That was a very thirsty day. Somewhere sunny in Austria, if you can imagine."

Michael peered at another jagged square of Kodak paper and two men looked back at him. The exposure was too long and they all looked like the sun burned about ten feet away from them. Michael made out Glenn with legs and arms crossed, leaning against the hood of a jeep. The other man was sitting on the bumper of something that looked like a box on wheels with an open cab. Michael pointed to the man and raised an eyebrow. Glenn nodded, "Jimmy Mulvaney." The silence grew fat until Glenn broke it with a whisper, "A real character, but an enigma none the less."

Glenn smiled because he loved surprises and waited for Michael to turn the next page. Michael's head jerked back from the page. Glenn looked through the photo and across the decades at himself and Jimmy holding a painting. Michael demanded, "Is that the..."

"That's right. That's the *Mona Lisa.* We held the most famous painting in the world in our hands."

Glenn and Jimmy posed holding all four corners of da Vinci's masterpiece, and their smiles were as broad as her face was coy. The photo was magnificently clear, as though it had been taken that morning. Every line of the portrait was as well defined as the creases in their own faces.

"How the hell did you get this?" demanded Michael.

"A photographer from *Stars and Stripes* took it," Glenn explained. "He was a real pro. He even had a Speed Graphic camera. You know, he just told us to hold still, took one click, and that's what he produced. Magnificent."

Michael held his annoyance with Anda's rambling, "Anda, I didn't mean the photo. How did you get the painting?"

"We found it."

"Found it? Next you'll be telling me 'it followed me home.'"

"Yeah. We found it. That was my job during the war."

Michael was getting confused. He wondered if Anda was losing it.

"I thought you were in the infantry."

"I was, but near the end, they transferred me to the MFAA."

"The what?"

"Monuments, Fine Art, and Archives," Glenn declaimed with pride.

Michael turned his attention back to the photograph, and Glenn let the strange words seep through Michael's confusion. "Our job was to find all the stuff the Germans had stolen from museums and people's homes." Glenn paused for the decades to fill the gap between them before adding, "and get it back."

"So that's how you got the *Mona Lisa*?"

"She was just one. There were twenty-two thousand others on our list."

Michael was having a problem dealing with the numbers, so Glenn explained.

"The Germans just took anything they wanted from anybody they hated, which was just about everybody. They hated lots of people, mainly rich people. Sometimes they stole stuff while they were fighting and sometimes they waited until the fighting stopped and then they grabbed stuff by the trainload."

"What stuff?"

"I mean real quality stuff. Rembrandt, Rubens, Vermeer, da Vinci, Michaelangelo. You can't flip through an art book without hitting on some of the stuff that went through these hands. We found it all - well almost all. But we got enough to make sure people could know enough about art to feel sorry about how much they were still missing."

Glenn knew the heartache of robbery; he had seen too many lost loves and stolen lives. What amazed him was how people could grieve the loss of things they never had, like orphans mourning unknown parents. Michael's question dragged him from his thoughts. "How can you find twenty-two thousand pictures in the middle of a war?"

"It ain't easy, I can tell you, but we had a great bunch of guys. There were just fifteen of us, at first."

The numbers started to percolate through Michael's confusion. Three point seven million dollars, twenty-two thousand works of art, fifteen men. The enormity of what he had witnessed at Sotheby's and what he was hearing from his grandfather formed itself into one question. "Fifteen?" he asked.

"Counting the eight who were back in England doing the paperwork. We had seven in the field, and Jimmy and I were the drivers."

"So you just went out picking up pictures?" Michael prodded.

"Sort of, but you had to know what you were picking up."

"I guess they knew you were interested in art."

"No. The officers knew I could drive."

Michael's mind was juggling masterpieces, so Glenn explained. "Before the war, I was shoveling coal for the General Electric Company in Schenectady. I'd never even seen a museum, let alone a painting, until we got to France. I got interested in art because of what we did in the war, not the other way around. We were the strangest unit in the whole U.S. Army because we had more officers than enlisted men. Five officers and two sergeants. Everything was backwards."

"Sounds like a lot of saluting," said Michael.

"That was the great thing; there wasn't, except in the morning. Captain George Stout, now there was a real bonafide genius. He'd wake us up every morning at six thirty and we would all have to parade in front of each other. He would salute me and say 'Good Morning, Sergeant Carnehan,' I would return a real snappy salute and say 'Good Morning, Captain Stout,' and then everybody would salute everybody else and be really formal and then we would all call each other by our first names for the rest of the day. It was the damnedest thing. Of course, it was always 'Yes, Sir, No, Sir' when the brass were around, but the rest of the time it was 'Glenn, look at this,' or 'George, what the fuck's a triptych?' or 'Don't step on the mines, George.'"

Glenn pointed to a photo of a man in combat clothes with a sharp crease running down the sleeve of an arm holding a flashlight.

"That's George Stout, right there. He was the chief conservator of the Fogg Museum at Harvard."

"What's a conservator?" asked Michael.

"That's the old word for a conservationist, someone who restores paintings and statues. He knew everything from the canvas up. He practically invented the whole field of art conservation and without his talent, we might not have a single one of those paintings. They'd all be just dust and slime. He used to carry around rolls of army toilet paper, you know the kind that feels like a file running over your ass. We thought he was just prissy because he was always so neat and well dressed, even in his field fatigues. But then we found a whole load of paintings in a wrecked railroad car. There were bits and pieces of stuff everywhere. George picked up a painting that was about four hundred years old. He spread his fingers and just touched the face of the painting. That canvas looked like cornflakes floating in milk. If he'd have sneezed, a Rembrandt would have turned into a snow storm right there in that boxcar. He gently laid the painting on the floor and told me to get the toilet paper.

Kneeling there like we were in a church, he wet the toilet paper and bandaged that painting. He covered it with that wet paper and then painted the outside of the paper with plaster. He did this so carefully that the painting looked like a squished igloo. He wrapped it in an old overcoat and put the whole thing into an empty ammunition box and personally drove it to Holland. We both did. He didn't lose one flake. And that's why the *Portrait of Rembrandt's Wife* hangs in the National Gallery in Amsterdam to this day. Some people think that Mrs. Rembrandt looked a whole lot better after she got the Stout treatment."

"Were all you guys able to do things like that?" Michael asked in wonder.

"Not Jimmy and myself. We were just the drivers. You know, sort of the helpers. George called us 'Assistant Curators in Uniform.' He even got us extra money for danger pay."

"What's so dangerous about paintings?"

"Nothing, but the booby traps the Germans left behind could cut a guy in half. When the Germans left town, they'd even put grenades in teddy bears."

Michael was eager for more. Glenn was relieved to think that Michael was understanding the importance of what they had accomplished all those years ago. He hoped Michael was getting more than just the horror of an old man's war stories. Glenn turned the page and a handsome helmeted man squinted at them over a Clark Gable mustache. Michael was taken with the sheer beauty of the man. The face could tempt you into a movie theatre or sell you shaving cream; an intelligence that inspired trust was shining through his eyes. "That's Robert Posey," whispered Glenn.

"Were all you guys like that?" asked Michael.

"George Stout, James Rorimer, and Robert Posey were the real experts. I guess you could say we were the students because those last six months of war and the first six months of peace were our education. Even Jimmy said he'd become smarter just driving those jokers around. Jimmy was plenty smart, smart enough to play stupid to keep himself out of trouble."

Michael looked at a group of soldiers posing on the steps of an ornate building and Glenn explained, "That's the Louvre, the one in Paris, not the one in Queens." Glenn slid his finger to the man with the mustache standing with his head above the others. "That's Posey." The finger continued along the group to a frail, plain looking woman, "And that's Rose Valland. She was a French spy. You know she wrote down the details of every shipment of the stolen stuff." The group sported very broad, but thin, smiles. They all looked like they needed a good meal. Glenn recalled their disciplined informality.

They were some of the only people who could have ever completed such a monumental task because they were devoted to saving these cultural artifacts for posterity, a goal so much greater than themselves. The war had been saving the world itself from the Germans, but the Monuments Men had saved a substantial part of that world's heritage. This attitude toward work had given Glenn's life a value, and their rough and peculiar virtue had lifted him beyond shoveling coal. Glenn had learned that hauling beauty from the rubble gave us all a future that would be better than our past, and that was hope. Glenn thanked them for their gift. He rested his fingers below the photograph to hold Michael's attention.

"Lieutenant James Rorimer took that picture. He was something else. He was twice my age. He joined the army when he was a curator at the Metropolitan Museum of Art. Imagine that. He could've stayed at home with all his society friends, but he enlisted as a private and worked his way up to be an officer. And there he is, at the Louvre."

Glenn shook his head in renewed wonder and then turned the page to show Michael a newspaper cutting of Rorimer holding a camera, his friendly scowl defying the photographer to get it right. Rorimer's eyes beamed intelligence and the type of confidence that only comes with frequent success. Rorimer looked like he could smash his ample forehead through a brick wall. Glenn confessed to Michael, "Whichever way you look at him that face says, 'I know I'm right, but I'm too much of a gentleman to tell you that you're wrong.' He could be a real pain in the ass, but he was always on our side."

Michael sat drinking in the latest images. Some photos had faded to smudges of light and shadow, but Michael could recognize his grandfather's face smiling through the sepia of time. Glenn's reminiscences held Michael's attention, but it was Glenn's pleasure to remember such comrades and his duty to share their achievements with Michael. "They were all very special people. Yes, they were educated and some were Ivy League, but they were also down to earth and had a real respect for others. It was as if they were trying to be the art they loved, but they knew they were unfinished. I guess we all get finished, when we're finished, but these guys had talent. Most of us never know the talents we have. What they had rubbed off on the rest of us."

"Well they had the money and the time," added Michael.

"I don't know about that."

Glenn dropped his eyes and paused long enough to bring Michael back to the point he was missing. "Sure, George Stout was at Harvard, but he was like a working man or some skilled technician. He worked in the museum and I mean he worked with his hands. He'd been trying to do all this stuff to save paintings for years but the bosses wouldn't listen to him, so he just taught himself how to do it and then he just kept on doing it."

Glenn turned back the album's pages to the photo of Robert Posey. The light in Posey's eyes beamed straight at Michael through the shadows of his helmet. "And Bob was no Society Pages type; the fraternities wouldn't have him. He was a dirt farm boy from Alabama, where they think a pair of overalls is a tux. I saw him flip through a stack of paintings like he was judging sheep and goats at the country fair, and when he was done, there was one pile of Old Masters and another pile of copies of those Old Masters, and he divided them without blinking an eye. That's what I mean by talent. He told me that art is about the eye and music is about the ear and he'd gone into art because he was tone deaf. I heard him sing once. He was right. So these were normal guys. It was their talent and their drive that was so abnormal. Robert Posey had something extra. He was a real soldier, too, and we would have followed him anywhere."

Chapter 4

Portrait of a Man in a Steel Helmet

Dijon, France:
January 14, 1945.

Captain Robert Posey loved the army, almost as much as he loved his work and his family. Going to war made him understand how the three together made up his life.

Posey hunched his shoulders against the wind as he stood beside the road thumbing a lift, his body begging for the relief of a ride. He had landed in Normandy, after D-Day, following Patton's Third Army across France and picking up the remains of looted artwork as he marched east with the troops. A supply truck took pity on him and plowed through the slush to a thrumming halt beside him. The driver shouted "Hop in, buddy." Posey hauled himself into the passenger seat and wallowed in the heat of the cab. He thanked the driver and was relieved to have a ride all the way to Dijon. He tucked his head deeper into his helmet and slouched into an exhausted slumber, too tired to think, and slumped into a bundle of snores. The driver thought Posey resembled a mud-spattered, hibernating turtle.

Posey's journey through northern France as the Monuments Man for the Third Army had crumbled into a chaotic scramble. After a month of scavenging for cultural treasures, he felt himself an utter failure. Trudging along French roads was just the latest part of his long walk from an Alabama dirt farm. He had used the ROTC to drill his way through college, so he was as much a soldier as he was an architect.

Getting into college in the South in the 1920s was its own miracle, and paying for it was quite impossible. He had come up with a bizarre scheme to get himself and his twin brother an education. His family were farmers lurching from lien to lien, gambling their lives on an unforgiving earth and always hovering on the brink of destitution. Poverty was so normal that when the newspapers announced the Great Depression, they all just looked around and couldn't see much of a change. College was the escape and the army was the key to the college because, if he trained for the military, the government would pay his tuition. He applied to Auburn University and was shocked to receive a letter telling him to report for induction into the Class of 1929. The letter was addressed to Robert A. Posey, which he figured was a spelling mistake. He reasoned that if they could make one mistake, they could make one more, so he told his brother that they could both get through college by pretending to be each other. Brother John was more practical and wanted the details of how they were going to fool all those educated people. Robert reminded him that people had been confusing them all their lives, so "I'll do the first year and then come home to help Dad, then you'll do the second year, and then we'll trade places until we graduate." John knew this was impossible for a dozen reasons, so he politely declined and Robert graduated alone.

Posey idolized General George S. Patton Jr. The man exuded all the ability and self-respect that Posey had poured into his work. It turned out that his drive wasn't enough. Posey had designed a bridge in Pennsylvania for the army, but when they tested it with a tank, the whole structure collapsed, tank and bridge plunging into a river never to be seen again. Posey's superiors were not impressed when he gibed, "Well, back to the drawing board." After the Engineering Design Office, he was sent to Canada, the cold part up in Churchill, Manitoba, and told to turn prairies into landing strips. Posey kept to himself and suffered through the loneliness of drawing endless rectangles to be reproduced on land flatter than a table. It was a waste of his degree in architecture, for a child could do just as well with a grade school geometry set.

If he stood on his toes, he thought he could see the Rocky Mountains and the curvature of the earth. The Northern Lights and marauding polar bears kept him awake. He ruefully accepted the fact, stark as the drifting snow, that this was his dead end. He'd joke that "the middle of nowhere is a good place, when you're going nowhere. That means you've arrived." Just to get rid of him, the Canadians sent him to London and buried him in a unit nobody'd ever heard of: Monuments Fine Arts and Archives. His bosses didn't mind if he disappeared into the MFAA as efficiently as the tank had drowned in the runoff of the Allegheny.

His drive returned the closer he got to the front lines and to Patton. Once he got to Normandy, two years of failure and frustration were just water, and tank, under the bridge. He was a loner who enjoyed the solitude of his work. The army had a way of organizing people so he could avoid them, and keep to himself.

The closer he got to the front, the more the soldiers seemed to understand this. The prospect of your own death does concentrate the mind wonderfully. It also loosens soldiers' tongues in a peculiar way. The trucks ferrying them to battle were like crates of magpies on wheels. They would talk about anything and argue over who burned the supper last night, just to assure themselves that they were still alive. You can't talk about how scared you are, so you talk about your job. With the first bullet, shell or explosion, silence erupted and nobody said a word until the next hint of safety. It was the fear of dying alone that made them such efficient killers and kept them alive. Mindless chatter coupled with practical discussion and punctuated by terrified quietude, that was life. Posey developed a gregariousness which belied his isolation. He could pretend to be one of the boys, even though he was twice their age, so that they'd leave him alone once he got down to work.

It was the mission that was important; the people came second. Posey's mission was simple: "Locate the art and significant cultural artifacts looted by the enemy and report your findings to the designated officer in charge." The order was straight-forward, but it was left up to Posey just how to accomplish his mission. One of Patton's aides had simply told him, "You have your orders. Fulfill them." That one statement was Posey's license for success.

The success was long in coming, though, mainly because he was always too late on the scene. On the few occasions when the Intelligence Section would reveal where the Germans were hiding a collection of paintings or a statue, the Germans would move on and take their loot with them before the army could get there. Captured documents and a couple of hours with a dictionary would tell him, "the items from the Jew Rothschild's collection will be transferred to the Chateau de Colombe," but when he arrived, the chateau was a smoldering shell.

Posey didn't even have his own reliable transportation, and his mission was reduced to thumbing lifts on anything that could move. He once had ridden to the rescue of a priceless object while hanging onto the back of a tank. Supply trucks would only stop because they thought he was wounded and were shocked to see a solitary officer looking like a tramp. Because he was encrusted with the grime of a thousand French roads, the drivers mistook him for just another combat "dogface" and one of their own.

Some would ask him what he had for car fare and he would answer, "a joke and some scuttlebutt." This tactic worked better than begging or bribery, and soon he had worked out a patter of lies, exaggerations, and stories as filthy as his boots. He would sit in the back of a truck sharing the accumulated heat of a platoon of infantry and regale them with the stories that had earned his brother John more than one whipping from their father. Having learned the humor of his compatriots, he devised tales to suit their tastes.

One of the best was his earnest and very confidential account of Betty Grable's wooden legs. The mention of the million-dollar pegs always roused their interest and caught their attention. Posey would convince them that Betty Grable was a double amputee and the legs which adorned a thousand lockers were actually the lower half of a well-preserved grandmother from Sacramento. Mrs. Gertrude Houlihan had the same shaped mole on the back of her right thigh as Betty Grable. If word ever got out about Betty's tragic accident, the movie studios stood to lose millions. They had to fake those missing legs. Betty herself needed the cash because, after the operation, she was in such pain that she was a hopeless morphine addict who kept falling off her trolley. The studio photographer would take pictures of Mrs. Houlihan's legs and butt, and then they'd cut and paste both pictures together to restore Betty's image and her legs. Posey knew all of this because "Cousin Jethro has been banging Mrs. Houlihan for three years and he keeps quiet because they get a load of money from the deal. Jethro has sole use of the part of Betty Grable that works and doesn't have to put up with the part that talks." In such manner, Posey had zigzagged through the landscape newly reconquered by the Third Army as he'd slogged his way to minimal success in his mission.

It was all very irregular and unpredictably infuriating. Without a jeep, he was doomed. The madness was frustrating and he felt he was playing Hop Scotch all over northern France with a clock hung round his neck and voices in his head screaming, "I'm late! I'm late! For a very important date!"

Even so, Posey was full of hope as he entered the municipal buildings in Dijon. He was finally led to a small office claiming to be "Transportation Allocations - Third Army. Leave all weapons in the hall." He obeyed the notice, parked his rifle against the corridor wall, and entered the room. Posey approached a paper-littered counter and read a name plaque proclaiming the office as the domain of "Master Sergeant - Thomas T. Eckert - Transport and Fuel Requisitions." Posey saw a soldier dozing with his head nestled into folded arms on his side of the counter. He figured the meat-faced man hunched over piles of army forms on the other side of the counter must be in charge, so Posey identified himself, "Captain Robert Posey presenting orders."

Eckert looked up from his paperwork, pressed his palms onto the counter, and rose to face Posey. He stared into Posey's eyes, pointed to the name plate then to himself and said, "Eckert." He sprayed a mischievous smile over Posey and beamed a conspiratorial cheerfulness when said, "Oh, yeah. You're that guy out saving the world."

Posey was taken aback by Eckert's casual attitude. Eckert showed no deference to rank, and Posey realized this man was all that stood between him and abject failure, so he decided to try his newly invented rough Southern charm.

"That's me, Master Sergeant, one painting at a time. But to do that, a fellow like me just gotta have a jeep. You yourself can see I'm no spring chicken and my rheumatism is making it mighty difficult for me to keep up with the young 'uns."

Eckert howled, "I love it. Talk some more 'cause it sounds like *Gone With the Wind* without that annoying bitch."

Posey went into his Southern Good Ol' Boy routine and Eckert was enjoying every twist of his whiney drawl. Posey laid it on so thick that even the soldier leaning over the counter beside him raised himself on his elbows to chuckle. Eckert said, "I knew you was coming. Sorry I couldn't bake a cake." He extended his arm to present Posey with the soldier hunched over the counter. He opened his palm like a cabaret master of ceremonies and said, "I got better. Captain Posey, meet Sergeant Mulvaney."

Posey looked down at all five feet six inches of encrusted dirt saluting him, as Eckert wondered "how they could pile shit that high." Even Mulvaney's face was coated in something that looked like grease peppered with sand. He also stank. Eckert assured Posey that "Mulvaney may look like a fart in a frame but he's your man for this job. I got better than some jeep jalopy. You can take Mulvaney with you." Posey could just make out the Screaming Eagle through the dried mud on Mulvaney's shoulder. If this guy was Airborne, he looked and smelled like he'd parachuted into a lake of sewage. Posey looked into Mulvaney's eyes and got the hint of something below the filth. Posey was an officer and was becoming a gentleman, so he returned Mulvaney's salute and said, "It's a pleasure to meet you, Sergeant."

Master Sergeant Thomas T. Eckert beamed approval from his side of the counter, which was the limit of his kingdom and his protection from both demanding drunks and the violently disappointed. He knuckled the counter and leaned into a rare compliment. “Awe. Ain’t that nice. I like it when officers show a little manners. Okay, cut the bullshit and get down to work.”

Eckert opened a bulging folder and spread out sheets of government forms in quadruplicate. Posey thought there were enough forms to buy a house back in Alabama. He masked his impatience with feigned interest because the signatures on those forms looked suspiciously like a future. Mulvaney patiently ignored the Master Sergeant’s patter. That’s what officers were for.

“These are your Vehicle Requisition Certificates,” said Eckert. “Don’t lose them ’cause you’ll need them when your vehicle gets stolen.”

Posey started to put both certificates into his pocket, but Mulvaney darted out one beckoning hand while casually leaning on the counter with his other arm. Posey shared the certificates, and Mulvaney returned to his snooze. Enjoying his earnest warnings and kindly admonitions, Eckert thrust two more little booklets at Posey. They looked like Food Ration Cards stapled together.

Eckert’s fingers waved a piece of cardboard inches from Posey’s nose. “This is gold dust. It’s a F.A.C., a Fuel Allocation Card, and you’ll need it if you don’t want to spend the next year in a parking lot. I’ll give you two, so’s you can trade on the black market, which means trading with our guys for stuff you’re going to need. Keep it away from the Frogs; they know a good thing when they see it and are selling them back to our guys.”

Posey was so captivated by Eckert’s knowledge and his willingness to share it that he became suspicious. Nobody else had ever done so much for Posey’s mission. Mulvaney leaned against the counter with the bored expression of people at a pawn shop who had no money and nothing to trade. Posey looked at them both and cast aside his doubts to accept his good luck. Eckert wound up his performance.

“Okay. That’s it. There’s a transportation park two miles from here. Go out the main door. Turn left and keep walking. The road’s a little iffy after the bombing, but the engineers cleared a good path a couple of days ago. Just keep going and you'll find it on your right. As they say at the gas stations, 'Happy Motoring.'"

Posey was so relieved that he warmed to Eckert's friendliness and asked, "How did you know who I was?"

"Hey. This is transport. Every driver within three hundred miles drags his sorry ass to this office, if he doesn't want to hoof it with the rest. I'm the spider and this is the very center of my web. The guys have been coming through here for weeks and they been telling me all about Betty Grable's wooden legs. I just had to give some credit to the Master Bullshitter."

Posey was confronted with a genuine hand of soldierly respect and was very confused about what to do. Mulvaney winked at him. Posey took the hint and shook hands with his indispensable fan. As he thanked his Fairy Godmother for the compliment and the assistance, he quickly stuffed the papers into his pockets with his other hand. Mulvaney uncurled his body from the counter, wrapped his face into a smirk, and turned to walk out first. Posey followed him into the hall, and they collected their weapons. They shrugged against the winter winds as they left the building and with a smart left turn onto the road. They slogged along, looking the place that would get them to even more roads, without all the walking and bumming rides.

In less time than they thought, they had woven themselves along the zigzag the engineers had cleared through bombed out houses and minefields, and stopped at the entrance to a vehicle park. Posey's heart sank into the socks he had been wearing for two weeks. It was a junk yard. Before them stretched miles of wrecked tanks, shot-up jeeps, trucks without wheels and every imaginable sort of military and civilian vehicle that had at one time claimed to move on its own power. Mulvaney recognized three French taxis, German staff cars, something the British called a Universal Carrier, tow trucks with broken cranes, and almost every American vehicle on the quartermasters' lists. Posey's disappointment rooted him to the frozen mud, but Mulvaney looked like it was his birthday and scurried amidst the wrecks looking for something.

Posey didn't know what could be of any use whatsoever in this pile of twisted rust, but he kept a close eye on Mulvaney. Mulvaney was opening boxes at the sides of vehicles and then slamming the lids in disgust. He moved from one jumbled mess to the next with growing irritation and started rummaging beneath the seats. He jumped up into the cab of a truck and cleared away a pile of camouflage netting and then triumphantly held up an old ammunition box as if it were the Holy Grail. "I found it," he whooped, and Posey came running. Mulvaney popped open the lid of the ammunition box to present four monkey wrenches, two screwdrivers, three sets of pliers and a hammer. "And it's almost complete," he said.

Posey gaped at the paltry collection of ordinary tools, "So. It's a toolbox."

"So. It's our ticket," answered Mulvaney. "With this, we can have any of those. Which one do you want?"

"A tank?"

"Lousy mileage. Yous knows, those things get four gallons to the mile. Not four miles to the gallon, but four gallons to the mile."

Posey surrendered to Mulvaney's logic. "Well, we need something that can be locked."

"Let's see what's we can scrounge."

Posey and Mulvaney walked the metal graveyard for an hour rejecting one green jalopy after the other. There was an ambulance that looked like Swiss cheese, and they both stopped to ponder if its wounded had survived the attack. There were holes in the big red cross on the roof, so they figured it was hit by an airplane. A truck was lying in two pieces and they both knew it had hit a big mine. Each bundle bore the scars of battles lost, but Mulvaney ignored the obvious and kept lying down to inspect the underside of anything he thought would work. They both stopped when they saw a small truck with an open driver's cab and a boxed-in body.

The body was perforated and a corner was missing, but both doors at the back opened with protesting squeals.

" What is this thing?" Posey asked.

"This is the answer to our prayers," Mulvaney assured him.

Posey wondered what type of god would answer supplications with such a bad joke. He also doubted Mulvaney's sanity in seeing salvation in a rusted out wreck of metal with no wheels. "This thing will never go," blurted Posey.

"Have a little faith, Captain. I seen worse, let me tell you, far worse."

"It doesn't even have wheels," protested Posey.

Mulvaney swung his arm to a line of trucks standing on tires. "Yeah, but those 'uns do,"

"Let's try another one," Posey sighed in disappointment

Posey walked a few steps up the line in search of something more suitable but realized he was alone. Mulvaney had wandered back down the line and was dragging a long piece of metal that looked like a silver floorboard out of the back of a two and a half ton truck. Mulvaney's casual insubordination annoyed Posey, but he decided to see what the smelly dwarf was up to before reprimanding him.

Mulvaney dragged the ten feet of perforated metal to his chosen wreck. It was a sand channel, used to guide mired truck wheels out of soft sand and deadly mud. Mulvaney had seen trucks buried up to their axles in wet earth, but two sand channels had allowed the driver to drag his chariot out of the quicksand. Posey decided to help and grabbed the other end of the channel. Mulvaney silently accepted this as Posey's admission that he was wrong. Posey took his demotion to Mulvaney's assistant with as much good grace as he could muster and followed the little man's lead. Together, their mouths grunted winter fog as they shoved the sand channel as close to the back of the wreck's bumper as they could. Mulvaney jumped from one truck to the other kicking spare wheels to the ground, if they looked like they had at least enough air in them to keep a generally circular shape. When they had six, they herded the wheels back to their open air garage like children playing with hoops.

They stood beside their tires catching their breaths, and Posey asked, "How do you know they will fit?"

"This is a Dodge. The chassis is the same as a truck, just shorter, so the wheels are interchangeable."

Posey had failed to look beyond the destruction of the car to the basic chassis and felt humbled. Mulvaney found a big jack, placed it on the sand channel, and fitted the tongue under the lip of the bumper. He wedged his foot along the side of the jack and pumped the handle. Posey watched the big box on the back of the car slowly rise, as Mulvaney's foot gently nudged the jack into vertical. He saw that Mulvaney was working the jack to let Posey place a wheel on the studs of the wheel hub. They got both back wheels in place and lowered the car to sit on straight but flat tires.

"Hey that's great. They're only flat on the bottom," Mulvaney bragged.

They manhandled the jack and the sand channel to the front of the car and repeated the process. Mulvaney supplied a running commentary as they worked.

"This is the best. It's a Dodge Command Car."

"Isn't this the same car Patton uses?" asked Posey.

"The exact same model, but he don't go in it where the guys go, so he's safe. He can stand up in the passenger seat and hang on to the machinegun mount so's he gets a good picture in the newspapers. He's got a whole fleet of these, like his very own limousine company with silver stars on the hood and flags all over. He knows he's gonna be OK 'cause he's at least three miles from anything dangerous. The Germans see this coming down the road and it's got "High Ranking Officer" written all over it. They think they'll get someone important, so they open up with the works and spray the thing. That's why this is such a wreck. Some trigger happy Kraut probably thought he was going to get the Iron Cross for hitting this baby."

Posey listened in wonder as Mulvaney initiated him into the mysteries of army transport. “So that’s why I’ve never seen one of these before,” he said.

“Right. They’re all in this Elephant’s Graveyard and the drivers are fertilizer someplace back in Belgium.”

Mulvaney didn’t like talking about the dead; he left officers to speak of “casualties,” but they were still dead. He took refuge from his nightmares in chatter.

“These come in three models, WC 56, 57 and 58. The 56 is your common or garden variety gruntmobile, also useful for suicides. This is a 57 ’cause it’s got the big nose in front and the winch. The 58 was for the radio boys.”

“So why are you so interested in this?” asked Posey.

“Cause it’s got the 58 box on the back and the 57 winch in front.”

Posey tried to clarify his question, not realizing that Mulvaney was trying to avoid the answer. “I meant, why are you so interested in this assignment?” They both wished Posey had not been so insistent, but Mulvaney took a deep breath and split the awkward silence. “We’re on a mission, or so I hear, and that mission involves paintings and stuff and they’re well out of range of the snipers.”

Posey respected the man’s honesty and returned it. “You’re right about that.” He also let them take cover from their confessions. “Back to the vehicle. Why this particular one?”

“Some joker put this big box on the back and you said we needed something that could lock. I figure you want it for the pictures and stuff.”

“What do you think the box was for?”

“You know what some of those guys in the motor pools are like. Give them a blow torch or a welding outfit and they think they can make the Brooklyn Bridge. For all I know, this is a cathouse and the boys were raking it in on the side.”

They circled the Dodge, searching for clues to the vehicle’s purpose and hoping it would not disappoint them. Posey speculated, “I think it was something to do with communications. There’s some sort of table and shelving back there that’s just the right size for a radio.”

“You could be right,” Mulvaney admitted. “Even these little French broads are too big for that table. They’d keep falling off and banging their heads on the floor.”

Posey sensed that Mulvaney’s conjectures about the possible alternative uses of a six foot by four foot steel box on the back of a command car were very like his Betty Grable story. There was just enough conviction in Mulvaney’s tone to make Posey accept the miniature French women as plausible. He confessed, “I don’t rightly know,” but added, “It’s looks to me like some sort of mobile office. Do you think it will go?”

“We’ll see.”

Mulvaney’s feet danced between the starter button and the gas pedal and the machine produced a lazy snore. He turned a switch and a dim light appeared in the speedometer. He switched it off quickly, conserving precious electricity in the battery. He jumped down from the cab and played with the fuel cap. He bent his nose close to the open gas tank like dogs getting acquainted. “I think we might have a chance.”

He found two fuel cans and a rubber hose and gave one of the cans to Posey. They went from vehicle to vehicle sucking as much gasoline out of each as they could, until both cans were full. Mulvaney poured the contents of each can into the gas tank of their new chariot, making sure not a drop was lost. Posey thought of Alice and Woogie, his family back home. Woogie would spend hours constructing castles out of backyard dirt. He had the same concentration on his projects as Mulvaney was applying to the Dodge. He looked at Mulvaney and remembered counting out a stack of pennies for Woogie’s allowance.

Mulvaney jumped back into the driver’s seat and waltzed with the starter button. The machine wheezed like it had tuberculosis. Mulvaney rummaged under the passenger seat until he found a hand crank and gave it to Posey. Posey inserted the long twist of iron through the hole in the front bumper and waited for Mulvaney's signal. Mulvaney raised his right hand like a conductor before a waiting orchestra and poised his boot over the gas pedal. Posey cranked in time to Mulvaney's gesturing hand, swinging his shoulders through circles, cranking a slow steady cadence until the engine squealed into a syncopated overture punctuated by Mulvaney's tapping foot. The engine settled into a rasping purr and kept going. They both sat in the cab waiting for the engine to gather its strength because Mulvaney wasn't going to risk their prize's life due to impatience. He kept jumping down to bend over the engine until, so slowly that Posey wanted to scream, the engine hit its rhythm and hummed a smooth idle.

Mulvaney squirmed in the driver's seat and coaxed the car onto the path separating the wrecks. The car staggered ahead in a cloud of its own exhaust. Mulvaney steered a slalom around abandoned engines and guided the car like a nurse leading a patient through the first steps back to health. Mulvaney listened to the engine until he could hear its delight in its own ability humming through the exhaust. They couldn't have been going more than four miles an hour, so Posey jumped down and walked beside the truck checking the tires.

They drove around the junk yard as Mulvaney adapted to the car's odd ways. He tinkered with the carburetor and coaxed the engine into a little more effort, until she could sustain twenty miles an hour, and the brakes could stop on a five dollar bill. The whole sorry mess wheezed and hissed exhaust in places there shouldn't be exhaust, but it moved, it turned, and it stopped. Mulvaney looked upon his work and saw that it was good. Posey was astounded. This stinking gnome had solved his nightmare with a couple of wrenches and some deep knowledge of machinery which had always evaded Posey. Posey was smart, but he knew that he was smart because he could appreciate people who were smarter than he was.

"That was a great job, Soldier."

"Thank you, Sir. Not bad if I don't say so myself."

“How did you learn to do all this with automobiles?”

“By stealing them.”

Posey thought he should change the subject. However he had acquired his talents, Mulvaney had gotten them on the road and off their feet. You don’t care which college the doctor went to, after he’s cured you.

“Does the heater work?” Posey asked. Mulvaney paused long enough to tell Posey the truth. “We can get it going, but I think we should wait until we can clean up and maybe get new uniforms. If you don’t mind me saying so, Sir, you’re getting a bit gamey.”

Posey cackled through his own arrogance. Here he’d been turning up his nose at Mulvaney and not even smelling himself. This was something he’d have to write home about to Alice and Little Woogie. His wife and child would just love to have a good laugh at his expense. For all his jokes, he loved the one’s about himself the best. He played it straight with Mulvaney and said, “So, let’s find a headquarters with a shower and a mess hall and make ourselves presentable to civilized people, James.”

Mulvaney’s face threw a sideways question mark at Posey, and he said, “People call me, Jimmy, Sir.”

“People call me Bob, Sergeant.”

“Yes, Siree Bob, Sir.”

Captain Bob settled into this new and unlikely friendship and found it both troubling and cozy. The resurrected Dodge gave Posey his chance to shine, but the assignment was Mulvaney’s ticket out of the firing line. Finding the looted masterpieces would unlock a brighter future when peace came. Posey had the education to appreciate artistic wonder. He could deal in abstractions; he found a peculiar comfort in ideals and a familiar assurance in concepts. They were like mathematics; they could be trusted. Mulvaney’s world was free of such vagaries. His arithmetic was the body count. He was the only survivor of his platoon, and his only ideal was to escape the butchery with his skin in one piece. Where Posey feared failure, Mulvaney was terrified of mutilation. Yet Mulvaney was indispensable. Mulvaney needed to be the driver of this college joker on his treasure hunt, for it took him further from the death he expected. Posey knew that art followed life, but for Mulvaney, following the art was life itself.

The grinding protests of the engine and transmission and the lurching wheels became their transport of delight because both would win and both would live. Posey smelled his helmet's earthy aroma from the dirt trapped in the camouflage net. His nose caught the scent of his own sweaty hair oozing from the interior straps. The top of his helmet smelled like sweet home Alabama and the straps conjured memories of Alice offering him a towel as he pulled his head out from under the stream of water cascading from the backyard pump. He could feel his feet thawing out and realized that Mulvaney had turned on the heater. They both looked straight ahead.

For a moment, Posey cradled his helmet in his arm and it became his first caress of his newborn son. Robert settled the helmet back over his head. The weight felt good. He snapped the straps under his chin and pulled the tiny peak down over his eyes to have a sleep. Just as he dozed off, he saw his own face half hidden under his helmet in the rear view mirror. He looked the part of the conquering hero, but only he knew just how scared he was. He would keep holding his fear to himself until he returned to Alice and Woogie, and he was grateful that his uniform hid both the father and the husband.

Chapter 5

Triptych

Michael flipped through the album and hovered between the images and Glenn's commentary. Anda's tales had become an avalanche, and he was having trouble concentrating. Like most veterans, Glenn didn't want to talk about his experiences. He would share the basic facts, but these were general and could be found in any soldier's service record. Enlisted 1941, European Theatre of Operations 1944-45. Discharged 1947. Never much detail and just the thinnest veneer over the events that were better not recalled, but never forgotten. Michael wanted answers to his big question about the big money, but Glenn was pouring forth a torrent of details. Michael wanted the big picture, but Glenn was making a mosaic and insisted on placing every tiny pebble in its place. Michael mustered enough patience to concentrate.

One photo was folded with two creases running from top to bottom like a letter left over from a long discarded envelope. The photo almost split into three pieces, and Glenn delicately opened its wings to reveal a group of soldiers clustered around a fountain in a town square. Michael recognized Robert Posey standing beside a statue and talking to a semi-circle of soldiers gathered in front of him. The scene looked like an open-air class. Glenn's eyes narrowed in admiration as he drank in the picture. "That was how Bob Posey got the guys interested in art."

Michael couldn't make out any of the other faces, but Posey was standing on the rim of the fountain with his arms in the air talking to the group. The background was a pile of ruined buildings, but Posey's face was illuminated with the joy of teaching. Glenn took Michael's interest as the signal to continue.

"He'd hauled that statue of Venus into the square from a house just down the street, and the men followed him out of sheer curiosity, saying things like 'Hey, buddy, does you girlfriend have a sister?' and he would answer 'No, but her mother's a friendly sort of lady.' He kept this up like he was the Pied Piper until he had a trail of laughter following him into the square. He introduced the guys to that marble woman and invited them all to 'take a good look at this fat girl with the big tits and an ass like a Thanksgiving turkey.'"

Michael chuckled, "I guess that drew a crowd."

"The statues with the tits drew the biggest crowds. When they all rushed over, he'd show them this Renaissance goddess and give them a lecture on classical ideals of beauty. You know, we hardly ever saw anything nice. Letters, pictures of wives and kids, even a pin-up was about as close as we ever came to having something good. The guys weren't horny, just homesick for something nice and normal. Even a smile from one of the Germans would really brighten up the day. We were all starved for beauty and here was this joker dragging a quarter ton of beauty down the street to share with us."

Glenn paused to see Michael paying attention and continued when he was sure Michael was looking and listening. "Now, that was something. He'd tell us all about the statue and joke about the artist who made it, but that was just his warm-up. He'd let them leer over the statue and laugh with them when someone asked if she was his mother. He always said his mother had arms like this lady, but her looks were kinda spoiled because she had only one eye, right in the center of her forehead."

Michael concentrated on the joy beaming from Posey's eyes and noticed there was no blurring in the group. There was no movement in the audience, but there was a fuzzy aura of smudges along Posey's arm. The soldiers were very still and listening intently to Posey; but he was waving his arms in excitement.

"When Posey would talk, he could make them all laugh," Glenn said. "They would really listen to his lecture on the idea in the painting or the sculpture. He could take us from the gutter to the clouds. He was amazing."

Glenn saw that Michael's eyes were wandering over the photo. Just as when Michael was a child, Glenn let Michael's attention waver. He called it their "recess" when Michael grew bored with the picture book.

Glenn ran his finger over the photo, following a jagged line of half a wall cut through a glassless window frame. Through the frame, he could see into two rooms in two stories of a house missing one wall. The camera's fast shutter had caught furniture, a mattress and some books tumbling from the upper room onto the pile of broken bricks below. Dust wafted through the holes. Michael could almost smell the pungent rubble that used to be someone's home. With a gentle shove of his hand, Glenn pointed to a perfectly normal house at the side of the photo. His finger traced the outline of the house and pulled Michael's attention along the gutters and up the chimney, over the roof and down the walls. "Not even a cracked window," he said. They savored the contrast of ruins piled around one untouched house.

"People think war is a hurricane. It isn't," said Glenn. He recognized that old frown of confusion creep over Michael's brow and explained, "It's a tornado that hops, skips, and jumps. There's no telling where it will touch. You can't even get out of its way."

Michael now understood why Anda was being so slow in answering his question about the expensive picture. There was no way Michael could really understand without all of this detail, without this sense of the thing Anda had lived through. Wars and strategies may be planned, but fighting is a very hit-or-miss experience. So was searching for and saving art. Anda was trying to show Michael experiences that were peculiar and unique. Posey with the statue in the rubble was defying the destruction, making his stand against the stupidity and the ignorance that had brought them all to that place. Anda had been there to record it, and this little photo was what he had left of that one, pregnant moment.

"Anyway, I think the lectures worked. Posey and Stout used to say that if more people went to museums and concerts, there would be fewer wars, but we knew that the Germans were music lovers.

What it actually did was make the men more aware of the art. They'd get into a town and think twice about what they were burning to keep warm. Every soldier who heard those lectures would go back into the line and be just a little more careful with his machine gun. We noticed there were fewer portraits with bullet holes after Posey gave his spiels about big asses and beautiful souls."

"Art appreciation with a tank?" Michael asked.

"A little more than that."

Michael waited for Glenn to get to the meat of his tale. "Some of the guys in that photo were dead one minute after I took the picture. Some German wanted to show what a real hero he was and let loose a machinegun. Two died and one was severely wounded. The Germans were beaten and everybody knew it was all over. There was absolutely no need to do that. It was murder. Somebody thought he would get in one last shot and that's what happened. The wounded guy was blinded. I felt sorriest for him. Lucky thing was the dead guys didn't know just how useless their deaths were. That's what hit the rest of us. It really made me think that the last thing those guys ever saw was something beautiful and they only knew it was beautiful because Posey had a great line in smut. I guess that's why we became art collectors."

Together they let the photo speak its last words to them. Glenn's memory jumped over the triangle of helmets to meet Posey again and to renew their love of beautiful things in ugly times.

Chapter 6

Venus

Markheim, Germany
March 4, 1945

The men jostled each other into a mud-coated, sweaty half-moon, half-listening to Posey's lecture and leering at the statue of Venus, complete with arms. Posey reveled in his lecture and the men's laughter. He was explaining that the woman was a perfect example of the Renaissance ideal of beauty when the bullets tore through them. They turned and scattered from the burst of machine gun fire. The lecture erupted into a desperate clatter for anything that could shoot at the building behind them. Jimmy stood with his rifle pointed over the men's heads at a window across the street while Posey fumbled with a cracked holster at his side.

Jimmy's eyes scanned the building parallel to the square. He saw the glint in the window and carefully fired into its empty space. He neither panicked nor hurried but kept up a steady fire of one shot every five seconds. He wasn't trying to kill the man who was trying to kill him, just pointing out the target for the others. The slow rhythm of his rifle broke the panic as each man started to shoot in the general direction of the window. Posey played second fiddle with his pistol to Jimmy's rifle.

A monster of metal, half truck and half tank, crunched to their rescue. A man sat on top of it and casually released the safety catch on a .50 caliber machine gun, swinging it in the direction of the window. The gun could kill a low-flying airplane, and the men all knew what it was going to do to the building with the squinting windows.

The next few minutes proved the soldiers' joke that their job was months of boredom punctuated by minutes of terror. The

German in the window was a fool or a fanatic or a suicide or all three, but soon he would be just another corpse. They hated him because there was no need to do any fighting. This one fool had to prove himself, had to go out with a bang and take someone with him. Nobody gave a damn for the German's motives. They just wanted him dead. He was darting from window to window along the second floor, and the town square resembled a shooting gallery at Coney Island, except here the bullets were real, the screaming was of pain, and nobody was going to get a Kewpie doll.

Everybody ducked as the next burst sprayed them from the second window, except Jimmy. He stood with his eye rigid along his sights, the rifle never wavering and his trigger finger as steady as a metronome. Posey reloaded as the spent casings cascaded over his feet like hail. His hand was shaking so violently that he wondered if he were even hitting the building let alone the windows Jimmy was zeroing in on. But it felt good to shoot, to do something, for he might soon be dead and not even know it. The shaking snaked along his arm until the muscles in his chest ached to keep the rest of his body steady. As he listened to his heart through the explosions surrounding him he wondered, "Am I going to die of a heart attack?" His mind saw the humor through the irony, and he bellowed laughter.

The men took up Posey's chorus and the firing became a vaudeville act. The German would shoot through a window and duck behind a wall. The men roared "Get him!" when the German popped up at another window. Jimmy kept a steady bead on him and the rest followed his sight. Their laughter became squeals as the murderous Jack-in-the-Box jumped and shot his way along the second floor.

The machine gunner on the half-track was bored and decided to end the game. Sitting behind the armored screen with his head almost even with the second floor, the gunner pulled the cocking lever, flipped the safety with a thumb as if he were flicking away a lit butt, and squeezed a couple of rounds into a cloud, just to make sure all was in working order. The bullets were a half-inch around, coated in a steel jacket and nestled in six inches of brass. Each round was in a belt of two hundred and fifty friends and they could punch holes through steel armor and soft human flesh and keep going for two miles. The army had named this machine gun the M2 Model 1917, but to the soldiers she was just "Ma Deuce." Nobody knew if "ma" was "mine" or "mother," but everybody felt better when she was around. There was something so maternal about this thing that could shoot five hundred times a minute at anything that could hurt you. Ma Deuce was a comfort. When they saw Ma turn to the house, they all became very quiet as a respectful silence descended on the square. Posey saw the reverence in the silence and knew that some of the men slept better when they could hear Ma Deuce's lullaby off in the distance.

The gunner pointed the barrel at the building and barked to Jimmy, "Where?" Jimmy let off one shot and the gunner took careful aim at the little puff of brick dust between two windows where Jimmy's shot had scratched the wall. The men all whooped as Ma Deuce ate the second floor. The front of the building erupted into horizontal clouds of brown powder and spewed forth a hail of brick splinters. The cloud had a silver lining of plaster and bits of furniture with a halo of sticky crimson.

The gunner paused to let the cloud settle, and the men stared at the jagged hole of bricks where a body half hung out of the opening. They jeered the corpse, and the gunner kept firing into the lower segments of the hole. The steady stream of bullets shoved the body back through the hole into the gutted room. The gunner would not let up. He kept shooting at the corpse until what was left had disappeared back into the rubble that used to be safety. His thumb eased off the butterfly trigger and everyone sighed and giggled or wept and screamed.

The street was a litter of brass, brick and blood, but the men walked over to congratulate the gunner on his handiwork. The town square resembled a midway filled with Freak Shows, but most of them were alive and grateful to the gunner. They filed past his metal box offering cigarettes and admiration and he accepted each with professional grace. They all knew that his work was life to them, and so did he.

Posey stood shaking beside the Venus, but Jimmy looked straight into his welling eyes and asked, "So how come she's so beautiful?" Posey rotated his head and fixed his shocked stare on Jimmy's eyes, wondering if his ears were still ringing from the gunfire.

"What?

"So how come this one's more beautiful than some other broad?"

Posey's ears were fine; it was his brain that was shaken. Jimmy seemed to be asking about the Venus, and Posey was confused. One minute ago they were caught up in death and destruction and now this short little bundle of attitude was asking about his lecture as if they had just taken a break for coffee. Posey could only stare at Jimmy, but Jimmy was in complete control of himself and the situation.

Posey had often wondered how nothing seemed to faze Jimmy. Such composure was troubling. He didn't seem to register the danger around him as other people did. Maybe Mulvaney was some sort of psychopath. If that were the case, Mulvaney might actually be more dangerous than the Germans. "Then again," Posey mused to himself, "we all might be a bit crazy." He shook a question out of his muddled head, "You want to know why she is beautiful?" Jimmy waited and then prompted Posey, "Well, ain't that the lecture?"

Jimmy really did want to know, and that was even more astounding than the possibility that he was just shell-shocked and out of his mind.

"So what do you remember?" Posey asked.

"You were saying she was beautiful because she was mean."

"No, the idea is that she's a Golden Mean. She is proportional."

"So why is she so proportional and Sally down the street is just ugly?"

"Jimmy, what the hell are you talking about?"

"That's what I've been axing you. Sally is this woman who lives near me in Jersey and she's maybe two hundred and fifty pounds and got an ass on her that could lift a transmission, so I want to know why is this girl beautiful and Sally's just a sack-a-shit?"

Posey laughed himself into a sitting position beside the Venus and tickled a pack of cigarettes out of his breast pocket. He was still chortling as he offered one to Jimmy. Jimmy fumbled with his lighter and giggled like a naughty little boy. He sat beside Posey and was really curious about "the Venus broad." Posey didn't know if it was the cigarette or the laughter or just the simple incongruity of lecturing on aesthetics in the aftermath of a battle, but he had stopped shaking. Jimmy watched Posey's steady hand lift the cigarette to his lips and waited patiently for enlightenment. Posey blew smoke and a demand, "Tell me all about this Sally."

"Well, she ain't too bright, but she's got a heart of gold. She works in the laundry and always smells of carbolic soap and has long hair that looks like she's wearing some dead animal."

"Probably her hair's like that because of all the heat in the laundry," Posey said.

"She's also huge. About as tall as you but you's could get three of you outta her and still have enough left over for a puppy."

Posey coughed laughter through the smoke, but was intrigued by Sally.

"Does she look like a pear or does she have a big gut like an apple?"

"Neither. She's just big all over. Like maybe she's really triplets in one skin."

"What about her ass?" Posey asked pointing the Venus, "Is it like this ass?"

"Yeah. Kinda. Just more of it."

"Are Sally's arms long?"

"Long enough, but don't get me wrong, she's no knuckle scraper."

"Knuckle scraper?" Posey asked.

"You know. Like a monkey with its hands scraping along the sidewalk."

"Okay. So Sally is big and doesn't look like a monkey. What about her head?"

"Like a melon."

"You mean a watermelon?"

Jimmy pondered different types of melon and dredged his memory for a description of Jersey Sally, "Like one of those Spanish melons. Whatdja call 'em?"

"A cantaloupe?"

"That's it."

"So she has pockmarks all over hear face?"

"No no. Really smooth but a bit puffy. And she got really beautiful eyes, all blue and really clear."

"Ah, eyes that see right through you."

Jimmy was watching Posey relax into his explanation. He had purged Posey of the battle rage, but now Posey was making him hot for Sally. He just had to disagree with Posey.

"I don't know about that, but when she looks at you her eyes are like that cellophane in the butchers when they wrap up chickens."

"She's got a face like dead chicken bits?"

"No. She got eyes like cellophane. Clear and shiny and a bit wet."

Posey was getting into his stride. He was proud that he could teach and not so surprised that Jimmy was keen to learn. "Okay. Now we're getting somewhere. So you think she has beautiful eyes. How come?"

"I dunno. But she looks like she wouldn't hurt a fly."

"So she's really big. She has a powerful body and her eyes say that she isn't going to hurt you. Is that it?"

Jimmy was pleased he had lured Posey out of his panic. He was also getting very interested in the man and the woman he was describing.

"Yeah. You know I never thought about that before. Most guys just look at her tits and ass and think they'd break a bone if they fell off her, but I guess I looked in her eyes."

"And saw something the other guys didn't see. That's how we find beauty."

Jimmy followed Posey's lead into the depths of silent marble standing beside them. He yanked a thumb at the Venus.

"But this one doesn't have any eyes, so how's I to know she's beautiful?"

"Take a look at how she's set up. Does she look kinda regular?"

"Now that you mention it, she does. How come?"

"Look at her nose. Does it fill her whole face?"

"No. She ain't no Jimmy Durante with a schnoz like a potato."

"You mean Sally or this statue?"

"Both."

Posey waggled his index finger to pull Jimmy's attention to the statue's nose.

"How about her nose in relation to the rest of her face?"

"Yeah. The nose fits."

"Go pinch her nose," Posey suggested.

"You kidding?" Jimmy retorted.

"Pinch her nose from the top to the tip," Posey commanded.

Jimmy spread a finger and a thumb and Posey guided him, "Keep your finger on the top of her nose and then turn your hand but keep your thumb straight." The triangle of Jimmy's hand swung to the left of Venus' face.

"Where's your thumb?"

"In her ear."

"Now have your thumb do an 'About Turn' but keep it rigid."

Jimmy rotated his hand like a compass and Posey asked,

"Where's your thumb?"

"In her other ear."

Jimmy felt a bit foolish feeling up the face of a marble woman but was enjoying the experience. He listened to Posey, who was now calm enough to make a lot of sense.

"Okay. So her nose is proportional to her ears. That means her face is regular."

"Wow. That's amazing," Jimmy said.

"Do the same to your own face."

"What?"

"Do the same."

Posey gently placed the tip of Jimmy's thumb at the top of his nose and stretched his index finger until it was resting on Jimmy's ear hole. "Now swing your thumb over your own face just like you did over hers." He watched Jimmy's finger search for his ear. "What happens?"

"They don't match."

"That's right. Our faces are what's called asymmetrical. They don't really match up left to right, but her face matches perfectly. Her nose and her ears. Is Sally's face like that?"

"I ain't going to try this with her 'cause I might lose a finger or two, but yeah, she's kinda like this."

"Now if you take the distance between her ears and add just a little over half, you'll get the distance over her chest. Try it."

Jimmy started measuring Venus with his splayed fingers and his thumb lighted on a nipple. Some other soldiers were enjoying the performance of one of their own feeling up the statue and called out "Hey, Buddy, save some for me." He ignored them and let his fingers walk his curiosity over the Venus to a new understanding.

Posey watched comprehension dawn in Jimmy's eyes and felt a fatherly pride in his new and surprising student. This was not a new experience for Posey, for he had repeated the magic hundreds of times in lecture halls, university classrooms, and church halls to anyone who showed any glimmer of interest in art and who took the time and paid the fee for the experience. But to have his classroom move to the town square of a ruined German town in the middle of a battle was something to tell his grandchildren, if he ever had any.

"So what do you think of Sally now?" he asked

"I think she's the Jersey Venus, but I think I'll just look and not touch."

"Sounds like that would be the safest bet."

They gazed over the litter that was the town square. The corner house was smashed along with the German who had attacked them. The street was a river of vitreous sparkles punctuated by stone fragments and little crimson lakes. Jimmy was still astounded by how little blood it took to kill a man, and he and Posey watched some friends load their own dead into the back of a truck. The medics and the morphine were working on the wounded man. He was calm as they bandaged the jagged line sliced through his head just over his nose. Jimmy shuddered at the torn face and thought of the surgeon's fingers that would be drawing lines across the face from ear to ear in, he hoped, a shorter time than it took the morphine to wear off.

Everybody knew the medics kept the morphine in pairs of syringes in their bags. "One for Hell and Two for Heaven" was their motto because the hopeless cases were always released with two quick and mercifully fatal jabs. There was as much pain in the face of the wounded as there was beauty in the face of the statue and they both screamed to Jimmy for release. He did not want to look at the soldier gabbling to the medic, and he did not want to think that another life was ruined for no reason. He gazed into the eyes of the statue. Jimmy thought Posey was a stone face and kept everything to himself, but Posey could read the secret fears in the quivering of Jimmy's nose. Posey left him to his terrors but was grateful for Jimmy's steady hand.

Jimmy's reaction to the firefight and to the statue forced Posey to admit there was something special about the little man. He felt calm, and thoughts of death were far from him because Jimmy had taken such an interest in the statue. Jimmy's life had not offered him much beauty. Posey understood that Jimmy's questions about the statue were an awakening. He admired Jimmy for making the connection between the statue and Sally. Sally was now Jimmy's Jersey Venus, and Posey felt that familiar glow of understanding run through him. Posey was grateful to the Venus and to her sculptor for giving them just enough proportionality for he and Jimmy to know one another.

They looked at the wounded soldier in the back of the truck and turned their gaze to back to the statue. Her blank eyes stared past them, and both were glad they could see her and all her sisters. "We better get her into the truck before something happens to her," Jimmy sighed.

Posey and Jimmy took hold of her feet and shoulders and lifted her onto a mattress in the back of their Dodge. Jimmy jumped up and secured her to the truck with the rubber belts he had scrounged from a burned-out tank. They worked with all the care of older brothers tucking their sister into bed, and she seemed to appreciate their rough civility.

Chapter 7

Landscape

Southern Belgium
January 20, 1945

In the two weeks that Sergeant Glenn Carnehan had been driving Lieutenant George Stout through France and Belgium, they had become Glenn and George. They had also become a team that worked with quiet efficiency borne out of mutual respect. When Glenn had been assigned as George's driver, he didn't know what to make of either the dapper officer who was his immediate superior or the definitely inferior battered German jeep he was supposed to keep on the road. Both the man and the machine looked like they could be problems. The thing he was driving had originally been a Volkswagen, but the Krauts had carved it into a bathtub on wheels. Glenn had been surprised to see a naval officer so close to the front lines, but soon figured out that, although he was Navy, he was all gentleman. Glenn saw Stout's pants had a sharp crease in them and his clothing was clean under the filthy parka. This was not going to be an easy job.

The man had been a "conservator" at Harvard, whatever that was, so Glenn expected him to be a pain-in-the-ass snob. Glenn soon discovered that first impressions could be very misleading, for George Stout was as easy to work with as the jeep was sweet to drive.

The Germans called their jeep a "kubelwagen" or a "tub bucket car," so the thing had become the "Stout Bucket." They had painted huge white stars in circles on the hood and both doors to make sure they weren't killed by one of their own, but the bucket was such an oddity that its very weirdness was a shield. Anyone looking at it through a rifle sight would stop for a second and ask himself, “what the hell’s that thing?” That second of curiosity had saved both Glenn and George from being listed as “casualties of friendly fire.” If George, Glenn, and the bucket were not exactly famous throughout the Twelfth Army Group, they were at least recognizable; their very outlandishness made them safe from impatient trigger fingers.

Stout would sit in the passenger seat poring over his maps and papers and telling Glenn where to go. At first, there didn’t seem to be any rhyme or reason to the directions. Glenn would drive George over half of Belgium and the next day they would do the other half. Glenn was glad that the American zone in Belgium was so small for it cut down on the driving. George appeared every morning with two mugs of coffee, a list of destinations, and his map case. They would then drive around putting “Off Limits” signs in all sorts of out of the way places. George plastered the signs on the walls of village churches and smeared a paint stencil over the windows of a cafe claiming that it was a historic monument. Glenn couldn’t figure out what was so important about a French boozer.

They had even put a barbed wire fence around a pile of two rocks with a big stone over the top of them. This was insane. It was like saying a gravel pit was a “protected site by order of the Commanding General.” They once spent a whole afternoon gluing signs and nailing boards to the two remaining walls of a castle. Glenn tried to make small talk and said, “the Germans really did a number on this place.” George just smiled that smile which said “I’m now going to give you a lecture” and dove into a two-hour talk about how Napoleon’s army did the damage in 1815 on the way to the Battle of Waterloo. Glenn was learning as much history as they were covering geography. They went on their journeys in much this manner, Glenn driving to wherever George directed him, until George’s impatience landed them up to the steering wheel in a ditch.

George was reading the big map and had told Glenn to hang a right and then go straight for three miles. Glenn had protested,

"That's not such a good idea, George." Stout had one of his very rare bursts of irritation and pulled rank. "To the right, Sergeant." Glenn had obeyed with a grudge. Fifty yards later, they jumped a little rise in the road and started tobogganing straight along the ice of a winding track. Stout was thrown out of the car, and it was just luck as sheer as the ice that kept Glenn's head on his shoulders. The Stout Bucket bounced off a couple of trees and tore through branches before it tipped into six feet of a snow filled ditch.

Glenn and George stood in freezing embarrassment, looking at the back end of their ride rising into the air. The tub really looked like a sinking boat. They had to walk three sullen miles to the town to beg for help. The only luck of the day was meeting Posey and Jimmy. Posey was assigned to the northern sector of the Third American Army and Stout was patrolling the southern half of the Twelfth Army's area, so it was just the luck of rapidly moving armies which brought them together. If George and Glenn didn't have a guardian angel, at least they had Jimmy, the Dodge command car, and the winch. It only took five minutes to get the tub on level ground. The two parties then went their separate ways, after arranging a rendezvous in two days in Antwerp.

But it took about half an hour for Lieutenant Stout to climb down off his high horse and tell Glenn, "Look. I'm sorry I was such a fool back there. There's really no excuse for that sort of behavior and I could have got us killed. I would really appreciate it if you would accept my apology." Glenn's simple, "That's OK, George. We're all pushed," covered the simple truth that Lieutenant George Stout had just proved himself to have the stature of the man Glenn thought him to be. The equally simple fact that Glenn did not use George's apology to browbeat an officer was clear to them both. There was never another bout of temper from George, and Glenn would forever think of him as "Gentleman George."

Glenn gingerly guided the Stout Bucket through the winding curves, and George asked, "How did you know we took the wrong road?"

"Whatdja mean?"

"When I told you to turn right, you said that it wasn't a good idea. How did you know?"

"The map," answered Glenn wondering why he had to state the obvious.

"But I was reading the map. How could you see it when you were driving?"

"The red's big and there's a lot of ice around, so I knew we were going to go ass over tea kettle."

"What red?"

"The red on the map."

George pulled the map out of his case and examined "the red." The map was covered with so many red and blue contour lines it looked like it had varicose veins. Sure enough, a careful look at the dip where they slid off the road showed the little rise they went over and the place where they ditched, but it also showed slight changes in elevation on the ground. George had been looking at the road marked in black and hadn't paid any attention to the contour lines which described the actual ground the road passed through. He had been so intent on getting to their destination that he had ignored everything else. Glenn hadn't, but how had he read the details on a map from three feet away when he was supposed to be looking at the road? Glenn could only have seen the map for a few seconds. George was intrigued and needed to get to the bottom of the mystery of Glenn's map reading.

George knew Glenn was right when he said "We're all pushed." There was only one Monuments Man and a driver assigned to each army and not all armies were equal. Stout's Twelfth Army was concentrated in northern France and southern Belgium, coiled to strike across the Rhine at Germany. Posey and Jimmy were with Patton's Third Army and Patton had a habit of conquering huge tracts of countryside. Countries usually stay in one place, but armies grow and move and shrink and disappear in surrender. Each American army had its own woefully inadequate monuments team charged with saving what the fighting hadn't destroyed. Nobody really knew what they were doing because, before the invasion of Europe, nobody had ever thought of preserving art in the middle of a battle. In the past, the conquerers just waited for the wars to finish before the looting started. But this was different. Stout was one of the very few detectives on the trail of a gang of thieves who had stolen entire countries. The Nazis were the most organized of plunderers, and it was Stout's job to get to their loot before they could destroy it. "Pushed" was an understatement.

They had been looking for a German who was reported to be living in the vicinity and who was an art expert. Stout knew, if he could get such a person to talk, he could get to the next hiding place before the artifacts were evacuated further east. After their ditching, Stout decided they really needed a rest and spent the rest of the day following a relief column in the hope they would eventually stumble upon a chow line. They drove into the square of a little town and almost into a line of very happy soldiers shuffling toward the cooks and their first hot meal in over a week. The cooks had set up a mobile kitchen and were ladling hot stew to anybody who was hungry, whether or not they wore a uniform. To the soldiers, it was like Christmas, but to the Belgium refugees, it was a reminder someone cared enough for them to share their food. The dinner was hot and meaty, and George now commanded that they both stop for the night and eat. George knew Glenn would be ecstatic at the prospect of real coffee, so he decided to postpone Glenn's interrogation until after they were fed and cupping the warmth.

After their meal, George opened the map between them, pointed to the place where they ran off the road and asked, "There's where we turned right off the road. Tell me what you see?"

Glenn stabbed his forefinger three times at the map, "There's the hill. There's the hollow. There's the ditch."

George demanded, "Show me the elevation."

George expected Glenn to follow the red contour lines with his finger and was amazed that Glenn hovered his hand over the map, moved it from west to east, and raised and lowered his hand following the rise and fall of the land.

"Do that again."

Glenn was used to George's little experiments. He thought George could not understand anything that could not be repeated. This was Glenn's explanation of why they were criss-crossing entire countries on the same roads. Glenn had not yet learned that George was a scientist as much as an artist and had to repeat procedures to make sure they worked. For Stout, trained in the science of art conservation, repetition was reality. For Glenn, repetition was boring. Glenn humored George and slid his hand absentmindedly over the map.

George had spent his life restoring masterpieces and had great appreciation for unique virtuosity, but Glenn's talent was different. Glenn was neither a painting nor an artist, so Stout had to test his observations, because he couldn't really believe what he was seeing. He took out a map of western Germany, one which Glenn had never seen and which represented places they had never gone. This map was virginal to Glenn's experience.

"Do it again on this map. Start from Wiesbaden and move from east to west."

Now it was Glenn's turn to get irritated, so with a sigh as if giving into to a child's demands to "Do it again!", he did it again. He placed his palm over the town of Wiesbaden and headed west. His hand never touched the paper but rose and fell following the red and blue contour lines. His palm dipped down to the Rhine valley and slowly rose over the hills of Belgium. He kept going just to please George until his hand hovered over the Ardennes with his little finger almost touching Bastogne.

"That's amazing," said George.

"What's so amazing?'

" What you just did."

"Ah come on. I just did what you said."

"What is amazing is that you can see the map in three dimensions."

"What the hell are you talking about?" Glenn asked.

"This map is in two dimensions, left and right, up and down, along northings and eastings."

"So what?"

"But you can see the land in three dimensions. You can see left and right, but you also see high and low. It's as if you're looking at the real thing."

"Doesn't everybody?"

"No, it's very rare. It's like you have perfect pitch," George explained.

"I don't even play baseball."

"Perfect pitch is when someone can give you the name of a note and you can sing it perfectly because you just know it. Here you have the same sort of talent, except that you use your eyes and not your ears."

"You mean everybody can't read a map?"

"Not the way you can."

"Ain't that amazing."

"That's what I said. Amazing."

From then on, Glenn navigated and George drove.

They parked the tub on the side of the little road the next day and walked up the hill. They knew better than to go barreling over hills where anything could be waiting on the other side. They kicked their feet through the last of winter's pebbled slush. The last days of January had brought relief from the worst winter in fifty years, but they hadn't stowed their winter coats. The feeble spring sun would soon come into its own, and then they would throw away their winter wardrobe because there was no way that this war could last until the next winter. The Germans were beaten and victory was a matter of not "if" but "when." Everybody sensed it, so everybody was just that much more careful. Nobody wanted to be the last death of the war, even though they all knew somebody would be.

That was the stupidity of the whole thing and it made George angry. There was no need to continue the hostilities. But whatever twisted motives the Germans had in starting the war, those same inspirations kept them from ending the fighting. As a young man, he had admired the art and the culture of Germans, but these last months had brought him to an understanding of Germans he didn't want. Now he loathed them, not just for what they had done, but for what they persisted in doing against all reason.

The Germans had five years to loot the lands they had conquered and the people they had destroyed, but now George had weeks at most to get it all back. He was dog tired but kept going. He had almost let his soul slouch into not caring - doing enough to get by and get home - when a soldier had brought him a sack.

Weeks earlier, a simple infantryman had walked up to him and said, "Hey, Sir, you're that museum guy ain't you?" George had confessed to the honor and the soldier had handed him a gunny sack. "I don't know what it is. Looks like a big rolling pin, but it's got writing all over it. Maybe you've been looking for this stuff."

The "stuff" was what everybody called works of art, and people would bring him any stuff they thought was the real stuff, or tell him about some place where they had seen lots of stuff. Stuff could be anything from a Dresden plate to a Michaelangelo sculpture, so George was always aglow with anticipation whenever he heard the word "stuff."

The stuff in the gunny sack was a 17th century Torah. George touched it, and generations of fingers reached out from the parchment to touch him. He felt sure that the last person to cradle this scroll in his arms had long since been murdered, so it was with the reverence which comes with understanding that he had placed it in the care of Chaplain Pomeranze, who added one more Torah to his collection of hundreds of others stored in the warehouse. Each was a silent witnesses waiting for a congregation which would never return. After the soldier had given George the rolling pin, he had sped with Glenn to their next assignment with renewed faith that what they were doing was worth the effort. In moments of exhausted dullness, he thought of “the rolling pin” and always found it strangely exhilarating.

They sweated their way to the top of the rise and stopped. Below them winked the waters of the Rhine and they stood silent upon the peak above Cologne. This was the end of the line, until the line moved forward. Glenn was unusually concerned. “Do you think we’ll make it?”

George’s mind traveled through the lists complied from interrogations, detailed reports, consolidated reports, gossip, telegrams, letters and whispered confessions and knew that just across that water was the greatest store of stolen treasure they had ever heard about.

Glenn had helped to compose those lists and had transferred the information to the maps. George had been very careful to place red triangles over names of locations where the Germans had collected their loot. He was just as assiduous in recording the names of Germans who had information and circling in deep blue ink the places where they had last been seen. The maps now had a second coating of red and blue and as the snakes moved west, the ladders followed them. Glenn was invaluable in making the maps a reality because he could visualize the terrain so accurately that George could determine whether to send a truck or a half-track to get to the place before the loot was moved further east. There was one place where all the red triangles and blue circles were converging. It was the town of Siegen, just a few miles on the other side of the river. And so, it was with renewed urgency that George answered Glenn’s question, “We have to.”

They shared their determination and faced the challenge. George asked, “What does the map tell you?”

“It’s downhill all the way once we get over the river. The whole area is a donut of hills and once we get over the hills, it’s a bowl down to Siegen and then up the other side to the east.”

The previous night, it was George who had shared his fears of being just a little too late, and Glenn had performed his magic over the map. His finger had circled Siegen as if he were coaxing a note out of the rim of a crystal glass.

Chapter 8

Nocturne in Neon and Amber

Glenn fussed at the kitchen sink, washing the evening's glasses and plates. Glenn's memories and the album had exhausted Michael, so he had dragged himself to bed. When Michael had moved out and finally married Anne, Glenn and Ellen had turned Michael's room into a combination study and guest room. Studying there was rare because Glenn loved to use the living room for pouring over books and collections of reproductions. Having guests was rarer because they almost never invited anyone into their fortress of domestic felicity. So the room had kept both Michael's bed and his name.

It had been a long day for the little fellow. Even though he was in his late thirties, Michael would always be their "Little Fellow." This had irritated Michael in his mildly rebellious youth, but he had come to accept Glenn's teasing about the arrogance and thin skins of young people. Glenn would recall Oscar Wilde's quip that "Youth is wasted on the young." Now that he was truly old, Glenn loved Wilde's deep knowledge that experience and understanding of the finer things in life had to be learned, slowly. Wisdom didn't come from thirty-second commercials. Michael's day was so tiring for him simply because he'd had to deal with so many fine things in such a short space of time.

Glenn had decided to share his own past with Michael, so Michael could appreciate the money that was going to ensure his future. Michael was now caught between the cash and his first wave of understanding of how Glenn's life had generated all that money. Glenn was a firm believer in understanding the principles behind anything because he thought there were some fundamentals in life. His basics were knowledge, which he had spent a lifetime accumulating, and dignity, which he had practiced to the limits of his ability, if not beyond. That was why he shunned others' company, for so many of them ridiculed dignity, and their cynical sneers or bellowing ridicule were too much for him to bear. He knew such mockery was moral vandalism, so he hid his treasures.

When he cleared away the dishes, he walked down the hall back to the living room. He stepped through the light shining under the door from Michael's room, but he could not ignore the excitement seeping through the wooden panels. Michael was probably calling Anne to tell her the good news of The Leprechaun, the pot of gold and the rainbow, so Glenn left Michael to the phone. They both had had enough for one day and they could continue tomorrow where they left off tonight.

Sleep did not come easy to the old man. After midnight, he would end the day in calm repose, sitting in a chair before the living room windows and gazing at the street below, stirring his "Old Man's Nightcap" of Metamucil. He liked to see the store signs blink and watch the people passing through the gaudy neon kaleidoscope. The street was his very own color tube, and it would change shape every few seconds and present its random patterns and scene changes, and he didn't even have to turn the tube.

People's faces took on lovely expressions as they passed beneath the primary colors of the Seven Eleven or whatever was occupying the store at the corner these days. He had seen every sort of light over half a century and no longer really cared what they were selling. But he liked the latest light, which always resolved itself into green and bathed the shoppers in fuzzy, verdant sparkles.

There was much that Michael had to understand before he could comprehend the meaning of van Meegeren's *Head of Christ*. Glenn hoped that a weekend was enough time for Michael to grasp the worth of something priceless. If only such complicated things could be as easily understood as the street signs touting "Sale" or "Adult Toys" or "Best Coffee Lowest Price." Nothing really valuable was that simple.

The signs blinked on and off leaving their lurid afterglow to dance in Glenn's eyes. They were better than sleeping pills because they conjured visions in subtle shades and had the manners to leave the mixing to Glenn's imagination. He would look up the street to see the fugue of electric colors merge and separate in their own time and then look down the same street to find a counterpoint of color. He kept coming back to the living room chair, amazed by such artificial artistry continually changing like a painting without an artist.

Glenn would not sleep until he saw the image of Ellen wander through the colors. She had been gone these two years, but every night the store signs resurrected her. Sometimes he would see her stately shuffle in the back end of a young woman ambling into a late-night convenience store. Other times, he would watch a young couple and imagine they were young Glenn and Ellen looking for the milk they'd forgotten to buy for Jessie's bottle. But most often the colors would gyrate in his head until the soft magenta of her mouth would blow him a kiss and he would nod off in the chair.

When two people had become one over sixty years, there was only half left when one departed. The doctor had assured Glenn that his heart and lungs were fine and that a mere enlarged prostrate was a bit of a miracle in a vigorous man over eighty years old. But Glenn cared nothing for his health when every second heartbeat was missing. What matter lungs, when there was nobody to talk to? What miracle kept you alive, when all that was worth living for was already dead? But Ellen wasn't. In the neon world of Seven-Up chartreuse and the vermillion of "Eat at Joe's," Ellen walked again by his side and made him the luckiest man in the world. And so sleep would never come until Ellen rose again to hear of all that had happened in the day.

Glenn laughed her through the sale at Sotheby's and almost forgot to tell her that they had visited Balto, just the same as ever. She wanted to know how Michael had taken the news of his new wealth and shared a chuckle as Glenn said, "Shock." They wondered what Michael was going to do with all that loot, and Ellen hoped that the first thing would be to get out of that drafty hovel they called a Pennsylvania homestead. She had hated the idea of Michael “moving the whole tribe to the wilderness in the hills,” but Michael had claimed that it was “a better place than Brooklyn, with really good schools for the kids.” Ellen had hid her skepticism behind her disappointment because “he’s a grown man and is entitled to his own mistakes.”

Glenn told her that Michael was still reeling from the sale, but soon he would see some sense and invest it wisely as Anne would, no doubt, suggest. Ellen was glad that Anne was the rock in Michael’s life. Their marriage had been a relief to her. Anne had good sense and, sometimes, Michael listened to her. Glenn felt amber invade his peripheral vision, and Ellen disappeared.

For a moment he thought there might be a fire in the drug store below him. There were also sounds less dulcet than Ellen’s whispered “Good Night, My Love,” and they annoyed him. He turned to see the blinking light on the telephone. It was probably Michael phoning home about the kids. Glenn saw the clock on the phone and realized that it was after one in the morning. Michael wouldn’t be calling home at this hour. Why was Michael using the apartment phone, when he practically had that cell phone glued to the side of his head? Glenn did not like those phones because they seemed to be everywhere. Phones should stay in their places on top of telephone books resting on telephone tables in hallways and living rooms, firmly tethered to walls. They shouldn’t be implanted in ears. The only times Glenn became a real curmudgeon was when people with aggressive elbows holding cell phones bumped into him on streets. Roads were for cars. Sidewalks were for pedestrians. Phones were for apartments. Getting them all mixed up together was a mélange of annoyances and just a plain pain in the ass. Michael had bought him this newfangled phone with mysteries such as “Speed Dial” and some foolishness called “Caller ID” and insisted that the thing would be a real life saver if Glenn fell and broke a hip. Glenn had finally surrendered if only to stop Michael pestering him, so the phone sat perched on the living room window sill like some anorexic Buddha.

He glanced at the black number etched in the amber of the telephone display and saw a strange area code. The telephone number was not one he recognized, and he knew that Michael was in more trouble than Michael realized. Glenn's puckered his lips at the neon signs and whispered to Ellen, "We got a problem."

Chapter 9

Kaleidoscope in Sepia

Glenn sat at the kitchen table watching the morning sun slink across the album. As in most things, Ellen had been right; the room trapped the morning sun and the heat marched down the hall following the sun's saunter through the day. Winter nights were always as cozy in the front room as the heating bills were low. The table was a chrome construction, still gleaming as the day they bought it in 1957. Ellen would run a knife along its metal ridges and scour the hell out of bread crumbs lurking in the crevices. Crumbs and a wet Brillo pad always brought her back to him.

He sat with his jaw resting in the triangle of his hands and elbows and gazed at the jagged square of Kodak paper from the album. Young Jimmy and young Glenn peered back at him over the long exposure of their lives. He remembered that day so clearly, his legs and arms crossed, leaning against the hood of a jeep and Jimmy sitting on the bumper. It felt good to salute the boy he used to be, when he was so young and so ignorant.

Glenn's eyes were hidden in the shade of his mischievous brows, but Jimmy's steady glare was the same as through a rifle sight. His thousand-yard stare jumped through the camera lens and bored through the decades. Jimmy didn't smile much. When Michael first saw the photo yesterday, he had missed the expressions in their eyes. He had been trying to take in the whole outline, searching for his grandfather, until he recognized the smile connecting the man in the picture with Anda.

Glenn kept an ear cocked down the corridor to hear Michael fussing in his room. The telephone was bothering him, and the curiosity was scraping at his skull. The amber light on the phone last night screamed trouble in Michael's family. It was too late for Michael to be talking to Anne or the twins. The phone number wasn't home, so Michael had not been talking to his wife after midnight. Anne would have tucked Teddy and Frank into bed at least four hours before Michael called whoever was at the other end of that number. Glenn did not know what was the source of the trouble, but he knew that Michael himself was the cause of it. Glenn picked up the phone and held it in a fist that could strangle a rattlesnake.

These new gadgets did so many things that Glenn lost patience with them. Telephones were supposed to let you talk with people; they were not supposed to run your life. Glenn had never bothered to learn how to use all the buttons, bells, and whistles on this phone. His interest ended after the numbers 9 and 0. The only reason he had agreed to keep the infernal thing was because Michael had insisted he have a new phone with something called "Speed Dial." Such things were fine for young people, but Glenn had accepted the phone just to stop Michael's whining.

When Michael had set up the phone, Glenn flipped through a little booklet the size of a car manual and his brain didn't care for the English any more than the French, Italian, German, Spanish or volumes of lines and dashes that said Japanese, Chinese or Korean. He had lost interest and had thrown the little Tower of Babel into a drawer, where he kept everything he wanted to ignore and forget but sensed he shouldn't throw away.

The phone sat neglected on the old telephone table, standing at attention in its little guard house, but Glenn couldn't ignore the niggle at the back of his brain. He perched himself on the edge of the chair and methodically pressed buttons and watched the display window. The damn thing made noises as if it had gas and, sometimes, it even talked to Glenn. He kept pressing the buttons until the display flashed "Call History." He pressed an arrow, and the last number dialed magically appeared on the screen. Trusting to what he called "old technology," Glenn picked up a pencil and wrote down the number on the corner of a menu from a Chinese restaurant. He'd never seen this number before. It was new and irritating and smelled of something he wanted to put into the drawer, but he couldn't. His suspicions grew with his curiosity. He had to know.

Glenn pulled a three-year-old phone book from under the telephone table. He had thrown away the phone books left abandoned at his door for the last two years, and sheer laziness had kept this one nestled on its little shelf. His thumb and forefinger did a drunken stagger through the yellowing pages until they stopped at a map proclaiming "U.S. Area Codes by State."

Ever since Stout had revealed Glenn's strange ability to locate information on a map, the flat worlds had been a comfort to him. There was something absolute about a map, which both fascinated and frightened him, for the very truth of a map could not be denied. People and their words would slither through different meanings, but you couldn't manhandle Pittsburgh over a map and make it fall into Nevada. No, places were set as firmly as the geological faults on which they rested. The people, like the bear, could go over the mountain to see what they could see, but the mountain remained. The familiar contours of the Eastern states were a higgledy-piggledy pleasure to his eyes, and he found solace in the regularity of the Western squares. He had always wondered about the shape of the country, but now his mind demanded to know why he was losing himself in all of these facts and details. He admitted that the facts of the map were his way of avoiding the phone number. By staring at the map he wouldn't have to deal with the other end of the line. Finally, his courage took hold of his cowardice and together they played Hop Scotch over the map with his finger, until they landed on the code. It was 570. That was in Pennsylvania. Michael's code was 607, the wilds of New York straddling the border with Pennsylvania. There could be some innocent explanation or a mistake, but he knew there was no mistake.

Glenn glowered at the pencilled number on the restaurant menu and punched buttons on the phone. His thumb hovered over the "Talk" button like the safety catch on a rifle. After his thumb fell on that button, there would be no turning back. There would be no way he could put what he would discover in the drawer and just leave it there. His thumb fell. A woman's voice said "Hello?" and Glenn could not bring himself to speak. What could he say? "Hi there. I'm Michael's grandfather and I'd like to know if you're banging my grandson." A second "Hello" pierced the silence, and Glenn's voice was aged velvet as he said, "Hi, this is John from Card Services," and he sweated a moment until he heard the relief of the click.

Two "Hellos" were all he needed. She sounded like a sweet young thing, but behind the voice, Glenn smelled sugar-coated cyanide. Two "Hellos" and Michael could say "Goodbye" to his family. Just two "Hellos" separated Michael and Glenn from their loves. He had to do something about those two "Hellos," but what? He gently placed the phone into its little cradle and quietly hated it.

The album spread open its leaves as if in supplication to the days of Glenn's youth. The amber of the phone melted into the faded sepia of the black and white photographs, and the colors mixed in Glenn's mind demanding that he make the connection. So many pictures were spiraling together: Jimmy, himself, the jeep, mountains, and a woman saying "Hello." He looked at the photo of himself and Jimmy and was happy that his old friend was gracious enough to just sit there, leaving him to his memories of himself. But his own eyes glared back at him, and the old man was caught by the determination in the face from his youth.

He knew what he had to do. He must take those adventures from his past and give them to Michael. The album wasn't open for a history lesson or an art lecture. It was open because the Leprechaun had squawked "three million seven hundred thousand dollars" and because Glenn saw the hurt clouding Anne's eyes. Michael must be brought to an understanding he could barely acknowledge. He did not know how to do this, but it had to be done.

Glenn had to reach back to his young manhood, grasp something by the throat, and drag it through the time of both their lives. Then he had to offer it to Michael. What Michael would do with it was up to Michael, but Glenn had no choice. He had to catch the knowledge gleaming from those young eyes in the photo and bring it to his grandson. Michael had to understand what was behind those eyes, if he were to know what was right in front of his own face. That was the mission. That was his duty. He had to offer his own understanding. Michael would have to choose.

He heard the door open and Michael's bare feet scamper across the corridor to the bathroom. Glenn was strangely tired. With a morning yawn and a sigh of resolve, the old man breathed in the vigor of his youth.

Chapter 10

Avalanche

Namur, Belgium,
February 14, 1945

George Stout was exhausted. Six weeks of following the armies east across four countries had given him shooting pains from his shoulder to his foot all down the right side. They had been driving from town, to castle, to city to barnyard, criss-crossing the rear echelons of the army, chasing the artwork. Sometimes it felt like they were in a giant game of connect-the-dots between burned-out buildings and flooded mines. He tried to shrug it off as the cost of sitting for hours either in the Stout Bucket or at a desk, when he could find one, but he also knew this was his age telling him to stop. George envied Glenn's youth and energy, wondered if these six weeks would take six years off his life, and grumbled to himself, "What I need is a young man's body."

George had made Glenn their navigator, but there were times when Glenn insisted that he drive and the old man rest. Glenn was driving them through masses of equally exhausted troops. It was hard work keeping the wheels on roads which were like icing melting on chocolate cakes. They plodded along at ten miles an hour. Their work was as sluggish as the roads they travelled. Every crossroads was an hour's halt as they waited their turn while frantic MPs sorted out the traffic jam of two armies headed in different directions. When they stopped, Glenn felt the bite of spring icicles and played tug-of-war with the canvas top until he had it secured on its frame over their heads and snapped into the top of the windshield. There were no side panels, so the slush would billow up and splash over their feet. With the rain, the mud, the jams, and the accidents, Glenn knew that it would take them most of the day to get to Siegen.

Glenn had also been feeling the pressure, for the work was getting harder as the final weeks of fighting became fiercer. The more German territory the Allies conquered, the more intelligence reports and prisoner interrogations there were to process. He admired the way George held all that responsibility on his tired shoulders, but George, the officer, had come to rely on his driver for much more than directions. Glenn supplied the young man's body and brought along with it the enthusiasm of youth. There were days when George would give up everything for a good night's sleep, and Glenn would give him that respite. Glenn took charge of the lists, as he called the Full Reports, and the little lists, which were their field missions.

Headquarters in London would send reports the size of telephone books which listed everything the Germans had stolen from nations and individual people. The reports contained millions of items, and it would take years to go through them all, when George had weeks at the most. The war was dying and so were the people. Every day the fighting continued, the casualties grew; the lists of the dead started to match the lists of the looted art. Those two lists drained George's strength, for he knew that the same criminals who looted whole countries were still robbing people of their lives in a war already lost.

When he was Glenn's age, he had admired the Germans because of their art and their culture, but seeing the war face-to-face had made George detest them. It was not just the criminals at the top who were to blame, for even if Hitler were some sort of evil genius, he could not accomplish such destruction on his own. He had to have help; the people themselves had to assist in this monstrosity. Nothing else could explain the magnitude of the evil George had witnessed. When he drove through miles of needless devastation his mind dredged up half-remembered lines from school-boy Shakespeare and posed the question, "Why is Caesar such a wolf?" The more he saw of ruin and the more he heard the feeble excuses, the more the answer rang true, "T'is because the Romans are but sheep." Shakespeare had been right, more right than George could ever have imagined or been willing to admit. The great destroyers are so efficient because the majority of people just allow them to destroy, by following the leaders to destruction. He did not want to acknowledge what was staring him in the face, the blatant conclusion and simple fact that he could no longer believe the Germans were even human beings. The artwork now had more humanity than the people.

Glenn had confessed he was thinking the same way, though he had neither the education nor the words to express it. "The stuff is like another person," he had said to George, and George had to agree that the war had made the things into people, just as it had made the people into things. The two were merging in their minds in ways they did not really want to think about. George had spent his life with paintings hanging on walls, but the sight of corpses slumped up against those same walls would haunt him forever. Something had to give.

The Full Reports were an avalanche of documents, names, places, intelligence reports, prisoner interrogations, and just plain rumor. Some of the information was culled from pre-war auction catalogues and was six years old. Another report was yesterday's interrogation of a prisoner, happy to trade whatever he knew, or could make up, for a cigarette. The catalogues and the half-page POW reports were equally unreliable, and the uncertainty just added to the strain. The reports would keep art historians busy for lifetimes, but George didn't have much time left.

George had been ordered to a top level briefing where a very senior intelligence officer had explained "The Nero Order." Hitler had decided the war was lost, so the German people had "failed the test of history." In his twisted mind, the Germans did not deserve to have a future because they had proven themselves inferior to his ideal of the Aryan Superman. Since they had failed him, they had to pay the price of failure; he ordered the retreating German armies to destroy everything. They were to "leave nothing for the enemy" and to destroy all bridges, railroads, water systems, electricity plants, factories. Nothing was to be left. The intelligence officer told them, "as we drive deeper into Germany, we will encounter greater levels of destruction, but it will be the result of the Germans' own scorched-earth policy." George appreciated the irony of Hitler finishing the job which the Allied bombers had started. The Nazis would destroy the German infrastructure on the ground more efficiently than the Eighth Air Force could rain ruin from the air. Since Hitler lost the war, he was also going to rob the German people of any future they might have.

The intelligence officer had given them a summary of the "cultural extermination in Russia and Poland." The Nazis had dynamited Russian palaces and gutted the entire center of Warsaw. They left smoking ruins so as to say, "If I can't have it, no one will." In Belgium, George and Glenn had met an old woman who had explained to them, "The Germans came in like gentlemen. They left like rabid beasts."

George did not like the comparison, for no animal behaved like the Nazis. An officer of Ordnance Engineers had told him of the booby traps he had encountered in the wake of the retreating Germans. Animals didn't leave hand grenades in teddy bears for children to find; demons did. The artwork was also slated for demolition because Hitler had decided that, if the Germans were unworthy of a bright Nazi future, neither would they keep their beloved German past. German culture itself was to be the last casualty of the conflict. At any moment, some Nazi official could decide to blow everything sky-high. Delay was dangerous and deadly.

Relief came with Glenn's "Little Lists." Throughout the late winter and early spring, Glenn had attacked the paper mountain. He liberated four large ammunition boxes from an artillery battery and named them "Big List," "Little List," "Maps," and "Other Stuff." George was skeptical until Glenn explained the system. "All the reports you've been losing sleep over are in 'Big List,' and the reports we make up are in 'Little List.' We put 'Big List' on the back seat and 'Little List' sits on top 'cause you fuss more with 'Little List' than with 'Big List.'" George resented all the time he had wasted pouring over 'Big List' because he thought it was the main source of information. But Glenn had picked up the most recent intelligence reports and put them into what became 'Little List,' and George had come to rely on the smaller, and much more useful, collection. Once Glenn opened "Maps," George was convinced that he could finally get a good night's sleep.

While George had been trying to do everything on his own, Glenn had been quietly burrowing into the mountain. If "Big List" was the history of this enormous crime, "Maps" held the key to their future work. Glenn had been meticulous in mapping everywhere they had inspected and had organized their trips in chronological order. George could follow the pencilled lines Glenn had drawn on the main map and read the dates of their inspections beside every important place name. It was a complete record of their travels.

Glenn rummaged in the map box and produced a small booklet of newspaper clippings. "I've been cutting out the maps of the Advancing Front Line from *Stars and Stripes*. I figure if they're going to put this in the papers then we're not giving away any big secrets." George looked at the little booklet, and each page showed the Allied front line from the invasion to today. It was like a child's cartoon flip book. When George let the leaves ripple under his thumb, the line moved from left to right across France, Belgium, and Holland and stopped just inside Germany. He flipped a second time just to make sure he wasn't hallucinating. The fluttering pages reminded George of his son's toy books and he reveled in the delight of the animated image. Glenn watched the pages fly past George's thumb five times and wondered if George was going a little battle crazy from too little sleep, but George was appreciating the simple efficiency of Glenn's invention. The line marched west to east and compressed nine months of death and destruction into three trembling seconds. Glenn protested, "Hey, don't wear out the comics," but George's smile pulled his head up and his eyes beamed back at Glenn. "This is very good work," he said, and he saw Glenn's chest swell under his approval. George carefully placed the flip book back into "Maps" and settled into a relieved snooze.

By this time Glenn had developed an interest in the artwork, and George responded eagerly. The drives from inspection site to headquarters to wherever they would bed down had become a classroom on wheels. George had asked, "What's in 'Other Stuff'?" and laughed to be told, "That's the stuff I don't have a clue about." "Other Stuff" held a field message book with an artist's name and some dates on each page.

As Glenn rifled through "Little List" to make up the maps, he had copied out the names of painters and tried to put them into chronological order. He had a growing affinity for the paintings and was full of questions about the images and the artists. When Glenn drove he would listen to George lecture from the passenger seat with the message book open on his lap. George would tell Glenn everything he could remember. He was the professor and supposed to be the font of all knowledge, but he was frequently stumped by one of Glenn's entries and had to admit "I can't remember a damn thing about this guy." The admission of ignorance was a relief to Glenn because it proved that George respected him enough not to bullshit him. Days later, George would remember some detail and write a note beside the name. Glenn was a sponge. He loved the details and hoarded everything in his notebook.

George spent so much time talking about the artists that their trips eroded the barrier between officer and enlisted man. When George was pushed to the limits of his memory, he sometimes lost patience with Glenn's insatiable curiosity. Once he had shouted in exasperation, "No, no. Raphael was Italian and Rubens was Flemish." Glenn was secure enough to retort, "Hey keep your shirt on. I just want to know the difference between a Rubens painting and a Reuben's sandwich." George had to laugh and the laughter vanquished his temper. He apologized, so Glenn said mildly,

“Sheesh what a grouch. You’d think I’d burned the supper last night.”

Most of Glenn’s questions were simple appeals of “who,” “what,” “where,” and “when” and reminded George of the brighter students at Harvard, the ones who were not afraid to admit their ignorance before they leapt to “how” and “why.” The “know-it-alls” were almost unteachable because they were always trying to impress their fellows and teachers with their meager learning. The wisely ignorant ones who persevered became the best students because they were the most honest, and George loved them for their character. The bright sparks called such students Dummies, but George would smile and muse to himself, “Dumbo was the one who learned to fly.”

Glenn’s endless questions brought him back to the sanity of Harvard, and when he was dredging up some fact from his rapidly receding youth, he could smell the floor wax of the Fogg Museum and the musk rising from wet wool jackets in the library. His morning routine of walking up the two flights of concrete steps and under the scroll work over the main door was a delight. The warmth of the two electric lanterns guarding that door on early winter evenings meant that he could take home his pride in a day’s work well done. It was a very short step in George’s mind from work to home and his wife and son. Now, his journeys across Europe with Glenn became lectures on art history, but they were also bridges to his peaceful past and a hopeful future. So, George had little trouble swallowing his irritations and fed Glenn a thousand years of art. While they were driving, Glenn was learning to fly. George had guided him through the lists of Rembrandts and relics, but Glenn put them on the map. He was eager to actually see all the stuff they had been talking about for weeks. It was something anxiously magical to have an impression in your mind and not know if the impression corresponded to the reality.

George had told him Rubens was born in Siegen and it was an irony that his wife’s portrait was reportedly hidden in a copper mine just a few miles from where the artist was born. There were other masterpieces on the list, other names on the maps, but Glenn had become entranced with the story of Hélène Fourment, Rubens' second wife. He had asked if Rubens had been divorced, and George chuckled to explain that, "three hundred years ago, divorce was only for the very rich and the very powerful." Glenn reminded George, "Oh yeah. A king just cut off the wife's head when he wanted a new one." George commented wryly, "You mean the new wife, not the old wife's head." He clarified that Henry VIII was an English king in the 1530s, but that Rubens was a Flemish painter in the 1600s. "Artists usually didn't decapitate the Missus for being ugly or not producing boy children. That was a luxury left to kings."

Glenn loved the story of Hélène and how Rubens had married a fifteen-year-old when he was fifty three. He also was happy to learn that the first Mrs. Rubens had died of natural causes and hadn't been murdered or otherwise disposed of. They had driven through so much killing and sordid theft in the last three months to find that there was solace in a man who had been faithful to his wife. Glenn didn't know why this touched him so deeply, but he accepted the feeling, along with the fact that Hélène was not a replacement.

Glenn was weaving along a road lined with resting infantry. He slowed to avoid an exhausted platoon huddled around a fire. George was recalling clusters of facts from his old lectures. Glenn asked, "Do you think Rubens was thinking of his first wife when he was painting the second?"

George recounted the tale of Rubens' father, Jan, who was "a happily married Protestant guy, but the Catholic kings were persecuting the Protestants, so Jan protected himself and his family by becoming the lover of Anna, Queen of Saxony. Since Jan was the queen's advisor, both in the court and in the bedroom, everything was hunky-dory until the king blew his stack and threw Jan into jail. When Jan got out of the hoosegow, he was so happy he immediately got his own wife pregnant, and then died ten years later."

He explained that, in the case of Jan Rubens, religion and politics made very strange bedfellows. Glenn followed the maze of all the religious intrigue. He wondered how a life could hang on a set of rosary beads but concluded that "Daddy Rubens and his wife did just about anything to keep themselves safe." George agreed that "the whole mess was crazy" and Glenn asked "how did the kid became a painter?"

"Young Peter Paul's mother moved him to Antwerp and they became Catholics. Momma didn't know what to do with the kid, so she made he an artist."

"You mean just like that, you could become a painter?" Glenn asked.

"It was a bit more complicated. His mother was Maria Pypelinks."

" Pypelinks?" laughed Glenn.

"They had weird names in those days. Well. Maria paid for Peter to get a good basic education in Latin at a special school. I think that's why they became Catholics. In those days you could be hanged by the Protestants for being a Catholic and burned alive by the Catholics for being a Protestant."

"Sounds like a pretty grim sort of choice."

"You bet it was. In this part of Europe, France, Germany, Holland, they were fighting over religion for almost a hundred years. They figure about a million people died in that squabble."

"So being a painter was a way out of the mess." added Glenn.

"Kinda," said George. He paused, looking for a way to bring Glenn from the facts of Rubens' life to the times in which he lived and painted. "You could keep your head if you painted the right things. Peter Paul Rubens produced Catholic images for Catholics, but he also did a great line in portraits of rich people for rich people, so he became rich himself. He knew what they wanted to look like, so he painted them that way."

"Smart guy."

"Yup. And he had the talent to pull it off."

"So that's how he became rich, painting rich people," mused Glenn.

"Not just rich, influential," said George. "He became the advisor to kings. The king of England even made him Sir Peter Paul Rubens."

"And all because of the paintings."

George let the information sink in and waited for Glenn to change gear up the hill. The engine labored through the incline, and when Glenn crested the rise in the road, George continued. "Artists in those days were servants, but some became the trusted friends of their patrons. You know he was a bit like an ambassador and a spy put together."

"So the painting was really about doing what the kings said," Glenn added.

"And making sure they got what they wanted. It could be a very dangerous job, but there were rewards."

"Like being made a Sir."

"Like keeping your head on your shoulders and money in the bank."

Glenn fell silent for a few miles, concentrating on driving and avoiding the dog-faced and dog-tired soldiers slogging along both sides of the road.

"Looks to me like young Rubens was following in his old man's footsteps."

"How so?" asked George.

"His daddy kept the queen happy to help his own family and the son kept the king happy to do the same. Painting the king wasn't so much different from banging the queen."

George's laughter spluttered onto the windshield, and he told himself he had to remember this observation for future classes. He flipped over the page of Glenn's notebook and read "Elsheimer" with a big question mark beside it. "Why are you so interested in Elsheimer?" Glenn was studying the muddy road and guiding the front wheels through ridges of slime that threatened to slide them into a ditch. They could feel the Bucket slipping along, and Glenn kept the speed as low as he could without stalling the engine. He commented casually, “That name keeps popping up in the lists.”

George racked “Elsheimer” over his memory, but drew blanks. Glenn was right - the name kept appearing in the Big List, but George didn’t know why. He could understand why someone would want to steal the *Mona Lisa*, but for every famous and expensive work of art on the “A” list, there were also dozens of minor or obscure or completely forgotten German artists from the “D” list. George would have relegated Elsheimer to the “F for Footnote” list and would not have bothered to even mention the name to a gaggle of undergraduates. Yet Glenn was absolutely correct, for he could count on an Elsheimer popping up in every consignment of stolen goods.

The lectures on wheels revealed something important to George. “Big List’ was so complete that one could make neither rhyme nor reason out of what the Nazis had stolen. “Big List’ said that they had taken everything, but this was clearly impossible, so George had searched for some pattern in the Nazis’ actual selection. Glenn had written down every name of every major painting they were searching for, and George had to tell him something about each of those names. The famous names were easy and George could churn up the miles with biographies of Rembrandt, Rubens, Michaelangelo, and Leonardo da Vinci. When George couldn’t remember anything about an obscure artist, he would wonder why the Nazis had bothered with it in the first place.

The thefts of both the famous and the forgotten had intrigued George. It all seemed a giant jumble, as if they had really raided a pawn shop along with the Louvre. But Glenn had been noticing the pattern that evaded George. The stolen works had only one thing in common; the thieves just wanted something, so they took it. Glenn had never seen these paintings, but he had appreciated the taking of them. George realized that the lists did not reflect the quality of the artwork. The lists expressed the tastes and the prejudices of the thieves. A professional art thief would make his choices according to resale value. That was the basic sanity demanded by money, for no cat burglar would waste his time on an Elsheimer when a Rembrandt was on the same wall. Why had the Nazis bothered to take both?

Glenn's questions about Elsheimer pointed to the answer. The Nazis were looting not according to the monetary value of the painting, but according to their own artistic values. This artwork was for them to keep, not to sell. Their choices reflected what they thought of themselves, just as the kings commissioned Rubens to project their images of themselves. Glenn had been right. There wasn't that much of a difference between Rubens painting the king and his father pleasuring the queen. The royals were getting what they wanted, and that was the key to the looting. Goering and Hitler were getting what they wanted, and what they chose reflected who they were. George had asked himself, "What would demons hang on their walls?" and always drew a blank. Such musings on the lists and on Glenn's questions forced George to admit it wasn't the Germans who were doing the looting; it was the Nazis. He was after the big fish and had to distinguish between the sharks and the barracudas.

George flipped through Glenn's field book and scanned all the names he had written down. Sure enough, the names of the artists spanned the entire spectrum of art, but Glenn's question marks revealed the colors of the rainbow the Nazis had taken. Glenn's lists were from the looted works, not from a history book in an art class, so his question marks revealed the Nazis' choices. The answer to George's question was in Glenn's punctuation. The thieves had no taste; they couldn't really tell a Rembrandt from an Elsheimer, so they grabbed both. George drew a huge exclamation mark at the end of Glenn's list.

They drove along Spring roads, their thoughts muffling the light rain and keeping out the cold. The tires squooshed through the gauntlet of exhausted troops sleep-walking one foot in front of the other to wherever they would collapse that night. Glenn and George would only stop when they reached a numbered map reference four miles west of Siegen, where they had a date with Mrs. Rubens.

Chapter 11

Déjeuner Chez Dora

Glenn puttered around the kitchen and living room listening to Michael gargling in the bathroom. Glenn pulled up the blind, and the window stared back the first frost of winter. The heat had come on during the night and spewed a summer's worth of dust through the apartment. Glenn pressed his palms against the window pane, and it told him winter was here to stay. He welcomed its chill, for he loved the change of seasons. Michael walked down the hall into the kitchen, impatient and hungry.

"What's in the fridge?" Michael asked.

"It's Sunday."

"So?"

"Sunday, we go to Moïse's."

Michael looked at his watch and admitted, "I suppose we have time."

They walked out of the apartment and into the foggy wash of a Brooklyn morning. Michael snuggled his chin into his scarf like a turtle, but Glenn carried his gloves in one hand, savoring the crispness of the day. Glenn could feel his cold breath dribble over his chin and enjoyed walking the four deserted blocks to Dora's Cafe.

Glenn and Michael were announced by the sprung bell over the door that had been warning the Wisemans of customers for decades. Young Solly waved a happy few fingers from behind the cash register and scurried around the counter to shake hands with Mr. Glenn. "It's been months. I was thinking about coming 'round your way but I can see just by looking at you that you're fine."

Young Solly was Michael's age and was the latest in a line of three generations of Wisemans to own the cafe. Glenn had seen all the Wiseman men emerge. They didn't grow; they just seemed to hit six feet of solid muscle and stay there for the rest of their lives. Solly's grandfather, Moïse, had started as a bus boy, and after ten years of wheeling, dealing, and tips, became the owner. The Wiseman tribe made their living selling huge portions of food, but they never seemed to gain an ounce of fat themselves. "That's because they give it all to the customers," Glenn had decided. That Jews would resemble heavyweight prize fighters was a happy realization to Glenn and a shock to anti-Semites. It was just another reason why they had all come to love one another. The Wisemans and the Carnehans had been in and out of each other's lives longer than either needed to remember.

The cafe had been a neighborhood institution for over sixty years, and each of its six citations by the Health Department just added to its popularity. The customers laughed at the health inspectors and nodded knowingly that "Those bastards just find fault so they can make money on fines." They debated the health warnings with, "Have you ever seen a rat in here?" and the universal testimonial to the cafe was always, "No, never. Dora is a clean woman." These opinions were supported with a chorus of "I would drink out of Dora's toilet bowl before I would accept anything from one of those 'spectors." So, Moïse tacked the Certificates of Violation to the wall behind the cash register, and the customers just kept coming.

Moïse was a real joker. When some teenage punks came in and loudly ordered bacon and eggs for breakfast, Moïse rolled up his sleeve, picked up a pen and held the nib poised over numbers tattooed on his forearm. He asked the giggling kids, "Sure thing. Gimme your telephone number and I'll give you a call when they're ready." The cafe erupted in laughter, and the four wiseguys slunk out the door under a barrage of hoots, Yiddish cat calls, and red faces. The "wiseguy" story was always the prelude to the tale of how the Wisemans got their name and everything else. Glenn could hear the distant growling of Moïse's voice and his laughter.

"It was 1948, and the whole world was parked in the Hudson River. We were a cargo of DPs unloaded at the Island, and the first time we all met up was in the main hall."

* * * * *

Moïse was wobbled by a crowd of passengers disgorged along a gangway and nudged along through double doors that looked like a huge mouth into an enormous building. The multitude of steaming coats shuffled around the hall in confused worry. An official looking man in a blue uniform came up to "a bunch of us and said in Yiddish, 'All the Jews over to this side.' There were about a hundred in our little herd and we all had the same papers. The shipping company was lazy and they put the same name "Jude" on each of the forms. The official looked disgusted. He asked, 'Who speaks English?' I stepped forward and he said 'Good.' He led me to his desk, but it had only one chair, so he sat and I stood.

"He had a stack of forms and picked up a huge pen. He chose one form and sucked on the end of the pen's nib. It was very funny because, when he opened his mouth wide and shouted in a whisper, I could see the line of black ink running down the center of his tongue."

"How old are you? the guy asked.

"Twenty eight."

"That's old enough to be married. Go find a wife."

"What?"

"Look over there. Is there any girl you like?"

'Yeah.'

"Go get 'er and bring 'er 'ere."

"I very politely went up to a young lady and asked her to come to the desk. The lady didn't say a word, but her eyes looked me over and said, 'I do.' The official asked her name, she said 'Dora' and he wrote down 'Wiseman, Dora, Married to Moïse Wiseman.'

The official said to me, 'Your name is now Wiseman. Meet Mrs. Wiseman.' And that's how I met my Dora."

"The official said that we needed parents, so Dora was to pick an old man and an old lady and I was to do the same. Dora caught on to the trick immediately. We found some people who fit the official's description, and with her smiles and her winks, she told complete strangers what to do. Her eyes made them keep their mouths shut. She did all this without saying a word. The official wrote down their names, also Wiseman."

"The official asked me if I wanted to have kids and I said 'Sure, if they're free.' He left and returned with a nurse carrying a baby and gave it to Dora. There was some more scribbling, which took about an hour, and then he gave us each a bundle of papers."

"'This says that the Wiseman family has all they need to enter the United States. You keep these papers and if you lose them, you get sent right back to Pollock Land. Understand, Wiseman family?' The whole group said 'Yes,' in five languages and we all trooped out the building. And we've been together ever since."

"I thought that was a myth about Immigration giving people different names. I don't know about the others, but that guy not only gave us a new name, he gave us an entire family. We had to go buy dictionaries in German, French and Polish just to figure out who we were. We settled into the neighborhood and only really got to know each other in English class at night school in the college. After that, everything was easy."

"You know, I still can't listen to the songs from *Fiddler on the Roof* without remembering Mr. R. Jenkins, the guy who signed our papers. He was one hellova matchmaker."

* * * * *

Over the years, Moïse had explained the whole process to Glenn. Glenn understood that it was an old Jewish tradition in the East not to marry anybody with the same name or even people who lived in the same town. It used to be quite normal for a couple to meet for the first time on their wedding day because the elders had arranged everything for them. The system had worked for hundreds of years in the old country, wherever that old country was. To Glenn, the real magic was that a complete stranger, purely out of the goodness of his heart, carried on that tradition, without even knowing it. Just like the Wiseman family, Glenn had to consult the dictionary to learn that Moïse's word "exogamy" was a real word for "breeding outside your family." Glenn had always admired the Wisemans' strong bonds and was not surprised by their origins on Immigration Form B-3268-4.

Each member of the Wiseman clan was the sole survivor of their own families. Ellis Island made a clean slate in every possible sense and proof of Moïse's old saying that "what you're given is what you get." Glenn knew that they had made a life for generations with what they were given. The cafe was the Wisemans' masterpiece created out of blank government forms.

Glenn breathed in the aroma of times past and spoke to Michael through the fumes of his boiled beef.

"You know they were all gentle giants."

"Who?" asked a bored Michael.

"The Wiseman boys."

Glenn dredged-up the image of granddaddy Moïse Wiseman and smiled through his memory to a man who demanded respect.

"Moïse was steady, but David had a real edge to him," Glenn said.

"David the old man?" Michael asked.

"David, Solly's father and Moïse's son, but it was Moïse who took care of the rent fires."

"What's that?"

"That was before you were born, but it was a thing that almost destroyed the whole neighborhood. The landlord wanted to raise the rent, but the tenants couldn't afford it, so he set a fire. The tenants cleared out, the insurance paid to rebuild, and new tenants moved in who could afford the rent."

"That's disgusting."

“Yup. But Moïse put a stop to it,” Glenn said.

“All by himself?”

“Practically. He figured out that the insurance companies could make more money by prosecuting the landlords, so he went to the university and found an expert, some guy with a law degree in arson. Slowly, Moïse went around the neighborhood talking to the cops, the firemen, many people. He even found the people who’d been burned out and he just wrote down everything and took it to the guy at the university. The professor knew a crusading politician who wanted to get elected, so they fed all Moïse’s information to him. The politician got elected, the professor got promoted, the insurance companies got even richer, and the judges fined the landlords and told them not to play with matches any more. It worked out well all ’round, but that was about half a century ago.”

Michael was intrigued and asked, “Were David and Solly part of that?

“David was just a baby,” Glenn explained. “Good thing he was a baby. David was too hot for Moïse’s ways. David was direct. You know, he used to keep a pistol in the ice cream freezer. People would come in to rob the cafe and he would pretend to be really scared and offer them an ice cream. They were so confused they said ‘Yeah’ and he would put his hand into the freezer, and say, ‘I got vanilla, strawberry,’ pull the gun out from behind the ice cream barrels and say, ‘or brains on the wall.’ He would have killed them, too, and they knew it and left.”

Michael’s cell phone rang, and he sprang to answer it. Glenn resented the ease with which the damn thing destroyed their chat. He reminded himself that “chat” was now something you did with your fingers and not your mouth. Michael’s elbow leaned into a smile as he told the machine to not worry, “I’ll be there soon.” His thumb flicked over a button, and the intimacy was broken. Glenn saw that far away look and knew that something was very fishy. Michael parried his quizzical stare with “Work,” and Glenn thrust under Michael’s guard, “On Sunday?”

Michael explained that snow didn't respect the Sabbath and that there was a front coming in from the west over the mountains and that he had to alert the crews and that if they didn't keep the roads clear, Monday morning would be a huge traffic jam snarling at him because they couldn't get to work and that he had to keep the roads safe for the school busses. The more Michael babbled, the less Glenn believed him. People like Michael just didn't smile and talk so sweetly to the morning road crew.

Chapter 12

Mrs. Rubens

Siegen,
Westphalia, Germany
April 2, 1945

They could smell Siegen miles before they could see it. George was hanging onto the windshield as Glenn coaxed the Stout Bucket up a debris-littered goat track. When they drove into a valley, acrid smoke crept up their nostrils and formed grainy lumps in their throats. They could only breathe freely when they rose out of the low-lying and lung-hacking cloud. Juddering up the hill was a relief.

The weeks of collecting every scrap of information had revealed that the Germans had collected their loot in mines and caves well within enemy territory. Glenn's magic maps were their work lists and their battle plan. But when they followed the army to the place, they found empty rooms and burned out walls because the Germans kept taking the treasure with them. "They're always one jump ahead of us," grumbled Glenn, and George explained, "That's because we're following the front line and they keep moving everything behind the line."

Chasing shadows always just beyond their reach exhausted George and Glenn, and their frustrations erupted into arguments. "If we keep on this way, there won't be anything left to salvage," Glenn had burst out and George had to agree with him. All the most recent reports pointed to a copper mine just east of Siegen, and Glenn demanded, "This time we got to get the jump on them." George had countered, "They will also get the jump on us." Glenn just shrugged and said, "Hey. That's war." Siegen was just out of reach, but almost within their grasp. They both knew the risks and had to convince themselves that such a gamble was worth it.

George's talks had given Glenn an abiding fascination with the art and a deepening awareness of its worth. They now had to ask themselves if the art was worth risking their lives, even more than usual. Glenn was used to the idea of his own death; it was just part of living. But memories of his wife and dreams for their two children haunted George's decision. They both knew their decisions were not for them alone, but also for everybody connected with them.

George finally admitted, "I don't want to go home a hollow hero. I don't want a medal on my chest knowing in my heart that when it came to the crunch, I was a coward." They had looked at each other in those seconds which made an eternity, and Glenn thought to himself, "This is when I have to be a man or forever keep my big mouth shut." He simply said to George, "Yeah. Me too." Thus they decided to put themselves at the head of the armies, just behind the front lines, to "get the jump on the Germans."

The top of the hill west of Siegen was their map reference to rendezvous with a Captain Hodges, who would lead them to the Aladdin's cave. They were now at the sharp end of the Allied spearpoint. It was terrifying.

They crested the rise and were halted by a single man slowly waving them to a stop. He walked up to Glenn and asked, "Are you the Monuments Men?" George replied that he was "Stout" and the man said, "You must be Carnehan. I'm Hodges. Follow me." He turned to walk up a steep rise and waited for them in a stand of trees. George and Glenn scampered in his footsteps and at the top, the three of them looked into the valley below. Hodges said, "The flyboys fucked over the town," as they looked into what was left of Siegen.

"Fucked over" was Hodges' polite way of describing an Allied Joint Air Operation. The British had perfected the technique of raising a firestorm over Hamburg and Cologne. They divided their bombers into two strike forces. The first wave carried high-explosive bombs to rip open buildings, oil pipes, and gas mains. Half an hour later, the second wave dumped incendiary bombs, and the night erupted into day. Different waves bombed from different altitudes at different times, so the raid was a loom of shuttling bombers and stabbing searchlights. The night became a tapestry of flame that would turn itself into a superheated tornado over the town. The British bombed by night and the Americans by day, so that each attack added more fuel to the fire. A joint air attack was limited only by the gas tanks of the planes and could last for days.

The three of them looked into a dust bowl. In his head, George heard Frank Sinatra singing snatches of Cole Porter. His eyes tried to follow the vague outlines of streets to the tune of "Night and day, you are the one, / Only you beneath the moon or under the sun," but his vision was lost in distant sand dunes and gravel pits. He could hear the far-off thrumming of engines, "Day and night, night and day." He thought he could see somebody walking in the town, but it was only a white sheet dangling from a half-eaten window frame. "There's oh such a hungry yearning burning inside of me, / And this torment won't be through..."

Glenn saw miles of scorched rectangles and it looked like someone had taken a hammer to a thousand crates of beer bottles. Each charred square was a rubble filled box topped with a jagged crown of broken bricks. He didn't have to wonder what had happened to the people who used to live there. Months earlier, his squad had broken into a basement and waded through greasy water - until they realized that the people had been melted in their air raid shelter.

Hodges looked at Siegen and just saw a road block. "The mine is four miles east of the town, as the crow flies," he explained. George thought that any crow flying over Siegen would have to carry his own lunch box in his beak. Hodges looked at the devastation and complained, "We'll have to side-saddle the place." Neither Glenn nor George had any idea about side-saddling, other than a lady riding a horse. Hodges saw their uncomprehending eyes and gently explained, "We can't get through that mess, so we'll have to circle 'round and follow the road along the rim of the hills."

Glenn and George swung their heads from the valley to the hills circling Siegen. Through the trees, they could just make out a road running along the crest of the ridge. Hodges' side-saddle meant swinging around the town on the heights and then running down to the mine. One look at the hills told them that they would be playing Peek-a-Boo with any sniper behind the rocks and trees. They nodded and walked back to the jeeps.

Glenn saw that Hodges had his pistol holster tied to his leg. The holster cover was draped back and tucked behind Hodges' belt for a quick draw. There was also a lanyard chord running from the butt ring of his pistol up his chest and around his neck. Glenn thought of the idiot mittens his mother made him wear to school in winter and smiled to think that Hodges would never drop his pistol, just like Glenn would never lose only one mitten. Hodges paused between their parked jeeps and explained the maneuver. "You follow me into the middle of the patrol and just go where I go. Got it?" George and Glenn would follow this guy just about anywhere. He looked like any dogface on the line, but his very sweat exuded confidence. He was almost nonchalant when he added, "HQ thinks there are Werewolves in this sector." This was so serious that Glenn forgot the usual joke about silver bullets.

George had been to a pow-wow at headquarters about continued resistance. The generals had come to the conclusion that die-hard SS units, fanatical Nazis, and escaped prisoners would keep on fighting after the surrender. Captured orders and prisoner interrogations detailed how the fanatics were going to turn the Bavarian mountains into a partisan fortress. The Nazis christened those units "Werewolves." Suddenly, the trees in front of George and Glenn were more menacing than the smoldering ruins before them.

Hodges jumped into his jeep, and gunned the engine. Glenn popped the clutch in silent obedience, and the two jeeps toggled up the hill. They drove over the top of the rise, and Hodges wove them through a staggered line of vehicles parked on each side of the road. They slowed to an idling halt in the center of the column.

This was a fighting and reconnaissance patrol - the absolute sharp point of the army. Everything in front of them, save the guarded Siegen mine, was determined enemy. Behind them was the rest of the Allied armies; they were friendly and nervous and sometimes even more dangerous than the enemy. This patrol was not going to take anything on the easy. Safety catches were permanently in the "off" position. There was no horsing around with these guys because they would shoot anything that even winked at them aggressively. Glenn could not imagine this bunch wailing out a chorus of "Over hill, over dale, looking for a piece of tail." Alertness was how they stayed alive. Hodges was completely in control and everybody knew it. The recon patrol was their guide to the artwork and their safety along the road. George leaned over to Glenn and whispered, "I don't know what they do to the Germans, but they sure scare the Hell out of me." Glenn nodded in the affirmative and they sat idling behind Hodges until a single thrust of his left arm motioned, "Forward."

They passed little clusters of one truck surrounded by three jeeps and could not help staring at their guardian angels dripping with weapons. Hodges pulled over near the head of the column. Glenn saw there were four sets of trucks and jeeps and George heard their engines all running in time. Unlike the usual convoy, no exhaust smoke coughed from these vehicles; the steady beat of their engines told him everything was well oiled and finely tuned, just like the men who drove them.

A steel box on six wheels passed them. Glenn and George watched a Greyhound armored scout car take point position on the next rise before them. A second Greyhound stood beside them, its turret swinging the 37mm cannon to the rear while the commander stood tall in the hatch pointing his Ma Deuce straight ahead.

Hodges signaled them to “Stay” and they watched the first Greyhound glide forward up the curving hill. It stopped just before the the crest of the hill so the commander could see what was ahead. The long barrel of his machine gun was like a school teacher’s pointer stabbing at the blackboard. The Greyhound inched forward to stand atop the rise with its cannon scanning the horizon. The commander jerked his machine gun skyward twice, Hodges motioned “Follow” to Glenn and George.

Glenn kept the Stout Bucket on Hodges’ tail until they pulled up behind the Greyhound. They could not see what was over the little hill, but the armored car beveled over the rise and Hodges spurted forward to the top. Glenn and George watched the Greyhound snake down the road with its turret cannon traversing slowly from left to right. The commander played counterpoint with his machine gun so that the cannon and Ma Deuce scissored over each other’s fields of fire. Glenn saw that nothing would escape their steel jacketed vigilance and felt relief running up his legs to his heart.

They followed Hodges down the rise, like ducklings, into the winding valley. George’s leg was shaking because this was his first time in the cross hairs. Glenn knew that if he could hear the bullets, they had missed him. The suddenness of death or wounding was its own comfort, and the idea helped him cope with the combat jitters. George imagined a rifle aimed at him from every branch and pebble and took deep breaths to hide his fear. Glenn heard him gasping for security, smiled, and thought to himself, “Well, he’s no longer a virgin.” The two jeeps wove through the road curves and pulled up under the Greyhound’s protective wings. Trucks and jeeps followed them until the column reformed itself before another hump in the road. They had traveled two miles. The second Greyhound purred past them, and George asked Glenn why the turret was pointed to the rear. “That’s in case they were letting us go ahead to hit us from behind,” Glenn answered.

George kept up his courage by reveling in the iron-clad choreography. One Greyhound pierced the territory before them, the ducklings would follow into the safety it had created, and then the second Greyhound rushed forward to take the point position. George thought it was like knights in shining armor playing leap-frog or Chinese Checkers and was astounded by their skill. These soldiers had acquired combat experience undreamed of by George. There was artistry in this. As much as any apprentice learning to grind pigment and mix oil into paint, these men had mastered the techniques of staying alive. They painted with rifles and carved with cannons.

And so they travelled the ten miles to the mine. With every changing of their guard and every syncopation of scout car and jeep, George cast his fear aside. Hodges escorted them to the administration building of the mine, and once they parked behind him, the teacher felt as much of a veteran as the student was. George would remember those last miles for the rest of his life, until fear became a distant memory hidden in the trees lining a simple country road.

Glenn and George unfolded themselves from the Stout Bucket and stretched the tension from their legs. The Greyhounds stayed on the main road guarding the entrance to the mine complex, but the soldiers scattered to start portable fires for coffee. George told Hodges that his men really knew what they were doing, and Hodges slid his helmet off his sweaty scalp, "They should. All the dumb asses are dead."

Hodges' gaze followed Glenn's eyes scanning the piles of rubble encircling the complex. People were moving over and through the mounds of broken walls, pipes, and boulders. "DPs," he said, and all three watched the people. Some were like feral cats scratching the earth. Others scampered out of sight. The defiant and the desperate stood rooted by their curiosity on the rubble, looking down at the convoy. George had to know, "DP?" Hodges eyed the mounds and explained, "DP... Displaced Person. Some joker in Civil Government came up with the name. They're ‘displaced’ because they have no place. They’re hobos in their own place, or what’s left of it.” Hodges nodded to a soldier bringing them cups of coffee. George was grateful for the consideration. Hodges fisted the handle with a tremulous hand and yelled, “Mendelson, Front and Center. Pot and Words.”

They watched Mendelson separate himself from the crouching drinkers and saunter closer to the rubble pile. Mendelson held a bubbling pot of coffee in his left hand and his Colt .45 in the right. He tapped the pot with the mouth of his pistol and wafted the aroma to the bravest of the DPs. “Kommen Sie. Sicher, Sicher Sicherheit.” Mendelson sniffed the coffee pot and assured the Germans that the stuff was so “Mmmmm.”

He was Hodges’ translator because weeks ago, Mendelson had beaten a basic vocabulary out of a bilingual prisoner. After a quick pistol whipping, Mendelson could fluently tell any German “You with me fuck, You I kill.” They were entranced by the pot and tamed by Mendelson’s “schmackhaft zo Geschmack” and warned by his gesturing pistol. He smiled like a billboard touting “Maxwell House” and even without the translation, the Germans knew it would be good to the very last drop. He cajoled them with a friendly “Hier,” and two men in civilian clothes pussy footed down the hill and cautiously approached them. Hodges smiled at the homey scene and said, “You could clear a whole town with one pot of coffee.”

George wanted to get into the mine as quickly as he could, but Hodges restrained him. “Hold your horses, Sailor. Here we do things my way.” Hodges’ glare held George and Glenn in their places. He raised his eyebrows and his voice to four soldiers lounging beside their truck, “Boom Boom in the hole.”

The four soldiers picked up their equipment and grumbled their way to the mine entrance. Hodges saw George’s forehead wrinkle into a question mark and explained. “Engineers. Those grave-diggers will make sure it’s safe enough to get to your treasure trove. At Ease.” George gulped down his impatience with the coffee.

All those weeks of compiling splinters of information and composing reports on borrowed typewriters had worn him down. He and Glenn had traveled 13,000 miles through France and inspected 224 monuments, but it had been no Grand Tour. At first, there was the excitement of getting on with the job, but then the job itself became a soul-destroying disappointment. They kept missing the moveable loot and liberating buildings that had already been obliterated.

In the German sector alone, sixty percent of the historic buildings, castles, palaces or cathedrals had been pulverized. George had shaken his head at each monumental shambles and said to Glenn, "They invented the blitz and now it's come back to them with a vengeance." Glenn had tried out one of his new phrases and called the whirlwind bombing a "boomerang." George had found the phrase so apt and so keen to cut through their despair that they had added crescent-shaped "boomerangs" to their maps to show complete destruction by Allied air raids. In conversation, they just referred to a place as "boomered." It could be seen as a spelling mistake if anybody in authority ever read the reports, but the words and the humor and the comfort of the joke, like a shared blanket in an ice storm, kept their diaries and reports from reading like the collective obituary of civilization. Glenn's creativity helped George to keep going. Whatever they were doing, and George frequently wondered just what they were doing, they were doing this together.

Here they were waiting at the entrance to a mine that might be a treasure trove. George knew they were barely two miles within enemy territory; he had to follow Hodges in everything. He could hear the artillery just over the hills rimming Siegen, but it no longer mattered. They had "got the jump" and now they had to wait for the rest of the army to catch up with them. Glenn had told him that "enemy territory is five inches or five miles." There was comfort in facing the fear and in Glenn's wisdom. Failure was more frightening than death.

George had first thought of Glenn as just a driver, almost an extension of their vehicle, but after he witnessed the miracle of Glenn's map reading and saw the boxes of reports, he had to change his mind. Glenn also had a collection of little books, pamphlets, and a notebook which he kept in a haversack stowed behind his seat. The little booklets were called "Pointy Talkies." They had columns of English and French phrases running down each page. The idea was that you could look up a phrase in English, point to the translation in French, and have someone answer you in turn. It was a great idea, but the authors had forgotten that there were many illiterates in the reconquered countries, so the print was often as useless as the encounters. Glenn had taken to pointing at the French side himself and guessing what the English translation would be. He said it was like collecting baseball cards, but after a while you could swap words. In a month, Glenn had collected enough French to function on more than a basic level. The German Pointy Talkie was useless. If they kept heading east, they would be collecting phrase books in Polish, Hungarian, and Russian. If that happened, the war would continue and the little booklets would look suspiciously like a death warrant.

What impressed George so much was that Glenn was oblivious to his talents. It was just a game or an interesting diversion for him, but George had seen generations of Harvard undergraduates take years to gain the same proficiency in a foreign language. Like his three dimensional vision over a map, Glenn took his abilities in his stride, thinking that he wasn't so special because "anybody can do this." It was only Glenn's limited social experience which allowed him to believe that he was nothing special. George's estimation blossomed every time Glenn first acquired a talent and then used it to get the job done. Glenn reminded George that he had probably spent too much time in the conservation rooms and the museum galleries. He had lost contact with people, and Glenn was bringing him back with many a jolt along smashed roads. Here they were chasing things and their very mission presumed that finding and saving those things was more important than the people who huddled around them for warmth, trying to save themselves.

George looked at Mendelson and saw that the DPs were very happy to obey orders, when the recon patrol was sharing coffee. The two old men savored their cups because it had been years since they had tasted real coffee. The German government had issued an ersatz brown swill they called Kaffee. George had been told that the Germans referred to this foul liquid substitute as Braunwasser. The name was a joke about Hitler's mistress, Eva Braun, whom they derided as an ersatz wife. George marveled that even such a childish joke about Hitler's choice of women had to be buried under layers of language. What was wrong with a people who couldn't even laugh without looking over their shoulders? This was just another example of what they were fighting against, and it frightened him.

The soldiers reappeared at the mine entrance and ambled over to Hodges. He raised an eyebrow, and the lead engineer reassured them that it was "All Okay, Sir. Pretty amateur stuff." Hodges dismissed the bomb crew with a nod and grinned at George and Glenn, "Now it's time for your magic." He raised his cup, pointed a pinky at the squad leader and casually commanded, "Boom Boom will go with you." Boom Boom was not one for small talk, so George and Glenn just followed him until the mouth of the mine swallowed the day.

The darkness slitted their eyes, but the smell flared their nostrils. The surviving population of Siegen had been huddling in the mine's tunnels for weeks. They could feel the shocks of their homes exploding, and some were thankful to be alive. Many had been driven out of their minds, so the conquerors said the DPs were "just plain poggled." George was careful to follow in Boom Boom's footsteps and they proceeded single file down corridors crowded with unwashed humanity. The stench was suffocating and only the desperate hope of survival had driven these people to squat in the crevices of stone picked over by generations of

Siegen's copper miners. What water they had was for drinking; washing was a half-remembered luxury.

The lights hadn't worked since the last bombing, so George, Glenn, and Boom Boom followed their flashlights. The little circles of light would sweep along the floor and up the walls to land on faces. The flashlights turned the tunnels into a portrait gallery and each face revealed a life. An old man's eyes beamed hate, while a middle-aged woman's forced smile was caught in the rim of Glenn's beam. George's light landed on a child playing with a sock encrusted with weeks of sweat. A young couple posed for a second, and the husband bared his teeth at the barbarian invaders, hoping that his silly grin would shield him from the bullets he expected to end their lives.

They had all been convinced that the Americans were savages who would kill their children after enslaving them. They all believed that these untermensch were capable of any atrocity, for they had only to scan the swirling dust clouds for their proof. Refugees had told them stories of American tanks driven by negroes who would grind anyone in their path under the treads and drive away laughing. All feared the gas these savages would unleash on the living and the dead, and only those who had given up all hope of survival felt the calm of not caring. Their poggle was their refuge and their strength. Some hoped the visitors would kill them quickly, so they could join their departed loved ones in some vague Valhalla that had to be better than this living Hell. Boom Boom's light was glued to the floor and his footsteps played Hop Scotch with the beams.

George, Glenn, and Boom Boom stepped over sprawling legs and huddled forms in the shadow world of the mine. George took it all in. With every fearful step, he looked into empty souls and wished he'd never come here. George stepped on a DP's foot and Glenn chuckled to hear him say "Excuse me." Glenn mumbled to himself, "Sorry for stepping on your toes," when he couldn't even tell if the foot was still attached to a leg.

Boom Boom skirted a hole in the floor, a dusty circle around a metal pot. They all stopped to stare at the thing, and Boom Boom explained, "That's an S mine. It jumps up knee high and then it explodes. Blows off your balls and your legs." George wanted to know why this little birthday cake in steel was intended to maim and not kill. "They don't want to kill you quickly 'cause they figured out that one wounded can get them at least five live guys. So, you're crawling around on your bleeding stumps. You know you got maybe three minutes to live, so you're screaming like all fuck. The trick is that all the other guys panic and they run around like chickens and step on all the other mines waiting for them."

Boom Boom picked up the mine, now harmless in his hands, for their closer inspection. George and Glenn stared at the five-inch can. The plunger raised itself out of the top and had three little prongs splayed out like mutilated fingers. Boom Boom had inserted a steel pin into a hole in the plunger shaft; it was all that stood between them and oblivion. Glenn shivered at the thought that this thing, looking like a can of soup, could be so deadly. In the gloom of the mine shaft, George imagined Boom Boom holding a rattlesnake with a popsicle stick behind its fangs, and his throat tightened around his terror. Boom Boom felt their fear and unscrewed the top of the mine. As he poured out the powder in libation to the devil that had invented it, the tension flooded out of George and Glenn, but it took some minutes for them to remember why they were there.

George looked down the mine shaft to see rows of little holes dug out by the engineers and breathed, "Diabolical." "You think?" answered Boom Boom. "I'll tell you about diabolical. We went to clear a department store. The guys got there before us and they hear a baby crying. Being like fathers and all around heroes with no brains, they rushed in to get the baby. The fuckers had put the baby in a box and placed the box on a pressure plate. When the guys lifted the baby, they detonated the rest of the charges. And it was Rock-a Bye-Boom, baby and all."

Glenn and George held their tears behind gritted teeth and clenched jaws. Glenn asked, "A baby as bait?" and George demanded, "How did you know?" Boom Boom confessed that "We could tell from the bits.... We couldn't even hose down that place."

They were the spearpoint of the army and had cut through to the heart of the evil. This was not war; this was mass suicide. The Nero Order was stark in its simplicity; everything and everyone was to be sacrificed. Baby and all. The essence of this evil rattled in George's growing hatred of the subhumans who could even think of this, and Glenn's mind was punch-drunk by the baby. George turned, pointed his flashlight down the tunnel and hosed light over the huddled masses. He whispered to Boom Boom, "What about them?" Boom Boom and his crew had ripped out the detonators, cut wires, and were experts in "making safe." All their experiences spoke, when Boom Boom replied, "Them? Nobody told them they're the baby." Boom Boom brought them back to the job at hand. "Come on. There's the place." He led them further down the tunnel into a cavern lined with massive shelves holding crates.

Their flashlights played over a collection of large wooden boxes housed in sturdy shelving. The place looked like a split-level stable with stalls piled up one upon the other on both sides. George moved his beam from box to box reading the stenciled names of the contents. Boom Boom asked incredulously, "Rembrandt?" and George answered, "That's him." They had "got the jump." Here was a cache of carefully hidden masterpieces. That such care had been taken to preserve them was proof that someone had some sort of faith in the future. The boxes were the survivors of the fate carved out for them by the Nero Order. They had heard their own execution order read out to them, but the boxes screamed, "We remain."

George's chest swelled with pride. Boom Boom walked down the bank of wonders and read, "Da Vinci." He stretched forth his arm and sprayed light over a top shelf like a garden hose and whispered, "Michaelangelo." He turned to Stout and fired the question that was bubbling through their minds, "Is this for real?"

George and Glenn looked at each other to muster the courage to answer. George broke their stare and replied, "Only one way to find out." The three pulled a large crate labeled "Van Dyck" from the lowest level of shelving and wrestled it onto the cave floor. Boom Boom complained in surprise, "Hey, shouldn't we be more careful?" but George simply said, "The Old Masters are a tough bunch. Otherwise they wouldn't have survived so long." George and Glenn raised the box until it was leaning against the scaffolding supports, and George examined the edge, looking for a way to open it. Boom Boom threw his arm behind him and yanked a small crowbar from his holster belt. George smiled, "The very thing." He wrenched the cover half off at the bottom and revealed the head of a man staring back at them with aloof annoyance. "Well, well, well. If it isn't Johan the Younger, Prince of Nassau-Siegen."

George had first seen this painting as a very young man on the Grand Tour, except his tour wasn't so grand. When he was a young undergraduate, every student of art had to go to Europe to see the paintings they studied. George and his wife ate sandwiches for six months to save up the boat fare for George's six-week tramp through Western Europe's great museums. While the other students whooped it up in the hotels and casinos of the Old World, George moved from flophouse to masterpiece, from soup kitchen to the Louvre to gain the experience others called a holiday. Van Dyck's *Portrait of Johan of Nassau-Siegen* was especially memorable because when George had first made the prince's acquaintance, he thought the old man was looking down his nose at George's empty stomach. Now, Johan's face was upside-down looking up at George, Glenn, and Boom Boom. Boom Boom ran his stained finger along the edge of the frame and gulped, "Is that real gold?"

"Yup." said George, "They poured a lot of money into their pictures and even around them."

"How much is this worth?" Boom Boom asked.

“More than either of us could imagine,” said George.

Boom Boom’s fingers closed like a five-bladed switch-knife, but his eyes bored into Johan’s smug mouth.

Glenn looked at the cavern full of loot and asked, “What are we going to do with all this stuff?” The three raised themselves to scan the rocky treasure trove again and Boom Boom stated the obvious, “We’ll never get this out of here on our own.” George gave the equally obvious response, “It’s foolish to leave it all here. The moisture, the stale air.”

Glenn protested, “We don’t have trucks,” and Boom Boom added, “You’re gonna need a whole bunch of movers.” George acknowledged that they were right and said, “We don’t even have a safe place to take it.” Boom Boom volunteered, “We’ll post a guard.” Glenn added, “You guys aren’t enough for this.” Boom Boom assured Glenn that, “Yeah, but the relief column will be here in about an hour.” George was reassured that there would be sufficient guards and decided to rest on this battle won. “We’ll come back tomorrow and find out just how much there is. But we can’t take it out. Not until proper arrangements are made. But don’t worry, this much at least is safe. Nothing will harm it now.”

The three stood surrounded by the treasure and in the center of their decision. The real value was in their choice, and they knew it. Boom Boom had cleared the booby-traps and the deadly surprises. George had guided them through the shock of their discovery. But together they had resolved their action. Nothing would be touched. Everything would be saved. All would share in this, their first victory of preservation over destruction.

George ran his flashlight down the side of one packing case and shone his schoolboy German on the bill of lading. “Let’s meet a lady before we leave.” They manhandled the crate onto the rippled floor of the cavern, and George took extra care with Boom Boom’s crowbar. As he slowly pried off the cover’s grumbling wood, George whispered to Glenn, “You’re going to enjoy this one.” George bent back the cover to the protests of squealing nails.

"Gentlemen, allow me to introduce you to Hélène Fourment, Mrs. Rubens."

George exposed the full-length portrait of a young woman with a fur coat almost wrapped around her ample middle. The three flashlights sprang to attention to take in every inch of her almost naked body. Boom Boom held his beam stiff and sure over her red nipples and suddenly the cave was warmer than he had realized. Johan stood on his head beside Hélène's portrait, and his eyebrows shot reproach up to her nakedness. Glenn's light cascaded over her rippling thighs. Boom Boom could not hide his admiration under his silence, "That's one feast of a woman."

Hélène's vital beauty spread through the cave's darkness. Boom Boom thought, "This ain't no tits'n ass pinup." Glenn stared into the face of the woman whose story had so fascinated him. Hélène stood before them with her smile more welcoming than her body. Rubens had posed her as if he had just walked into her room and she had grabbed the closest garment to cover herself, unsuccessfully. But it was the look in her eyes that beckoned Boom Boom and Glenn. Boom Boom did not see the suggestive leer of the coquette, for there was nothing of intrigue in her face. She stared straight at them, ignoring Johan's aristocratic smirk, secure in her own knowledge of herself.

George let them drink their fill of Hélène for he knew there was no desecration in their rapture. This was no time for a lecture, for intrusion would destroy their experience. He tucked his thumbs into his holster belt and waited with the teacher's patience for the pupils' understanding. He didn't care if they sat there all night, for this was what they were fighting for, that others would be able to have this beauty, even if they didn't fully understand it. And so he simply waited, sharing in their wonder.

When he sensed Boom Boom's feet shuffling, he stepped forward and held the lid over Hélène's face. "We'll see you tomorrow, Old Girl." That was the sign to return her to rest alongside scowling Johan. They carefully replaced the lids and nails, like grave-robbers feeling guilty beside their abandoned theft. When all was as they found it, they wended their way through misery to a different level of reality at the surface.

Darkness had fallen during their inspection, so they brought their night vision with them out of the mine. George and Glenn walked over to Hodges sitting on a rock beside a fire. Boom Boom had already joined his engineer crew to regale them with the tale that had to start with the exclamation, "There's gold in them thar hills." They looked down at Hodges balancing both his Dixie cup and a Lucky Strike in his left hand. "You guys find what you were looking for?" "That and more than we can deal with," said George. "I thought so." Hodges paused to give his good news more punch. "I sent a message back to HQ and they're giving you two infantry companies for guard." Hodges' arm offered a canteen of whiskey "just to take the edge off the air."

They squatted in a circle to end the day. Hodges told them the details of how the relief column would arrive in two hours and how George was to command operations inside the mine. George was more interested in Hodges' head. Wearing the helmet, Hodges looked like a mature man in his mid thirties, but with the helmet wobbling on the ground beside him, Hodges had the bald scalp and etched lines of a pensioner. George was struck that there were thirty years separating Hodges' clenched jaw and stone-carved lips from his receded hairline. It was like looking at two men of different ages in the same face. He mused to himself, "I guess that's what recon patrol does to a man."

George breathed in the fumes of the whiskey. The liquor flung a soft blanket over his exhaustion and he fought sleep like a little child protesting bed-time. He wanted to stay awake just long enough to be sociable with Hodges, to say "Thank you" with the shared jug. He looked at the DPs and recalled the huddled refugees in the mine. They didn't even know that they were to be sacrificed. Everything became clear to George in those two letters. Somehow, the DPs were still persons. Even if they survived, The Nero Order was designed to rob them of a place where they could be persons. That was what was so hellish about the Nazis, everything and everybody had been reduced to nothing. Everything was to be smashed, so it could never be rebuilt. It made the art all that more vital. Without some foundation, nothing could grow. Diabolical.

Glenn raised his gaze to the hills that had been so pregnant with terror just a few hours ago. His eyes followed a truck bouncing down the road to the mine, its driver oblivious to the safety Hodges and the patrol had created in those trees. The fear was gone and Hélène had filled the vacuum. He thought that Hélène was "one Venus who has really fixed this Venus Fixer." It was not just her magnificent body but the beauty wrapped in character like the coat around her body which so fascinated him. He knew in ways he could not express that Hélène Fourment would be "forever mine."

Chapter 13

Cream Cheese Sfumato

Glenn sat staring at Michael across the table. Michael ignored his bagel just as Solly was ignoring his customers. The deli was a family business, for family and friends of the family. "Drop-ins" got a dose of Solly's disdainful tongue. They seemed to like his irritable foul mouth and thought the place "quaint" and "so real New York." Solly chuckled to have his fashionable customers waiting for the waiter.

The cream cheese had dripped over the edges of Michael's hot bread and congealed as it cooled. Glenn looked at the knotty circle smeared in titanium white and asked, "Something wrong with the bagel?" "No. It's fine" was Michael's unfocused response. Anda's stories had filled his mind more than his stomach. "I just never knew you had all those adventures."

Glenn was a little embarrassed, as if he had been talking too much about himself and not listening enough, but he had felt the urgency to share with Michael. He looked at the frost creeping from the edges of the windows and wondered if the roads would be clear later in the day. "They're only adventures in the telling. When it's happening to you, it's no adventure."

Michael's mind was digging itself out of the blizzard of Anda's stories. "I never knew about any of this." Glenn shrugged his shoulders and said, "So, now you know." It took Michael a thoughtful pause to finally say over his bagel, "But you were a real hero."

Glenn looked through the frosted window and explained to Michael, "I just saw a little slice of the pie. There were others who did even more."

"Others? Like Posey?" prompted Michael.

"Guys who have been forgotten, even if anybody ever heard of them. There was James Rorimer. He became the Director of the

Metropolitan Museum of Art. There was a man. I saw him drive through Hell and back to get a statue. But it wasn't just men, you know."

"Huh?"

"There were women involved in this, real classy women like Edith Standen, She'd been to Oxford. We called her 'Battle Ax Edith' but we all loved her. But the cream of the crop was a woman called Rose Valland."

"Rose?"

Glenn paused to conjure the image of a petite and not too pretty woman, who could easily be ignored in a crowd, and introduced her to Michael. "She was a French woman who worked with the Nazis in Paris. While they were stealing everything they could lay their hands on, Rose was memorizing the stuff they stole. She even wrote down the addresses where they shipped their loot and hid those addresses until she found someone she could trust with her knowledge. For four years she did her job, not knowing if that someone would ever come. All those years, they could have just shot her, if they suspected what she was really doing. The Germans could have killed her as a spy, and the French could have shot her as a collaborator, but nobody knew what she was up to."

Michael was intrigued and asked, "Did they catch her?"

"No." Glenn said, the mischief sparkling in his eyes, "She caught them. It took Rorimer months in Paris, but eventually he got her to trust him, and she gave him a book with all the addresses of the looted art, the same book she had been scribbling in for four years, hidden under the bed."

"That's amazing."

"Yeah, amazing. Some of those guys got killed doing what they did and nobody ever knew what they were doing, just like Rose in Paris. I don't want to talk about them. You can read all about them in the library, but it'll take you a while to find the book."

Michael sat toying with his bagel, looking through his Anda to the man who did all these wonderful things. His mind was approaching a place he'd never been, a realization of quiet heroism. "And you knew all of these people?" he asked.

"Yup, but I didn't know who they really were until I got to college."

"You went to college with them?"

"Kinda, in a way. I went to college on the G.I. Bill to study the history of art, mainly because of all the trips with Stout, and would you believe it, those guys had written the books I had to read. There wasn't a course where I wasn't pouring over really big books, all by people who had been Monuments Men during the war. You see, they were the geniuses, and when they got back home, they just went back to their old jobs in the universities and the museums where they could write their books and continue being geniuses."

"That's even more amazing."

"That's what they were. Every last one of them."

Michael looked at the approaching snow and thought he should contact the depot to make sure that the crews had been called. If there were flurries in the city, there could be a blanket of clouds rolling down the hills into Pennsylvania trailing blizzards along their path. He was keenly aware that what happened in the city was very different from in the country. City Slickers always had other ways to get to work or school when snow sprinkled over them like powdered sugar on a cupcake. The Country Mouse had no such choice; he just had to sit tight in the car until the police or the road crew hauled him out of the ditch. Snow was fun to New Yorkers, a little relief, a quaint decoration over garbage cans, and the accepted excuse just to stay home. Out in the country, a snow storm was no such holiday, and it was Michaels's job to make sure that the roads were clear. Michael yanked himself out of the fog of his job and blurted out, "You could have been killed at any moment."

"Lucky for you I wasn't," Glenn calmly stated.

The words whistled through Michael's ears as the thought sent chills along his neck. His grandfather's survival was responsible for Michael's very life. If the cave had fallen in or a stray shot had hit Anda decades ago, Michael would never have been born. It was hard to think that one little twist of time and Michael wouldn't even exist. Michael's appetite disappeared and the bagel lay abandoned on its plate.

Michael evaded the thought by claiming an urgent call to work. "I'll have to get going."

"What's the hurry?"

"I have to make sure that the guys are out working the roads. This looks like it could get really nasty."

"Call them," Glenn challenged.

"They need me to be there."

"Just tell them you're snowbound in New York."

"No. I really have to go," Michael insisted.

Glenn could taste the lie in Michael's insistence. Nothing could be clearer than Michael's need to leave, except that he wasn't needed at all. The County Road Works Section did not have to be led to snow blocked intersections by Michael. They could find snow all on their own. Glenn decided to pull rank. "We've got someplace to go."

"Where?"

"Jersey."

"Jersey? On a Sunday?" Michael protested.

"Yeah, on a Sunday."

"Why?"

"It's important," said Glenn simply.

"What's so important in Jersey on a Sunday that can't wait until Monday."

"A check for three point seven million dollars."

Glenn's eyes narrowed on Michael's uncertainty. He waited for the numbers to melt into Michael's mind, then commanded, "Make the call."

Michael rummaged under his coat pocket and pulled his cell phone from the holster on his belt. Glenn noticed that Michael's thumb hit "Speed Dial" without even looking at the buttons. He smiled to himself that he was getting used to this new technology but was glad that he preferred the old kind. Michael turned away from Glenn, seeking privacy in a three-quarter profile. Glenn heard him apologize into the phone, "I'm not going to be able to make it," and anticipated the silence that was filling Michael's ear. "I know I promised but..." Glenn knew that "Hello Hello" was having a first-class pout and giving Michael a disappointed nag at the other end of the line. Michael was not giving orders to someone in a checkered shirt with a sagging beer gut behind the wheel of a snowplow.

Glenn turned his attention from Michael's wheedling to the window misted over with the first breath of winter. He heard Solly clank open the lids of the meat steamer and become enveloped by the peppered cloud. Solly pulled a mass of smoked brisket out of the steamer with a fork and started slicing through it with a butcher's knife. Each cut released a wraith of tantalizing spices. Glenn drank in the aroma of smoked pastrami and recalled introducing Smelly Eddy to the secrets of sfumato.

It must have been three decades since his lectures had bubbled up the Italian word when he tried to explain this Renaissance technique of painting. The class had written down "sfumato," dutifully copied "to make the image fuzzy," and locked the word away in their notebooks to be dragged out for a test. Glenn knew that ninety-nine out of a hundred would never utter the word again and would soon forget it. Its only use was to gain yet another point, on yet another test, in a long line of exams that would lead them to a job with benefits and a company car. But Eddy was the one who really wanted to know about it.

Eddy was a stranger to showers and not an aficionado of deodorants, so the other students called him Smelly Eddy, with some justification. But Glenn loved his curiosity and savored Eddy's questions while dodging his bad breath. After the class had stampeded at the bell, Eddy remained to know more about this strange word. Glenn believed showing was always better than telling when it came to art, so he led Eddy into the studio and spread a glamor magazine over the workshop table. "So, what do you see?" Glenn asked. Eddy responded with the pleased leer of a naughty little boy, "A naked lady." "Good. You're not blind." Glenn picked up a bottle of Elmer's Glue and squirted daubs of creamy cellulose over the woman's nakedness. He grabbed a brush, dipped it in a water jar, and pushed the bristles through the sticky mess until the woman was wearing a semi-translucent coat of glue. He worked the brush over the woman's face and breasts, until Eddy had to squint to make out her form. "So Eddy, what's the difference?" "Now, everything is kinda fuzzy," Eddy admitted. "Glenn spluttered through his laugh, "That's an excellent translation of the Italian 'sfumato.' Kinda fuzzy." But that was what had happened to the nude in the girlie mag; she had become a drunken blur.

Eddy watched Glenn clean the brush in the water and force the excess glue and water onto his cleaning rag. "Now see what happens." Eddy watched Glenn drybrush the glue from the woman's eyes and mouth. The eyes stood out from her face, and the subtle suggestion of pleasure curled at the corners of her mouth. Glenn worked the brush along the woman's neck, ran it down her cleavage to her stomach and wiped the glue from her knees. She stood out in a composition of clarity and obscurity, and Eddy was amazed to see her photograph turn into a three dimensional Venus rising out of the shellack.

"So, Eddy, what's the difference now?"

"Now she's beautiful" Eddy said, entranced by the image.

"And before?" Glenn prodded.

"She was just sexy."

"That's what sfumato does. It is the contrast of fuzzy and unfuzzy that the artist uses to bring out what's under the surface."

Eddy stood looking down at the lovely form and marveled at how easily Glenn had made her even better. Where she had been brash and coarse, she was now soft and mellow, and her skin was a silken billow. Glenn watched the understanding seep into Eddy and would not interrupt his reverie. He remembered how Stout had let him drink in Mrs. Rubens and repeated the courtesy with Eddy.

Michael's fingers clicked at buttons and his face was magenta with suppressed rage. "Everything Okay at work?" Glenn asked with a mischievous twinkle. Michael was trapped between guilt, pressure, and annoyance. Glenn read all of this in Michael's eyes and hunched shoulders. "Work can be a real pain in the ass," Michael complained.

"You make me glad I'm retired."

"Where are we going?"

"Jersey"

"Yeah, you said. I know. Jersey... But where in Jersey?"

"You'll find out when we get there."

Michael's mood was on the verge of resentment, and Glenn knew it. "Let him fume a bit," he thought to himself. "You got the car all gassed up?" "Yeah." "So, let's hit the road then." And Glenn rose to leave. Michael sat with his cell phone in his hand caught between the phone and his grandfather. For a moment he wanted to tell them both to "Go to Hell," but a lifetime of Anda's kindness lifted him off his chair and frog marched him to the door.

Glenn said "See you next week." to Young Solly, who replied, "Always good to see you Mr. Glenn," and the door bell chimed them into the morning. The air was clearer than the windows, so the road to Jersey wouldn't be all that bad.

They walked around the block and down the alley to Michael's car, and Glenn numbered off the techniques of Renaissance painting he had memorized as a young man on his G.I. Bill scholarship. "There's 'cangiante,' to change the color from dark to light or light to dark." His mind's eye ran over the robes of Michelangelo's prophets on the Sistine Chapel. "'Unione' will bring together different colors," and he could almost touch the blue and green in the Madonna's neck. But it was the contrasts that had always fascinated him: "That bold 'chiaroscuro' makes everything dark and light and stand out clearly." Rembrandt faces beamed out of blackness to hover before his face, and Glenn nodded to them like old friends.

But 'sfumato' whispered to him of his loves. There was so much in life that was uncertain, so many experiences that were fuzzy. Glenn also had matured into the disappointing awareness that people were just too lazy-minded for clarity, when it was all around them. Sometimes he thought that he was unable to knit together the frayed textures connecting people, but eventually he had to accept that there were just too many threads to weave into a whole pattern. People seemed to want the excitement of confusion, so chaos became normal. Life was confusing enough on its own, but sfumato helped him live with other people's cherished messes.

In his own world, Ellen had always kept the apartment spotless, and it was a habit that connected him to her. Everything had a place and was in its place. Even when she was old, there were no lines etched into her face, and her eyes were as bright as Mrs. Rubens smiling in a cave. Nothing could ever change such beauty; it was his beacon in a world of chilly collisions.

They climbed into Michael's car. His finger touched a button, and the engine hummed into life. He turned on the heater, and they felt the cold retreat to their feet. Glenn looked at how neat everything was. "This car is cleaner than the day it left the factory," Glenn kidded. "I hope so," replied Michael. "Those people really don't take care of what they make."

Even as a child, Michael had been a bit of a fuss-pot. He never had to be told to clean up his room because it was always clean. Glenn had thought there was something wrong with a boy who hung up his own pants every night. It was as odd to Glenn as when he had seen Stout neatly fold his pants under his sleeping bag. It was Stout's way of keeping himself a gentleman with pressed pants. Later, he realized that Ellen had given Michael her wonderful sense of making a home. Gradually, Glenn had learned to follow her lead and to relax into a clean and neat state. Every time she ironed a shirt, Ellen had smoothed the fuzziness out of his life, and when she swept the floor, she vanquished sfumato with her broom.

Glenn was now old enough to appreciate what he hadn't understood when he was a kid. Stout had known: what we do makes us who we are. People had told Glenn to choose his battles carefully, but he just shrugged off the platitude. There are some fights you just can't leave alone. Sometimes, the fight picks you. Stout knew Glenn would have to find this out for himself. Michael would have to learn the same lesson: what men choose makes them men. The thought was so simple; it could run around the inside of your skull for years. You just had to let it fall and then decide what you were going to do. This was not an easy thing.

The windshield wipers waltzed before Glenn, even though Michael had not flicked any switch. "Isn't this one of those SUV thingeys where you can go anywhere and still get Hi-Fi radio?" Glenn asked. Michael decided not to say "It's Wi-Fi these days," and stretched a finger to the dashboard. Glenn felt the warmth rise up his thighs. Even the seats had heaters. He remembered Jimmy driving a truck way back in Germany, pointing at a bullet hole in the windshield, and saying, "I bet that warmed some guy's ass." Michael's car was like a spaceship compared to the old "Deuce and a Half" truck Jimmy kept on the road. Glenn liked the luxury of this living room on wheels and jibed, "Wow. This car even kisses your ass." Michael lost the frown he had been nursing since breakfast. He laughed through a smile, and Glenn found joy in Michael's chuckles.

Chapter 14

Whispering Gallery

Merkers,
Thuringia, Central Germany,
April 8 - 12, 1945

Jimmy was flying the Dodge along one of the few clear stretches of that main road the Krauts called an autobahn. He slalomed around each wrecked vehicle and shell-hole but just ran over the smaller battle-junk littering the road. Posey sat statue rigid, but his worry was as intense as his buttocks grasping the passenger seat. Third Army HQ had informed Posey that "some old pictures had been found in a mine at Merkers," and then had casually added, "Oh yeah, the mine is full of gold." Instantly, Jimmy knew if some officer was telling Posey about some old pictures in a gold mine, there would be a stampede of dogfaces. "If we don't get there first, those vultures will strip the place clean." So they piled into the Dodge to tear up the fifty miles between Frankfurt and Merkers, desperate to outrace the rumor.

The rumor had started the previous night. Two MPs on a dull patrol found two French women walking alone on a country road after the curfew. More out of boredom than duty, curiosity, or even desire, they stopped the women. They were bombarded with desperate appeals and excited kisses in incomprehensible French. One women pointed to the distended belly of her friend and pleaded "docteur." The two policemen saw she was waddling in the last stages of pregnancy and instantly became Knights in Crumpled Olive Green. They helped the women into their jeep.

The women tried to explain that they were forced to work in a mine outside of town, but their frantic chatter was lost on their rescuers. The MPs sped into town heading for the nearest Medical

Aid Station. They screeched to a halt, and the driver yelled, "Anyone know what to do with a Frog Broad with a bun in the oven?" The medics found a nurse who disappeared with the expectant mother, but left her friend standing at the door of the Aid Station. Being complete gentlemen, who would never leave a lady stranded, they offered the unpregnant woman a lift back to the DPs' shacks out of town, and with a hearty "Hop in, Babe," they drove into the middle of the night and the middle of Germany.

The woman sat in the passenger seat, guiding them along twisting lanes out of town to the place where the Germans stashed their slave laborers. They passed a ramshackle collection of industrial buildings, and the woman pointed her boney finger at a wrecked crane and breathed "or." The driver asked, "Or what?" and the woman kept repeating "or," until she remembered "gelt," which she finally translated into "gold." The brakes screeched at the word. A fifteen-minute inspection of the Kaiseroda Mine revealed the location of the entire gold reserves of Germany.

The boredom of their midnight patrol evaporated, and the MPs called in their first report over the radio. That was also their first mistake. Their sergeant responded if they didn't sober up before they returned to HQ, they would wake up in the stockade "thirty seconds after I finish kicking your sorry asses." They drove back with the woman and ten bars of gold as proof of their sobriety. The sergeant saw just enough glint in their hands to know instantly that this report had to go all the way up the chain of command. He was not going to be left holding the bag, even if that bag held enough money to buy a small town in Nevada. So the sergeant got on the radio to the captain.

The captain was not happy to be disturbed in the midst of his first chance to "fraternize with the enemy" in over a year, but had to cover his ass with a phone call to his major. The blonde former enemy lounging in the first real bed she had seen in four months was impressed that the American was so respectful to his superiors, for even buck naked on the telephone, he stood at attention. The major was pleased with the captain's interruption because it was the only good luck he'd had all night. An important message was the best excuse to leave a poker game holding a losing hand, so he took his time in copying down the details from the captain. His report to the colonel at headquarters lasted just long enough for the other gamblers to give up the game.

The colonel woke up the general and took an earful of abuse for annoying the general with civilian matters and commanded the colonel to "go bother that Bernstein." It took a while for the colonel to find out just who Bernstein was at Finances Section, Department of Civil Affairs, Third Army Headquarters. It took even longer for Bernstein to understand the telephone call. The colonel sounded like he was yelling something about millions of dollars in hard currency through a wad of tobacco.

In the middle of battles, an economist in uniform is not "essential personnel," so Bernstein had been waiting, bored sick in Frankfurt, for some real work. His official duties involved "the recovery of economic assets from the enemy," but the Treasury Department had hinted very clearly that his real mission was to make sure Patton kept his sticky fingers off the loot. When he could finally make sense out of the phone call, Bernstein gobbled the colonel's report like bread to the starving and, within minutes, was leading the charge of a convoy of accountants, economists, bookkeepers, and one German-speaking private, who actually knew where Merkers was.

Each time the report climbed to a higher level of authority, it also spread horizontally to everybody who had a radio, a clear telephone line, or an unwaxed ear. By morning, the single word "or" had blossomed into a full-grown tree and, under its spreading branches of piled-high greed and wild exaggeration, all hell broke loose.

Jimmy thumped the brake and halted before a tank turret pointed straight at them. He knew they had lost the race. MPs with no-nonsense scowls demanded identification from Posey. He immediately became the senior officer, presented his papers, and said, "He's with me." Jimmy sat "At Ease." He hadn't seen this much concentrated firepower since Normandy. Tanks were lined up in a roadblock wedge. Posey and Jimmy had to weave through staggered squads of guards and then a jeep full of MPs led them up a winding road to the main building.

Another officer ushered them into an office, and Jimmy smelled the panic. The room stank of anxiety and exasperation. People in glasses and helmets stabbed pencils at each other and barked a thousand questions and a million answers. He was unnerved by officers wading through corridors ankle-deep in papers, so he kept close to Posey. A fat guy in glasses glowered at Posey, until Posey stood to attention and announced, "Captain Posey, Monuments, Fine Arts and Archives, reporting for duty, Sir." The "Sir" reassured the man in the glasses that there was some order left in the world, and he thrust a grateful hand out to Posey. "I'm Bernstein, Civil Affairs. This is chaos." Posey grasped Bernstein's hand, and they melted into comrades who were going to help each other. "I'll show you just how chaotic."

Bernstein led them through the litter of wrecked furniture and ruptured filing cabinets to get out of the building. He walked them along a footpath around banked hills of mine slag to an elevator. Jimmy followed at the safe gap of three paces behind the officers, the distance every soldier knew was necessary to keep out of trouble, and well within range of every word. Bernstein was a little apologetic. "Patton had a blue fit when he heard the word was out."

"I wouldn't want to be on the sharp end of his tongue," Posey confessed.

"Some idiot gave an interview to a reporter and mentioned he'd fallen into the German Fort Knox."

"You're kidding!" Posey gasped.

"Can you believe it? Every replacement knows you don't talk to anybody about anything and then this Sad Sack Nobody blows open the biggest story they've ever had," Bernstein grumbled.

"I haven't seen any newspapers."

"It came out this morning in *Stars and Stripes* with pictures of bags of gold. Patton fired the censor on the spot and threatened wholesale courts martial."

Posey scanned the scuttle of troops moving between lines of armored vehicles and said, "I bet there's more muscle here than at Fort Knox."

"Uh-huh. When you get inside, you'll see why."

For the tenth time that morning, Bernstein presented his ID badge to the guards, who escorted them to the elevator. The tame German operating it neither smiled nor spoke to the three conquerors. There was plenty of time to think in the silence of descending over half a mile underground. Jimmy hated confined spaces and being squeezed into a box on a string operated by a suspicious DP was not his idea of fun. The German was used to the descent but not to all the attention by these Amerikaner, so he stood rock rigid guiding them into the lower depths. His hand rattled on the handle in time with the protesting motor. Posey's ears perked to the squeals of the elevator gear, and he smothered his fear beneath his hope that someone had remembered to grease the cables. Squealing machinery was just as dangerous as screaming artillery shells because you never knew what would happen until it happened. A simple elevator ride could be as lethal as a full-scale attack, but "if it happened, you wouldn't know, so stop worrying about it," he convinced himself. Bernstein fidgeted more out of impatience than apprehension. He wanted the whole thing finished as quickly as possible and was annoyed with anything that got in his way. The German eased back on his little throttle and swung open the cage that served as a door.

They stepped out of their vertical coffin and were immediately blinded. At such a depth, they expected almost complete darkness, but were attacked by dozens of lights. They squinted until they could see a vast cavern lit by search-light lamps dangling from the roof of the cave twenty feet above their heads. They looked down the long funnel of the cave. It was a rectangle scooped out of the solid rock, and the jagged walls made Jimmy think that they'd been scraped by giant teeth. Generations of miners had hollowed out the salt with picks and shovels, leaving this undulating cavity in the earth. The whole chamber stank of sweat and salt that seeped into every pore.

Bernstein led them down a central pathway that was a little railroad track. Posey felt he was walking in a busy cemetery. He estimated the cave was the same area as two or three football fields. Jimmy looked up at the lights dangling from the ceiling and thought the cables were twenty lynchings that someone had forgotten to cut down. Posey scanned from left to right to see serried ranks of burlap bags.

On either side of them, the bags stood shoulder to shoulder. Jimmy shuddered with old nightmares of ending up in just such a bag. Salty sweat trickled down his neck and slithered under his shirt to wallow in his armpits. He could hardly breathe through his nose and saw that Bernstein and Posey were open mouthed for air. The atmosphere was both cold and hot, and only when he raised his chin to gulp more air did Jimmy think of the half mile of earth hovering over his head. He saw that the little sacks, each about the size of a loaf of bread, were stacked four deep. Twenty bags huddled in each group with twenty groups in each row. When he looked up, there were more bags than he could count. He gave up the mental multiplication when his brain clicked ten thousand bags and ran out of zeros.

Bernstein beamed at them, circled a wide arc with his arm to encompass the whole cave and announced, "You're looking at the entire gold reserves of Germany, Holland, Belgium, France, and Norway."

Jimmy had to lean his ear into them just to pick up Bernstein's words. A rackety generator at the back of the cave pumped electricity to the lights and water to hoses. Soldiers were spraying water over each other. A soldier emerged from the gloom and offered Jimmy and Posey a handful of dirty rags. "Take these and cover your nose." They obeyed with the conviction this man knew what he was doing, even if they didn't. "It's the mineral salts in the walls," he said. Jimmy noticed everything was covered with a thin white dusting and fumbled to tie the rag around his head. "Use it to wipe down your boots when you're back up top," the soldier advised. They nodded approval like bandits in a movie, and the soldier explained, "That salt water will eat through leather in a day." Posey thought if they dallied much longer or even looked back, they would turn into pillars of salt. Jimmy could feel the crystals seep into his groin and was thankful that someone had thought of the hoses.

Bernstein stood beside Posey wiping his face and neck with a handkerchief and whispered, "So far, we've found seven more rooms, all bigger than this one." Posey now knew there must be tens of thousands of such bags. He looked down the railroad track to the back of the cave and saw a little railroad cart, like a child's red wagon. A soldier dragged a bag up to the cart, and Posey saw the man was smaller than the cart. The soldier struggled to lift the bag, and Posey could see the wagon was really a very large ore car. The dusty light and brooding shadows had combined to play tricks with his eyes, and he realized the perspective was all wrong.

Jimmy kicked one of the bags, and it didn't move. Bernstein encouraged his curiosity. "Pick it up, Soldier," and he winked at Posey. Jimmy lifted the bag like groceries, slung it under his left arm, and opened the top with his right hand. Bernstein's smile disappeared. Jimmy looked small, but Posey had seen him lift an engine and gently lower it onto concrete blocks. Posey grinned at Jimmy's strength, and Bernstein gaped at the brilliant stream of coins cascading through Jimmy's fingers. They could not take their eyes off of the satchel deflating under Jimmy's arm to create a golden pool welling at their feet. "Twenty-dollar American gold pieces," Bernstein said.

Jimmy's thumb felt a stray coin wriggle through his fingers. He dropped the rumpled sack and casually thrust his hands into his jacket pockets. Bernstein continued his tour. "They've organized this cache according to the value of the gold in each of the currencies." Posey pointed to the strange lettering stamped onto the bags a few rows along, and Jimmy stepped on two bright circles in the salt dust. When Bernstein moved them along the line, he ignored Jimmy retying a boot lace. "We've found French francs in those packing cases." He didn't hear the clink in Jimmy's pocket. He led them along the track, pointing out a line at the back of the cave bearing the seal of the U.S. Mint. Jimmy whispered the question Posey was too much of a gentleman to ask, but which he sensed Bernstein was so eager to answer. "How much is all this, Sir?"

Bernstein beamed like the kid in school who always had the right answer. "In today's precious metals market, a helmet full of these coins would be $35,000." You didn't need advanced math to know half a bag was one helmet, so each bag was more money than Jimmy could expect to make in a lifetime driving a New Jersey taxi. "What would you do with this money, Soldier?" Bernstein prodded, and Jimmy had the simple honesty to say, "I have absolutely no idea."

The German salt miners had been replaced by uniformed accountants wielding clipboards. Dozens of officers calmly examined each burlap body and entered their calculations into hand-held ledgers. Teams of soldiers followed the officers and carried the bags to the waiting ore cart and then manhandled the millions to the surface. The sweat and the salt oozed over their collars and seeped into their hands. They were systematically clearing the cave and leaving no mark, franc, lira, pound, or dollar unturned.

Jimmy looked up at the ceiling gouged out of the rock, and it looked like an upside-down frozen wave. He mumbled to himself, "If I stood on my head, I could be at the beach." Bernstein led them over the treasure rows and pointed out holes in the walls down the gallery of the chamber. "This is Room Eight," he told them. "Seven more of this?" Posey asked. "Yup" bubbled Bernstein, "This is called The Treasure Room. The others have your kind of treasure."

Bernstein did a quick right turn and marched them up to the wall. A steel door like a bank vault was nestled into the wall, perfectly cut into the salt and rock, but to its right, was a jagged hole four feet high. Bernstein said, "The engineers couldn't open the door, so they just blew a hole through the wall." "Practical," grunted Posey, and Bernstein hopped them through the jagged circle into another gallery.

They tiptoed along a tunnel curving to the right and then to the left, and shone their flashlights through open doors crammed with crates. Posey inquired, "They didn't dynamite into these chambers?" "Didn't have to." answered Bernstein, "The previous tenants left the keys in the locks when they moved out." Bernstein led them into the first room that was an underground warehouse and politely commanded, "You gentlemen get to work here. I've got to get back." He left Posey and Jimmy to figure out what they were supposed to do.

Jimmy started looking over the boxes piled high to the ceiling and said, "They all have labels on them." Posey shook his head. "That's our good luck. They've left all the shipping labels. We can identify at least where they came from, if not the contents." "We're gonna need help." said Jimmy. Posey nodded his head in time to his flashlight beam. "Bernstein called Stout. He'll be here soon."

They stood stymied by the sheer quantity of the crates. Jimmy figured there were thousands of boxes and suggested, "Let's snoop around." They returned to the main corridor and walked its length looking into the rooms to the left and to the right, as if they were clearing a hotel after a convention. Getting an overview of the place before Stout arrived would at least tell them the extent of the job.

Jimmy entered every chamber and memorized as many of the labels as he could. He read. "Louvre," "Kaiser Wilhelm," "Nationalgallerie," and many more than he could hold in his head. He asked Posey for a pencil, and Posey offered a stub and a few sheets torn from his field message book. Armed with the pencil and making sure his sidearm was handy, Jimmy started to copy down the strange names, knowing that Posey and Stout would need these to make any sense out of this regimented jumble.

Posey wandered the corridors more intent on the geology, for the moment, than the art. There was just too much for him to take in, and his mind rebelled against the onslaught of information. His brain demanded rest, so he ran his hands along the crystals of salt and felt their warmth at his fingertips. He remembered his college classes and started to talk to himself from distant notebooks, bringing to mind the afternoon lectures of his geology professor.

"Giant crystals often occur in remote areas, which are difficult to visit even these days." He'd have to tell his old professor when he got back just how difficult this visit was. The professor's voice tinkled in Posey's ear, telling him "the Merkers potash mine is the largest known salt crystal cave in Middle Europe."

Posey was exhausted by the physical effort of moving at such depth and steadied himself with both hands pressed against the wall. He leaned forward, his palms wrapping themselves over the sharp crystal rectangles. He swayed and breathed deeply, as if doing vertical push-ups, and let his mind retreat to the Geology Lab of his college days. He mumbled to himself through sweat-drowned lips, "Halite salt rock is generally a very ductile type of rock; that is, under pressure it tends to flow quite easily." With each labored breath, Posey's lungs were filling with moist salt. He started to giggle at the long-forgotten lecture notes "a cave was partly filled with giant halite cubes up to more than one meter of edge length."

Jimmy heard Posey's laughter echoing down the corridor and scuttled along the tunnel. He followed the pulsing gasps until he turned a corner and saw Posey babbling to the wall. A few steps brought him alongside, and he gently cooed into Posey's ear, "It's OK. Let's get outta here." Posey submitted to the soft arm around his shoulder and wandered off with Jimmy. He turned to tell Jimmy, "You know, Jimmy, the formation of these extraordinary halite cubes is, notwithstanding their size, quite simple." Jimmy guided Posey back to the blast hole in the far wall with the assured experience of coaxing many a drunk buddy to his bunk.

Posey was intent on explaining just what they were walking through. "Wherever there is free space in a salt mine," he said, "the ubiquitous migrating salt brines tend to crystallize on the walls of this space."

"You don't say," said Jimmy, feigning a special interest in the very thing that was poisoning Posey.

"But I do say, Young Jimmy me Lad." Posey waggled a crooked finger in the air. "Mostly these crystals are only small due to the small space available." Jimmy pulled him through the dynamited door and into the main Treasure Room where there was enough air to drag Posey back to full consciousness.

Posey looked up at the ceiling as he had when he was a boy searching for Santa's sleigh. "In this case the available space was large and so the crystals could grow to giant dimensions, not even filling up the whole void." Jimmy wobbled Posey to a ventilator shaft and let him collapse into a sitting position. He held Posey's head back to ease the air down his swollen throat. "That's right. Nice deep breaths. Now you gotta fill up your own void." Posey swayed back and forth, his head and shoulders nodding with the rhythm of a thoroughbred nearing a sure finish line. He looked long and deep into Jimmy's eyes and exhaled, "Whoo. That made me a bit whoosy." Jimmy tenderly told him, "You'll be OK now. Let's just sit and watch the rest of those jokers do the work."

Jimmy rested Posey until he was breathing normally. He was trying to figure a way to keep Posey out of the tunnels when he was jolted to attention by the rattle of the elevator. The doors opened, and Stout and Glenn stood in the backglow of the lift lights. Jimmy whistled to them and called, "Over here." When Stout stood before him, Jimmy jumped up to blurt, "You won't believe what's here." Posey lifted himself to his full height to say, "The motherlode." Stout just nodded his head and looked over the bullion bags to say, "I know. We got HQ reports and all the signs pointed to this place. We're only here because the Germans collapsed so fast, they couldn't take it with them." Glenn added, "Yeah. And that's because they had no place left to take it."

Jimmy brought Stout to one side to tell him about Posey's fainting fit, and Stout immediately organized their work. "Robert, you stay here while Jimmy gives me the tour. We'll need you here by the elevator to check everything that leaves this facility." Jimmy led Glenn and Stout past the gabbling accountants and threaded them through the tunnels beyond the Treasure Room. They were back in forty-five minutes. Stout had spent the time devising a method of cleaning these Augean stables. "I've had a word with that Bernstein fellow. He says we can have labor from a DP camp. Muscle is needed, but we also have to do this with brains." He added that the art work would be removed with the gold. "If we leave it to the end, it will never get out."

Putting the art together with the gold was a brilliant solution because the art would get as much attention as the money. Stout had explained the situation to the people at Civil Affairs in terms they could understand. These were not just bits of culture, but also things of outstanding monetary value. He got everybody's attention when he told them one crate of art could be worth as much as a million dollars, and there were "an estimated four thousand crates secreted in that mine." The economists' eyelids blinked like cash registers on goofballs. Now that Civil Affairs had something they could work with, they gave Stout everything he needed. He'd linked worth and value and put dollar signs over the artwork. With this new level of official support, he was ready and able to work, where before he was just willing to do whatever he could, with what little he had.

Glenn, Posey, and Jimmy watched Stout's boot drawing rough plans in the dust on the floor when the elevator rumbled again. It disgorged ten officers, who just stood waiting near the door. Something extraordinary was happening, so Stout led the team into the shadows. They stood well back watching the growing crowd wander through the mine's gloom. With each trip to the surface, the elevator returned to deposit more officers of even higher rank to add to the collection in the Treasure Room. Jimmy said the elevator was a sardine can full of officers. "We'll just wait and see," Stout commanded. After an hour, Jimmy counted twenty-two colonels, fifteen majors, and some captains. A solitary lieutenant looked like he had gotten on the wrong train.

The last load landed with greater care, and the doors were opened with a respectful smoothness. Two men in helmets and one in a peaked cap emerged with their hands shading their eyes. Stout examined the man behind the shiny brown peak and whispered, "That's Eisenhower." Posey looked at the polished helmet of the second officer and recognized Patton. Jimmy and Glenn knew "the little guy with the swollen mouth is Bradley" because they had been avoiding him every time they were sent on an errand to headquarters.

The whole party surrounded the big three at a respectful distance, and Jimmy took a long look at what was going on. The place was crawling with brass. Patton joked into Eisenhower's ear, but the words grew louder as they scurried through the chamber, "if the clothesline snapped in that contraption, promotions in the United States Army would be greatly stimulated." Eisenhower was fed up with Patton's gruff wit and told him, "OK, George, that's enough. No more cracks until we get above ground," and then turned to greet a saluting general.

Jimmy noticed that "there were so many generals' stars and colonels' eagles that the cave looked like a flock of birds flying south for the winter on a clear night." Bernstein hovered on the edge of the group, eager to report to the Commander-in-Chief-Supreme-Allied-Headquarters-Europe. Stout whispered to the others, "I wonder if Bernstein is going to ask Eisenhower for his autograph." They had to suppress their chuckles. Patton stood with his fists on his hips not twenty feet from them. Posey could see the slash of Patton's mouth and the squint of those steely eyes clear through the murk in the air.

The whole group shuffled along the rows of money bags, stopping occasionally to peer down at an odd sack, as if they were on a quiet stroll in a garden. Another general, with only one star, headed them towards the entrance blasted into the tunnels. Bernstein ran up to Stout to tell him, "You better come along to explain the art." So, Stout led his little squad of Venus Fixers to bring up the rear of the procession.

They all filed through the hole into the connecting corridor, and Jimmy could hear a voice from the front explaining to Eisenhower that "the enemy used this as a storehouse for everything they wanted to keep." There was a low growl and an answer, "They were certainly willing to destroy everything above ground." Jimmy was impressed by how obvious the answers were. He could have told the generals just what was happening, if anyone had asked his opinion. The tunnels barked with crunching feet as the VIP party was ushered into one of the rooms. Stout felt his ears pop from concussion of marching boots. He wondered if the miners who had dug out this hole were all deaf. It would have helped.

Bernstein was glowing in his role of tour guide of the treasure, but he had to remind Eisenhower that he was Chief Financial Advisor for Civil and Military Government. Bernstein's title seemed to evade the Supreme Commander's memory, so Eisenhower beamed his fatherly grin and said, "Lead on, young man." Bernstein led the top brass single file along the corridor and into the next chamber. They scanned the shelves holding frames, and Bernstein beckoned Stout to join them. George was introduced as "our art expert" and he explained, "these paintings are from the German State Museums. They seem to have been evacuated in a hurry." Bradley perked up interest and wanted to know, "How have you come to this judgement?" Stout pointed to the haphazard wrapping around one painting and then to the boxes which had not been specially constructed for the contents. "They collected everything and just threw whatever they could into whatever they had."

Soldiers were opening boxes for general inspection. Bradley ran his hand around a frame inside a box and waggled his jowls at Stout. "There's a lot of space between these paintings and the crate," he said. "And the frames are all of different sizes," Bradley observed. Stout replied, "which indicates a hurried packing." "Where is this museum?" asked Bradley. "Berlin," answered Stout. Bradley filed away the information in the card-index of his brain for proof that their bombing offensive of the Nazi capital was working. To him, the aroma of sawdust and smoke wafting from the open boxes smelled like victory. Stout urged them over to the racks of framed paintings lining the walls.

Eisenhower was intensely interested in the paintings and flipped through a shoulder-high stack of frames. Jimmy thought he looked like an old man selecting wallpaper at Woolworth's Five and Dime, but Glenn noticed that every time Eisenhower pulled a frame from left to right of the stack, he wiped his hand on his belted raincoat. He couldn't decide if Eisenhower was trying to get the dirt off of his fingers from the last frame or making sure his hands were clean enough for the next frame. The three generals examined every painting in the stack, and Stout was on hand to interject a footnote. "That's a Caspar David Friedrich landscape, also from the Kaiser Wilhelm Museum." Eisenhower nodded. Stout turned to Bradley to add, "The Kaiser Wilhelm is on an island in the center of Berlin." Bradley's chin shook once, and his mind drew a map of a river running through a bombed city.

The impromptu exhibit continued until Goya's *Nude Maja* opened before their fingers. The three stared at the canvas. Patton stood on tiptoe to get a better look over Eisenhower's shoulder at Maja's plump thighs, and delivered his opinion: "That's worth about $2.50 and I can see it in any saloon." Nobody chuckled, but Glenn caught the twinkle in Stout's eye and saw that the Hero of Bastogne didn't know much about art because he didn't even know what he liked. Their brief glimpse of Patton made Glenn speculate that "maybe even the generals can't tell a Rubens from a Reuben's sandwich." Stout was convinced that Patton was "just another millionaire ignoramus." Eisenhower turned to Bernstein to ask "What's next?" and they all trooped out along the narrow, winding tunnel to the next cache of loot.

They gathered around Bernstein who displayed piles of suitcases, over-night bags, rucksacks, and ammunition boxes. “This room contains items earmarked for the SS.” He opened five of the suitcases, each one crammed with gold and silver household items, all of them smashed flat. The generals rummaged through the objects. Eisenhower picked up an ornate candelabra which looked like a steam roller had run over it. His face held a thousand questions and one realization before he dropped the thing back into the suitcase. Bradley asked “why would anybody take all these useless things and spend so much effort hiding them in the middle of such a desperate military situation?” Bernstein was stumped, but that never stopped an economist from delivering an opinion. “We think they were more interested in the monetary value of the material than in the usefulness of the objects.” Patton picked up a silver cigarette case, and his finger traced a heel print in the metal. “But you could buy this in any store,” he queried. “They’re not your usual Smash and Grab thieves,” Bernstein explained, “first they grabbed, then they smashed.”

The three looked around the room trying to understand the significance of this place, which reminded them all of the left-luggage depot at a busy railroad station. “We even found cases of eyeglasses.” Patton was incredulous, “Glasses?” “Yes, Sir, spectacles.” Eisenhower shook his head in disbelief at the sheer pettiness of such theft on such a massive scale. Glenn was struck by how cheap the Master Race was, “if they had to rob the blind, they couldn’t be all that smart,” he thought. Patton’s face scowled as if he’d caught a servant purloining a spoon in his California mansion.

Bernstein was silent, and Eisenhower sensed there was something Bernstein didn’t want to say. He had heard this silence a thousand times, when officers had to report bad news but were afraid the messenger would be shot. He loaded his voice with as much kindness and approval as he could muster when he asked Bernstein, “Is there anything else I should know?” Bernstein’s feet shuffled in indecision, but his arm reached with firm resolve for a suitcase. He opened the lid to reveal the interior, full to overflowing with velvet bags. He picked up one of the bags, which Patton recognized as the same as those that held expensive whiskey. Bernstein's fingers pried open the bag's mouth and he emptied the contents over a crate. They gazed at a river of gold teeth cascading through Bernstein's fingers. Bradley saw twenty-two-carat molars wobbling over silver bridgework. Patton squinted at the sparkles set in ivory. Eisenhower's fist went to his upper lip as his eyes followed the trail of glistening, irregular lumps. Patton's face billowed crimson outrage. Bradley held tears behind his glasses. Bernstein breathed slowly, "We found five such cases." Patton grimaced "How?" through clenched teeth. "We think they are from prisoners. They might even be battlefield casualties."

Eisenhower straightened parade-ground tall and inspection rigid, turned on his heel, slowly walked out of the room, sauntered along the corridor, stepped over the jagged threshold, and marched through the Treasure Room to the elevator. He was followed by the cortège of his party. The elevator door was open, and the three most powerful men in Europe stood like statues awaiting delivery. Patton and Bradley snuggled beside Eisenhower, and the German at the controls had the good sense not to look at them. Glenn, Jimmy, Posey, and Stout stood listening to the elevator disappear up its noisy ascent. Bernstein joined them and said, "We'll get the next ride."

The Monuments Men were going to wait their turn, but Bernstein jumped the brass line and all four crowded into the elevator with him. Stout listened to their nostrils sucking in air and exhaling disgust and whispered to himself, "Domine dirige nos." Glenn remembered the words and would ask Stout what they meant, but now was not the time. His ear landed on "dirige" and he thought, "maybe it's got something to do with a 'dirigible' like a blimp, or maybe that's Stout making one of his jokes only Julius Caesar would find funny." Later, Stout explained that it meant "Lord lead us." and was impressed with Glenn's idea of the "dirigible" because "One could not be led unless one is lifted up."

The elevator did just that because all were happy to get to the surface. They knew they would have to go below again.

They stood breathing freely, surrounded by the activity of the two whole regiments of motorized infantry which Eisenhower had ordered to guard the mine. Stout explained that they would have something to eat and two hours sleep because "after that there will be neither rest nor refreshment until the whole damned place is cleared."

Bernstein nodded to them and walked off on his own business. Jimmy followed him with his hand in his jacket pocket and stopped him. "Excuse me, Colonel, Sir." Bernstein turned quizzically and asked, "Yes, Sergeant?" Jimmy produced three gold coins from his pocket and offered them open-palmed to Bernstein. "I think you dropped these in the elevator, Sir." Bernstein knew he had dropped nothing, for his pockets had been empty all day as a security precaution. He stretched out his hand and accepted the three coins from Jimmy. He gently stroked the three shiny discs in his palm because they were physical proof the world was not completely poisoned. He said, "Thank you so very much, Sergeant," and Jimmy accepted his relief.

Jimmy watched Bernstein walk away with a clenched fist toward the main building and heard distant traffic jams whisper in his ears. He lit a Lucky Strike, inhaled the relaxation of safety, and breathed to himself, "That's the first time I ever gave a tip to a colonel for an elevator ride."

Chapter 15

Pastoral

Glenn never liked driving the expressway, so he ordered Michael to "Take Flatbush." The SUV glided along the avenue as a phantom rider in the empty, Sunday morning mist. Michael drove slowly, trying to take in Anda's stories. Flatbush Avenue was an arrow pointed northwest to the city, and where it landed nobody knew. Glenn's eye caught the gaudy sign of The Perfect Dept. Store touting "Uniforms for School and Work... Graduation Gowns and Fashions for the Trend Conscious Boy Scout and Nurse." He mumbled to Michael, "We used to call it the Perfect Debt Store." Michael thought Anda was talking to himself but asked, "What was that?" "The store," Glenn replied. "It used to sell all sorts of army surplus stuff. You know, sporting goods and hunting rifles." Michael couldn't see the sign shrinking in the rear view mirror and grunted a confused "Huh?" "You could get credit," Glenn recalled, "but it would cost three times the price."

Michael wondered if Anda was losing it. Most of the time he was tight-lipped about himself. Anda would talk about pictures, tell an anecdote, or rant about something in the news. He seldom reminisced about "the old days." Michael had speculated Alzheimer's, but Anne dismissed the possibility: "His mind is as strong as his body." Michael had to agree that he was very healthy and had the constitution of a sprightly sixty-year-old. But all this talk of things long gone was making Michael concerned. Anda had never been like this when Nanna was alive, so Michael supposed this was just what happened when you are old and alone. Michael's finger touched the blinker arm, and they veered to the left into Prospect Park.

Whenever they entered the park, Glenn could smell the luscious change from concrete to grass. As soon as they drove through the park gates, he heard the tires humming to a different tune. Glenn loved the crescendo of the transmission singing in time with the wheels. Even in winter, he loved to imagine the grass sleeping under its white blanket. He didn't care that people thought such musings childish because he no longer cared what people thought. He was content to enjoy life, even if he were ridiculed for his pleasure.

He caught the whiff of wet branches mingling with Michael's new-car smell. He asked Michael, "Do you use the same deodorant as the car?" Michael laughed to hear the jibe; it reassured him that Anda's mind was as sharp as his tongue. Glenn gazed at the carousel and told him, "Pull in over there." Michael obeyed and stopped the car in the little parking lot, and the merry-go-round filled the windshield. "Let's stretch our legs," Glenn said, and they left the car in the morning fog.

The carousel stood silent before them, its gaudy horses caught in mid prance, waiting for the first rider of the day. Glenn caught the glint of distant skyscraper windows peeking through the trees and recalled mixing pigments of yellow ochre and burnt umber with a palette knife dragged over the ridges of stretched canvas. The relationship of landscape and portraiture had always fascinated Glenn. Sure, people looked at the face, but rarely did they notice that the same colors in different combinations could be billowing clouds over verdant fields. "Just add a little Payne's Gray to the mix and you have all you need for a face," he said to Michael.

When Anda started talking about painting technique, Michael knew he was up to something. But there was no use rushing him. He accepted Anda's obsessions because he had grown to realize there was method in the madness. Anda would hide something behind hints, and Michael would have to figure it all out. If Anda wanted to play mental Hop Scotch, Michael was ready to jump. It was like waiting for a present after Anda made you guess what was in the box. They walked slowly around the carousel, and Michael was content to follow and to wait.

Glenn pointed to a patch of green in the snow surrounding a concrete fountain and asked, "You ever wonder why there's always some grass here, even in the middle of winter?" Michael smiled, for he remembered the same question from years ago. "I know this one," he said. "So, tell me," and Glenn waited for the answer. Michael rose to the test and enjoyed the explanation, "The fountains are drained in the fall and covered with burlap sheets for the snow." Glenn smiled that Michael was playing the game, "That's true. Otherwise they would freeze and crack. But why the grass when there's snow everywhere else?" As if remembering the punch line of a forgotten joke, Michael explained, "There are pipes running under the ground. Some are sewers and some are the heating pipes between the buildings of the zoo." Glenn dug deeper, "So there are pipes. But why the grass?"

He let Michael build fact on fact and listened for the conclusion. Michael beamed as he explained, "The animals in the zoo aren't used to winter, so their buildings have to be heated. The pipes carry the hot water and heat under the ground. There's just enough heat to keep the grass growing." Michael was proud that he remembered the answer to the puzzle Glenn had forced him to solve when he was a kid. Glenn was pleased Michael could remember the facts. Now it was time for grown-up puzzles.

"That little fountain always makes me think of Jimmy," Glenn said. Michael looked at the circle of concrete wrapped in its burlap coat against the winter blasts. The fountain gushered refreshment in heat waves, and Michael remembered the first time Glenn had asked him the fountain question. "How so?" asked Michael.

Glenn took a long look at the fountain before elaborating, "There it is snuggled up in its winter coat and sits in its own little patch of green." Michael looked at the drips of melting ice falling from drooping branches. "Yeah. It sure is weird," said Michael. "And beautiful," added Glenn. "It's always surrounded by the grass." Glenn waited and Michael was confident in the question, "Why does it make you think of Jimmy?"

"Because of *The Mystic Lamb*," Glenn breathed.

"The what?"

"The Adoration of the Mystic Lamb."

"You mean that painting?"

"Yup. That painting by Jan van Eyck."

Michael snapped at the bait and was happy to be played. He asked, "Didn't you tell me it was something really special?"

"More than special. Unique." Glenn fell into his thoughts, and Michael waited. For his own reasons, Glenn wanted Michael to remember that picture. Michael picked up the silent hint and waited until Glenn said, "Van Eyck was one of the first to use oil paint."

"Oh yeah," said Michael, "didn't they use eggs and stuff before that?"

"Right," Glenn continued, "but van Eyck changed all that."

Michael was prepared for the professor to emerge. He had long become accustomed to the cascade of information flowing out of Anda. Usually, he zoned out and just waited for the fit to pass, but sometimes the story was too interesting to ignore. Anda's enthusiasm was drawing him to a place he didn't know.

"Well, there are masterpieces and then there are things so special that they have a life of their own. That's what *The Mystic Lamb* is."

"Didn't you show me a picture when I was a kid?" Michael asked. Glenn reeled in Michael's curiosity, as patient as an angler with a new lure. "Many times," Glenn sighed with relief and fond memories. "That's why you loved the little zoo." Glenn nodded in the direction of Prospect Park Zoo, and Michael nodded in tune with his own memories.

The zoo was a favorite treat, even though Michael was a little too old for such places. The first time Glenn had taken him to the zoo, Michael was about eleven and felt embarrassed. He was bigger than the squealing children running around him. He didn't want to be such a little kid, but he also wanted to touch the animals. Anda fed dimes into a slot like a bubble gum machine and filled their pockets with tiny food pellets. The baby donkey scared Michael, but Anda held Michael's hand through the fence. Michael felt the wet rasping of the tongue across his open palm, and the little creature licked away his fear. After that, they were free to make friends with all the small animals, until their pockets were empty. "The sheep in the zoo," Michael remembered.

"You really liked the lamb," Glenn said. "You'd stroke its wool and when we got home, I brought out the big book and showed you a double-page spread of *The Mystic Lamb*." Michael knew Anda was getting the painting into his head, just as he'd gotten Michael's fingers into the wool.

"Didn't it have three ears?" Michael added.

"You remember," Glenn glowed.

"And you told me that someone had tried to make the painting better, but they forgot about the ear, so the lamb ended up with an extra ear."

"So much for restoration in the 19th century," grumbled Glenn, "but good you spotted it."

Michael held back. If this story was going somewhere, Michael would prod Anda to lead them.

"You told me the picture was just one of a whole lot."

"Yup. It is a polyptych. A huge screen with doors, and it holds all sorts of pictures on the inside and on the back of the doors. In those days they didn't paint on canvas. They used wood panels to make their pictures, so they came up with the idea of making a big cabinet out of the panels. When you open and close the doors, you get a whole load of pictures, every one of them a masterpiece."

"Is that why it reminds you of Jimmy?" Michael asked.

"Yes and no. He heard about it from Posey and Stout, just like I did. In those days, we couldn't tell a triptych from our elbows, but we were so involved in the hunt that the stuff just took us over."

Michael looked over Glenn's shoulder, and Glenn caught that faraway look when Michael was really thinking. He smiled at those two little embers of understanding in Michael's eyes, as if greeting old friends. Now Glenn had to keep his mouth shut and wait.

"So why Jimmy?" Michael asked.

"That painting got under his skin. It got to all of us, but Jimmy had a way of hitting on the target. He zeroed-in on *The Mystic Lamb*. When that guy got something in his sights, he just wouldn't let go."

"So you found the Lamb?"

"No, not me," Glenn protested, "We were all looking for it."

"But you knew about it."

"It was in the reports," Glenn clarified. "Jimmy and Posey had met us for a briefing, and the four of us were figuring our assignments for the next week. *The Mystic Lamb* had been mentioned in about a dozen reports, so I asked Stout about it. He got really excited and gave us one hell of a lecture. We sat like Boy Scouts 'round a campfire and he just took us away. Posey knew all about it, but he got fired up too. Jimmy was quiet, like always, but then asked 'How big is that thing?' Stout pointed to the back of a truck and said, 'It wouldn't fit in there.' So Jimmy rubbed his chin and said, 'Then it won't be in a house. It's too big to get through the door.' That was obvious, but not until he said it."

Glenn slowly walked Michael along the paved path between two rows of benches. Melting ice was welling over the cement blocks, so he held on to Michael's arm, as much to lead Michael as to keep from falling. Glenn gazed into the distance and stopped at a bench close to the parking lot. He let the mists of his breath cast sparkles at Michael and said, "Let's sit for a while."

Snow had drifted over the bench, so Glenn sat on the top of the back rest with his feet on the seat. He took out his cigarettes, and Michael sat beside him, upwind. Glenn looked into the lighter flame cupped in the circle of his hands. His fingers tightened against the wind and he said, "In some ways, he was a lot like you."

Michael was hooked. "How am I like Jimmy?"

"Because you both really get it, when you get it."

Glenn looked over the rolling parkland, his eyes darting from zoo to fountain to the distant giants touching the clouds and mused,

"I guess they had more of a sense of the picturesque when they made this place."

Chapter 16

Into the Woods

Trier, Germany
March 29, 1945

There was nothing picturesque about Trier. Posey and Jimmy drove into town, but Jimmy said they were driving "over it." Thousands of Americans crammed Trier, either headed to the front or taking their Rest and Recreation - a hot meal, a cold shower, and nobody trying to kill you. The place bustled with military activity, but Trier was a ghost town, with two thousand years of spirits oozing through the debris. The few Germans left in the ruins had nowhere else to go.

They missed their Dodge. It had become their home as they criss-crossed liberated territory, searching for anything that had not been obliterated. Patton had run out of Command Cars, so he ordered a trade. Posey thought "trade" a funny description. A jeep had pulled up beside them, the driver kept the engine running, and they were commanded to transfer their gear. Patton got the Dodge, and they got a new jeep complete with a radio bolted to the back fender.

The radio was a blessing and a curse. Jimmy figured out how to work the thing so they could contact Stout and, through him, the other teams. Jimmy would fiddle with the dials and threaten to shoot it. It would die without warning, and Jimmy would bellow, "that damned thing won't work when we need it most." Posey agreed, "It's worse than a bunch of drunks on a party-line back home." Because of its perverse way of going silent in a crisis, Posey named it "Lucy" after a spoiled brat who would stamp her foot and refuse to talk when she didn't get her way. She used so many batteries that Jimmy called her "Juicy Lucy" and added, "I wish I could spank the bitch." At least they had a connection to Stout, even if it occasionally pouted.

When the armies crossed the Rhine into Germany, a committee in London had prepared maps and lists for the inspection teams to "survey damage to historic buildings," but in Trier it was difficult to find the buildings. They could trip over fragments of ancient wonders jumbled with last week's washing and the kitchen sink on top of the pile. A poet in stinking fatigues penned Trier's obituary: "The air had lost its power to hold atoms together. Gravity had a dogfight with matter, and matter lost." Posey was not so poetic when he shouted into Lucy's handset, "Trier is smashed." Stout already knew Trier was frozen desolation and sighed back, "Do what you can. Survey the main damage, and we'll just hope for the best." Just as Lucy was about to sulk, Posey heard Stout's fading voice say, "Report to A.M.G.O.T."

With the occupying troops had come a skeleton government and the hope of order. Posey and Jimmy had more hope than faith as they stood before a tent bearing a sign proclaiming this was A.M.G.O.T., the office of the Allied Military Government of Occupied Territories, G-5, Civil Government Affairs.

Posey knocked on the sign, and an old voice told them to "Enter." The man inside sat on an upturned ration box, apologized for not being able to offer them a seat, and introduced himself as "Simmons, AMGOT. What can I do for you?" Posey relaxed to see Simmons was no hard ass; he would probably help as much as he could. Jimmy looked back at the sign and then at Simmons and dubbed the tent "The Office of Aged Military Gentlemen on Tour." Posey saw the faded eagles on Simmons' shirt and realized that this ancient colonel was in charge of everything to do with the civilian government in this part of the liberated territories. Posey introduced Sergeant Mulvaney and himself and explained, "We need your help to do a preliminary survey of the monuments of Trier."

Simmons sighed in understanding of their predicament. Simmons was one of those very nice people who are given nothing and told to do the impossible. A government overseeing "Displaced Persons" was as absurd as a culture of "Endangered Objects." "Well, Boys, I can't help you very much, but I can help you find people who may be able to help you." They listened to Simmons speak of creating the remnant of a civilian administration out of "a few tame Germans huddled around a stove in the old mayor's office." He added, "The Germans are shell-shocked. Completely poggled. But they'd rather consort with the enemy than live like hobos in their hometown." Jimmy thought, "This is a guy who can get stuff done." Simmons volunteered to ask the Town Council "to organize a team of civilians who will try to assist you."

Posey wrote notes in his field message book as Simmons gave him more advice, but couldn't keep up with the torrent of names and places. Simmons saw Posey rubbing his jaw and asked, "Is there anything else you need immediately?" Posey said, "You have been very kind, Colonel. Anything you can suggest would be greatly appreciated." Simmons sniffed, "I meant is there anything you need, personally?" Jimmy jumped in, "Yes, Sir. We need a dentist."

Simmons looked at Jimmy as if he had asked for a manicure. "Can't help you anytime soon, son. The closest dentist is a hundred miles west at the hospitals." Jimmy nodded his helmet at the obvious. Simmons turned fatherly eyes on Posey and said, "I know you're from the South, young man, but you're talking like you have a wad of tobacco stuck in your cheek." Posey laughed through the pain. Jimmy smiled and thanked Simmons for his help. They made arrangements to meet the next morning, giving Simmons time to "rustle up a few Germans." They saluted him and left the tent.

They had been in town for three days when Stout delivered rough street maps taken from the *Baedeker's Guide to Germany.* They were to supposed to draw crayon marks on the maps identifying the damage. There were three categories of destruction: green for Minimal, yellow for Emergency Repairs, and red for Total Destruction. They skirted the rubble from every era of Trier's past, seeking any connection between the streets on their maps and the debris before them.

The next day, Simmons appeared with a string of dusty Germans. He ordered them in German, and Posey heard that Simmons was fluent. Simmons gave them a German and a bulldozer complete with an American engineer to drive it. The German would tell Simmons where the streets used to be. Simmons would command the bulldozer forward until the German told him to stop. The German, Simmons, and the driver could figure out which pile belonged to which street. Posey and Jimmy could then recreate the streets of Trier according to the lines in the *Baedeker.*

Once the area around the cathedral square was roughly cleared, they could see where the rest of the town had stood. Posey and Jimmy drew big black lines along streets on the map. Jimmy paid attention to the dark outline of Simeonstrasse because he had read in the *Baedeker* that it was called the "Street of German History." He grunted, "Now it's just another shit-pile." Posey told Jimmy, "Simmons is organizing the Krauts to keep clearing the roads, so let's get going." They were glad to get on with their job of coloring-in the map.

They walked the area, scrambling over crumpled castle walls sprinkled with fragments of Romanesque mosaics. The cathedral had survived, but the exterior walls had third-degree burns. "The church looks like it will stand," Jimmy said, and they craned their necks. "Let's see what's left," Posey said.

Jimmy scrambled up a little hill of pulverized brick and fragmented stone until he stood before a gaping opening in the cathedral wall. Posey was below him, and to Jimmy it looked like Posey was walking up a giant's tongue and into its mouth. Jimmy hung onto the crumbling wall and peered through the big hole. Posey heard Jimmy yell, "Say 'Ahhh.'" They laughed and turned back to look at the town. They watched the bulldozer carve straight lines through scattered debris.

"The inside don't look too bad," Jimmy said. Posey agreed, "The inner walls are largely intact. Green." Jimmy's nose pointed to what looked like a huge dirty champagne glass upside-down in a pile of cracker crumbs. "Looks like the bell came tumbling down and took the tower with it." In its grotesque way, the remains of the bell tower gave them a feeling of hope. "At least the walls are up, though the tower is down," he said. Posey nodded approval of such optimism and was startled when Jimmy said, "I wonder if we could get the bell to ring again?"

Posey had noticed a change in his companion. Before he had been efficient, but sullen. Lately, however, Jimmy was more interested in the work and had taken to saying "at least" when they were inspecting damage. Somehow, Jimmy had moved from grunts of "Kraut junk" and "stinking shit-pile" to "at least." "At least, the walls are still standing, sort of." "At least, Lucy works some of the time." "At least, we have plenty of water to wash down this crap." Posey valued the positive notes seeping out of Jimmy just when they were running out of hope. Jimmy turned away from the cathedral to look at Trier again. He crossed his arms and said, "At least, we have a few Squareheads left in the town to tell us where everything used to be."

They started the descent to the jeep, and Posey winced with pain. Jimmy stood beside him in case Posey tumbled. A few weeks ago, Jimmy had noticed that Posey was often in pain and had asked, "What's eating your ass?" Posey had responded, "It's nothing. I fell into a landing craft in Normandy." Jimmy knew that a fall from a scramble net wasn't so bad. It was the abrupt stop when flesh met steel that hurt. "You could have gotten a Purple Heart." Posey chortled and told him, "That guy who got shot in the ass on Omaha Beach, he should have gotten four Purple Hearts." Jimmy asked, "Why four?" Posey explained, "He got hit side-on, so the bullet went in, out, in, out, that makes four." Jimmy roared at the thought of medals dangling from a pair of perforated buttocks. Posey had refused the Purple Heart and a ticket home because, he said, "That medal is awarded for wounds received in action from the enemy. I just fell on my ass."

A couple of weeks later, he noticed Posey's limp, and Posey told him "the foot got run over thumbing a lift in France." Now they were in Germany, and Posey's right jaw was swelling. Posey's body was collecting hurts, breaks, bruises, and swellings like luggage stickers. The more Jimmy heard of the little accidents, the more he respected the man. Posey was in constant pain, but he kept going anyway.

Jimmy's respect for Posey had become concern for the old man. After all, he was "at least forty-five." Posey stopped halfway down the slope, took off his helmet, and spit blood. There was no coughing. Jimmy was relieved it wasn't his lungs, at least. It was that tooth again. Posey rested, growled, and spat for a few minutes.

Jimmy told Posey, "I'll drive." Posey slumped into the passenger seat, and Jimmy drove the jeep at a walking pace. He was searching the faces they passed for a civilian, but it was an endless parade of tired dogfaces. There was no use asking these guys for a dentist. Most of the Squareheads were hiding until they knew more about the occupiers.

Jimmy spied a patch of white hair sticking up over a window ledge. He pulled the jeep close to the window and hoped the hair was attached to a head, one which was still on some shoulders. He got out of the jeep and took off his helmet as he approached the building. People seemed to be reassured if they saw a bare-headed soldier. The helmet in the hand said, "I'm not going to hurt you."

The white hair rotated and a pair of creamy blue eyes beamed fear and indifference at Jimmy, who scrounged up a German word and said, "Bitte" to the head. The head was still attached to an old woman. She rose and peeped around the door. Jimmy stood his ground so as not to frighten her and repeated, "Bitte." It took some courage or desperation for the old woman to take two steps closer to him. He did not approach her but spread his palm over his jaw, groaned, and mimicked pain.

The woman went into the house, leaving Jimmy standing at the door and Posey sitting in the jeep. When she didn't return after a minute, Jimmy sniffed the air, marched to the back of the jeep, and dragged his Thompson sub-machine gun out of the back seat. Posey said, "Don't think you'll need that." Jimmy pulled the sling over his shoulder with the barrel dangling down his back. "Just for friendly," he said, and turned to the house.

Posey smiled. He knew what Jimmy was up to. Germans were used to weapons, but Jimmy had figured out that they became friendly when they saw a Thompson. The gun was no more lethal than any other, but its shape made an impression. They had discussed the strange reactions to the Thompson, and Jimmy had decided the Germans thought the gun was a "Chicago Typewriter, so any dogface with this is Al Capone and the Squareheads know all about him." Posey had tested the reactions to rifles and pistols. Faced with a carbine or a .45, a German could be really bossy, but show him a Thompson, and the atmosphere was instantly jovial. He agreed with Jimmy that a Thompson put the frighteners on the Germans. Posey appreciated the Thompson M1928 A-1 as a wonder of form following function; Jimmy saw that its function was to threaten. A man with this weaponry might just be a gangster, and the movies had convinced them gangsters always got their way. The Germans were all very nice to Posey when they thought he was Jimmy Cagney.

They waited for the old woman long enough to get first annoyed and then worried, but she returned after several minutes with a small child. Jimmy couldn't tell whether the little gnome was a boy or a girl. The child's eyes shone through a dirty face, and Jimmy melted. He rummaged in his pants pocket and found three wrinkled strips of Pop-O-Mint gum. The old woman cooed something gentle in German and the child clawed at the gift. Jimmy stood armed to the teeth, and Posey thought him overdressed for the occasion.

Sweet saliva jumped the child's delighted lips and carved mint runnels down the grimy chin. The child grabbed Jimmy's hand and led him around the building. Jimmy turned his head back in appeal to Posey. Jimmy's expression said, "Well, what else am I going to do?" Posey waggled his fingers in farewell, but could not restrain his laughter at Jimmy being dragged along by the little ragamuffin. The pain ended the laughter, and Posey suffered through the attack with clenched eyes. When he opened them, he saw the old woman's eyes full of sympathy and her hand nodding to him to rest.

Jimmy returned 15 minutes later with a portly middle-aged man and said, "This clown's a dentist, and he speaks English, sort of." The man took off his hat and bowed to Posey. "Allow me to introduce myself. I am Doktor Emil Schlossmeyer. It will be a great privilege for the Doktor to attend to all the dental needs of the Herr Officer." Jimmy thought the dentist was going to click his heels and salute, so he took control. "Hey. That's great. Let's get to work."

Schlossmeyer took the hint and asked Posey to "please to open mouth and keep open." Posey dropped his jaw, but his eyes scanned for trouble. He saw Jimmy's thumb swelling under the sling of the Thompson, and so did Schlossmeyer, so everything was friendly. "Shut, please," He told Posey, "There is cervical decay in der Zahn nummer fünf."

Jimmy growled, "English, Bitte."

"He has big hole in tooth," Schlossmeyer proudly exclaimed.

"Can you do anything about the hole?" Jimmy demanded.

"Of course, I am dentist. But you to my surgical office must go."

Posey and Jimmy were surprised there was a working office and were suspicious of the offer. Jimmy broke the silence and commanded Schlossmeyer to "hop in." The dentist wriggled his bulk into the back seat, and Jimmy's foot thumped the starter. He turned his head to order, "You show and I drive." He knocked the stick-shift into first with the heel of his hand and gently let out the clutch, so that Posey's head wouldn't be jolted and Schlossmeyer wouldn't fall off the back.

Jimmy followed Schlossmeyer's directions over, around, and sometimes through the bits of Trier that were scattered into giant sugar cubes. The farther they drove from the center, the less damage there was to negotiate. Posey made a mental note to "put this on the maps, when my head stops thumping." Jimmy saw houses with bullet holes and the occasional destroyed wall where artillery had come a-calling, but the place wasn't very beat up. Sheets hung from windows as if surrender was confused with laundry day. They saw few people. Schlossmeyer commanded Jimmy to "Stop" in front of an old house with a pointed wooden door and invited them into his office. The pain drove Posey through his suspicions and into the building. He felt some comfort in seeing Jimmy flick the safety catch on the Thompson to "Off." Schlossmeyer led them down corridors and through clouds of plaster dust into a dark room filled with medical equipment.

Schlossmeyer offered Posey a seat on a dust-covered chair, but Jimmy positioned himself at the window, so he could keep one eye on the jeep and the other on Posey. Schlossmeyer was bubbling over with energy, as if it had been a long time since he had seen a patient. He bumbled around the room chattering about how it was so good the Americans had finally arrived to free them from Hitler, and how he had never agreed with those terrible people, who got us all into this mess, but now everything was going to be just fine because civilization returned to Germany on the points of American and British bayonets. Posey just wanted him to shut up and get on with his work. Jimmy kept his right hand glued to the Thompson's pistol grip.

Schlossmeyer told Posey to "say Aach" and explained, "I give you an sprint of Novocaine to make dead the nerves." Confident Jimmy could take care of any trouble, Posey surrendered to the relief of the syringe, and soon the pain had shrunk to a dull thudding in time to his heart. Schlossmeyer would not keep quiet. He seemed to know all about Posey and the Monuments Men and was fulsome in his praise of their efforts for German culture.

Posey was wondering about the disjoint between the ruined town and the functioning dentist's office. The place looked like any dentist's office in America, the kind which charges good money. The people in town hardly had anything to eat, but this rotund little clown seemed to have escaped the worst of the war. There was no explanation. All Posey knew was that he was sitting in a fully equipped dental room on the rim of a wrecked city, and the sooner the chatterbox finished, the better for them all.

Jimmy watched Posey almost horizontal with his mouth gaping and took in Schlossmeyer's every movement. There were plenty of sharp things in the room, but he hadn't seen a weapon, and he doubted this fat Squarehead would be foolish enough to stab them with a blunt scalpel. Schlossmeyer's arms made a circle around Posey's head to deal with the cervical decay, which Jimmy thought funny, "At least, he's doing the tooth."

Posey looked up at the dentist's head looking down at him and was sprayed with waves of bad breath. He was talking about someone called Hermann, who seemed to be related to Schlossmeyer. The Novocaine had worked well enough for Posey to be getting thoroughly annoyed with the dentist, who kept asking him questions he couldn't answer with a mouthful of drill bits and prods. It seemed this Hermann was Schlossmeyer's son-in-law and he was a professor of art at some university, but Posey could not connect the dots to Hermann, who was "so refined and a gentleman just like you." Jimmy heard Schlossmeyer say, "You will have much to discuss when I introduce you." Posey got the impression Schlossmeyer was making a dinner date for him.

"There," said Schlossmeyer, "you have a temporary plug in the tooth and you will feel better when the swelling subsides. But you must see one of your American medical practitioners as soon as you can. Now we go to visit Hermann."

"Hermann who?" Posey asked.

"Doktor Professor Herr Hermann Bunjes. It will be such a pleasure for him to meet you."

Posey and Jimmy froze. Jimmy remembered the name because it had cropped up in reports, but they had very little information. He had read it aloud as "Bungies," and Stout had corrected his pronunciation to "Boonyays," so the name stuck. Now this Schlossmeyer was going to lead them to the name, and they were as confused as they were intrigued. They stood by the jeep waiting for Schlossmeyer to collect his things.

"What do you think?" Posey asked.

"We heard that name before."

"I know. But where?"

"It was at the meeting last week," Jimmy recalled.

They stood scratching their memories for anything about this mysterious son-in-law. Posey realized the name was important when he recalled he had seen it in a Consolidated Report. Posey prodded Jimmy, "He's some art expert."

"Yeah, that's right," Jimmy confirmed. "Stout talked about a couple of museums."

"What do you remember?"

"They were in Paris," Jimmy blurted.

"You sure?"

"Dead sure."

They quickly changed the subject when Schlossmeyer appeared at the door. The dentist was as jovial as a schoolboy on holiday and started to heave himself into the back seat. Posey grabbed Schlossmeyer's arm and guided him to the passenger seat. "You've been so good to us, please sit here, Herr Doktor." Schlossmeyer nodded his gratitude. To be the passenger in a car that actually worked made him feel important, but to have a chauffeur was heaven. As Posey was squeezing himself into the back seat, he heard Jimmy whisper, "Paris. Red Flag."

Jimmy drove forward, and they pondered the "Bunjes, Hermann Red Flag" note which Stout had shown them on the index card. Only the most important targets merited a red flag on Consolidated Reports of the Art Looting Investigation Unit. They had talked targets and assignments with Stout, but that was to coordinate their inspections. Tracing the stolen art was the mission, but finding the thief was the quickest way to the looters' hoards. Stout had a list of German looters in alphabetical order, but there were too many names and too few Monuments Men. Stout and Glenn had made index cards of the biggest fish; they were his flash cards at meetings. Posey and Jimmy had been dog tired, but Stout had made a joke about Jimmy's pronunciation of the name to make them remember it. Jimmy knew the fat Kraut beside him would lead them to this Bunjes. They were sniffing out a trail.

Schlossmeyer guided Jimmy out of town and onto a country lane. Posey felt every bump and was glad the Novocaine had not yet completely worn off. They were only a few miles out of the city, but they could have been in a different world. Posey saw fields and neat little houses huddled around hills the war had never touched. The people who lived there were either very smart or very lucky.

Jimmy felt a wobble coming from the right front tire and knew a rock was lodged in the tread. The rhythm proved the road was dry dirt with no shell craters, and he didn't see any ruts. Nobody had driven this stretch for a while, and it made him wonder why they were the first vehicle down this road. His nose gulped the air, and the smell of cows flew through the jeep. This was so much better than breathing the bone meal dust in town.

Schlossmeyer pointed to a house on the left and said, "We must make one stop here." Jimmy warily pulled over, and Schlossmeyer waddled to the front door where a woman offered him a can. They chatted in high-speed German while Jimmy scanned every window, tree and rock. He turned to Posey and said, "This is not a good idea." Posey agreed but added, "What are we going to do?" Jimmy replied, "This might be a High Roller Win or Fatso could be setting us up for an ambush." Posey had the same thought. If they just dumped Schlossmeyer here and scootled back, there was no harm done and Posey had a tooth. If they kept on, this could be a wild-goose chase, or they might be the geese. Jimmy was content to follow Posey's call, so he nodded when Posey told him, "We'll go on."

Schlossmeyer returned with a covered pail and was so effusive in this thanks that Jimmy thought he was going to kiss them. "I have not eaten any milk for weeks." Jimmy watched a woman leave the house and walk down the street looking back over her shoulder at them. The look gave him the creeps. She turned quickly off the road and walked down a track. His eyes followed her until she disappeared into some trees. Jimmy scowled and asked, "Where to, Doc?" Schlossmeyer waved his hand forward, and Jimmy caught the slyness seeping through the dentist's smile.

Posey felt Jimmy's dread and unbuttoned the cover of his holster. Schlossmeyer was too enthusiastic about their meeting with his daughter's husband. Jimmy was using every inch of the road to look around bends before they got to them. The road was leading them into a little wood. Jimmy slowed and his mind jumped to high alert.

Schlossmeyer told them "a cousin's house is just down the road to the right," and it would only take a minute for him to pick up some more supplies. "The country people have had it so easy," he complained. Posey was rethinking their decision. Afternoon was running to dusk and ten kilometers of isolated road at night was a very bad idea. They were alone and being taken to meet a complete stranger by an annoying bumbler visiting relatives. While Schlossmeyer was in the cousin's house, Jimmy said, "I just remembered something else. The red flag was beside his rank, Lieutenant in the SS."

When Schlossmeyer returned, the smiles had disappeared. He sat and told them, "We have one more stop." Posey took charge, "No more stops. We go to your Herr Hermann or we go back." Schlossmeyer caught the command in Posey's voice and waved his hand at Jimmy, "Straight ahead."

After a mile, the trees opened onto a little clearing, where they saw an isolated farmhouse. Jimmy stopped where a cow track led off the road to the house and asked, "Is this the place?"

Schlossmeyer told him, "Yes, we are here." Posey saw the pistol grip of Jimmy's Thompson wedged between his leg and the stick shift and nodded them forward. Jimmy drove down the track to the house. "Here is Hermann's house," Schlossmeyer said. Jimmy pulled to a stop but kept the engine running.

Schlossmeyer unfolded himself out of the jeep and waddled to the front door. Jimmy slung the Thompson over his shoulder and stood beside Posey, looking at the house. Jimmy whispered, "Hey. No gingerbread." Posey laughed with the confidence that they were a fully armed Hansel and Gretel.

Schlossmeyer invited them into the house, his pride bubbling through his introduction. "Allow me to present to you the distinguished Herr Doktor Professor Hermann Bunjes." Posey was confronted by a tall man in tweeds offering his hand and asking, "And you are?" Jimmy looked through Bunjes' cheesy smile and over the fat neck and noticed Posey wasn't shaking hands. "Posey, Captain, U.S Army." Bunjes spread his rejected hand to take in the room and to offer them seats at a table. Posey saw that the table was set with three chairs. They had been expected. Jimmy thought of the woman in the street looking back over her shoulder and guessed she had sent a message ahead of them. Bunjes introduced a fearful looking woman as "my wife, Hildegarde," and a ten-year-old girl as his daughter. Jimmy counted three generations all lined up for inspection. "Very nice to meet you," Posey assured them, and Bunjes offered, "Please, to sit."

Jimmy's eyebrows bowed into question marks and Posey returned a sly shrug. Jimmy wandered through the room and into the kitchen to make sure nobody was waiting with a grenade. He opened a door and stepped into a back yard. He could see nothing out of the ordinary. There were no farm sheds or outbuildings, so he figured the house was a holiday place. He circled around the house and saw the woods had been cut down for fifty feet, leaving the house sitting in its circular lawn. He stopped to smell the grass and the trees. Silence was always trouble, so hearing the birds sing meant the place was safe enough to open the front door and return to the little party.

Posey and Bunjes were sitting at a table, so Jimmy pulled up a chair and sat between them. Bunjes blinked at Jimmy's effrontery to sit in the presence of superiors. He said, "Cognac," and Hildegarde disappeared into the kitchen. Bunjes was talking to Posey, and ostentatiously ignored Jimmy. "My father-in-law has informed me of the wonderful work you are doing for my city." Posey could not interrupt Bunjes' stream of compliments and his fulsome praise of Posey's "important mission to save our culture from the devastations of war. So unfortunate." Jimmy looked over the room, and his eyes followed shelves of books on three walls and dozens of photographs thumb tacked to the wooden beams.

Bunjes was explaining his doctoral thesis on "The Medieval Monuments of the Moselle Valley" and was "so impressed by you people from America, doing so much good work to save these same monuments." He offered Posey a copy of his book on Trier, "to assist you in your work." Jimmy was bored with Bunjes' bragging and rose to look over more of the house.

He wandered along the book shelves and peered into a small room near the kitchen. Schlossmeyer and Hildegarde's daughter were sitting on a bed. They looked worried, but the girl mustered a pleading smile. Jimmy felt sorry for them and thought of the three generations nervously wondering what was going to happen in the living room. He made a mental map of the house in case of trouble. He took his time inspecting the photographs of ancient buildings and recognized some of the places he and Posey had inspected after they were wrecked. Bunjes' eyes followed Jimmy, but his mouth was aimed at Posey. "My work has been mainly with the medieval artifacts of the Ile de France and it is my dream to continue that work."

Hildegarde brought in a tray with a bottle and three small glasses, and Bunjes poured drinks. Posey lifted the glass awkwardly and followed Bunjes' lead when he tossed the contents to the back of his throat. Jimmy ignored the third glass. When

Bunjes lectured on art, Jimmy noticed how eager Bunjes was to explain his own resumé. The more Bunjes talked of his academic achievements, the more Posey remembered what was on Stout's index card. When Bunjes spoke of his time as the Director of the German Cultural Institute in Paris, Posey remembered that Bunjes' main job was looting Jewish art collections. Bunjes shared his "most gratifying accomplishment, the saving of the Bayeux Tapestry," but Posey knew Bunjes had led an SS commando team to steal it. Posey's memory was teasing out the truth from every lie that drooled over Bunjes' lips. "What an experience!" Posey complimented him, and Bunjes smiled, "It was an adventure and a duty to save such wonders for the world." Posey could see Stout holding up the index card between his thumb and forefinger and reading to them the words, "SS Lieutenant." Bunjes felt confident he was impressing Posey, so he went into detail of the art work he had rescued. Posey was itemizing the wonders Bunjes had stolen.

Jimmy left the table to wander around the room. He looked at the books and listened to every word. The books were in three languages, and he guessed they were mainly French because he could just make out some titles. The German ones were incomprehensible. He picked out one heavy volume and studied the bookplate on the flyleaf. The name was not Bunjes. He could feel Bunjes getting annoyed that someone would dare to touch his books, so Jimmy carried on his inspection. He examined the bookplates in five more books; they all had different names. Jimmy's face aimed a knowing smile over one book straight into Bunjes' eyes. Bunjes' eyelids closed in contempt and opened to Posey.

"I began writing my book with Arthur Kingsley Porter, an Englishman. You may have heard of him." "I certainly have," Posey said. Bunjes was keen to compliment his guest, "But of course, an educated man such as yourself would know such people. I studied with him at Harvard." Posey knew that Kingsley Porter hated the name Arthur. Posey had mourned a man he had never met when he had read of Porter's death a dozen years ago. Porter had disappeared from a beach in Ireland, but none of that was on the index card. Posey did not need an *aide memoire* when it came to Kingsley Porter, for the man's writings had made his life.

The first thing Posey learned at university was just how little he knew. That first semester was a horror. The other students knew everything the professors were saying, but the only lesson he took from lectures was shame at his own ignorance. When he could take it no more, he confessed to a kindly professor, who just smiled and said "Here. Have this," and gave Posey a book. It was *Beyond Architecture* by A. Kingsley Porter. The professor had told Posey to "keep it." He was not used to expensive gifts, but the professor leaned over his desk to confide, "I'll let you in on a little secret. We're all stupid. Porter just has a way of making us all smarter."

The professor had been right. Posey read the book, and every page was an assurance. Porter wrote in common language about the most rare experiences of art. When Posey read "architecture is really part of landscape and both are just where people live," he made the jump. He had thought of architecture as complicated construction work, but Porter was telling him that making a building was just like creating a poem or a painting. A building was as much a portrait as a Kodak flashed at a wedding. The kindly professor, with Kingsley Porter's help, told Posey, "you may be ignorant, but you don't have to remain so." With every turning of every page of Porter's book, Posey grew to the honorable state of manhood in his mind, and never looked back.

Posey accepted Bunjes' Harvard lie; the index card showed Bunjes had attended a Harvard course in France. But listening to Bunjes forge a counterfeit link to a dead hero was a robbery Posey could hardly stomach. He knew he had to tolerate this charlatan and suffer his elaborate fraud, until he figured out what to do with him.

Jimmy sensed the table was some sort of Mexican standoff. He walked behind Bunjes and saw the tension rise in the German's fat neck. Bunjes' face filled with outrage that this inferior had interrupted them. Posey looked up and asked him, "Have you talked to Lucy lately?" Jimmy stepped forward with his back to Bunjes. "She ain't been saying nothing." "Why don't you give her a call?" Posey suggested and glanced at Bunjes. Jimmy hesitated. "You think it would be a good idea?" Posey assured him, "That girl is just itching to hear your voice." Jimmy walked to the door saying, "I'll give her one more chance."

Bunjes eyes bored onto Jimmy's back. Posey listened for the door to shut and told Bunjes, "He found a woman in Trier." Bunjes nodded a knowing smirk between "men of the world," but glowered at the door. He thanked Posey for removing his driver and confessed, "I am personally in a very difficult position."

"How is that?" Posey asked, pretending sympathy.

"People do not understand my situation," Bunjes whined.

"You can tell me."

Bunjes took a deep breath to emphasize the importance of what he was about to say and leaned over the table to whisper in confidence, "I knew Goering."

"Really?" said Posey with feigned admiration.

"Yes, in Paris," confided Bunjes, but Posey already knew Bunjes had been Goering's main art thief. Bunjes had confiscated "abandoned Jewish property" after he had condemned the owners to concentration camps. He was a dealer in fine art with a gun to the owners' temples. Bunjes picked up the interest in Posey's tone and started reeling off the names of the top Nazis he had worked for. But refinement was more important to Bunjes than his former associates, and this was what he was trying to sell to Posey. He knew Americans would be in the market for superior European taste, and he had the publishing history to prove his expertise. This American sitting at his table would be his first step to a deal.

He explained that his work for the Nazis was all dictated by necessity. It was the only way he could save the art. "Really it is all a great misunderstanding" and "people could get the wrong idea" and hang him. He had to escape to civilization, "in Harvard, or some other institution of learning where I can make my contribution to world historical research." Otherwise, his neighbors would put him up against a wall, "without even the courtesy of a final cigarette."

Posey's brows knitted with concern. "People here think I was a Nazi, but as you see, I am a simple scholar. It was a terrible strain working with the Nazis all those years, but you will appreciate that I only did what you are now doing, preserving the culture for future generations. You see, I was protecting the art. It was conservation by acquisition."

"So by taking control of the art, you were able to preserve it?" Posey asked.

"Exactly. You understand. The Nazis are boors. Complete frauds. They don't understand the beauty of art, only that it is somehow valuable."

"Not the most cultured bunch," Posey agreed.

"They robbed the silver service from the Rothchilds, and then used it for their own tables. To see them dribbling food off those priceless forks made me sick."

The door flew open when Jimmy returned, letting a cold blast fill the room. Posey sucked in the night air, and it helped him swallow his rising bile. Bunjes' wide grin could not hide his annoyance at the driver interrupting him once again. Posey half turned to ask Jimmy, "How's Lucy?"

"She's fine. You were right. She was really glad to hear me, and can that girl talk!"

"Oh yeah. What did she say?"

"She having a party later at Simmons' place, and we're all invited."

"A bit late for a party."

"She said to show up, the later the better, 'cause she's gotta square it with Simmons."

Posey understood Jimmy had gotten through to Stout, but Stout needed some time to coordinate with Simmons at G-5. He turned back to Bunjes, showing eagerness for more tales.

Bunjes was relieved his plan was working. His father-in-law had told him of these Monuments Men when they first arrived, and it was sheer good luck which brought this American buffoon to his table. If he could only convince this idiot and his driver to arrange an introduction to a higher authority, he was sure he could make a deal. The American was so obviously impressed with all the important people Bunjes knew, he decided to name some more. His eyes pleaded for Posey's approval when he said, "You see, we are actually colleagues."

"I don't know what I can do for you," Posey answered.

"You can contact higher authority and tell them about me. I am most willing to offer my expertise in the service of culture and the American government."

"Professor Bunjes, I am not in a position to make such a decision."

"Please, please, why so formal? Call me Hermann."

"Thank you, Hermann. I am Robert. I know what you have done for art, and I can see from this room, these books, that you are a truly educated man. I am willing to do all I can to help you. I just don't know what a higher authority would do."

Posey felt the contempt oozing through the charm and the cheery good humor. Jimmy saw the monster beneath the velvet and knew he had to keep the safety catch on his Thompson and his temper. They needed what was in this joker's brain, and it would do them no good to have it splattered over the walls.

Jimmy walked over to a row of photographs tacked to a wall. The first picture was a double display of Romanesque arches holding up an aqueduct, and Jimmy recognized the ruin they had themselves photographed in Luxembourg. Jimmy's inspection of the photos made Bunjes nervous, so Jimmy took his time. He slowly moved along the shelves, stopping before each rectangle to stroke his chin in contemplation. Posey had to grind his teeth to keep from laughing, for he imagined Jimmy as one of the patrons at a private viewing of a new exhibition.

Jimmy stared deeply into one of the photographs. He noted the title and mumbled, "Het Lam Gods" and remembered this was

Dutch. He heard Bunjes cough, so he raised his voice to say, "The Ghent Altarpiece."

Bunjes stopped talking, and Jimmy could see a red glow of indignation creep out from under Bunjes' collar. Jimmy's sensed his interruptions were a real pain in the ass, so he continued reading out titles. One book was written in English, so he read aloud in his most unrefined Jersey accent, "*The Adoration of the Mystic Lamb.*" He caught the glint in Posey's eye, and almost shouted, "van Eyck." He aimed his voice at the back of Bunjes' head, "Flemish. 1432."

Posey was asking about the trains which took the French art to Germany, and Jimmy heard Bunjes complain how difficult it was to get the shipments coordinated. Jimmy hated Bunjes, and to keep himself under control, he concentrated on the angels in the van Eyck painting.

Posey was explaining how he would need more information, if he were to help Bunjes. Jimmy had now reached his limit. His fingers grasped the bottom of the photo. Bunjes saw what he was doing and yelled, "Do not touch those. They are my work." Jimmy slowly pulled the corners of the photograph from the thumb tacks to make the sound of ripping paper scream throughout the room. Bunjes glowered at Jimmy and turned his face to Posey, shrugged and said, "What can you expect of such people?"

They hardly heard Bunjes. Jimmy was sick of happy Germans. This one had lips too large for his face. Jimmy was repulsed by the little white bubbles that formed at the edges of his mouth. He saw the lips were very moist and watched Bunjes drawing his thumb and middle finger from the corners of his mouth to meet under his lower lip. It was like pulling grease along a tire rim.

Posey heard Bunjes' tone of high seriousness punctuate his superficial charm. He mused, "This creep would not be out of place at a lodge meeting, regaling his brothers with tales of Hitler's private life. He would be a star performer at dinner parties, where he would trot out the same anecdotes for the hundredth time and think his amusing table talk was the hit of the evening."

Jimmy slowly and deliberately paced back to the table, sat on the chair, and spread the photograph before Bunjes. Bunjes recovered his oily charm and sighed, “Ah. Van Eyck’s masterpiece,” and started a lecture. Jimmy knew all about *The Mystic Lamb*. Stout had shown Jimmy and Glenn the very same picture, and Jimmy had fallen in love with it. The picture had captivated him. Stout had said, “Wherever they have stashed this, there will be the treasure,” and Jimmy had offered his opinion, “If it’s that big, it sure ain’t going to be in a house.”

Jimmy paid close attention when Bunjes casually admitted, “I know where it is.” Posey and Jimmy strained to keep silent blank faces so he would talk. When he could no longer bear their silence, Bunjes said, “It is part of the consignment for Hitler’s personal museum.” His eyes beckoned to Posey. Posey returned Bunjes’ casual tone and said, “That would be of interest to my superiors.” Bunjes smirked, “Quite possibly they would like to trade my knowledge for a secure place in an American university.”

Jimmy’s loathing lifted his hand to action. He pulled at the sling on his shoulder, and Bunjes stiffened. Posey watched Jimmy lay the Thompson across his knees and remove the magazine. Bunjes saw the empty gun and relaxed for a moment. Jimmy grasped the magazine in his left hand and let his thumb push bullets into his right palm. Bunjes told them, “I know where they have secreted the Ghent Altarpiece.” Jimmy looked straight at Bunjes and flicked another bullet from the magazine. “This is the information I would be willing to share.” Jimmy thumbed another bullet and rattled them in his right fist as if he were at a crap game.

Posey saw Jimmy was now making Bunjes sweat and sat back to enjoy the show. Jimmy shuffled his fist and rattled more bullets. Bunjes looked deep into the photograph of *The Mystic Lamb,* trying to ignore Jimmy. He pressed his finger nails into the table beside the photograph, and Jimmy saw they were neatly cut, cleaned, and manicured. He had only seen such a shine on the nails of women who had time to waste. Bunjes finally spoke to Posey, and his pinky finger gesticulated with a golden index ring that splayed his fingers apart. "I can tell them everything."

Jimmy fingered the bullets in his palm and held one between forefinger and thumb in front of Bunjes' face. Bunjes stared in arrogant fear as he watched Jimmy carefully place the bullet on a corner of the photograph. The bullet stood straight up, and Bunjes could see the point had been cut to a blunt edge. Jimmy smiled back, and the smile said, "I did this to this bullet and when it hits you, it makes a little hole in the front of your chest and rips out your back as it leaves."

Jimmy was putting the frighteners on Bunjes and was going to keep him frightened. Posey suppressed his laughter when he saw Jimmy place another bullet on another corner of the photo. Bunjes blubbered, "There is a repository near Hitler's country home at Berchtesgaden." Posey was hoping Jimmy wouldn't overplay his act. If Jimmy said, "You dirty rat," the spell would be broken and Bunjes would clam up.

Jimmy watched the bubble of saliva appear in the corner of Bunjes' mouth and placed a third bullet on the photo. Bunjes tried to bluff. "Only I know the exact location." Jimmy saw that Bunjes didn't have much of a poker face. Others surely had this information, but they weren't sitting two feet from his trigger finger. He lifted up the magazine in his left hand over the table, and his thumb launched a fourth bullet onto the table. Bunjes watched it spiral in little pirouettes on its dull head before tumbling to rest on its side. Jimmy dug his elbows into the table and read the indecision in Bunjes' eyes. He picked up the bullet and gently placed it on the last corner of the photograph. He felt the breath wheezing through Bunjes' nostrils and kept his eyes glued to the face. He pushed the magazine back into the Thompson so slowly that the screeching metal echoed through the room. Bunjes turned to Posey to proclaim, "I will tell them everything."

Posey yawned and said, "It's getting late. We can give you a lift into town." Bunjes said it would take him a few minutes to pack a bag and they both heard the relief in his voice that told them they had won without promising anything. "We'll wait outside," Posey said, as they left the house.

Jimmy started the jeep and let it idle to warm. They were both shaky and stood in the glow of the headlights holding on to their triumph. Posey had to ask, "You got through to Stout?" "Yup. All we have to do is get him back." They waited for their passenger, barely believing what he had told them. Jimmy was looking at the photo of *The Mystic Lamb*. He'd picked it up off the table along with the bullets. He didn't know much about art, but he sure knew he liked this picture. Posey watched him for a moment and looked back at the house. "I was wondering what monsters hang from their walls," he said. Jimmy raised the photo to Posey and said, "Angels." They had a good laugh until Bunjes emerged with a small suitcase, looking like he was rushing to a waiting train.

Posey peered past Bunjes to the front door and said, "We can drive your father-in-law back to Trier." Bunjes impatiently waved away the suggestion, "He stays here." Bunjes settled himself into the passenger seat. Posey wriggled into the back seat and Jimmy turned the jeep onto the cattle track.

Jimmy's foot thumped the gas pedal and kept up the speed all the way to Trier. Bunjes slouched into the seat, confident he had taken the first step to a position far away from his vengeful neighbors. Posey was hanging onto the hope they would get him back without any problems. He felt waves of success whirling under his helmet. They would make it and deliver their prize just in time. Jimmy was flying along the road, eager to get rid of this bastard before he emptied a magazine into his smug face. Somewhere ahead of them, Simmons waited at a roadblock with a squad of bored military policemen and a requisition for a prisoner to be transferred to the authority of the Allied Military Government of Occupied Territories, G-5 Civil Government Affairs.

The jeep skidded along the road, but nobody complained about Jimmy's driving too fast. All three were happy that their hopes would be fulfilled and their dreams come true.

Chapter 17

The Giant's Causeway

Michael was so captivated. His mind was floating in a sea of questions, but Anda's answers were like a life jacket. As he listened, his admiration for Anda rose to the surface. There was nowhere to hide from such questions; they all led back to the man sitting beside him, his own grandfather. This was perfect, so Michael loved him. "I had no idea," he admitted.

"Maybe I should have told you earlier," Glenn sighed.

"I wouldn't have understood," Michael confessed, "I was too young."

"But now you're not. Look at you, a husband and a father."

Glenn's own pride was clear, so Michael said, "It's amazing what you did."

"I was just a small part of the whole shebang," Glenn answered. "You know, I didn't understand it until many years later."

"You mean you had to think about it?" Michael asked.

"What was there to think about, when I didn't know? Jimmy told me all about capturing Bunjes twenty years afterwards."

"You kept in touch?"

"Yeah. We used to meet at Dora's every few months. He'd show up with a fistful of papers. He wanted to talk, to try and fill in the missing bits. So did I. That's how I can tell you all this now."

Michael was reaching out for the mosaic pieces of Glenn's life. Each pebble was becoming precious in itself and not just for the bigger picture it painted. His mind rebelled at the missing pieces.

"So what happened to Bunjes?" Michael asked.

"Huh... He turned out to be an even bigger coward than a phony."

"How?"

"He was arrested and tried to make a deal with the Americans," Glenn said, "He promised to tell them everything, if he got a job at an American university. Claimed that all he wanted was to finish his research. They were to throw in a 'safe passage' for his wife and child."

Michael could practically smell Bunjes and said, "The wife and kid were pretty low down on his list." Glenn's voice rose with his temper. "All that Harvard stuff was just bullshit. Sure, he was an art expert, but he just did a summer course from a Harvard lecturer in France, and palmed that off as a degree. It was the Harvard name he was trading. He had nothing else."

"Was he tried with the war criminals?" asked Michael.

"They didn't get the chance," Glenn sighed. "It's all a bit confused. Jimmy told me there were two stories going the rounds. You know, Jimmy was a real magpie, picking up everything he thought nobody else wanted. He told me that either Bunjes had killed his wife and child and then shot himself or that he hung himself in jail."

"So he was a suicide?"

"That's about the worst type of coward. Shot or hanged himself, it doesn't matter. What matters is he left his family destitute in the middle of the worst poverty anyone can imagine; that is, if he left them alive. Coward."

Michael grasped the word, and "coward" brought Anda's hatred of Bunjes within Michael's reach. What could be worse: being left by your husband with a child and nothing to raise that child with or murdered by your husband? Either way, it was the worst thing anybody could face. The betrayal was the badge of cowardice. Glenn's anguish pulled Michael's thoughts through the fog. "That's what ambition can do," said Glenn.

"Ambition?" asked Michael.

"I don't mean success or achievement or getting rich or anything like that. I mean the ambition when you expect others to give you what you can not earn yourself."

Michael was confused. Anda was talking out of left field again, but now Michael could not dismiss what he said as the confusions of an old man. This was Michael's own confusion, and he owned up to it. "Anda, I don't understand," Michael simply said.

Glenn took a deep breath and dragged the meaning through the shadows. "Put it this way. For Bunjes, his career was the most important thing in his life. He wanted status and recognition more than money. What he wanted more than anything was a position. He sold his soul for a title, if he had one to sell. When he couldn't do the deal, that was the end of the line, so he killed himself. Success meant more to him than his own life, more than the lives of those who loved him."

Michael seethed in silent loathing until he admitted, "That's frightening."

"What's even more frightening," Glenn continued, "is I've seen plenty of Bunjes' types in faculty rooms. It wasn't just the one German. It's so many of the people who are supposed to be the smartest turn out to be the worst. That's what really scares me."

Michael sat staring at the circle of the carrousel, glimpsing Anda's profile as he spoke. Michael was crossing the shadow line into middle age, and Anda was holding his hand.

Glenn sat studying the horses on the carrousel, their wooden manes held stiff under layers of gold and silver. Their harnesses were bejeweled with metal lumps and glass beads the size of eggs. The saddles gleamed with the polish of a million riders, skewered by the twisting poles that kept them prancing through the generations. Glenn wondered how much lead was covering those statues for they were caparisoned in decades of gaudy paints.

Michael saw the sadness invade Glenn's eyes. Anda's hurt was hiding beneath his anger. Michael reached beyond his own confusion to stroke his Anda's shoulder and said, "Let's go see the Giants." Glenn turned to Michael, and the joy shone through his surprise. "Yes," he said, "Let's go visit the Giants."

Michael led him back to the SUV and they left the park. The traffic was gearing up for the day. Waiting at the red light, Glenn pointed to the entrance of the Brooklyn Public Library and asked Michael, "Remember when Nanna used to bring you here?" Michael pulled over and parked on the Flatbush Avenue side of the building. "Yes. She was wonderful. Every Thursday after school."

They got out of the SUV and shuffled along the snow dusted sidewalk to the entrance. The building's massive two story triangle snuggled perfectly into the apex of Flatbush Avenue and Eastern Parkway. Michael had once told Nanna that it was a huge piece of cherry pie. She had laughed and told him "you can have a piece when we get home." Glenn and Michael approached the scalloped steps to the main entrance. It was like an ancient temple or some other exotic place, but the front was a welcoming semi-circle holding the door. Michael remembered how Nanna had pointed to the door and joked to him, "If it's a big piece of pie, a giant took a big bite out of it."

Glenn and Michael stood dwarfed before the massive doors between columns where golden figures looked down in sympathy on hurrying mortals. Nanna's finger would point out the statues and tell him stories of Tom Sawyer, Captain Ahab, and a Raven, and Michael was entranced by figures four times his size. He had loved the birds, boats, and whales, and once brought a carrot for the golden Easter Bunny. She had coaxed Michael into the library with tales of giants, gnomes, fairies, and mermaids, just like the ones decorating the doors. She taught him to read in the Children's Section of the library, but he warmed to the soft pleasure of following her finger across the pages, until he could do it himself.

Michael had to know, so he asked, "Anda?"

"Yeah?"

"I really want to know how you got the painting?"

"I picked it up in Merkers."

They stood before the main entrance, staring at the ornate letters of the dedication carved into the wall beside the door in foot-high letters. Glenn was evading the subject. Michael wanted facts, and Glenn needed to give the meaning behind those facts. They stood silent before the inscription, until Glenn read out the top line of the poem. "Here are enshrined the longing of great hearts and noble things."

Michael had to share with Anda, "Nanna read the next line to me. She told me there is a place where the beach turns into a rocky road and heads into the sea. That's where the giants walk into the ocean, so they can 'tower above the tide.'"

"That was so like her," Glenn recalled.

"She said they were stepping stones and they disappeared under the sea. She called it 'The Giant's Causeway.'"

"You know there really is such a place. She didn't make it up," Glenn said with pride in his recollection.

They remembered the woman who loved them and silently finished the rest of the inscription: "the magic word that winged wonder starts, the garnered wisdom that has never died."

Glenn was ready to reveal all to Michael, patiently waiting. "Those paintings were the 'longing of great hearts' and they were buried in a booby trapped mine along with the people."

"So you just took one as a souvenir?"

Glenn faced the wall and the decades separating them. The frustration poured through him. There were things about his own life he barely understood. His experience was trapped within him, but he knew Michael had to share that experience to make his own decisions. He gently offered the answers to Michael.

"Lots of guys were sending home anything they picked up."

"Like helmets, and daggers, and flags, and stuff like that?"

"Yeah. Those were very popular. You can see them in any veteran's living room. But there were other things."

"Like the painting?"

"The painting is small potatoes. One guy even put a stamp on a crown and mailed it home to a gas station in Texas."

Glenn waited until the memory of Ellen gave him the courage to tell Michael how he got *The Head of Christ*. Glenn's eyes shone with the determination to tell Michael the truth, simple as it was.

Michael's face screamed in silent patience, "I want to know now," and Glenn's mind jumped back six decades. "It was the last night, when we had cleared the Merkers mine. We were dog tired."

Chapter 18

Souvenirs in Chiaroscuro

Merkers,
Thuringia, Central Germany,
April 14, 1945

Jimmy and Glenn were as exhausted as the sun dragging itself behind the mountains. As soon as the generals left, the people from Civil and Financial Affairs ripped through the area like a tornado. Stout had figured a few weeks to clear the mine. They gave him forty-eight hours. Merkers was in the area allotted to the Russians, so the Army had to grab all the stuff they could before the new guys moved in. Jimmy stood watching as the last convoy of recovered loot left the compound.

The trucks carrying the gold were almost empty; their loads were so heavy they could do only ten or fifteen miles an hour without overheating the engines. Every inch of the art trucks was crammed with crates of silver dishes, paintings wrapped in burlap rags, and statues forced into castoff German overcoats. Glenn thought they looked almost comical as the treasure chests on wheels swayed down the mountain. There was no room left for Jimmy and Glenn, so Stout told them to stay behind with the skeleton guard, and he would come back to get them in the morning.

The last truck had disappeared in a purple haze of exhaust, and they all settled down to enjoy the quiet after the frenzy. A lone tank stood guard near the road with its turret gun at rest, so Jimmy and Glenn shuffled over to see if the crew was open to a meal. The tank commander was a friendly type and invited them to share rations and some warmth. The crew was busy setting up for the night.

Tankers always slept well away from the gas fumes and never crawled under their tank for protection. Glenn had seen what happened when a crew had ignored the advice of the old hands and bedded down under their armored fortress to seek shelter from the rain. While they slept, the tank settled into the soggy earth. When their buddies dug out the bodies, one of them had no finger nails from scratching at thirty-five tons of indifferent steel pressing him into the mud.

Jimmy and Glenn knew tankers had a way of making everything cozy, so they were extra polite with their new friends. Everybody was so tired they couldn't sleep. Glenn had quipped to the others that the last two days "was like moving day after everybody had been evicted," and they all laughed. There was discarded junk everywhere. Bits of boxes, ripped burlap bags, splintered wood, and the rusted trucks from the mine littered the area.

When night twittered around them, the cold snapped at their aching bones and seeped into their exhausted muscles. The four guys of the tank crew started policing the area, which meant they were picking up anything that could burn. Glenn thought they looked like chickens scratching in a barnyard, but he and Jimmy joined them in the hunt. The young gunner crawled up the bow of the tank, swung himself over the gun, and untied a large metal box full of holes. He kicked the steel rectangle over the side and onto the ground, and Jimmy saw it was a bullet-riddled ammunition box. The gunner jumped down, and together they carried the box twenty-five yards away from the tank reeking of gasoline vapors. Glenn, the commander, the driver, and the radio-man returned carrying bundles of anything that could feed a fire. They piled the trash into the box and the driver doused the pile with gasoline. He spit a lit cigarette butt, and the box whooshed into a pyre to burn off the night frost.

The commander took off his helmet, flipped back the hinges holding the chin straps, and separated the liner from the steel shell. He put the liner back onto his head because it always made him feel safe, even if it was useless to deflect a bullet or ward off jagged lumps of whizzing shrapnel. He passed the helmet around as if he were taking the collection in church. Each of the six soldiers rummaged in packs and pockets to produce a can of rations each. Without a word, the commander skinned open each can with a knife and emptied the contents into the helmet. Beans, spaghetti, Irish Stew, prunes, and buckwheat all congealed into the helmet. The commander announced, “This evening I will be your chef.” He snapped the chin straps together over a metal rod and dangled the helmet over the fire. Jimmy mused that he looked like he was fishing, but everybody knew that this was “slumgullion,” when the soldiers shared rations of whatever they had.

These potluck suppers wouldn’t win any prizes, but they were always hot and welcome and usually a nice surprise. The helmet bubbled as the commander regaled them with his rendition of a Bill Mauldin cartoon from *Stars and Stripes* about the dogface brewing up slumgullion and telling his buddy to “Drop those cans in the coffee real easy. There’s a chicken in the bottom.”

Bill Mauldin was the cartoonist beloved by every dogface who could read or look at a picture because he was so irreverent. Patton yanked Mauldin before a court martial for “spreading dissent” and threatened to “kick his ass into jail.” Maudlin had answered the dressing down with a cartoon of Patton demanding that soldiers shave every day and wear ties, even in combat. “Old Blood and Guts” hit the roof and wanted this “disruptive force” shot at dawn. Eisenhower thought of reminding Patton what happens to kings who kill their court jesters, but decided to simply order him to leave it alone. Years later, Glenn read an interview with Mauldin which summed up what they all thought at the time: "I always admired Patton. Oh sure, the stupid bastard was crazy. He was insane. He thought he was living in the Dark Ages. Soldiers were peasants to him.” They’d all heard and told the chicken joke many times, but it was one of those jokes that got funnier with the telling because it was so true. Glenn thought to himself that the truth of the joke was that they were all still alive to laugh at it.

While the commander was brewing the slumgullion, Glenn watched the rest of the crew folding their coats into neat squares. Glenn was curious to see them carry their woolen rectangles to the back of the tank. The driver squirreled himself through his hatch and started the engine, and Glenn watched the other two hold all the folded coats over the exhaust pipes. The driver gunned the engine, the pipes glowed crimson in the night, and soon the coats were steaming with heat. They returned to the metal cooking range and offered a warm bundle to each of the diners. Soon, each sat crosslegged on a coat around the fire waiting for his supper. Jimmy complimented the commander, "That's a neat trick yous guys have figured out." The commander passed off the praise with a casual, "Yeah. It sure keeps your ass warm." Jimmy scrunched himself deeper into his seat and said, "Wish we'd had this in Belgium."

"You were at Bastogne?" asked the commander.

"We both were," said Glenn.

The commander glanced at Jimmy's screaming eagle shoulder patch and grunted, "That figures." After some moments to decide whether to trust these newcomers, he said, "So was I. Patton's bunch." Jimmy laughed, "So was you the taxi driver what took four days to make a call?" They all laughed at the complaint because it was Patton's tanks which had driven the hundreds of miles to the rescue of the Bastogne garrison.

It was a military feat that was already being compared to the cavalry columns of the Old West, hard-riding to save the day. Patton's tank army had fought for three days, blind in blizzards, and arrived in Bastogne on the day after Christmas. Those tanks meant life to every soldier. They had jumped out of the foxholes under igloos, and danced like the Snowmen in the Macy's Parade. Glenn smelled the tanks before he could hear them. That year, Santa came on a steel sleigh clad in white camouflage to both the naughty and the nice, passing out survival to all who still had enough strength to run away. To Glenn's frostbitten ears, even the guns were shouting "Ho, Ho, Ho." They all hid their gratitude under their gripes.

"You fucken' crunchies complain, but if it wasn't for us, you'd still be there," said the commander. The laughter rippled around the tank crew, but Jimmy had to ask, "What's a crunchie?" The driver informed him, "That's the sound you dogfaces make when I run over you." All agreed this was the best grouse they'd heard in a while. Glenn told them of the British and their first-class griping. "I heard one of those Limeys grouse to the other, 'If we gave you a mermaid, you'd ask for chips and mushy peas.'" Feigned gripes and exaggerated bellyaching were soldiers' chit chat, but the longer the service, the shorter the complaining. The veterans griped or insulted just to say, "Hello, I am not going to kill you." Replacements would even complain to officers, which was as useless as it was annoying to both the officers and the dogfaces.

After all the shouting from "those assholes in Civil Affairs," Glenn welcomed the silence. They chatted about "why was it that garritroopers had to scream orders at the top of their lungs." It was so unnecessary, "so uncivilized." Glenn pointed out, "They shout because they don't think anyone is going to obey them." The knowing laughter fanned the flames, and they settled into a binge of warmth and rest.

Glenn gazed at the faces in the firelight and tried to place them. Only the commander's face bore any recognition, but the grime and the pain settled into similar patterns. He knew that sometimes only the commander survived a battle. The Germans called the M4 Sherman tank the "Ronson" because it lighted up every time. There was more truth in the German humor than Glenn wanted to remember. He searched through the combat lines etched across the commander's face trying to conjure anything familiar, but drew a blank. Glenn could not connect the man's face flickering in the firelight with the four days he spent in an ice-hole in Belgium.

* * * * *

That first night in Bastogne, they had been digging in. Glenn had been scraping the frozen earth and cursing the rocks and tangled tree roots. The little entrenching tools they carried would fold out into a miniature pick and shovel and could dig about an inch before the handles broke. When the first German shell hit the trees, everything went into quadruple time and they all scraped out two feet of safety in seconds. They were like cartoon mice munching through Swiss cheese.

The first night was Glenn's terror time, but by the next morning, he had accepted that he was going to die in this hole, so he set about making it as comfortable as he could. Inch by reluctant inch, he made his own grave three feet deep and two feet wide. There was just enough space to keep his head down and his ass in the air. The exploding shells were bad, but not as bad as the trees they hit. With every overhead shot, the trees splintered and whirled through the men.

One guy got caught out of his hole and half a tree went through him. There was no screaming and no blood; the guy just crouched down with the end of the tree sticking out of his ribs. The other end of the tree kept his body off the ground, so he hunched over as if on a football line. The first day, the guy bloated up and then deflated like a beach ball and froze. For four days, he kept Glenn company because it would be suicide to crawl out of the hole, and the guy was already dead twenty yards in front of him. He had to look over and peep around the body to see if the Germans were attacking. Glenn finally took his eyes off of him when he could smell gasoline and heard the American engines behind him. He never looked back, just jumped up and ran to the tanks.

* * * * *

Glenn hadn't felt much for "that guy what was skewered," and was dissatisfied with the word, until Stout gave him the dictionary. Glenn had discovered "impaled." Now he could feel a deeper regret for the tree-man in the snow because "skewered" was just something you did with meat. "Impaled" made the man somehow more human because Glenn couldn't think of an animal being impaled. Warm, tired, and safe in the circle of the rescuing tank crew, Glenn now could solemnly remember him and mourn for a complete stranger. Before that, the man had just spoiled the view.

Firelight sprayed through the holes in the ammunition box and danced over the men huddled around its glowing sparks. The flickering played over faces, tracing the outlines of hidden thoughts, and each man remembered the moment he was desperate to forget. They were all so exhausted they couldn't sleep, and in the waking snooze Jimmy whispered into the flames, "We weren't the first wave but damn close to it." Glenn did not look up from the fire. "But you are the last wave."

Glenn knew Jimmy was talking about the first jump on D-Day, but for the paratroopers, it was actually D-Night. Their first taste of angry steel had been around midnight. Jimmy sat trying to sweep memory out of his head, but he couldn't. He saw the planes lined up back in England and himself waddling to the door. Each man was so overloaded that his buddy had to push him up the little ladder and into the plane.

Jimmy could not look at Glenn, so he spoke to the fire and let Glenn eavesdrop on his confession. "They took off just before us.... a big stream, must have been a thousand planes. There was a traffic jam in the air," he confided to the glowing embers. "The first guys were lucky. They just woke up the Germans. Then it was our turn. The Germans were just awake enough to let all Hell loose."

* * * * *

They had been only an hour in the sky, and Jimmy watched the others just to keep his fear under control. He sat on the bench near the door, clutching the safety rope. Thirty-two men lined both sides of the fuselage, silent in their terror or shouting their bravado over the roaring engines. From up front near the pilots' cabin, laughter waved over the men, and Jimmy heard a voice shouting, "Her mother was in the kitchen the whole time." He grinned to think someone had to brag of a conquest when he might be dead any moment. Two guys in front of him were talking about a cartoon, and you'd think Mickey Mouse was the most important thing that had ever happened to them. One soldier was thumbing his rosary beads through trembling fingers and whispering, "Now and at the hour of our death, Amen." That was hard to listen to, so Jimmy concentrated on Mickey Mouse.

The cockpit door was open, and Jimmy could see past the pilots right out the front window. A crazy curtain of lights was thrown up from every angle, and moved across the window. Nobody else looked through the door, but Jimmy could not take his eyes off the pilots. They sat there headed straight into that tracery spewing through the night. Jimmy was reminded of bus drivers who just sat there and drove through blinding snow storms like it was the most natural thing in the world. Those pilots must have been the bravest of them all because they knew what was going to happen to them.

The Jump Master stood and opened the doors to port and starboard, and a roaring ice age invaded the plane. He yelled through the wind "Stand Up!" and the whole troop obeyed as one. Each man held a clasped hook in his right hand. The hook was the head of their static lines, twenty feet of canvas webbing that snaked from their parachutes to the plane. When they stepped through that door, they would tumble to the end of the line, and their their chutes would jerk open. The Jump Master screamed, "Hook Up!" and thirty two metal hooks clicked over the metal bar that hung from the ceiling and ran from the front to the back of the plane. All turned to face the door, and each man cuddled the man in front of him. They all looked at the red light glaring at them over the doors. When it turned green, they would run through the door and cross the shadow line of their lives.

Jimmy turned his urgent eyes to Glenn. "We were all lined up and hooked up facing the back door. The light was red and nobody could move until it went green. Then we all piled out as fast as we could. I was near the door and the plane was thumping itself like crazy."

Jimmy watched the light and breathed as much and as slowly as he could, but his left leg was starting to cramp and shiver out of control, and his chest was trying to break through the cross straps of his harness. The leg wobbled in time to the engines that were straining at different speeds. The pilots leveled off and lifted the nose just enough for each man to press into the back of the other. It was embarrassing, but it would only last a few more seconds. Jimmy's ears picked up the symphony around him. From outside he heard a spiraling soprano wail of metal dancing over the bass of the men's lungs. The engines trumpeted their protests at the staccato of bullets hitting their cowlings. A thousand different tempos all playing at the same time.

Glenn sat as close to Jimmy as he dared. "I don't know what happened to the guy in front of me. I didn't hear anything, but the inside of the plane lit up like a light bulb."

Something tore through a wing tank and into the pilots' cabin, trailing burning gasoline. The flames flashed through the cabin door, hurtled over the ceiling, and spiraled down the walls. Jimmy's head jolted to see men walking in the flaming tunnel. "I think I got blown out the door."

Jimmy fell forward, face down, headed for the quilt of farm fields below him. The chute burst open above his head. One jerk later, it held him in the sky, and he was gazing up at stars. "I was just floating in the air."

Jimmy sat quietly in his harness. The cacophony of the plane was gone because his ear drums just couldn't take any more. He was completely alone with the night, and it was so peaceful. He nestled himself into the seat of his harness and raised his hands over his head to clutch the guide wires running up to the canopy billowing over his head. The silence wrapped itself around him. It was no different from a Ferris wheel ride at a county fair. His breathing was normal, and his heart was slow. He judged he was two thousand feet above the ground with about five minutes to just sit there. “The plane was above me and was on fire and clumps of fire were falling out of the plane. It was like somebody took a blowtorch and ripped open the belly of a bird, and she was still flying and dropping stuff out of her.”

He looked around and saw the mushroom field of opened chutes all around him and planes flying at different altitudes so their propellers didn’t shred their falling passengers. The sky was full of fires, but they were far away and everything was silent. Jimmy turned his head to look over his shoulder and up to see if anything was close. One of the little flares burst into flame, like someone struck a match, and looked as if it was going to fall on him. The flare got closer, and it was a man on fire, but he was still in his chute. He was swinging in the air like a pendulum, and burning from his chest to his head. His mouth gaped open, but Jimmy could not hear the scream. Spinning pieces of molten metal zoomed past them, and the hissing was either a violated air pocket or swishing angels’ feathers. Jimmy was too terrified to think. The fireball’s arms were windmilling and smashing at the flames on his chest, but the hands had caught fire. Jimmy started running. He was a thousand feet in the air and his legs were pumping like a track sprinter, desperate to get away from the burning horror headed straight for him.

The flames jumped over the man’s head and slithered up to the silk canopy above him. It only took a second for the whole chute to turn into a plummeting candle and plunge to the earth. Jimmy kept running through the air as his pursuer hit the ground.

Jimmy grabbed at the strands holding him under his chute and pulled his elbows to his chest to collapse the canopy. The Earth whooshed up and he landed still running. He tumbled twice, and a wind gust billowed his chute. The canopy filled and dragged him along the ground. Terrified that the wind would blow him back into the sky, Jimmy played a desperate tug-of-war with the harness straps. The wind screamed through the holes in the silk, and the parachute rose up before him. Jimmy pulled his knife from his boot and slashed at the chords tethering him to the white monster. He screamed and cursed to cut himself free from the thing that would drag him back into the burning garden of the sky. One by one, each cord burst under the edge of his knife until he jerked backwards and the thing blew away from him. He stood weeping in laughter as he saw his parachute run away like a beaten dog. He watched it scamper into the night and then looked down at his chest. He was fascinated by the glinting metal of the release disc holding together the straps of his harness. He slowly rubbed the chrome circle and remembered his training. The sergeants had banged it into his head that all he had to do to get out of the harness was pull the release ring and the harness would fall away. Jimmy collapsed into a bundle of laughter, whimpering to himself, "Why didn't I just pull the stupid ring?"

* * * * *

"I guess I was lucky. I got down and found some other guys," Jimmy sighed. Glenn knew all about such pain and fear, and Jimmy did not shrug off Glenn's hand on his shoulder. He whispered, "I never saw any of my guys again." Glenn's hand pressed Jimmy's shoulder once to emphasize, "The important thing is you made it this far." Together they accepted their terror in fire and ice. "The sky just ate them," Jimmy reflected.

They had not noticed the creeping cold of night, but Glenn pulled his hand away when the driver stood up to announce, "I'm going to find some shit." They all stood, shook their stiff legs and scattered to search for more firewood. Glenn and Jimmy contributed an armload of broken planks, and the commander stood poised with the jerrycan of gas and his Zippo. The driver returned with a stack of paintings on his head.

Glenn demanded, "Where the hell did you find these?" The driver threw them on the ground and explained, "They were in some big can over there." He pointed to an overflowing garbage dump.

Glenn and Jimmy wondered why they had spent the last few days saving paintings only to find some of them cast away. Maybe they were forgotten or maybe they were spares or just maybe they were so worthless that Stout and Posey had left them to make room in the trucks for the good stuff. The driver fed one frame into the brazier, but Glenn pulled it out with a commanding "Wait a second." The commander flipped shut his Zippo, wondering what the crunchies were up to. Glenn and Jimmy sat poised between the paintings and the flames, not knowing what to say. Glenn came up with the best solution: "Let's keep these as souvenirs." The young driver complained that he couldn't fit the painting into his pack, so Glenn told him to leave the frame and take the canvas. The driver pulled at a corner of canvas and started to tear it from the frame.

Jimmy shook his head in disgust and admonished, "For fuck's sake, have a little class, will you. You don't just rip this shit." The admonition flared the driver's temper, and he threw the picture at Jimmy. "If you're so fucken' smart, do it yourself." Jimmy raised his arm to deflect the painting and quietly replied, "Yeah. I am that fucken' smart," and pulled out his bayonet. The glint of the edge was as keen as the look in Jimmy's eyes. The crew commander ordered, "Quieten down. No trouble." Jimmy ignored him and brought the point of the bayonet to bear on the broad heads of the nails in the frame. The commander was relieved to see Jimmy's blade go for the painting and not the driver's throat. Jimmy held the frame between his crossed legs and gently slid the blade between the canvas and the wooden frame. They watched him tease out the nails. He was as careful with the knife as if he were skinning and butchering an animal. The wood made little protesting squeaks as the canvas was flayed. It dropped from the frame, leaving only the little holes from the staples and the gouges along the edge. Jimmy gently placed the picture on the ground, and the frame looked like a wet cardboard box after the present had been removed. He flung the frame into the fire's embers, and they flickered over the smiles of the circle. "There. That's how you do it," he said.

The young driver was happy he didn't have to fight for his souvenir. "Roll it up with the picture on the outside," advised Glenn. The others followed his lead and he instructed them, "not too tight, or the paint will come off." Jimmy and Glenn, who seemed to know what they were doing. Jimmy added, "If I was yous, I'd wrap it in a couple of socks."

The others offered Jimmy their trophies, and he removed each of their frames. Glenn saw the crew had chosen landscapes. Their paintings were just like the postcards they would buy at Old Orchard Beach or in New York to mail home, just to prove they had actually been to those places. The men wanted to bring something home as proof of their war stories, the ones they knew nobody would believe. The landscapes were all rolling hills or mountain scenes. There were very few people in their selections, as if they had enough reminders of humans. The place was the thing they wanted to bring back. The people could all stay where they were.

Glenn had picked up a really cheesy face. It was a portrait of a man with shoulder-length hair and nothing special. In the firelight, the eyes looked sad, but in the dark chiaroscuro of a quiet night, Glenn was struck by the light from the forehead shining so brightly. He had spent so much time rummaging through masterpieces with Stout that he could now tell instinctively what was valuable. The face didn't move him. The whole composition was what he and Stout had come to call Woolworth's Five and Dime. But the contrast inside and outside the painting made him choose this particular piece of junk for his memento. The picture was the proof, but the light and the dark were what he had lived through. The eyes on the painting's face didn't focus on anything. It was really a picture of the thousand-yard stare.

Jimmy had chosen a picture of a barnyard. He liked the place and could almost smell the cow shit oozing from the canvas. He laughed to himself that he was taking home some of the shit he had lived through. The canvases were secured to the frames by nails with big heads, like in upholstery, but his painting was transfixed with a neat row of staples running around the frame. He was surprised by how easy it was to remove them. The nails on the other frames needed a lot of pressure to pry them out, but these metal lines seemed to jump at the mere touch of his blade point. It felt like someone had stamped them into nail holes that were already there.

When he had the top of the canvas separated, he realized why it was so easy to remove the nails. The material flopped over his arm and he saw that there was a covering on the back of the canvas. Someone had removed the canvas and placed another piece of material behind it and than stapled both onto the original frame. He gently pulled apart the two canvases and looked at the top of another painting. There was something stuck to the back of the barnyard scene, and he laughed to himself, “Huh! I get a double-loaded doofer.” He rolled up the canvas, slid each end into an old sock, and made a woolen tube for his souvenir. He put it in his pack and didn’t even think about it for the next ten years.

Chapter 19

Manhattan Transfer

Glenn had that far away look that sometimes seeped through his squinting eyelids. The tale was now a trust and a test of Michael's own understanding. Michael knew this was leading to somewhere unknown, but the journey demanded he trust his grandfather. He turned to look at the huge golden figures on the columns of the library door and knew this was his time to lead. He put his hand on Glenn's shoulder and said, "Let's get going to Jersey."

Glenn smiled and followed Michael to the SUV. They were caught in a sudden gust and leaned against the little dust devil of snow the wind danced around them. Glenn was glad Michael's car was so cozy. He didn't mind walking in snow, but he also enjoyed the car's gadgets. These days, a car was a computer on wheels, so different from the bone-shaking jeeps of his youth and the stick-shift sedans of Michael's childhood. At least, they were out of the wind and on the road, and Michael seemed happy to drive.

They drove onto the Brooklyn Bridge, and the ramp tilted them up to see the clouds above the skyscrapers. "I guess you could say I stole it," Glenn said. Michael was glad the roads were clear, but kept well back from the few sleepy drivers plodding over the bridge. Glenn was happy to sit and enjoy the view, so Michael set a steady forty on the cruise control and glided through his thoughts.

There was just so much to take in from Anda's tale, so much was new and didn't connect with the quiet man he had known all his life. Anda had done something really important and kept it to himself. Michael thought if he had done all these things, he would have had to boast about them. Anda had kept his accomplishments and the photos in the hall closet, well hidden from admirers.

Glenn peered out his window, and his head traversed to the right to look over the Navy Yard. He saw only "To Let" signs and wondered where all the boats had gone. He remembered the Navy Yard when it was building ships and sending them off to fight. By now, they had all scattered, or sunk, or had been dismembered under a thousand cutting torches to become a million car doors, or whatever else they did with old battle wagons. The sixteen inch guns had been hammered into ploughshares, and The Yard had become an industrial and residential park. The women who had bent over old sewing machines had given way to executives for fashion magazines, and the sweatshops had been skinned of their moldy plaster to become media centers in quaint bare brick. He didn't turn to Michael when he said, "But I really just picked it up from a garbage pile that had been picked over by the Germans and the Americans."

Michael was confronting his own exploits, as they approached the hump of the bridge. What had he ever done to compare with his grandfather? The highlights of his life were in graduation and wedding photos and that was it. Anda had risked so much in the service, not just of his country, but for the world. Without Anda's accomplishments, those museums would be empty. But that was way back before Michael was born. He mourned the lack of opportunities of his own time. There had been no big wars. There were so few circumstances where a man could prove his own mettle. Michael's life had been so boringly normal that he felt a twinge of resentment for Anda's youth. If only he'd had the same chances as Anda. If only he too had seen the opportunity of a war in which he could shine and do heroic things. He finally confessed, "I envy you for what you did."

Glenn was surprised by Michael's reaction. "You wouldn't, if you had to do it." There was a new thought in his concerns for Michael. If Michael looked upon World War II as a good time, just a series of adventures, he wasn't telling the story in the right way and Michael didn't know the first thing about it, or him.

Glenn had seen this problem at veterans reunions. He had gone to four of them and soon lost interest. During the first two reunions, he had met veterans who shared their war stories and searched frayed maps to find out where they had fought. They would say things like, "I must have been in the foxhole next to you." But then the combat veterans melted away from the reunions to be replaced by men who hadn't been in the foxhole next to Glenn because they'd never been within ten miles of an angry bullet. These were the ones who bragged the most about their "war days." These were the loudmouths who wore their VFW medals on dry-cleaned blazers and showed up on Memorial Day to cry over the graves of people they had never met. When Glenn saw the combat veterans ignoring the reunions, he joined their silent boycott and kept his experiences to himself. The truth of his own life would remain silent, but the meaning of that life had to be offered to Michael.

Michael slipped the car over the bridge, thumbed the cruise control release, and poised his foot over the brake. The money they were going to collect was receding behind Anda's stories. Three point seven million dollars was the carrot, but the story was the stick. He knew he would have to grasp it and what it meant. Anda always had candy in one hand and homework in the other. This was going to be tough, but somewhere along the glide to Manhattan he decided to follow. The candy was just out of his reach. He asked, "Did you become a professor because of Stout?"

Glenn answered, "Now that Judy Collins. She's the one with the voice." Michael was shocked by the answer. He had expected a confession, but Glenn was going on about some singer he'd never heard of. "Anda, what are you talking about?"

Glenn was just as surprised by Michael's ignorance until it dawned on him, "Oh yeah. You would have just been born when those girls were singing." "Huh?" said Michael with mounting concern. Glenn enlightened him. "Those '60s girls. The radio was full of young women with straight hair and a guitar. They had three chords and one bad attitude. They were singing protests about Viet Nam, but I doubt they even knew where the place was." Michael wanted to jump over the digression and get back to the point, but Glenn had to be given free rein when he was thinking about something. “They all thought that just by saying war was a bad thing they could get people to stop fighting. Now that was just plain stupid.” Michael almost shouted back, “What does that have to do with Stout and the art?” Glenn was whipped out of his detour and explained.

“One day, Stout and Jimmy and I were unloading a truck in Wiesbaden, and I was asking Stout about a painting. He explained that the allegories of Venus and Mars were really talking about the human condition because people were always going between Venus, Goddess of Love, and Mars, the God of War. Well Jimmy perked up and winked at me. Stout went on to tell us that the two planets on either side of Earth were named Venus and Mars to show that we were caught between war and peace. Jimmy had seen enough of Mars to really want his own Venus and said, ‘OK. That’s just a high-faluting way of saying everybody likes all the fuckin and the fightin.’”

Michael bellowed at Jimmy’s aphorism and howled laughter at the windshield. Glenn was glad that Michael could see the joke and told him. “That’s just what Stout did, too. He dropped the box, shoved his elbows over the tailgate of that truck, and laughed for five minutes.” Glenn and Michael chuckled together, and in the mirth of the joke, the meaning emerged. Michael saw Glenn was getting at the difference between the love and the war. The contrast was what he was supposed to see, something about Glenn’s own humanity, and he surrendered to whatever significance Glenn was coaxing out of his stories.

Glenn swung around to the answers. It was time. “Yeah. I studied art because Stout gave it to me. You could say the rest of my life came out of our job and the back of that truck. So did Jimmy’s.” Michael understood that Glenn’s message had something to do with understanding what you do is connected to who you are, and relaxed into the uncertainty. If he knew anything about Anda, it was that he would always bring Michael to clarity. The murky meaning would eventually come out.

Glenn cast a sideway's glance at Michael and decided to continue. "That night in Merkers was when I got the painting. You gotta remember what that soldier said to us in the mine. 'The salt in the walls will rot leather in a day.' Well, the water in the ice will rot a canvas in a night."

"So that's how you got the *Head of Christ*. Simple as that." Michael added.

"Yup. Simple as that. And that's how you got millions of dollars yesterday. Simple as that."

"And how you got *The Mystic Lamb*," said Michael.

"No. Jimmy and Posey got Bunjes. He led us to the Lamb."

Glenn fell silent, wondering if he should tell Michael about the castle. The citadels of Manhattan loomed up before him, glistening streaks of silver and white like someone had scraped a palette knife through a cloud. Michael would have to know all, if he were to understand anything, so he whispered, "The last time we were all together was the best."

Chapter 20

Castle in the Air

Neuschwanstein, Bavaria
June 6, 1945

Glenn focussed on the distant dot winding up the road. The dot was a couple of miles below him in the the valley, but Glenn knew it was Jimmy before he could see him. Only Jimmy could make that speed winding through the curves of the hill and still get up to the castle gates without killing himself. He turned to look at the entrance and the walls and wondered again about the man who had created this gigantic wedding cake in stone.

Stout had told him that Schloss Neuschwanstein was the brainchild of a Bavarian count called "Mad Ludwig. Ludwig was his first name." "Why was he so pissed off?" asked Glenn. Stout's eyebrows arched into a question mark before flapping into a laugh, "Mad didn't mean angry. In those days, mad meant crazy."

"So why was Crazy Luddy so nuts?" Glenn prodded. "Did he eat children or something?"

"Worse," continued Stout, "He wrote poetry."

"Wow, what a time. Painting could get you hung and poetry could get you thrown into the looney bin," Glenn mused.

Stout led him through the castle's corridors and the twists of Mad Ludwig's mind. Glenn heard of Ludwig's relatives, who wanted him committed, so they could grab his property. They stood at the main entrance to the courtyard, and Stout said, "Back then, if you were a count or a king, they let you build your own nut house, so Ludwig created this place, Schloss Neuschwanstein." Stout knew Glenn would be puzzling out the words, "Schloss means castle. Neu is new, and schwan is swan, and stein is stone, Castle Neuschwanstein."

Glenn packed away the facts as he did any time Stout "told him stuff," and his eyes launched over the five stories of intricate stonework that made up the fairy-tale castle. "Boy, the Krauts really know how to pile up the words."

"Yup. That's their way," Stout agreed. "They pile up the words."

Glenn concentrated on the massive walls in front of them, "Kinda like the same way they built this place."

Stout looked over at the intricately carved blocks of granite and marble and had to admit he had never made the connection between architecture and grammar as Glenn just had. He had come to admire how Glenn took basic facts and made surprising connections. Everything was new to him, and Stout was proud to share his own knowledge and see Glenn blossom. The shared joy of learning was yet another proof for Stout there was life amidst all the ruin.

They had been at the castle for a week, but Glenn resented having to sleep because there was so much going on. He was like a kid who dreaded Mommy's order, "Time for bed." The work itself was routine and just plain boring. Lift the box, take it to another room, drop the box on your foot, curse the box, shove the box on a trolley, and then get another box, to be followed by still more boxes.

A company of replacements had been assigned to the castle. American soldiers were the laborers because the roads were full of homeless, stateless, and stolen people. There were not enough DPs in Bavaria to move all the stuff. The new boys were full of disappointment at missing the war. Each day was an endless procession of baggage wagons, trolleys of paintings, and stacks of splintered crates. Trained for combat, the young soldiers had to be satisfied with the exhausting labor of longshoremen. When they expected to be heroes, dead or alive, the army made them stevedores. The castle was like any other bustling warehouse. The only real difference was they were all manhandling the treasures of

Europe's museums. After a few days, all that civilization became just a backache.

The real treat was when Stout and the other officers opened a box. Stout always included Glenn in these little ceremonies, and Glenn immediately dumped his work and jumped into the discoveries. Crates were only opened when there was uncertainty about their contents. There could be anything inside an unlabeled box. They had found an Egyptian sculpture of a woman's head in a mess of wood and nails claiming to be "Meat Grade 6." Stout didn't trust the glue and paper labels, which never made it through the second trip or the first humid weather, so Glenn found a soldering iron and just burned the information into the wood. This was so effective that Stout called Glenn over for a "branding" every time they found something important. Glenn would kneel beside a crate, and a circle of officers would bend over with their hands on their knees and breathe in the acrid aroma of his flaming calligraphy. Glenn carved the names of the artists, the titles of the works, and the destination of the shipment onto the boxes. They really looked like they were cowboys branding cattle in the Old West, and the image stuck for the whole crew. When they had prepared enough boxes for a convoy, Stout would order them all to "saddle up" and the boys would fill twenty trucks waiting for the signal to "move 'em out." The convoys were organized exactly the same way as an old-time cattle drive, surrounded by guards and followed by a chuck wagon with their food. Instead of taking the cattle to the slaughterhouses, they were returning the art to those who owned it.

Stout admired the way the men organized themselves and their work. Where there had only been the pouting stillness of tedious repetition, they had created a lively hum. When he asked Glenn about the changed attitude, Glenn simply said, "The boxes." "I don't follow," Stout admitted. Glenn explained what had happened, "When we open a box and brand it, there's always a surprise. It's like Christmas or Cracker Jack." Stout saw the art was a new adventure for these men, so the castle's rooms bustled with contented work. Glenn found Stout's talk of "rooms" funny because the castle was really a series of cavernous chambers. Only fourteen of the rooms were finished, but every space was crammed with art.

When George and Glenn had first arrived, they thought the sheer volume of stuff would keep them hovering in mid-air for years, but HQ had flooded the place with experts, officers, packers, drivers, and secretaries. After Merkers, with Stout's trick of combining the art with the gold, the generals gave Stout everything he needed, and more. Jeeps and trucks appeared out of nowhere, followed by squadrons of tanks to guard the treasures.

Now that they finally had transportation, there was nowhere to send the convoys, so four collection points had been set up. It took a while to find suitable buildings that hadn't been wrecked, but Wiesbaden, Munich, Offenbach, and Frankfurt had been designated as the "Collecting Points." That way, the stuff could be processed and kept away from sticky fingers. In a week, they had cleared Castle Neuschwannstein, and and the treasures were dispersed to the four points around Germany.

It struck Glenn as odd that once they found a hidden trove, it had to be dispersed and then collected all over again. Stout explained this was really the way we all think. We get buried under information, have to dig ourselves out of it, and then pile up the bits of information in better order. This made perfect sense to Glenn, and there was the added benefit he had a brain and could use it. Along with the dictionary and the cigarettes, thinking became Glenn's third addiction and the greatest souvenir he would take home from the war. And so he stood on the pile of marble at the entrance to the castle sorting through all the stuff that was whirling through his mind and waiting for Jimmy to get his sorry ass up the road.

Jimmy was used to the "Hurry Up and Wait" of military wild goose chases, but this one at least got him out in the fresh air. He had been reassigned to Collecting Point Wiesbaden and really wanted to get away from people and the stuff. When he'd gotten the call from Glenn saying he had to get to some castle in the middle of nowhere, he grabbed the chance for the solitary drive. Glenn said both Stout and Posey had requested his assistance. A request was as good as an order, and he needed an order to get away.

The journey to some distant meeting with officers was the perfect excuse for some time alone. He had convinced his boss the jeep needed a long ride just to get everything working properly because it had been sitting idle for so long. Jimmy was an expert at making up official forms because he knew the Army wouldn't let you have a crap without a piece of paper in triplicate, so he created his own Transportation Requisition Form A-13-2670 for his boss, Captain Farmer, to sign. He offered Farmer the paper and launched a barrage of fictitious problems concerning the jeep which "had been standing in the compound for three weeks and needs a drive because the oil is all settling in the pan and that will clog up the motor and the long ride will get the ignition system working and the wheels needed greasing just because it's been sitting there so long and I think the carburetors are all clogged up and... and... and," and Farmer went for his pen to sign Transportation Requisition Form A -13-2670 as fast as he could just to get rid of Jimmy and get on with his work.

Jimmy walked Captain Farmer down the hall to the main door bombarding him with thanks, and Farmer blurted, "Good idea, Sergeant," while thinking, "Some people just can't take 'yes' for an answer." Jimmy assured him he would check the magneto and walked to the perfectly working jeep, thankful Farmer had signed him out of the compound for a day and relieved because "I was running out of bullshit."

The farther he drove from Wiesbaden, the higher the road rose, and the purer the air became. As he ascended the foothills of Bavaria, he sucked in the mountain air and watched the snowcaps whirl around him at each bend in the climbing road. His requisition was as good as a twenty-four hour pass, and he was going to enjoy every second of it. He did not plan on getting drunk, finding a woman, or winning his fortune in some barrack room casino. He just wanted to be alone. He would tell Glenn, Stout, and Posey whatever they wanted to hear as quickly as possible, scrounge a meal and some gas, and get back to Wiesbaden just too late to do any more work.

The jeep glided to a stop, and Jimmy asked Glenn, "So. Why all the hurry?"

"We found it."

"Found what?" Jimmy blurted.

"That huge altarpiece, the one we've been after for months."

Jimmy worked himself into a pleasant grouse and accused Glenn, "You made me drive fifty miles just to look at stuff? I got more stuff back at the shack than I can shake a rifle at and now I gotta come all this way to see some more stuff. This is a real busman's holiday."

Glenn waited patiently for Jimmy to finish his gripe and quietly said, "This ain't just any just stuff. It's *The Mystic Lamb*."

That was all Jimmy needed to shut up. He pretended not to be really interested as he remembered the night they nabbed Bunjes.

"You mean that thing we thought would have to be hidden in a airplane hanger cause it was so big?"

"Yup. Van Eyck's masterpiece," said Glenn.

"Oh. Well that's different."

Glenn turned to lead Jimmy through the main gates and bubbled on about the altarpiece. "It's amazing. It's ... it's ... huge. I can't tell you about it. You gotta see for yourself."

Jimmy followed Glenn into the huge castle courtyard, and the walls rose around him. The walls were so high he imagined they were mountains closing in on him. It was not a nice feeling. He couldn't see anything beyond the walls, and the hairs on his neck twitched because doors and walls always warned him of booby traps. Glenn could almost read his thoughts and said, "We got here last week and the engineers didn't find a single present."

"What? The Squareheads hadn't mined this place?"

"They didn't have time. Some airborne outfit got here real quick and grabbed the whole lot."

At this news, Jimmy's shoulders collapsed into his casual slouch and his steps fell into rhythm with Glenn's hurrying feet. They walked up stairs into a large room that was either a chapel or a throne room. Glenn thought it was a combination of both, where someone worshipped a long-gone king. Stout and Posey were sitting on chairs going over some paperwork, and everything was calm and peaceful. It was like the end of the day in a busy store when everybody is waiting for the bell to ring. They looked up to see Jimmy and Glenn walking towards them. They rose and beamed welcoming smiles.

Posey was very glad to see Jimmy and asked, "How's Wiesbaden been treating you?" "Not bad," Jimmy said, "Captain Farmer is a bit of a ball buster, but he's Okay." Posey gossiped about Walter Farmer and bragged about how Farmer's talents were indispensable because he'd been the adjutant of an engineering battalion and was the perfect man for the job of organizing the whole operation at Wiesbaden, although he was really an interior designer for a big department store in Ohio, until Jimmy just wanted to say "All right already. I get it. Farmer's a good guy, so enough with all the bullshit about what a great guy he is," but just nodded his head "yes" to each of Posey's effusive praises. Jimmy thought it odd that Stout would shake his hand. Something was in the wind. Stout shared a smile with Posey before turning to Jimmy to say, "We thought you'd like to see this."

Jimmy had seen thousands of bits of stuff, but this was the first time Stout had both shaken his hand and wanted to talk with him about an individual piece. Posey was wearing that grin which said, "I know something you don't," but the eyes said, "and I'm going to share it with you." Jimmy knew what Posey wanted to share, but he wasn't going to spoil the surprise. He had the odd sensation of waiting for his mother to light the candles on a birthday cake. Stout confessed, "You've worked so hard chasing this thing. You should be one of the first to see it." Stout walked to the end of the room, and Posey fell back just far enough to whisper to Jimmy, "It wouldn't be here without your work." Jimmy relaxed into Posey's praise.

Glenn fell in beside Jimmy, and Posey walked them slowly to the front of the room. Posey grinned to see Jimmy confused and remembered the little man combing through mechanized garbage in Dijon. He fully realized that if it were not for Jimmy's scrounging, Posey would still be "scratching his ass in the snow," as Jimmy had so eloquently put it. Posey would be going home soon. He had been put in charge of guarding the treasures at Altausee, but the mission was almost complete. Soon he would be handing over his responsibilities to Farmer in Wiesbaden. Posey had enough Demobilization Points to be discharged sooner than he had expected. He would now return to normal life, whatever that was, and re-enlist in his family to be a father and husband.

For a year he had followed the trail and now the mission was complete, or at least his part of it was. There would be no battle honors for his work. "Normandy," "Nancy," "Trier," "Merkers," and "Altausee" would not be blazoned on any flags. There would be neither unit citations nor awards for what they had accomplished. Nobody would ever put up a statue to these Monuments Men, and Posey didn't want such recognition. That the art had survived at all was a fitting monument. As he walked with Jimmy to the front of the room, Posey swelled with the honor of recognizing that the four of them had done their part in pulling civilization from the flames of barbarism.

Stout and Glenn had carefully raised the altarpiece, so it stood tall on a platform stage six feet off the floor. They had made a cradle of beams supporting the huge frame so that it rose above them as it would from an altar. The nearer they approached the front of the hall, the more Jimmy could appreciate its size. He had to crane his neck to hold the altarpiece within the compass of his vision. When he had swept the bullets from Bunjes' table, he had kept the photograph. For months, he had savored the photo and lingered over the angels singing and playing their strange instruments. But the real thing was so much bigger than he had been able to imagine.

Stout was above them fussing with the edges of the frame, preparing to open the triptych's giant doors. Its discovery was a tale for Hollywood, complete with spies, midnight intrigue, and hair-raising risk, but its recovery was a source of quiet pride for Posey, Stout, and Glenn.

Glenn had been with him, when the Germans led them to the treasure trove in yet another mountain. The local Nazis were determined that this masterpiece would not fall into the hands of the enemy and had placed five-hundred pound bombs throughout the tunnels, enough to seal the mountain forever. The miners wanted to save their livelihood and removed the bombs in the dead of night. The German army also had dynamited the mouth of the mine so their Nazi masters could not get at the treasure either. The Americans blasted their way in, and then Stout and Glenn had risked all to get it out. For Stout, this was his medal. If ever his manhood or his courage were put in doubt, he could thumb through any library book of "The Great Masterpieces" and say, "Because of me, this still exists." When they had placed themselves at the tip of the spear, Glenn and Stout had worried that they would not be able to finish the job. The very existence of *The Mystic Lamb* was the living proof of their courage.

Jimmy's breathing slowed, and his nostrils quivered when he stared up at it. It was so huge its very size beckoned to him and whispered, "Come to me and drink." Glenn was bubbling over with enthusiasm and information, the type of thing that left Jimmy cold. He didn't want facts about the stuff but he was going to get them anyway because Glenn just couldn't keep it in.

The altarpiece was twenty feet high, held together by strong wood frames. It was forty feet wide and each frame held pictures of strange people and magical places. Jimmy looked at two levels of frames and felt like he was looking into an apartment building with the outside wall removed. He thought of the house in France where they'd killed the last sniper and how the gunner had just eaten the outside wall with his Ma Deuce. That was how this picture looked. On the bottom story, there was an old man and what looked like his wife, and they were praying. Between them were two other pictures that looked like statues. Maybe they were praying to the statues. On the second story there was an angel on the left and a woman on the right, and you didn't need to be a genius to figure out the girl was Mary and the angel had some good news for her. The angel was holding flowers, and Jimmy joked to himself, "He ain't selling flowers door-to-door and he's definitely not taking her out to the Prom." He heard Glenn lecturing into his ear.

"Jan van Eyck finished painting it in 1432. Must have taken years to do this."

"So it's over five hundred years old," Jimmy said.

"And it's just like it was way back then," beamed Glenn.

Jimmy examined every panel. On the second level, right in the middle, he could look through a window and out into a busy street at the back of the house where the angel was talking to Mary. He looked up and saw three semi-circular rooms with people looking down. One of the people at the top was wearing a turban, so he must have been some old guy from the Bible, or something. There was another old guy trying to read a book, and he was looking down into the room with the angel. Jimmy thought he was saying "What's with all the racket down there? Can't you see I'm trying to read?"

Jimmy had to step back to take in the whole painting. Now he could see things he'd missed in the photo. It really did look like an open apartment building back in Jersey, complete with the gossipy neighbors in the attic, listening to all the kafuffle in the apartments below them. Glenn kept hosing information into Jimmy's ears and was being a "kinda pain in the ass." "This is really van Eyck's masterpiece. But wait 'til you get a load of the rest of it," Glenn enthused. "There's more?" Jimmy asked. He knew what was coming but looked surprised because Glenn was having so much fun telling him all about the stuff he'd already seen in the photograph.

Jimmy watched Stout march back and forth before the painting. Stout grabbed hold of a handle in the center, which Jimmy hadn't noticed, and walked the handle to the left of the stage. As he walked, half of the altarpiece opened, and Jimmy saw the painting open, like shutters after a rain storm. Stout returned to the middle of the painting and pulled the door on the right. The whole *Adoration of the Mystic Lamb* stood before them, spreading its full glory. Jimmy saw that the shutters were really a cover for what was inside. Only when the cabinet was fully opened did the painting reveal its greatest mystery to him.

With the shutters closed, the painting was a scene in a house in a busy street, but with the shutters opened, that world disappeared to be replaced by something not of this world. When Stout opened the picture, the three rooms of the cover became two levels. The three semi-circular attics at the top became a square room in heaven where God or Jesus or somebody important was sitting on a throne in the center. He was taller than the two figures on either side of him. To the left was a woman, and any fool could see she was Mary. Jimmy noticed she was the same girl who was in the room when the shutters were closed, but now she wore a crown and was wrapped in a deep blue dress covered in jewels. Jimmy thought, "The girl done good for herself. She became the Queen of Heaven." Jimmy looked to the right to see some hairy guy who looked like he needed a bath and a shave. Jimmy's eyes lovingly scanned the whole length of the upper level, and on the extreme left, he could make out Adam looking really pissed off. At the other end of the line was Eve. She was holding something that looked like a shriveled up lemon, so Jimmy figured that they had been having a really bad day in the Garden of Eden. Both were covering their privates with a hand over a fig leaf, but Eve looked pregnant.

Between Adam and Eve and Mary and the Hairy Guy were two panels with some women singing, and on the right there was a band. A woman was sitting at an organ, and she looked like she was about to fall asleep because she had been playing so long. Behind the organ other women were playing harps and bull fiddles and they all looked like it had been quite a party and they would be glad to get home.

Glenn was explaining to Jimmy that "the top panels represent heaven, but the bottom one is this earth. That's why they have an altar in the center with a lamb standing on top." Jimmy wished Glenn would just shut up. Stout sensed that now was the time for silence, raised one palm, and Jimmy got his wish.

Glenn remembered Stout explaining "the meticulously detailed *Adoration of the Mystic Lamb* was the work of the van Eyck brothers," and "it is the largest and most complex altarpiece produced in the Netherlands in the 15th century." The details fascinated Glenn and he had spent hours listing the intricacies of the painting. He had lovingly recorded the stars in Mary's crown, identified the household utensils in the room of the Annunciation, and even numbered the singers in the chorus of angels. He could have spent many happy years discovering the painting's secrets. But he often had to leave such wonderful labors behind to shift crates onto the convoys. There just didn't seem to be enough time to do everything he wanted to do.

Stout stepped to the right of the painting and stood poised beside a table lamp, which he had positioned so its light could flood the wooden panels. Stout had explained to Glenn that the painting was commissioned for a specific place, a chapel in a church in Belgium. The images became completely free only when the painting was bathed in sunlight streaming in from a window. To prove the point, Stout had aimed a light at the painting to recreate the light source of the original setting. Glenn was thunderstruck. Glenn wanted Jimmy to see the same effect, so he had pestered Stout to do the "thing with the lamp." Stout obliged and had set up their private viewing, so they could all appreciate *The Adoration of the Lamb* under the illumination of an office table lamp. Stout turned on the lamp and something strange happened.

Glenn looked deeper into the painting, but the figures jumped out of the background straight at Jimmy.

Glenn was excited to see it again. His eyes panned from right to left and top to bottom, taking in every detail. His mind triggered memory and was drinking in the azure skies of each panel and savoring the clothing and the textures and the flesh. Glenn's eyes would bounce from the jewels in Mary's robes, catch the dull glint of the metal in the organ pipes, and squint at the gold glistening on the horses' saddles and reins. He looked into the fantastic cityscape at the back of the bottom panel and gazed over the tall forests. Each feather in the angels' wings was as distinct as the blades of grass they walked on. He could have sat before this wonder for half a life and still not exhausted his pleasure. Glenn was starting to appreciate the technical magnificence of van Eyck's brush. This wasn't just a painting. It wasn't something to hang on a wall and forget. This was something which would call you back time and time again. There was a richness in this beyond anything he had ever experienced and he could barely admit to himself this was one of the signal experiences of his life. He would understand these things, even if it took a lifetime because van Eyck's monumental achievement was worthy of the demands it was making. The painting called to him, and the siren waves wafted through his mind, telling him this was just the beginning. There were more wonders, and he would make himself live within their majesty. The magic had produced this spell, and he felt himself walking into van Eyck's mystical world.

Stout could sense what was happening to Glenn and Jimmy. He quietly walked away from the painting and crept away to find a place where he would not intrude upon their wonder. Posey followed Stout's lead, and together they stood behind Jimmy and Glenn, as if posing for a portrait. But they were not having their picture taken, Stout thought, the picture was taking them.

The silence screamed wonder, and in that stillness Stout could listen to the small voice of his own life whispering to him of value. All the learning and studying and all the pain they had suffered to get to this moment and this place was all summed up in the sweat trickling down Jimmy's neck and the rapture in Glenn's eyes. Here he was, an educated man, old enough to be their father, and they were having the experience of a lifetime because he had served these things all his life. He was an art conservator, a repairer of pieces of old wood and paint, a craftsman dedicated to the preservation of these things. His whole working life had told him that each scrap on a canvas was not the painting. He was merely rearranging the dirt of centuries so the artist's vision could shine again in the dark places of the soul. He knew the things were not the real magic. The wonder was in the looking and the being with the thing. The frame, the canvas, the multitude of pigments, all the little bits added up to nothing, if the art did not shine through. The material was just a vehicle, mere things that talked over centuries. They were dead in themselves, but they had something living about them which people could experience. Now these two young men, not much more than boys, were having their experience. They would sit and bask in that wonder and he would not disturb them. If they sat there all day, he would stand vigil behind them and guard against any unwanted distraction.

Jimmy could feel Stout and Posey behind him and was grateful for having his back covered. As he had looked out for Posey, now Posey was looking out for him. When Stout had opened the panels, he had opened a complete world for Jimmy, but when he turned on the light, that world came parading out of the picture towards him. He thought he was hallucinating, but Posey standing behind him said this was real. The figures danced before Jimmy's eyes. They were alive. They were moving. The Jesus on the throne loomed largest, but it was Mary and the Hairy Guy who moved towards him just a little in front of Jesus. There they were, just hanging in mid-air, gently hovering a foot or two or three before his face. He had never experienced anything like this. Even the battle terror of falling through the sky did not bring forth the emotions this painting was pulling out of him. It wasn't bad; it was just more than anything else he had ever felt. "Am I going out of my mind?"

he asked himself. He knew he wasn't because he could feel Glenn's breath beside him. Out of the corner of his eye, he could see the light in Glenn's face and then he felt the heat on his nose.

The room was clammy cold like a subway station after the train has left, but he felt so hot. Sweat was welling around his collar, but the tops of his ears were like ice. Jesus and his mother and her buddy grew dim as the lower picture wobbled closer to him. There were people all gathering around an altar, and on top of the altar was a lamb. Of course, that was supposed to be Jesus too "'cause he was the Lamb of God," but Jimmy was more captivated by the little sheep itself than by what it represented.

The lamb was standing sideways, but his head and face looked straight at Jimmy. The lamb's eyes were small dots peering directly into Jimmy's face. He could not tear his gaze from those wooly eyes until the lamb itself blinked and looked down at his chest. Jimmy saw that there was blood flowing from the lamb's chest and splashing into the top of the altar. It was a serious wound, but the lamb just didn't seem to care. He still looked at Jimmy. Jimmy started humming "Mary Had a Little Lamb," and then the lamb smiled at the joke. "Sure, Mary was my mother, and she did have a little lamb, and that's me." Jimmy smiled back at the lamb to share the joke, but instead of laughter came the feeling of quiet peace which was such a stranger to him. The lamb blinked again and baaed "I have a new friend for you." "Who?" asked Jimmy and the lamb answered, "Me."

Around the altar the angels held up a cross, a crown of thorns, a hammer, nails, and whips, and the lamb looked straight through the things which hurt him to Jimmy and said, "They won't hurt you 'cause they're all tired out from hurting me." That was why the wound was so weird. The lamb didn't mind about all the pain and the hurt. They could only crucify him once and it was finished.

The lamb nodded to Jimmy and his eyes followed the stream of blood flowing into the cup, then to a fountain between him and the altar. The lamb forced Jimmy to look at the fountain. It became the most vital thing in the whole painting. Jimmy heard the lamb say,

“Nice fountain, ain’t it?” “You bet it is,” responded Jimmy. The lamb was keen to keep up the conversation. “You know what it really is, don’t you?” “I ain’t got a clue, Lamb.” The water in the fountain was so clear you could see right through it. At the bottom of the fountain, Jimmy saw where people had thrown in three coins for good luck. The water swirled around the basin in the fountain and flowed out of a pipe at the bottom. The lamb told him, “It’s a laundry. It makes all things clean.” Jimmy nodded his head and admitted to his wooly new friend, “Oh yeah. That’s what it is. Sorry to come to your house all crusty, but I been having a hard time getting soap and a new shirt.” “I know,” said the Lamb. Jimmy looked straight into the Lamb’s eyes and said, “I got a feeling you know a lot more than you’re letting on.”

The water from the fountain was flowing through the pipe and seeping into the earth, but the fountain was not on the earth - it was right in front of Jimmy’s face. He didn’t care about the saints and hermits in the picture. They were so intent on adoring the lamb that they were ignoring the fountain right in front of him.

He was glad the lamb wasn’t paying much attention to the cross and the whips. Since teaming up with Posey, he’d seen enough of crucifixion to last a lifetime and beyond. It was almost as if he’d rifled through a couple of thousand years of people really gloating about Jesus’ death. After you get strung up in every church and every museum and even on postcards, it doesn’t mean much. He’d seen enough of the real suffering, enough of body parts and red messes in the street not to be impressed with one guy hanging on a cross. It was just too much to take in. So, the lamb spoke directly to him.

“You know, the night before was the worst. Thinking about what would happen before it happened. It wasn’t all that bad. It only hurts for a little while.”

Jimmy saw the dawn of that first day in Normandy and the paratrooper hanging from the telephone pole. He’d been strangled by his own chute, the feet dangling six feet off the ground with something dripping from his boots. “It wasn’t all that bad.” But it was that bad. He remembered the baby carriage with one leg sticking out of it. It was the day before he met Posey. He was walking down a road west of Dijon. There must have been two thousand guys marching ahead of him, and every one of them had seen that carriage just sitting there by the side of the road. The little leg was chubby and about eight inches long. Nobody could take his eyes off of it, but nobody could break ranks to put it in the ditch. You couldn't help but look, and you couldn't do a damn thing.

"It only hurts for a little while."

It didn't matter if you were a young man hanging from wires or and infant slumped by the side of the road. "It only hurts for a little while." Jimmy hoped it had been a very little while for both of them.

The lamb was now looking over the heads of the angels and the crowds of people, looking directly at Jimmy and blinking at the fountain. Somehow the lamb wanted to keep Jimmy concentrated on the fountain. The pipe was just in front of Jimmy's face, and the sweat dripping off his nose was the drops of water sprinkling out of the fountain onto him. Glenn coughed, and everything retreated back into the painting, not because he'd scared the lamb, but because it was quitting time. The painting had done its job.

Stout turned off the light, and they all stood up and walked slowly back through the room. Nobody said a word as they walked across the courtyard to the entrance. They gathered for a moment around the jeep as Jimmy settled himself into the driver's seat. His foot pressed the starter switch, and he let the engine idle to warm up for the journey back to Wiesbaden.

He looked at Glenn and Posey and drank in their smiles. Stout leaned his elbow on the windshield and looked deep into Jimmy's eyes. All Jimmy could say to the three faces was, "That was really great. Thanks Guys." Glenn's farewell was, "I'll see you in a couple of weeks." Posey grabbed his hand, "I'll see you Stateside." Stout rose up, slapped the windscreen twice, and said, "Safe trip home." Jimmy slapped the gear stick and let the engine pull him over the rise and tilt him into the road.

Glenn watched from the top of the rise framed by the castle entrance as the jeep meandered down the road. Jimmy was going no more than ten or fifteen miles and hour and it was unlike him not to be tearing up the road. He perceived the driver was distracted, lost in thoughts that were higher than the mountains enveloping them. Glenn looked at the clouds hanging in the distance and wondered if there would be the usual afternoon shower.

Jimmy was recalling the lamb. The words and pictures were ringing in his head, but the rest of him was calm. Jimmy waltzed the jeep down the mountain with loose fingers on the steering wheel. His shoulders swung from side-to-side as he wove the jeep through the curves. He let his mind do the flying.

He pulled over and drove a few yards along a dirt track. He stopped at a stream, which could have been inches or feet deep, and plunged his head into its cooling current. The water was ice from the spring runoff. He welcomed the coldness and doused his head and shoulders into the water.

He would live. Three simple words were the lamb's little present for a future. He had survived the war and had no idea what the future would bring, but he didn't care. He would live. He would not end up scattered over the hillsides. His body would be whole and healthy until the end and that was not going to be today or even tomorrow. He didn't know how many days were ahead but felt the days would gather themselves into years. He would just have to stop counting.

The lamb had spoken, and the miracle was that Jimmy had listened. "All those hundreds of years that lamb was just hanging there talking to all those people." He felt good that so many others had had that conversation. There was no way of knowing who those people were who had talked with the lamb, but it didn't matter. Today, with Glenn and Posey and Stout, the Lamb had spoken again. What mattered was that he would live.

"It wasn't all that bad," he said to himself, "it only hurts for a little while." The conviction it would only hurt for a little while was what made it not all that bad. The thinking about it was worse than doing it. Death had been walking beside him for so long it was now time to speed up and just leave him behind. Death could push that baby carriage, but he could no longer push Jimmy. There was a strange loneliness in giving up such a traveling companion, but it wouldn't be all that bad. There would be others to share the road and, who knows, maybe that lamb would walk a little further with him. There were no promises; Jimmy was beyond believing in promises. Sometimes, you only knew they were promises, after they were broken. Sometimes you didn't know what you wanted, until you were disappointed. But now the promises had become a firm faith that "It wasn't all that bad. It only hurts for a little while."

He started the jeep and swung back into the road. The mountain air was fresh. He recalled his morning wish for a little fresh air. He wanted more. He shoved the windshield forward so more air could be sucked past him and into his lungs. His foot jammed on the gas pedal, and he chuckled to have put some distance between himself and his old fear of dying. Since he first arrived in Europe at the end of a parachute, he had known he was brave. When he had been most terrified, he had still done the work. But the future had held the greatest terror; the fear of what might happen had trapped all the hope of living.

The faster he went, the more he could breathe, and the greater was his courage. You had to be brave to survive a war, but surviving the peace also took courage. This was new and it was the gift of the lamb. Jimmy smiled to think of his new comfy friend and thought of a fat woman in Jersey. Somewhere in the winds along that mountain road, he stood silent upon a peak in Bavaria and could smell soap.

Chapter 21

The Golden Journey to Samarkand

Michael bumped the car off the bridge past East River Drive and told Glenn, "It's hard for me to get my head around all this." Glenn nodded and said, "I know. It took me years." Michael was glad the traffic had picked up. Concentrating on the road was a relief, for Anda was bombarding him with new knowledge. Glenn confessed, "When I was actually doing it, I didn't have a clue," and Michael glimpsed some order in his own confusion. They stopped at a red light and watched a file of yellow taxis pass before them. "How long were you a Monuments Man?" Michael asked.

"About a year, but not always on the same assignment," Glenn recalled.

"So you worked with other teams?"

"No. I only worked with Stout. Jimmy was assigned to Posey."

"So how long was that?" Michael prodded.

"I had eight months with Stout."

"What happened to him?"

"He got sent back to the States."

"Along with Posey?"

"Posey was put in charge of the guard squads at Altausee, the mine where they found the Lamb. You know, all the stuff was in another mine very close to Hitlers's home in the mountains. He was going build his own museum after he won the war."

"The guy had big plans," Michael jibed.

They laughed together with pride of Anda's part in thwarting those plans, and Michael had a break from his confusion. They waited for the light to turn green. Glenn's eyes jumped from taxi to taxi slowly filing past the windshield and said to Michael, "They look like camels all tied nose to tail." Michael's head nodded in agreement as his eyes moved from side-to-side, observing each little metal camel. He loved the way Anda could point out things he would otherwise miss. He was content for the tale to lead him wherever it was going and was in no hurry to get to Jersey.

The light turned green, and Glenn told Michael, "Those guys weren't in it for the money." "Of course not," Michael said, "I can't imagine how much money all that stuff was worth." Glenn smiled in the comfort that, like Jimmy, Michael was getting it and said, "Nobody could put a price tag on even one of the crates."

"So, it wasn't about the money?" Michael asked.

"Not for us," Glenn said. "Stout had a real sense the paintings would live longer than we would. I didn't know about that. I was just a kid. Sixty years later, I can understand it better."

"So why did you guys do it?" Michael asked.

"Because the art was worth more than its price." Glenn saw his answer had bubbled up the questions in Michael, and waited. "What we did made us better than we were. That was the real triumph of the Monuments Men. That's why we did it."

The taxis disappeared along Riverside Drive and their exhausts puffed frozen clouds at a florist's delivery truck. Michael wondered if the truck was doing its rounds of funeral parlors and slipped his foot slipped off the brake. "Are the others gone now?" he asked quietly. Glenn nodded and whispered, "I'm the last of the bunch."

Michael did not want to acknowledge Anda's end, but the reality was, at eighty-two years, the stark fact of Glenn's death could not be avoided. That was what this was all about. Glenn was preparing Michael for the final act and knew Michael wanted to ignore it. Glenn was selling the painting and telling the story just so Michael would be able to face the inevitable, just as Glenn was facing it.

Michael admitted to himself that Anda had every right to be proud of his experiences, but now he was old. He remembered Anda's kindnesses and his eyes squeezed back the tears. He knew just how unkind people can be. Glenn had frequently told Michael when he was growing up, "there are only two kinds of people in the world - good and bad." Glenn could not tell him why people were so often cruel, but Michael had to know the difference and choose which one he would be. Michael knew what Glenn was up to.

Glenn was looking over the buildings of Manhattan and wondering how many gazillions of dollars passed through those places every day. There was the Stock Exchange and those banks of long generations lining Wall Street. So many banks you couldn't count them, and all of the people in those places would have fainted in Merkers mine. All that wealth, and all it could do was make more money.

The great markets by the sea were all shut fast on this calm Sunday, so Michael could drive across town more easily than he could circle it on Riverside. Glenn remembered something from Wiesbaden and quoted to himself, "those long caravans that cross the plain..." and couldn't think of the rest of it.

Michael jolted Glenn out of his search for the slippery words. "What did they do with all that stuff?" Glenn was relieved to continue the tale because he didn't want to tell himself he couldn't remember those few words, so he explained to Michael. "Jimmy and I were assigned to the Collecting Point at Wiesbaden where they'd found an old museum that was just a little wrecked. You know, the old Nazi Party Headquarters in Munich was another Collecting Point, which was a good joke because we were returning the loot to the people from whom it was stolen by using the very building the thieves themselves had stolen."

"Yeah. That's neat" Michael said

"Jimmy was a kinda handyman in the place, and they had me in the guard. That's when we met Johnny Murray. What a guy he was, tall and skinny and bright as a button. They gave us four tanks to guard the four corners of the building, and Johnny was in charge of that little troop. We were three sergeants, so we had a bit of pull in the place, which was good because we could get all sorts of stuff from the quartermasters, including coffee."

"What was so special about the coffee?" Michael asked.

"You've heard about French girls and nylon stockings, but coffee was something else. Cigarettes were used like money. I remember one of the Wiesbaden officers bought a looted Picasso for half a carton of Pall Malls, and he gave it to Farmer free of charge. He said if he could get a hundred boxes of twenty cartons of cigarettes, he could get us a whole museum on the black market. Sugar was another big money item. Sugar was silver, but coffee was gold."

"Coffee?"

"That's right. Good old everyday java. You remember what I was telling you about those DPs at Merkers Mine? That was done with one pot of coffee. Jimmy found a way of getting all we needed and more, and Farmer used it to pay some of the DP workers at Wiesbaden. He used to say, 'We fight for peanuts, but the Germans work for beans.' He had a real way with words, did Walter Farmer."

"Wasn't he your boss?"

"Yeah. But you gotta remember, we did all the military mumbo-jumbo saluting shit only when there were senior officers around, just to make it look good and to keep them off our cases. The rest of the time there was no 'Yes, Sir, Yes' or 'Good Morning, Captain Farmer' or anything like that. It was just Jimmy, Johnny, and Walter working together."

Michael turned off Canal Street and into the approaches to the Holland Tunnel. Glenn gently quizzed him, "Aren't you going to take the bridge?" Michel flicked the flasher left and said, "You like the tunnel better." It was true, and Michael added his more practical excuse, "The road crews will have sanded the tunnel early this morning. The bridge will still be slippery."

Glenn took more than his usual interest in Michael's expertise at road cleaning and was following Michael's little lecture on how there was "an agreement between the New York and New Jersey Maintenance Sections to make sure they both took care of the tunnel and the bridge."

When Michael told him they had changed from road salt to a mixture of sand and pulverized gravel, he was pleased that Michael said, "Just like the salt in the mine that could rot boots, our salt rotted the cars."

Glenn lost interest in the intricacies of snow removal and road safety, but he was reassured Michael had really been listening to him. Putting together road salt and the salt mine was proof Glenn was getting through to him and that was all he really wanted.

They started to merge with a line of traffic from the left and slowed until each car found its place to enter the tunnel. Glenn's attention slipped to the barren trees in concrete planters lining the sidewalk, and his eyes jumped up to the old, pointy water towers on the roofs. He remembered more lines from that distant poem.

"Put forth no more for glory or for gain,
Take no more solace from the palm-girt wells."

The wells in New York were on top of the buildings, and the street was a long oasis of stone-planted palm trees. In the summer it looked good, all green and shining, but the trees spent the winter with splayed and barren branches, like bony fingers reaching up the sides of the buildings. "Of ships and stars" was from another line, and he recalled that George Stout was a naval officer and could see Patton's bestarred helmet glitter in the mine's gloom. He remembered them without mourning, in forgiveness of all their faults and joy in all their triumphs, for now they had reached those "isles where good men rest, Where nevermore the rose of sunset pales."

While they were waiting their turn to enter the tunnel, Glenn told of the time they got Walter Farmer drunk. "He wasn't really drunk, just a little tipsy because he was too much of a gentleman to go on a real bender. It was our last night, and Jimmy had scrounged enough booze to start a bar. The guys were singing and talking about what they were going to do when they got stateside, and Jimmy asked Farmer to sing a song. Farmer said he only knew ‘vulgar ditties,’ and we all roared because smut coming out of that man’s lips would be like a nun showing you her tattoos. So, he recited a poem, and his voice was amazing. When he finished, there wasn’t a dry eye in the house, and we clapped for him for five minutes. It was magnificent.”

“What was the poem?” asked Michael.

“I can only remember a few lines, something like this:

“They know time comes, not only you and I,
But the whole world shall whiten, here or there.”

Michael jumped to help Glenn’s memory. “Let’s look it up on the computer when we get back.” Glenn nodded to accept this partnership with Michael and simply said, “I’d like that.”

The traffic gurgled in a rush through the tunnel’s mouth. Two lanes merged along the road and Glenn’s eyes basked beneath the whirling light and sound. He squinted joyfully in the cascade of shimmering headlights and his mind was caught in the lighted hole of the white semi-circle before him. The wheels scattered sand in their wake and the gravelly grit echoed off the tunnel walls to beat a fanfare on their journey into darkest Jersey.

Chapter 22

Ali Baba

Wiesbaden, Germany,
MFAA Collecting Point
Landesmuseum.
June, 1945

Captain Walter Farmer was proud of himself. The war had brought the hidden parts of his character to the surface, and they surprised him. He reveled in his new personality and the power it generated. In peace, he had been content to follow, but that was a different Walter, and now he kept that one locked behind his confidence. He had become a leader, and war had given him roots in strange places. Now that peace had broken out, this was his time to bloom.

Walter sat on the bed he had constructed out of empty ammunition boxes and old boxes. He had built a little room for himself on the second floor of the reconstructed museum by piling up wooden shipping crates from floor to ceiling. His little cell had three sides made of anything solid and rectangular that the war had thrown away. He had even found a small table for the Primus stove, the coffee percolator, and a secure footlocker for the coffee.

He would spend the day supervising a motley crew of assistants opening, inspecting, classifying, packing, and repacking the cases of artwork delivered to his domain. The late evenings were reserved for himself, and the night was Walter's dream-time over coffee. He could be alone with his visions of Josselyn and plan the future they would make when he returned home.

They were war-bride and war-groom, having been married only one hundred days before he boarded the train that would take him to Wiesbaden, via boot camp in Louisiana, training in England, combat in France, and surrender in Germany. It was a long road, but thoughts of Josse made the journey bearable. Walter sat on his bed every evening to watch images of Josse dancing in the flames that tickled the bottom of the coffee pot. They would always make him smile.

Their first meal as husband and wife was when Josse came home with a live chicken and asked him what to do with it. Josse had never learned to keep house, and Walter was much better with textile scissors than a butcher's knife, so they ate sandwiches and kept the chicken as a pet. The Primus stove was a bit like that chicken, for it was now his portable pet. He appreciated the little wonder's simplicity. You filled the base with any combustible fluid, pumped the little valve to get up the pressure, and lit the ring. A perfect halo of blue flame could boil water in five minutes. The little fire would scatter the flame's light through his room and flicker over the names on the crates: "Rembrandt," "Vermeer," "The Louvre," "Kaiser Wilhelm Museum." Walter mused to himself, "No wonder the men call me Ali Baba." That he was able to sit amidst all these wonders was the real magic. The miracle was he also had real coffee.

He had quickly discovered that the Germans could be controlled with coffee because they were the masters of the substitute. When they ran out of gasoline, they invented ways of making it out of coal oil. They made tea from raspberry leaves, tires from synthetic rubber, and heating oil from food scraps. Ground up acorns became "kaffee." They were infinitely inventive and called these imitations "ersatz," but it was all inferior to the real thing. Even prostitutes were ersatz wives. Germans knew when something was phony, but they accepted the masquerade when there was no alternative. Walter was frequently reminded that what the Germans put into their stomachs was similar to what the Nazis had put into their brains.

Walter had the genuine article, and real coffee made him a millionaire in the land of paupers. He kept the precious grains in quarter-pound parcels neatly stacked in his office safe, ready to bribe and threaten the Germans working for him. Walter made sure the fumes permeated the building every morning and doled out a few spoons to the best workers every evening. When he was in England waiting for the invasion, he had seen posters of two boys following the scent of some gravy called "Bisto." All their mother had to do was cook some "Bisto" and she could drag them out of mischief with her gravy boat. The Germans were like those boys, and Walter's percolator made him into the Pied Piper. The magic of the beans kept the whole place running like a mainline freight station. So, it was with renewed pride he would end each day making his very own coffee on his very own stove. Tonight, he was waiting for Stout and Glenn to arrive with a new convoy of goodies. The regular tramp of the perimeter guards signaled they hadn't yet arrived, so he could talk to Josse and tell her of his world.

That world contained all of Germany's artistic past, and it was his job to save it for any future Germany might have. The building was the old Landesmuseum in Wiesbaden, and Walter had resurrected it. Until the war came, the museum had housed the town's civic pride and ancient treasures, but with the peace, the pride was gone and the galleries had echoed with the bickering complaints of the DPs. The treasures had first been squirreled away by the Nazis, but then the survivors rummaged through what remained, seeking anything they could trade for food. The building was a huge, two-story complex of three hundred rooms in the shape of a giant letter "E." It also had two thousand bomb-blasted windows. The structure was intact, but the holes in the roof let in the rain. Walter's assignment was to make the place "a secure refuge for those works of art recovered in the field." To make a secure refuge, he first had to get rid of the refugees.

Walter's first inspection revealed the interior full of DPs. They had scuttled through the exhibition rooms, setting up camp, and everything that couldn't be used or eaten was just thrown out of the windows or pushed aside. The shattered glass in the museum's Natural History galleries was two feet deep. The DPs looted the stuffed animals, and Walter was confronted by a moosehead drowning in a river of sparkling shards of broken glass and a lion's legs rising from a jumble of overturned display cases. He thought the vandalized animals looked like they had missed the boat on Noah's Ark. To clear the clutter, Walter had recruited gangs of DPs desperate for food. It took them a week to clear the rubble out of the main galleries, which included some of their neighbors and relatives. The pandemonium of shovels on glass and brooms on broken bricks continued until a welcome silence oozed through the empty building. Walter boarded up a few windows and patched the roof to create something that resembled an abandoned warehouse. It was a start.

Wiesbaden was a long way from Cincinnati and his job as an interior designer for the Closson Company. Closson's offered fine living in comfortable surroundings along the whole financial spectrum, from newlyweds with a few dollars to millionaires with more money than taste. Walter had spent seven happy years supplying both comfort and style to rich and poor alike. He never thought the army would have any use for his talents. Neither did the army, so they shoved him into an engineering battalion where he could do as little damage as possible.

He'd been assigned to making prisoner of war cages for the millions of Germans streaming west to avoid the Russians in the east. A POW cage was little more than a rectangle of barbed wire patrolled by a company of sour-looking guards thumbing rifle slings. The Germans were grateful to be his prisoner and some even gave him presents of watches and cigarettes, looted from the dead littering the roads to Wiesbaden. Each cage was a bustling hubbub of old friends and relatives who were meeting up for the first time in years. The noise and the laughter and the camaraderie were deafening. Walter wanted something more to do than listen to their too often repeated joke that they should "Enjoy the war. The peace will be terrible." Germans seemed to get fixated on one thing and didn't realize how a joke lost its humor, when it was repeated twenty thousand times. For variety, Walter had written a letter to the Monuments Men, one of those shots in the dark that can hit a target you don't even know is there and change your whole life.

Two officers appeared at Walter's cage. A sloppy-looking lieutenant introduced himself as Lt. Charles Kuhn and then presented a very neatly turned out Capt. Stout. They were both Navy. Their driver hovered in the background but seemed to be listening to every word. Once they started talking, Walter realized just who they were. Kuhn was a professor at Harvard, and Stout had reinvented the whole field of art conservation and restoration. Walter had read their books and admired their work but never expected to meet them. Here they were courting him. It was as if the gods had fluttered down from Olympus and asked very politely if he could repair their chariot.

Kuhn and Stout were the elite, being Harvard men with PhDs, knowledge, and reputations. Even without the uniforms, they would be men he saluted in his heart. He was just an interior designer for a Cincinnati department store with a degree in engineering, so low down on the food chain it would take him a few reincarnations to raise himself to the level of these men. But here they were, hanging on his every word.

They kept asking him questions, and it puzzled Walter that they should want something from him. They wanted to know about his work in the 373rd Engineering Regiment and took an inordinate interest in how he filled out requisition forms. They asked, "What do you do when the Quartermaster won't issue enough toilet paper?" Walter's grin flooded his face. "Oh, that's easy. I save all the copies of orders and requisitions in a big box and instead of throwing them away, we use them in the latrines. Some of the men like it better because it's softer than what they call G.I. sandpaper or ass rasps." Their laughter showed their admiration for a man who could solve a problem with the very bureaucracy which caused the problem in the first place.

"But what if you have an officer who won't listen?" Kuhn asked.

"Then I send him someone to whom he has to listen, like a more senior officer or someone who has something he wants. The soldiers march on their stomachs, but the Army moves on orders. The orders are all on paper, so the best way to control the army is to control the paper. I've even forged a general's signature, when we needed welding tools to make a bridge."

"Did the general ever find out about the forgery?" inquired Stout. Walter had to pause to think through his own experience of the generals. "Generals sign so many pieces of paper, they can't remember each piece, so if they see their own signature, they must have read the requisition. We got the welders, the bridge was completed, and the 12th Army crossed the Rhine. We wouldn't be sitting here today without that piece of paper and the general's signature, real or not." Stout and Kuhn exchanged glances and beamed back at Walter.

"When can you start?" Stout asked.

Walter thought through an awkward silence, and sighed his answer, "I have to get my superior's permission."

"We can request your transfer," Kuhn assured him.

Walter had to tell them there was no time to lose because his regiment was going home in two days. Stout and Kuhn did not want the answer to their prayers disappearing on a transport from Le Havre. They needed his expertise as much as he required his colonel's approval for a transfer. Arranging his own transfer to the Monuments Men would be Walter's first test. He would be dealing with the military command structure for the next couple of years, smoothing out a mountain of looted art which just kept growing. Kuhn and Stout reasoned, if this man can get himself to us through proper channels, he can use his skill in processing the artwork through those same channels. We need a guy who can use the Army system creatively to accomplish the humanitarian mission.

Kuhn told Walter, "We can make an urgent request through Third Army Headquarters. Will that satisfy your commander?"

"In that case, I can work it out with Col. Bell," Farmer offered, trying to suppress his enthusiasm.

So, it was with a sense of adventure that Walter, after the briefest of interviews, was put in charge of the Collecting Point in Wiesbaden.

Walter had been offered a palette of responsibilities fuller than his wildest ambitions. Stout had stated the problem with his usual clarity: finding the art was one thing, but preserving it from “the ravages of the mines and the itchy fingers of our own soldiers is something quite different.” The Monuments Men had naturally divided into Doers and Gatherers. The Doers were the front line of the rescue: engineers, restorers, academics in fatigues who could grab the stuff before anybody else could. The Gatherers had to make sure that the Doers’ achievements were not in vain. They had to protect whatever had been found. Someone had to create order out of this chaos, so Walter cleared the decks for action, along with the corridors and the exhibition halls.

After Siegen, George had drawn a square in the mud with the heel of his boot, and when Glenn had asked what it was, simply replied, “Square One.” He’d convinced the brass that if they didn’t find a safe haven for the art, it would all disappear into a cloud of pockets, kit bags, parcels home to mother, cellars and attics stashed by retired SS men, Hitler Youth, and people with big plans for the future of a resurrected Germany. The authorities had requisitioned the bomb shattered Wiesbaden Landesmuseum, so square one had no roof and no windows, but four walls and a basement. Then Farmer’s letter came with a note asking if Stout “could use the services of this officer.” George jumped at the chance to give Walter his chance, and the results were miraculous. The war was for the Doers, but the peace was the time of the Gatherers.

Walter sat sucking the coffee, until he heard the squeal of dusty brakes in the courtyard. Stout and Glenn would want it hot after a night ride at the head of a convoy, so he pumped the Primus stove. The echoes of hobnails clicked counterpoint with the muted bass of rubber soles and built to a crescendo up the stairs. Walter went to the missing third wall of his cell, leaned on the crate wall with one arm, and beckoned them with a wave of the other. "Come on in. I've got the brew going."

Stout and Glenn drew their canteens from their belts like Dodge City gunslingers.

"Pull up a box, Boys," Walter invited and then said, "There's no milk or sugar."

'We found both," Glenn said and uncorked his canteen to pour milk through the coffee. George put his canteen-full of sugar on the table.

"It'll be a party," said Walter and demanded cheerfully, "So what have you dug up this time?"

Stout settled into the warmth of Walter's cubicle as Glenn prepared the cups.

"The convoy is about ten miles behind, so we've got about an hour to kill," said George.

"How many?" asked Walter, and George turned to Glenn.

"Six full trucks and a moving van. I counted two hundred and twenty seven crates and boxes."

"He means we piled as much stuff as we could into whatever we could find that would hold it all," laughed George.

"The contents?" Walter asked, wondering where he could find some more space.

"It's the first shipment from the Berlin Kaiser Friedrich Museum. There must be a thousand other crates scattered throughout Bavaria."

"We figure there are three hundred other hidey-holes full of stuff," observed Glenn.

Such an avalanche had become routine for Walter, and he was thankful he didn't have to reinvent the wheel every time a convoy appeared out of the mist. The first shipment arrived when the Landesmuseum still looked like Swiss cheese in the rain. Thirty trucks escorted by a regiment of infantry dumped 6,000 crates containing everything from German paintings to the Guelph Treasure to Byzantine chalices. The paintings had survived only because Walter had told the officer in charge to set up a chow line for everybody. Field cooks banging frying pans organized everybody into an orderly line snaking around the building. That gave Walter just enough time to get the crates into the building. He didn't know what to do next, so he sat on a box for an hour looking like Buddha on a crash diet. He finally jumped up and attacked a six-foot wooden box with a hammer and in five minutes had three large pieces of wood. One of the soldiers had rummaged in a tank until he found some dark camouflage paint. With an old sock over his hand like a puppet, Walter had written the letters "A," "B," and "C" on the panels. He gathered the hammer and some nails and the soldier reappeared shouldering a ladder. Together they nailed a sign with a letter over the entrance to each of the museum's galleries. Walter gazed up at their handiwork with his hands on his tired hips and saw those three letters signaling the start of their crusade. He turned his compliments to the soldier and said "Thank you, Sergeant. What's your name?" The little man shrugged back at Walter, "Jimmy Mulvaney" and Walter was glad for a new friend. Jimmy decided this was going to be a good job, if officers were saying "thank you."

Walter had worked out a system where the German assistants would unpack the crates at long tables in Gallery A. American and British museum workers would identify, record, and tag the artifacts in Gallery B, and Russian ex-prisoners would repack everything under the all-seeing eye of "C." The Russians had to be taught that "C" was not "S" in their own language, but starvation, and desperation not to be repatriated to Russia, made quick learners of them all. The real genius of Walter's plan was that each stage of the process would be completed by a different group in a different language. This helped ensure the security of the artwork. He liked to think this was his "Tower of Babel System." If he confused their tongues, the Germans and the Russians wouldn't know what they had in front of them and would be less tempted to rob him.

Walter turned to Stout and Glenn and answered their questioning eyebrows.

"Well, we'll pile it up in the halls until we can figure out what to do with it all. The problem is the stuff is coming in faster than we can send it out."

"What about another warehouse?" Glenn asked.

"You try to find anything still standing with a roof. It's a miracle this place wasn't leveled," Walter said.

"So how come this one escaped?"

"Good question," George said. "Why didn't I think of it?"

"You've been busy," Glenn joked.

"This was a Luftwaffe headquarters," Farmer explained, "I guess we missed it when we bombed the hell out of the town."

"So, what about the other HQs?" Glenn posed.

"What other HQs?" Walter asked.

"I think Glenn's got the right question," George added, "If this building survived because it was important to the Germans, then other structures they considered important might also have fared better than the average apartment house."

"Yeah. They used this as HQ thinking it was safe, so other HQs might be safe." Glenn saw the reasoning behind his own suggestion.

"You're right. I'll look around the suburbs in the morning. Can you guys drive me?" Walter asked.

"I thought you had your own jeep, that going away present from the engineers."

"Posey was here yesterday," Walter confided.

They laughed in chorus because they knew Jimmy would make some sort of a deal on wheels.

"What was it this time?" George asked.

"He said he could trade it in for a better model," Walter admitted.

"We'll see when he finally turns up."

"It's bound to be a surprise."

Jimmy had quickly become notorious in Wiesbaden. Walter's first job was to secure the building from foreign and friendly pillaging. Jimmy had a knack for finding things and then making them work. He never looted; he just liberated the things nobody wanted. He could find a use for garbage, and it always turned out to be the very garbage Walter needed. Since Walter had built cages for POWs, Jimmy made a suggestion. Jimmy volunteered to "scrounge up some fencing from the vacated camps. The idea was to make a cage around the museum. Jimmy and Walter found everything they needed in one of the camps Walter had created weeks earlier. Jimmy had arranged for some of his truck driver friends in the Red Ball Express to make a detour when they were empty, and in one day they delivered enough wooden posts and barbed wire to surround the Central Collecting Point. Hungry DPs and American money constructed two stories of barbed wire fencing that made the building look like a transparent Fort Apache.

The DPs stayed on to work the galleries, and Walter had put the fear of a firing squad into anybody who was even suspected of pilfering any of the stuff. Jimmy found a German-speaking GI and gave him a Luger as a souvenir. The retreaded German-American stood behind Walter as when bellowed orders. The cowed DPs quickly became Walter's very helpful Gallery Assistants. Within two weeks, Walter had two hundred "trainee curators" working the humming galleries. English promises and German threats bounced off the walls. Walter could have been reciting "Mary Had A Little Lamb," but the tone of his voice and the glower of the translator made for a happy working relationship. The translator was tickled to have been transferred for special duties at the Collecting Point, so Walter had a linguist he could trust and a system he could use.

The dogfaces guarded the perimeter of the building, and the German police guarded storerooms. A secret policeman guarded the Germans, and Walter was proud to say, "and I guard the guards." The Germans were used to suspicion and found a strange comfort in their mistrust of each another. It was normal. Walter understood this when the translator told him about a phone call one of the DPs had made. The DP talked to the telephone operator, when they finally had both telephones and women to operate them. When the German asked for a number, the operator demanded to know, “Why do you want this number?” The DP did not hesitate to give his reason and thought it completely normal for a telephone operator to ask such a personal question. Walter realized there was safety in paranoia, if not in telephone numbers.

When the cage was up and the workers were sufficiently terrorized, Walter had to light the building both inside and out. Jimmy went back to Transport Allocations and appeared with one truck towing the front half of another truck. Walter was intrigued to discover what he would come up with this time. Jimmy and the driver looked over each other’s shoulders for wandering officers or MPs and then proudly pulled back the canvas cover to reveal hundreds of headlights pried from wrecked vehicles and two spools of telephone wire. Jimmy started hauling boxes of lights from the cargo bed and simply explained, “We put the lights on the fences facing the house and they'll scare away the cockroaches trying to get in at night.”

Walter saw the sense of this but had to get down to practicalities, “And just what are we going to use for electricity?” Jimmy proudly pointed to the wrecked truck and said, “That.”

The driver towed the wreck into the compound and parked it beside the front stairs. Walter was suspicious because the truck-and-a-half idling in the courtyard looked like a baby elephant hanging onto its mother’s tail with its trunk. He just couldn’t see how all this junk was going to supply power and light.

“We get the engine going and that will make the electricity,” announced Jimmy.

“You can’t power all these lights with one truck engine,” Walter complained.

“I know that,” agreed Jimmy, “But we can run the generator we found in the officers’ quarters, now the officers have all moved out.” Jimmy jumped into the passenger seat of the tow-truck and yelled at Walter, “We’ll be back in the morning with it.” Walter watched them rattle through the main gates and shook his head in gratitude of Sgt. Mulvaney’s extraordinary abilities to “liberate” just about anything they needed. Two days later, the Collecting

Point nestled in its own pool of light every night, and nobody ever had to disturb Walter's sleep with a gruff "Halt. Who goes there?"

Stout was tired. He would be heading Stateside soon and was counting the days. He just wanted a few more days, but not too many.

"When are you going back?" Walter asked.

"They say two weeks, but you know how it works. Two weeks become a month and then the months become 'Today.'"

"What about you?" Walter asked Glenn.

"I ain't got the points. I got another six months before I can go home."

"Glenn has added a second semester," added Stout. "You should see him take notes. He's going home with a bachelor's degree in art history."

"Don't knock it. I've learned more doing this job than I could ever learn anywhere. I've been thinking maybe I'll go to school when I get back."

"You're learning more here than you could ever learn at Harvard."

"How'd you figure that?" Glenn queried.

"At Harvard you'd listen to some professor talk about what he thinks about a painting. If you're really dedicated, you could go to the Fogg Museum and see the painting, but everything would be Off Limits. Don't touch. Don't even breathe too close to the canvas. Just write down what the professor tells you, copy it on a test, and then you get a grade. Six days later, you wouldn't be able to tell a Gauguin from a Gaudens."

The light went on in Walter's head. He had always thought himself inferior in intellect to the giants from Harvard. Now the giant had come down to him and said, "I'm just bigger, not better." Walter listened intently. "Glenn can keep things clear. He's the one who knows what we've been up to these last few months," Stout confessed.

Stout was fed up with the destruction. He'd seen enough waste, too much pain, and the despair that welcomes death. He was sick of the jumble of past, present, and future. The tenses were all cock-eyed. Even the story of his own time here was a muddle, and he felt his life was trapped in the squalor of time. He could remember each place, but the chronology eluded him. Everything was out of joint. His mind kept going over details deposited by waves of memory. Glenn kept a log of their mission, something between a work schedule and a diary and George would ask to see the book just to know on which date something happened. Glenn's book had become an anchor for his mind and he valued the man's dedication to order. Glenn had dismissed his diary with, "How else are we gonna know what we did?"

"That diary is like your map reading," said George.

"Speaking of maps, how goes the hunt?" asked Walter.

"We've been able to identify fourteen hundred caches." George said. Glenn was eager to contribute to the discussion, and George was relieved of the duty of telling the same story for the hundredth time.

"They shoved the stuff everywhere. In bunkers, mines, trains. There was even a butcher's refrigerator filled with loot from Belgium. Can you believe it?"

"Very easily. What did you call the repositories?"

"Hidey-holes. This is the biggest game of 'Hide and Seek' anybody could come up with." Glenn rode his enthusiasm like a new maverick just getting used to a saddle.

George relished the simple enthusiasm of Glenn's newfound interest. It reminded him of the time when he could get excited about a painting and then bore his wife with the details for the next week. She was so patient, and he yearned to just be with her and the children again, and never have to talk about this. She would know without him saying anything, and the silence would be balm to his soul.

Glenn kept up his tale of "the altarpiece of *The Mystic Lamb*" and regaled them with the bits of information they both knew from their adolescence but which now bubbled forth from Glenn like a water tap that wouldn't shut off. The more he talked, the more they appreciated the very things for which they had risked so much and worked so hard. Walter felt Glenn's new thirst for knowledge was catching. He welcomed Glenn's eagerness. Maybe this was why they were all going to such extremes to preserve the art. Maybe it was for Glenn and all the other Glenns out there who would be changed by these mere things. Maybe that was the real purpose.

"Hey. This is good coffee. Where'd you get it?" asked Glenn. Walter simply said, "Jimmy." They laughed together about the repeated obviousness and listened to the thrum of engines in the distance. The three looked at one another and could tell without saying that this was the time when their lives would change in different ways. Stout was ready to leave the present and crawl into the cocoon of his family. Walter would remain with the treasures until the galleries echoed empty triumph. Glenn was just taking his first baby steps into a future as uncertain as it was unexpected.

They waited and listened to the growling engines growing louder. The convoy halted at the perimeter gate and the lead driver stuck his head out the window and shouted to the guards, "Open Sesame."

Chapter 23

Cabinet of Curiosities

The windshield wipers were slapping in time to Glenn's heavy breathing, and the blades cleared segments of slush before their eyes. The window defroster kept the glass diamond bright, so Glenn could study the rows of neat houses all connected to the street by their little umbilical driveways. Glenn pointed to a one-and-a-half story pile of '70s chic in glazed white brick and commanded Michael to "Pull into that driveway."

They had been driving through that eclipse of soft rain and premature snow which makes a car cleaner after the journey than when it first sets out. Michael slowed to a crawl and maneuvered the SUV up the drive as if he were the captain of a supertanker squeezing through the Panama Canal. He set the brake and stood the car on tired wheels, dripping gritty road runoff.

Michael looked up the drive at a boy in a parka pushing a snow shovel past the garage doors. Glenn descended from his passenger seat. The boy turned, let the handle of the shovel fall, and walked to Glenn's side of the car. Michael got out of the car and walked around the front to join the boy, who was giving Glenn an affectionate hug. Glenn released his greeting cuddle, and the boy turned to Michael. The boy's mischievous eyes were framed in the furry halo of his hood. Michael gaped into the face of the trophy wife from yesterday's auction. Her pearl earring throbbed with noonday luster, and her smile beamed out of her hood and through the snow mist.

"I'm glad you were able to get here," the woman said.

"I had a good driver," said Glenn and introduced them, "Michael, meet Judith."

Michael was now beyond shock. The knowledge that Glenn had a bigger game afoot than his war stories pulsed in Michael's mind. Now he was looking forward to the pleasure of a revealed secret because Anda was leading him to something really good. He nodded and smiled at Judith to say, "Nice to see you... again."

Judith's teeth flashed a promise of more mischief to come. She clapped the snow off her mittens and methodically folded them into the pockets of her parka. "Come on in," she invited, and led Michael and Glenn along the little concrete pathway to the front porch. She opened the door and stamped slush from her boots before removing each one and stepping each wool-socked foot onto the hall carpet. Michael and Glenn followed suit, and soon she was leading their muffled tread along the shag-carpeted hall.

Judith ushered them into the living room and back to the 1970s. All the furniture was from Sears, and the walls were crowded with framed photos of a family. The sunlight bounced off the snow outside and streamed through the picture windows to blind them in the reflections from the wall of huddled glass rectangles. A large man raised himself from a Lazyboy reclining rocker to his full height, and Michael recognized the older man with the thinning hair from Sotheby's auction yesterday. The man demanded, "Hey, what took you so long?"

Michael asked, "You know each other?"

"Long time," the man roared. "I know all about you," he said, and offered his hand to Michael. Glenn's voice was soft but echoed through the room. "Michael, allow me to introduce you to Robert Posey Mulvaney."

Michael's hand was pumped by this bear of a man, but his gentle voice commanded Michael to "Call me Bobby. Robert is too formal. Nice to see you again, Michael."

"You mean after yesterday's sale?"

"Among other times, but you wouldn't remember me. You were too young, and I wasn't so fat back then."

Michael relaxed to hear the story that was sure to come and the answers it would give. So this was the man and his trophy wife. He turned to Glenn with a face full of questions. Glenn returned a knowing grin framed in a filigree of wrinkled merriment. "Sit down," Bobby offered, and they all formed a square and sat on anything that was close. Bobby burrowed back into the recliner like it was a beach ball, while Glenn sprawled on the couch. Judith pointed to an upholstered chair for Michael as she enthroned herself on a chrome kitchen chair between Michael and Bobby.

Glenn offered one of the big puzzle pieces, when he told Michael, "Bobby is Jimmy's son," but Bobby rattled another puzzle box when he revealed, "Judy is my daughter." All Michael could think to say was, "Well that explains why you look so much alike." They all roared, for nobody looking at Judith's dark hair and petite form would make the connection with Bobby's burly bulk. "I take after my mom," Bobby said.

Michael looked at the wall and saw the picture of Anda and Jimmy posed in front of the jeep at the castle and could see Judith's eyes and face staring back at him. Judy was Jimmy without the attitude, and Jimmy was Judith, without the earrings. "And Judith takes after your father."

"That's about the way it is," Bobby growled softly.

Thoughts of "yesterday," "the auction," and "how" hovered in the room, but Michael was patient. He did not want to intrude but he was desperate for answers. Glenn explained, "Bobby is a wonder at bidding, so he helped us in the auction."

"Hey, there ain't no price that can't be pumped," Bobby admitted with pride.

"So, you were pushing up the bidding all the time?" Michael asked.

"Let's just say we were encouraging those people to rise to their true price."

Judith's eyes blinked a merry chuckle in time to her swinging earrings, and yesterday's puzzle became clear to Michael. Glenn explained that Bobby had inherited Jimmy's business. Bobby was eager to add, "Yeah. Dad had a junk yard and we made good until my own little genius came along," nodding to Judith.

"It was a junk yard," Judith proudly stated. "Now it's a Museum of Automotive Heritage and Restoration Service."

"Yeah," said Bobby, "that's her fancy name, but we did have old spare parts for anything that couldn't move until Judy came up with the idea of going on the internet."

Bobby went into a father's long ramble of how he'd spent all that money for his only daughter to go to that college and how she hadn't found a husband at that college and came home from that college with no job. Judith interjected she had taken a course in electronic marketing ten years ago "when eBay was still kind of new." She had written a term paper for the course on the only thing she knew she had to sell, which was her grandfather's junkyard. After writing the term paper, she realized the professor had missed her point about the business potential of social networking. He had written a stupid comment that "Facebook wouldn't last ... it's only good for hookers and hookups." She kept the essay, as she kept everything, and talked about it to her grandfather. She showed him the professor's marginal note and said, "He probably types with one hand." They had howled together because Judith could say things to Jimmy she would never say to anybody else.

Out of their bond and Jimmy's questions came the idea of selling spare parts on the internet. Together, they tested out her theory by contacting the clubs for car enthusiasts. They had started with the Pinto Owners' Club on Jimmy's premise that "if people wanted to restore a piece of crap that was a rolling fire-bomb, then there would be other people who would do the same." She had spent a week with her grandfather collecting all the junk that could go into a Ford Pinto and then made computer lists of the numbers. Granddad encouraged this because he loved spending time with her, and the junkyard business was the best excuse.

Judith got on the club's network and contacted a man who "needed desperately to find a 1976 generator." Judith and Granddad beamed the joy of a shared conspiracy when the man thanked them from the "bottom of my heart" for making his dream come true. Jimmy whispered to her in the glow of the computer screen, "I guess his wife thanks us from her bottom, too." Judith's idea made them $12,506.72 minus tax that first month. Bobby finally got to the end of his tale and declaimed, "Our Little Girl made us a fortune with her fingertips."

Judith put an end to her father's embarrassing praise and asked, "Who's for something to drink?" They all suggested tea or coffee except Glenn, who asked for something stronger. Judith went into the kitchen, leaving Glenn and Bobby to explain to Michael what Judith had known all her life.

Glenn started. "When we came home from the war, I went to college and Jimmy drove a taxi like he had before. I invited him to my graduation, and we talked about him going into the junk business because he had been collecting car trash while he was driving. He'd see something in the road and throw it in the trunk, and pretty soon he had a garage full of stuff people had thrown away."

Bobby added, "But that was just the start. He put every cent he had into buying an old aircraft hangar from the War Surplus Board, and Mom kept on her job at the laundry. They thought he was crazy, buying a whole hangar, so they cut him a deal on the price 'cause they felt guilty about taking advantage of a retard."

Glenn and Bobby took turns telling Michael the whole story of how Jimmy had built up the junk yard by going to auctions of confiscated automobiles through the police department and city authorities. He'd wait until everybody got bored and then buy the stuff that was left over. "Turns out the back end of a head-on crash is full of stuff people want." Glenn's lips pursed into a warning shot at Bobby, so he quickly changed the subject to all the stuff his dad had salvaged over the decades. After a while, Michael felt like he was the loser in a tag-team wrestling match and was relieved when Judith returned with a tray of cups. She set the tray on a sideboard and they all rose as if going to Holy Communion. Judith brought another tray from the kitchen and placed a teapot, an old coffee percolator, and a whiskey bottle beside the cups. Glenn gurgled the whiskey over the coffee, swirled cream and sugar into the mess, and breathed in the welcome fumes.

Bobby guided Michael to a wedding picture, and they all looked at young Jimmy with the cat's meow smile arm-in-arm with a huge woman in a starched dress. "That was the day they got married," Bobby said. Glenn added that someone had once "busted Jimmy's balls, asking why he had married such a big girl." Jimmy had kept his eyes narrowed and his fists clenched when he replied, "My Sally is heat in the winter and shade in the summer." Michael looked at Jimmy's grin in the photo and got the impression that if there had been any more jokes about Mrs. Sally Mulvaney, there would be teeth on the floor and blood on the ceiling.

Bobby told Michael his mother had worked in "that laundry for twenty-five years." The laundry had been started by Chinese immigrants, became a war plant and then a front for a Mafia business, and had survived the demise of the small hotel chains until it was finally put out of business by "Throw Away Diapers." Sally Mulvaney had been the only continuity over decades of change and had retired to the junk yard to make their living. "It was a good living too. Dad bought this place with cash." The house was clearly where Jimmy and Sally had spent their happy lives and raised their son. "Judy lives here now. I got my own place in the suburbs." Michael wondered what could be more suburban than this place.

Judith asked them to follow her. She led them up the stairs to the rooms spread across the living room and the garage. They passed a bathroom and the open door to a small child's room, until she ushered them into the master bedroom. Michael looked at boxes of files piled on the bed while Judith stood before the long wall. She said, "I spread cork over this wall and just started pinning pictures to it."

The wall was divided into columns by lengths of ribbon descending from the ceiling. Glenn looked across the wall and saw a sign identifying the decade of each column. Neat rows of photographs and documents filled the entire wall. Judith also had placed folding tables against the wall. The tables held boxes of cornflakes, and Michael looked down to see each box filled with more documents.

Michael's eyes scanned from left to right starting at 1925 and ending in the 2000s. The first column held pictures of babies, small children, and the formal poses of grammar school classes, with one child picking his nose. The 1930s column was mainly a baseball team and a picture of the old taxi rank in Times Square. Familiarity burst forth in the 1940s when Michael recognized the same photo of Jimmy and Anda in front of the jeep as in the living room and in Anda's album.

Judith led them on the tour of Jimmy's life. "There was so much stuff Granddad had collected that I had to make this just to get it all in order." When her grandparents died, Judith had sifted through their possessions and could not bring herself to throw anything away. She realized she was as much of the hoarder as her Granddad. She was determined that his life would not be bulldozed into some landfill. "He kept papers in old cornflakes boxes, so it was easy to identify what was what." Michael saw that the boxes were themselves a chronological stream of all the advertising commissioned by the Kellogg's Company since 1950. The cursive swirls of the name carved themselves through the simple green boxes of the '50s and then started to disappear in the psychedelic "Fruit Loops" of the '70s. He laughed to see the leprechaun winking from a box of "Lucky Charms." At a glance, he could follow Jimmy's life and know it was good.

Glenn walked the circle of the room's rectangle and knew what this place was. "It's just like those Kuntscammers the barons used to have." He remembered the rooms in German castles which he and Stout raided for loot. "The gentry would have special rooms where they kept anything that struck them as curious," he said. Glenn had seen just such a room in 1945 and wondered why people collected skeletons of babies with two heads or paintings of werewolves. Stout had told him, "These are the places that are full of question marks. They exist because they not only hold items which are curiosities, but because this is where you go to exercise your own curiosity." Glenn called them "The Why Rooms" because that was the main question of these Cabinets of Curiosity. Glenn did not have to ask why Judith had created this place with the images of Jimmy's life marching across one wall. They all stood in silent admiration for the man who was their friend, their father, and their mentor. This was no shrine. There was nothing tasteless about this wall of memories, for it was a work in progress, though the subject had finished his work. Bobby turned, and they followed his signal to return to the living room.

When they were seated Judith said, "We have one question you could help us with." Glenn stared at them both and reassured them, "Anything I can do to help." Judith looked at her father, and he told her, "You know more about it than me." She turned to Glenn and said, "He talked to me of a woman he knew."

Glenn tightened with suspicion. He did not want to open some can of worms about a long-forgotten romance. "Did he tell you her name?" he asked with feigned nonchalance. "Yes," Judith said and paused as Glenn squirmed, "Edith Standen."

Relief flooded Glenn's voice as told them all, "Edith. She was one classy woman."

Chapter 24

Tapestry

Wiesbaden, Germany,
MFAA Collecting Point
Landesmuseum.
August, 1945

The Wiesbaden Collecting Point was collecting more than it could handle. One convoy of ninety trucks stretched their capacity far beyond its ability to process the shipments. Crates were piled so high Walter kidded himself he wouldn't have to worry about the roof because the walls were going to explode. Walter felt he was drowning and called Headquarters for help. The help arrived in the form of a wiry, skinny woman thrusting into his face papers introducing "the bearer is Captain Edith Standen. Transferred to CCP Wiesbaden." Walter read she was under the command "to assist Captain Walter Farmer in any capacity he deemed fit." They looked at each other asking, "Well, what's next?"

Walter knew the problem but was unsure this woman was the answer. The sheer quantity of art was matched by the volume of paperwork. The Germans had been meticulous in documenting their loot and this was supposed to make Walter's work easier. Even though the Collecting Point had enough people to sort, store, and ship the art, the paperwork was in at least three languages. There had been too much guesswork matching a document to a particular crate, and it had been disastrous. What was needed was a translator with a knowledge of art or an artist who was also a linguist. This woman looked like neither.

Walter led the lady into his office and offered her a seat, which she cheerily accepted with a "Thanks, Old Chap." At a loss as to how to answer her familiarity, he looked over her American uniform and stammered, “You’re British?” “Almost, but not quite,” she replied. “Canadian, actually, but I became American two years ago.” When Walter asked a simple, “How did you get here?” he could hardly breathe under her torrent of “funny you should ask that. Daddy was a British Officer in Nova Scotia and Mummy was from Boston, and you know what those people are like, and her grandfather was Nathan Stapleton, who made a bundle in textiles, so they raised me in Ireland, lovely place but the cold gets into your bones, so I took my degree, English, from Oxford, Somerville, but I like men, and got back to Boston where I could be with Mummy, but one must work, so I sorted Medieval textiles for The Society for New England Antiquities, which uncle Billy founded, don’t know what he saw in old pieces of fabric, still it kept the wolf from the door, but not really a challenge you would call interesting, so I went to the Fogg at Harvard, and wouldn’t you know it, Paul Sachs let me do his course in museum curatorship, fascinating stuff, and then Widener needed someone to take care of his collection, but it all had to be transferred to the National Gallery, something to do with death or taxes or both, money anyway, and Mummy moved back to England just in time for the Blitz, so I joined the American WACS, so I could get posted to England, but Mummy was just fine, doing something very hush-hush at the Foreign Office, so here I am.” Walter leaned back in his chair, as if for protection from Edith’s word barrage and all he could think to say was, “That’s good.”

She was amused by his response, and Walter was a little frightened by her cackling. He asked her if she had any languages, and she became very quiet. “Hardly any. Just the usual, French, Italian, German, a smattering of Danish, oh yes, I can order supper in Portuguese.” Walter put on his most relieved face to assure her, “Thank goodness you’re here. The servants never tell us what’s on the plates.”

Her cackling finished as abruptly as it started, so Walter decided to give her the tour of the facility. He walked her down the main corridor in the direction of Johnny Murray lounging at the main door. Johnny could stand witness to whatever this scrawny chatterbox would do. Johnny saw an unidentified officer, which meant possible trouble, so he stood to attention as Walter introduced Edith. "Captain Standen, allow me to present Sergeant John Murray. Sergeant Murray is in charge of the tank patrol which guards the compound perimeter." Johnny saluted smartly and launched an official and slightly threatening, "Good Morning, Captain Standen." Edith giggled, and Walter's shoulders cringed at the expected stabbing laughter, but Edith's voice was more matronly than manic when she said, "Oh, please, let us dispense with such formalities, Sergeant. I'm just a glorified secretary." Murray responded, "In that case, good morning, Captain Secretary" and cocked his head to the side as he watched Walter lead the giggling laughter down the corridor.

Edith settled in quickly because everybody simultaneously decided that she was more eccentric than insane. The ice and the suspicions of her sanity broke when Walter watched her work the first day. He had led her away from Johnny at the main entrance and along the corridor to a little room as far from his office as he could place her. There was a desk, a chair, and a mountain of paperwork. "Can you organize these invoices?" he had asked her, and she simply said, "Yes." She ignored him and started her day by clearing the dust from the desk. Walter left her to seek refuge in his own labors.

Three days later, Edith appeared at Walter's open office door asking, "What else do you want me to do?" Incredulous that she had ordered all those papers, he followed her down the corridor and into the dirty room where he had left her. The place was gleaming, the windows were open, and in place of the chaos he saw only boxes filled with bundles of papers held together with paper clips, chancellory tags, rubber bands, and string. "How did you do this?" She sat at her chair polishing her glasses and said, "Chronologically according to shipping date and linguistically according to German first, then French, and often there is a pile of Italian at the back." She had taken all of the paperwork that was lying with the recovered artwork and made sense out of it. Walter was impressed.

She had created her own way of doing the job. One morning Walter dropped by to gossip, but that was just an excuse to observe Edith in action. She was piling up invoices and shipping manifests on the floor beside her desk. Her work area always looked like a garbage dump in the morning, but Walter understood her system.

Every morning she emptied boxes of random documents onto the floor to the left of her desk. When the little mountain reached the top of her desk, she went out for a brisk walk around the compound and a good gossip with "Murray and the boys." Refreshed by their banter, she would sit for hours identifying each paper with a penciled note in a different color. Red circles were for paintings on canvas or wood. Green triangles identified sculpture, but drawings on paper or vellum received three slash lines of blue. The documents would halt before her concentrated curiosity to be interrogated in German, French, or Italian. They would huddle like relieved prisoners to her right before being herded into file folders for each color. As the day progressed, each piece of paper shuffled through the identity parade across her desk and the mountain eroded. The procession continued until the jumble of the morning became the rainbow of late afternoon. Walter admired how Edith destroyed disorder with the simplest of solutions, a child's crayon set. He left knowing he could trust her with any task.

Jimmy made a special effort to get to know her. Whenever he saw her carrying boxes down the corridor, he would rush up to help with a polite, "Let me help you with that, Ma'am." Edith responded to his overtures like an older sister. She would rib him about being too old for him to carry her books home from school, but she also liked the attention. The guys in the Guard House ribbed him about finding a girlfriend his own age, but did this only once. They got the hint of lethality in his cold stare and left him alone. Johnny seemed to understand this new friendship was very important to Jimmy.

Every morning, Johnny would run the tanks around the compound, more to blow out the exhausts than to frighten the neighbors. Edith loved to watch them weave through the main gate and then split left and right on the road outside. She seemed to take pleasure in watching two tanks slowly circle the block and pass within inches of the other two going in the opposite direction. After the first pass, Edith would position herself on the steps of the main entrance to see them back up into their places at each of the four corners of the building. Jimmy asked her why she liked the routine so much, and she told him of the Changing of the Guard at Buckingham Palace. "My mother used to take me to watch the soldiers," she confessed, and Jimmy did not wish to intrude further into her nostalgic gaze.

What she didn't tell him was that patterns fascinated her. Even the lines of chevron prints the tank-treads pounded into the street were a joy to her. Walter had seen a glimmer of this love in her work. The thousands of bills of lading, receipts, and telegrams associated with the art were just meat to her. She was instinctively seeking the patterns which all these transactions left behind. Her morning walks and her review of the tank guard became part of the daily routine, so Johnny always expected to see her on the steps when he was sitting on the turret hatch of the lead tank. He would wave to her with one hand while barking orders into the radio handset he held in the other. Within a week, Edith was a tradition in her own right. The rumble of the morning engines was Jimmy's cue to wander over to Edith's little viewing stand on the steps.

One morning he kept asking her if she had enough soap and a good place to wash. She was very confused by such solicitous interest in her personal hygiene and didn't know if she should be offended or delighted. No gentleman had ever asked her if she took a bath. She sensed he wanted to talk about more than the soap, so she prodded him, "Jimmy. Do I smell bad?" Jimmy flushed and drove straight to the point. "No. No. No not at all. You smell great. It's just that I'm a bit worried about the dust and the sickness."

She was speechless, which some would have thought impossible, and asked asked "What sickness?" Jimmy went on a rambling story about how "people came home from war and there was a lot of sickness and I was just a kid back then but half the street was sick and couldn't breathe, and my uncle died and my Mom said it was the Chinese thing that got him, so I been thinking about the sickness and I found a whole box of soap and was just wondering if you could use any." It took her a while to follow his reasoning but then she asked, "Do you mean the influenza epidemic?"

"Yeah. That's the one. The Chinese Sickness."

"Oh, that. It wasn't Chinese."

"How do you know that?" asked Jimmy.

"I was there. I worked in the hospitals."

The reminder that Edith was old enough to have worked in the hospitals when he was just a kid told Jimmy to mind his manners with a lady. "It's just that I can see there's a lot of dust in the pictures and I wouldn't want you to get sick." She was touched by his concern for her and accepted a bar of lye soap, more out of politeness than necessity. Jimmy left to take roll at the Guard House and assured her, "There's more where that came from." Edith sat holding the pungent rectangle as if it were a bullion ingot.

After two weeks, Walter had to ask how Edith had accomplished so much in so little time. She was thrilled to have the recognition of this man the boys called "Fussy Walter." He was fussy, and that was exactly what was needed. A nonchalant attitude to the art would cause havoc, and the men meant the word as a compliment. She explained her reasoning to Walter.

"When I completed that course in museology, I became aware that the collection is the soul of the place, not the building. It is the contents that demand our attention."

"But how does that relate to our work?"

"Well, we have the building and the other three collecting points, but that is exactly what they are, points at which the artifacts are collected. These are not their permanent homes."

"Quite right," Walter agreed.

"Therefore, we have to see ourselves really as continually preparing a traveling exhibition. Nothing here is permanent; everything is moving all the time. The point is to know both what you have and where you have it."

"So, this determines what you are doing?"

"Yes. It's simple. My function is cataloguing for an exhibition."

"But there are hundreds of thousands of documents you have to sort."

"And all of them relate in some manner to the moving of the artifacts, not to the ownership of individual pieces. All I have done is find the pattern of the shipments of the art and ordered them into chronological order from 1937 until the most recent paperwork."

"So that's the pattern."

"That's this pattern. If we look at the art as a traveling exhibition, we can trace its movements and follow each of the threads to some point where the threads cross."

Walter was taken aback. It was Edith's fastidious concentration on the dating of the documents that made her so indispensable to the smooth operation of CCP Wiesbaden. She had the most amazing ability to remember that a consignment of seventeenth-century paintings had been shipped from the Jeu de Palme in Paris to Berlin in July of 1942. She always knew "what" he was asking about because she already knew "when" it had been handled and "where" it had been sent.

Edith became such a fixture at the compound simply because she worked. The guards loved her because they were all veterans who hated shirkers. The Germans would do anything for her because she would ask about their families in their own language. When she stood her own guard at the delivery bay, clipboard in hand, the drivers all left feeling they were very special because she was so enthusiastic in thanking them for being so careful with such precious cargo. But most of all, Walter came to admire her for the sheer dogged determination to complete her tasks more thoroughly than anyone would have expected. She had a strange ability to connect all the different elements of the compound together, just by making them feel good about themselves.

Jimmy was no exception to her rule. He had confessed to her, "those guys make me feel stupid." She pressed him because she felt his invitation, and Jimmy allowed himself to say to her what he didn't want to say to himself. "Posey and those other guys like you. You been to those colleges and I just graduated high school." She was standing, watching Johnny maneuver his squadron for the benefit of any would-be thieves and pointed to the prow of the lead tank. "What's that thing on the front of the tank?" she asked. Jimmy didn't know what she was talking about and just said, "You mean the hedge cutter?" "The very thing," she answered. They both looked at the row of four steel teeth thrusting forward from the belly of the tank. She listened to Jimmy explain that "they put that steel on the front so they could plough through those big hedges in Normandy."

Edith knew all about the invention of the Culin Hedge Cutter and the problem it solved. After the invasion, the tanks became trapped in the bocage country. The farmers didn't use fences. Instead, they had grown hedges to separate their fields and had added to the vegetation for hundreds of years. When the generals were planning the invasion they saw these hedges and thought of neatly trimmed lawns at home. They didn't realize the hedges were actually earthworks with a little forest topping each one. Tanks would have to run up the hedge banks to cross a field. A tank at a forty-five degree angle in the air exposed its soft under-belly to the enemy. It was a perfect target. Hundreds roasted in their metal crematoria on tracks, and the army was trapped behind the hedges. For weeks there was slaughter at the end of every killing-field. Edith knew all this when she asked Jimmy what that thing was at the front of the tank.

"Got time for a little gossip, Jimmy?" Jimmy sensed that she was cooking up something, so he said "Yup" and listened carefully.

“I was at a meeting at HQ and Eisenhower spoke to us of what he called ‘the little sergeant.’ His name was Culin, and he had an idea. And Culin’s idea was to weld knives, great big steel knives, to the fronts of the tanks, and as they came along, they would cut right through the hedges at ground level. And this idea was brought to the captain, then to the major, to the colonel, and it got high enough that somebody did something about it, and that was General Bradley, and he did it very quickly.”

Jimmy chimed in, “I heard that he was a tank sergeant, like Johnny Murray.”

“That he was,” Edith agreed, “but the point is that there was a huge problem and he came up with the simple solution all on his own. They didn’t ask the college guys for an answer, and the officers didn’t know what to do.”

“That’s officers for you,” Jimmy said.

“That’s stupid officers. But Eisenhower and Bradley, they’re not stupid because they listened to a sergeant who had an answer.” She fell silent, waiting for Jimmy.

“Never thought of it that way.” Jimmy whispered.

“The next time you feel stupid, just look at the lights on the compound fence.”

“How come?”

“Because without you, we’d all be working under candles. Very romantic, I’m sure, but I would rather have the lightbulbs.”

Jimmy’s chest swelled, and he had to make his excuses to “gotta get back to call roll.” Edith stood listening to the tanks doing their morning dance and watching Jimmy walk through the compound yard as if he were leaping from cloud to cloud. She had to admit to herself that sometimes she felt like a dwarf standing on a giant’s shoulders.

Chapter 25

Paint-by-Numbers

Judith's eyes welled up with moist pride as Glenn recounted Jimmy's friendship with Edith. She understood why veterans are so silent and how they must keep the silence from destroying them. Glenn sensed Judith's quiet knowledge of her grandfather's locked memories. She had known Jimmy in ways only a loved granddaughter can know, but she also had the experience of sorting through his things after his death. She could understand with both her heart and her head, and this gave Glenn the confidence to say, "Edith is important to you."

"She was important to Granddad, so I've tried to find out everything I can about her."

"She was important to us all, but Jimmy had something special with her."

"It's very clear that she was special to him."

"I don't mean special in that way," and Glenn was embarrassed even to say it.

"I know. Granddad told me they were talking friends and left it at that."

Michael was trying to pull the pieces of the mosaic together. He sat listening intently to Judith and Glenn talk about Edith and Jimmy. Judith speculated, "She affected Granddad very deeply." Their talk was designed to uncover all the missing pieces of someone they loved, but each piece revealed yet another piece. They were trying to make a quilt out of all the jagged little squares of a life.

Glenn thought, "This is just like those 'Paint-by-Numbers' kits you could buy in any drugstore in the sixties." He knew it was just a great marketing ploy, but it was a cheat. Some printer had come up with the great idea that he could get an artist to draw an outline and sell the printed page on cheap canvas. Then all you had to do was paint all the squares and circles with the number of the paint that matched the number inside the shape. In a couple of hours you had "created your very own painting." He'd seen them on kids' walls and been presented with these daubs by proud parents because he was a college professor of art. The parents all wanted his approval, so Glenn had smiled and told them all, "Your child shows real promise." The paintings were nothing but a coloring book with a few tubs of water-based emulsion thrown in to convince the painters they were artists. He had always hated the little plastic envelopes that promised so much and delivered so little. The stark facts of Jimmy's's life and death were like those little blue lines, begging us to "just fill-in the blanks" and all would be revealed. The more they concentrated on the blue lines, the less would be revealed about Jimmy and all the people he had encountered, and it infuriated Glenn.

Judith had all the numbers and all the lines of Granddad's life laid out on the wall and on the tables, but she knew this wasn't the right way to sort and categorize Jimmy's life. This method didn't add up to anything as important as the feeling she remembered of being snuggled in his arms, warm and soft and drowsy on a summer's night. She had all his serial numbers, his driver's numbers, his account numbers, but they were just the borders of his life, not the hidden interiors and that was what she wanted to know.

Bobby was patient. They were going to find out something his father had wanted to keep a secret. It was a bit like listening to your parents when they thought you couldn't hear. And so, he was fascinated by the prospect of finding out the things his father wouldn't tell him. Jimmy had been distant with Bobby, when it came to anything personal. Bobby had accepted this as "Dad's way," but the silences had been a fence between them. Now his own daughter was revealing the father to the son. He was hungry for more.

Glenn made a new start, "You got to remember there was a big change when the garritroopers took over." Judith jumped at a word which would lead into the place in Granddad's life which so intrigued her.

"What's that?" she almost demanded.

"A garritrooper was a soldier who didn't fight. He stayed in the garrison away from the fighting."

"You and Granddad certainly weren't garritroopers."

"No. We were front-line dogfaces. We just got lucky working for Stout and Posey."

The gazes of Bobby, Michael, and Judith converged on Glenn, imploring him to continue, so he tried to explain to them that the garritrooper was "more dangerous to our guys than to the enemy." This was completely new to Bobby and Judith, but Michael nodded his head as if he knew all about such things. Glenn was puzzled by how easily Michael understood the threat of the garritrooper, but continued to describe the heart of the problem.

"Two of them showed up at the Collecting Point. Officers. That was the start of the big trouble. But it was a warning to us for many, many years." Glenn swung his head to see Michael oddly reflective and knew something had hit home. He just couldn't tell what it was.

Chapter 26

Fire Bell in the Night

Wiesbaden, Germany,
MFAA Collecting Point
Landesmuseum.
October 15, 1945

Walter Farmer walked the corridors of the Collecting Point on his first inspection of the day. He followed his morning ritual and slowly paced the long main corridor with his morning coffee, his slow steps echoing along the halls. He would inspect each of the three galleries leading off the corridor, waiting for the workers to arrive. The silence was reassuring because soon the galleries would hum with activity. The daily work was Walter's joy.

Walter loved the routine of petty problems which could so easily merge into a catastrophe, but never did. If a roof leaked, a painting could drip into a pulpy slurry. If the heating system died, frames would crack, and canvases would shrivel. The very dust of centuries could collect into deadly clouds, and one cigarette could explode a whole room. Gangs of DPs armed with brooms, mops, and rags kept the entire building clean and safe. The bald fact that the DPs had work and the means of survival was part of the building's magic. Lightning had been Walter's greatest worry; one straggling cloud could discharge ruin from the air. But this morning, Walter sauntered the clean corridors, gazed at the ceiling, savored his morning coffee, and let his joy rule his anxiety.

The hodge-podge of watertight tiles over the roof was all the proof he needed that "the facility" was precious. The local people had fished the tiles out of their collapsed basements. They would appear with an armful of slate tiles and say, "für unser Museum." Walter had just enough German to know they were speaking of "our" museum. The "our" said that he and all concerned with the preservation of the artwork were somehow connected. They thought of him and the building as "unsere" "ours" and Walter took renewed dedication from their embrace. Somebody else would deliver a load of twenty tiles in a baby carriage to raise the blocks of neatly stacked roofing material inside the compound. German roofers would talk sign language to American engineers, there would be a quick exchange of words and tools, and soon both would be perched on their knees over a beam. A few square yards of roof would be the fruits of their labor. The people told Walter's interpreter they were loaning their roofs to their museum. When Walter asked when he would need to return the borrowed roofs, they always answered, "When we have some walls."

The collections were now safe from any sudden deluge or stray flash of lightning. A company of engineers had rigged up a bizarre web of wires and antennae over the roof. The wires were scrounged from useless telephone poles, and the rods of conductive metal were assorted radio masts from an abandoned radar station. They had draped this contraption over the eaves to catch any bolt. The museum resembled a drunken porcupine inside its wire cage. Form always followed function in Walter's mind, so he accepted the whole hodge-podge as a battle won in the war against disaster.

Safe from nature, Walter had solved the problem of human predators with a squadron of tanks and a company of no-nonsense paratroopers who were glad to have their feet on the ground. Night and day, they patrolled the fences and manned the gate. One scowl would send any thief or casual scrounger scurrying back into the night. A more sophisticated gang of criminals had appreciated the value of the building's contents, but they had seriously misjudged the quality of the night watchmen. The sole survivor of a few burps from a sleepy Thompson was grateful to be charged with grand theft.

The Collecting Point nestled in that lovely quiet between waking and getting out of bed. The workers would arrive in thirty minutes, and the slumber would launch into the steady rhythm of useful work. Walter wandered from gallery to gallery and mulled over the thought that the Landesmuseum of Wiesbaden would have to continue its present duties for some time to come.

Gallery A was a work station with a loading bay and a counter that ran down the center of the entire room. The long row was constructed from tables that had seen better days when they were in a factory cafeteria. Here, German tradesmen, supervised by American art experts, worked from sunrise to sunset. The schedule soon would run twenty-four hours a day.

Trucks would back up to the loading bay ramp, where a team of German DPs would unload everything into trolleys salvaged from the ruins of a department store. They sorted the cargo into packed, damaged, and ruined and then delivered their loads to the tables. Wooden crates would be opened for history students to identify to which century the contents belonged. A painting would be tagged as "19th Century" and put on another trolley. When that trolley was full, a German assistant would trundle the load to Gallery B to run the gauntlet of art historians, insurance adjusters, and artists in khaki. As paintings and sculptures were processed through the human conveyor belt, they were identified from catalogues saved from city bonfires. An archivist would have to make a positive identification from a photograph in the relevant catalogue. An "unknown" would follow the route, guided by Edith's provenance work, until it could be tagged: "Date: 19th Century / Title: *The Angelus* / Artist: Courbet." Walter had created The Collecting Point as an artistic version of a Detroit assembly line, but instead of making cars and tanks, they were saving the past for whatever future they could imagine.

Gallery C was the quietest hive. This was where ownership was researched by the most experienced art historians culled from the auction houses of America and Europe. These people knew the business of art, and their knowledge was crucial to finding the last reported owner of the artifact. They could search through Edith's files to discover who actually owned the thing in front of them. Every painting, statue, drawing, stick of furniture or miniature that journeyed through all three galleries regained its name and an identity and waited to be reunited with its family.

Walter thought of the art as "the orphans of the storm" or DPs, "Displaced Paintings." Thus the human DPs made a living out of returning the artistic DPs to their rightful places. The system was as fool proof as the building was thief proof, for every object inside and every person entering or leaving was double, triple and sometimes quadruple checked. Walter had devised the whole system based on the Shipping and Receiving unit of the department store he had worked in before the war, connecting himself with his past before the war and his hope for a future after it.

Walter paused with the cup poised before his lips and realized he was very much like the paintings, the building, and the DPs seeking future homes and families. His only regret at the moment was that there was no sugar for the coffee. He heard boot steps echo from the distance, and in the crescendo of approaching thumps he recognized the tread of Sgt. Murray. At this time of the morning, Murray's appearance could only mean some trouble at the main entrance. With a smart salute and a "Good Morning, Sergeant" and a "Fine day for a fight, Sir," their formalities were concluded and Murray got down to business. "There are two jokers in the guard house claiming to be officers, but one of them has no identification papers."

"So, you've 'detained them until identification is confirmed.' What's the problem?"

"One of them says he's a colonel here on inspection," Murray said skeptically. "I wasn't told about any inspection."

Walter's eyebrows raised into a question mark, and Murray admitted, "There's something fishy about them."

"You did exactly what you're supposed to do. You say one has I.D.?"

"Yeah. A Major Bonner from the Department of Civil Affairs."

Walter appreciated Murray's conscientiousness. He was a stickler for details, and the men joked, "Johnny would shoot a cockroach without its I.D. card." But it was Murray's nose which so impressed Walter. Murray seemed to have a sixth sense about danger, and a very healthy paranoia. Walter had decided Murray could smell trouble because he was a tanker. "If I were trapped in a steel box filled with gasoline and ammunition, I'd turn psychic," Walter had said to himself. Trusting to Murray's unseen powers, Walter turned to lead him down the corridor. "Let's go to the office. I think I have something on them."

They walked back past the main hall to Walter's office, and he flipped through a clipboard of official looking documents until his thumb rested on a letter. "This came last week. It says two officers, yes, a Major Bonner and a Colonel Schwartz would be here today for a consultation, whatever that is. We better see what they want."

Murray stood fidgeting with his belt buckle. "They want to be away from here. They're a real 'Mutt and Jeff' routine."

"Which one's Jeff?" Walter asked with a grin to break the tension.

"Bonner. He's about half the size of the other one."

"What about Mutt?"

"Mutt is miffed because I wouldn't let him in."

"Where are they?"

"I put them both in the guard house with Mulvaney standing at the door to make sure they're 'not disturbed.'"

"Good. Let's not keep our guests waiting."

They walked out of the main entrance, marched down the steps, and threaded their way through parked trucks to the little hut beside the gate which doubled as a Guard House and shack for the patrol. Walter and Murray entered to see the major standing at about five feet four inches and barely controlling his impatience. The colonel was sitting in a chair, and from the mirror tips of his handstitched shoes to his expensive and unstained field cap, he was six feet four inches of lazy annoyance. Jimmy was standing "At Ease" beside them as if waiting for a child to finish its sulk. Mutt was oozing irritation, and after a quick glance at the captain's bars on Walter's shoulders, glowered pique. The glancing reminder of rank did not escape Walter, so he just stood there, silently counting to ten and letting Jimmy and Murray percolate.

Farmer saw the thousand-yard stare in Jimmy's eyes. He slowly turned his head to scan the line of soldiers standing around the entrance. The men guarding these two officers were seething in silent and righteous contempt. Neat uniforms and square haircuts were the badges of the garritroopers. They were postal clerks, cooks, secretaries, or anyone attached to an HQ. Serious gunfire was beyond their hearing, but they affected the style of the front-line soldier. Two months previously, Murray had been delivering reports to an Intelligence Officer ten miles behind the lines, and the officer's snotty manner prompted Murray to offer the man his helmet. "What's this for?" he demanded in a superior tone. Murray was stone-faced in his reply, "I'm about to fart and I didn't want to frighten you." Nobody could quite put his finger on the source of their hatred, but the garritrooper's breezy air of superiority caused universal anger. Wearing the same uniform as a dogface without facing the same dangers was the insult.

When a garritrooper was found with a .45-inch hole in his head, the men just passed it off as a flesh wound. Patton had once jibed they could finish the war in a week, if he could only convince the men that every German was a garritrooper. The officers were the worst because they had rank without risk. They were all sticklers for protocol and regulation and would demand a salute from anything that could wave an elbow. Jimmy's stare said it all. He had earned his safe job with Stout by surviving the horror. Farmer could practically hear "Vultures" and "Flock of Fuck Ups" ticking in Jimmy's brain and in the stances of the Guard Squad. Dogfaces with rifles and Vultures waving paper in a confined space was a deadly mix. Farmer smelled the type of trouble that ended with your back to a wall staring down twelve rifles aimed at the paper pinned to your chest. He would have to get the two visitors out of the guard house before it exploded.

"Colonel Schwartz, I presume, I am Captain. Farmer." Walter offered his hand. Schwartz looked at the outstretched hand with such contempt that Walter continued the motion of his handshake into a salute.

"You are in charge of this facility?" Schwartz asked, without bothering to use Walter's name or rank. Condescension dripped from Schwartz's tongue and oozed from his relaxed manner. Walter decided that two could play this game and omitted the customary "Sir."

"That is correct. I have a letter identifying a Major Bonner and a Colonel Schwartz. Sergeant Murray has confirmed Major Bonner's identity, and I must ask Major Bonner to vouch for Colonel Schwartz."

Schwartz wriggled in the awkward silence of waiting for an inferior to confirm his identity.

"I can confirm this person is Colonel Schwartz," Bonner said.

"Thank you, Sir. A mere formality but a necessary one, considering the value of the contents of this facility. Would you please follow me?"

Schwartz stretched himself out of the chair to his full height and waited for Bonner to open the door for him. They paraded past the guards' glares into the courtyard. Walter snaked them through the trucks, retracing his path to the front door. Behind them, the guard house erupted into a hubbub of laughs and chortles.

Walter eased Schwartz into conversation. "The letter from Head Quarters stated that you would be visiting us for a consultation."

"You and I will discuss matters pertaining to the Civil Government, but Major Bonner has a different mission."

"I am here to inspect your fire precautions and evacuation procedures," Bonner stated.

The "consultation" had become a "discussion" and then an "inspection." Walter was always suspicious when "orders" slithered through a variety of meanings, and there was a hint of danger lurking beneath Walter's unease. These two were in charge of something indefinite, but their manner proclaimed that Walter would have to do whatever they said. This vagueness was worrying because Walter knew that indefinite suggestions soon became very definite problems. He ushered them into the building and stood in the main corridor for an impromptu lecture on the Collecting Point.

Walter continued with his guided tour. "Our main objective is to identify works of art and match them with their owners. When caches of looted art are discovered, they are brought here. Our experts carry out the initial work and then dispatch the objects to holding facilities for return to the owners."

"I am told you have Germans working here," Schwartz said.

Schwartz spoke in a slow Southern drawl, and Walter had to turn an ear to understand what he was saying. Bonner was also Southern but had a nasal twang which sounded like razor blades cutting paper. Walter was accustomed to Southern accents and had come to appreciate the speakers by working with them. He was free of the usual prejudices of Ohioans because the Southerners he had met in Cincinnati had been customers who'd had the sense to follow his advice. Besides, the soldiers of the 373rd Engineering Battalion were no-nonsense people who just got on with the job and shared their pride with all who worked. It was one of the most endearing features of the Dixie people. They could accept others in mutual labor and in the pride of a job well done. But Schwartz and Bonner gave him no such respect.

Walter led them through Gallery A, and while he was explaining how the shipments were processed, Schwartz and Bonner wandered around the room almost completely ignoring him. Their behavior was intentional ignorance, and Walter had to raise his voice to follow their wanderings. He heard his own echoes and felt like he was delivering a sermon in an empty church. Their casual disregard of him was as infuriating as it was laughable. Their manner said "We are too important to listen to you and you are so insignificant that you must listen to us." There was not a thing he could do about it.

Schwartz wandered along the table peering into empty crates and stopped in front of a pile of material almost as tall as himself.

With a curving index finger, he beckoned Walter, who hid his rising bile behind a cheesy smile. "Could you explain to me just what is the purpose of these filthy rags?" Schwartz demanded.

"We use them for packing material. They are strips torn from German overcoats, and we wrap them around canvases to protect the frames during shipment."

"See that they are cleaned."

Schwartz turned on his heel and strode down the other side of the table. He stopped and peered into a bucket half filled with water as if he were staring down a well. "I was under the impression that this building was equipped with a new roof?"

"Yes, it is," Walter said, "We were able to seal the roof last month. This has been a major accomplishment in these economic conditions."

"Yet I see you have placed buckets around this room to collect rain drips. Please explain yourself."

"The buckets do not collect water from the roof, which is two stories above us. They are used to disperse humidity. We half fill the buckets so they won't tip over so easily. We have to keep the humidity at a constant level to protect the paintings. They are very susceptible to changes in atmosphere. The pails also double as fire buckets, although they have never been needed for that purpose."

Schwartz's finger ordered Bonner to join them, and he scurried to their side.

"This officer claims the buckets are part of the fire prevention program," Schwartz said.

Bonner was a walking catalogue of army regulations. He gave the impression he had memorized the whole set of Orders and Regulations, American Forces (European Theater of Operations). Bonner was happy to share the latest regulations with anyone who had to listen to him. "You may not be aware that we have recently replaced water in fire buckets with sand. This is much better for smothering fires and does not have to be changed as does water. Much more effective."

"We need the water to control the humidity," explained Walter.

"Then place them beside the walls where they won't be tripped over. Place other buckets with sand along the walls to be used in case of fire," Bonner ordered.

There seemed to be no way of actually talking with Bonner. He was fixated on "fire precautions" and so could not actually take in what Walter was saying. It was like trying to toilet train a very spoiled child. He tried to reason anyway. "But the water buckets have to be distributed throughout the area so the whole room can be properly and evenly humidified. Such humidity control is essential for the preservation of the artworks."

"Well, that's your problem. I have to insist that the fire buckets be filled with sand and placed against the wall. Humidity is your concern; my mission is to ensure the safety of this building."

Walter was as immobile as one of the statues, as much in shock as fury. He was trying to process the ignorance of these two hicks. There was no reasoning with them and he started to doubt they were capable of rational thought. They simply could not understand what he was doing because they would not listen. He remembered how he had dealt with wealthy clients at the Closson Company back in Cincinnati and decided to smile and agree with everything they said, no matter how stupid. The customer was always right, until they paid. He got the feeling Schwartz and Bonner would never be satisfied, so his function was to be as pleasant as possible until they were clear of the building.

Bonner immediately returned Walter's smile because he thought it was a sign of submission. He launched into his report. "I'm afraid to tell you that I have discovered fifteen infringements of the fire regulations in this area."

"I'm dreadfully sorry," Walter said, "and I assure you that I will take all steps necessary to conform to the code of fire regulations. Could you tell me specifically what is to be done?"

"The most immediate concern is the lack of an alarm system."

"What would you suggest?"

"I think a bell is the most appropriate system for this classification of building."

“Could we not designate someone as the Fire Monitor?” Walter suggested.

“I have found that this is not a very efficient way of alerting to fire danger.”

“Couldn’t the Fire Monitor be organized into a Fire Patrol?”

Bonner stoked his chin while thinking of an objection to Walter’s suggestion, “Such patrols take too long for word to spread. By the time everybody knows there is a fire, the whole place has gone up in smoke.”

“Yes, I see your point,” Walter admitted, “The fire spreads quicker than the warning.”

“Precisely. But I like your idea of a Fire Patrol. Please take steps to organize an internal fire brigade to contain the fire until the local fire department can deal with the situation.”

Walter did not point out that there was no local fire department because it had been burned out in the last bombing raid. Bonner seemed to think that he was still in an American city and wondered if Bonner had ever looked out a window since arriving in Germany.

“Ah yes,” Walter said, “we must address the problem of yelling ‘Fire!’ in a crowded building.”

“My point exactly.” Bonner agreed, happy that Walter was understanding the seriousness of the situation, “That is why a bell is the very thing. Do you have one?”

“As a matter of fact, I don’t. We are in very short supply of bells in the art world.”

“Yes, and banging one of water buckets wouldn’t do much good.”

“But where shall we find a bell?” Walter mused.

“I have a report of a large supply of confiscated church bells in Hamburg.”

“Hamburg? But how would I ever get a bell from so far away?”

“I would be more than happy to have my secretary arrange for delivery.”

"That is most kind of you Major. What other infringements of the code have you observed?"

"There is no fire escape and there is only one main entrance. If you would open the loading bays at both ends of this corridor then there would be three exits for the efficient evacuation of the building."

"You know, you are right," Walter admitted, and Bonner smiled. "We are in great need of efficient evacuation," Walter confessed.

Bonner sensed insubordination in Walter's tone, and the amiability evaporated.

"I will put this in Daily Orders," Walter added without a smile, "and instruct the troops to keep the loading bay doors open at all times."

Open doors at each end of the building would form a perfect wind tunnel. Any flame would quickly be fanned into a conflagration, and the entire treasure trove would spiral ashes to the sky. Walter decided to defy Bonner's open door policy.

Bonner offered Walter an Army Regulation form, as if he were conferring a diploma at graduation. "I have checked off the other relatively minor infringements on this form. My main concerns are the fire bell and the fire escape."

"When do you expect this work to be completed?"

"Two weeks from the delivery of the bell will be adequate," Bonner instructed.

"That is very kind of you," Walter smiled.

Schwartz was impatient to get out of Work Station A, so Walter guided him back to the office. Even if it meant dealing with Schwartz, Walter was glad to get rid of Bonner. Schwartz peered at Walter and said, "I presume that you have received your orders from the Headquarters of the Civil Government Administration."

"All I have received is an announcement of your consultation."

"The appropriate paperwork will be delivered to you in due course. You can then start your selection."

"What selection?" Walter asked with confusion.

"Your selection of paintings," Schwartz replied.

Walter was confused, for nobody had mentioned anything about a selection. The only time they selected a single piece was when it needed emergency repairs. He had to repeat to Schwartz the mission of the Collecting Point. "In this facility, we do not select. We collect and identify looted art so it can be returned to its rightful owners."

"Well, you will soon be identifying for a collection for Civil Affairs," Schwartz informed him.

Walter stood rigid, trying to decipher what Schwartz was saying and wondering if Schwartz himself knew what he was talking about. Schwartz broke the awkward silence, "I am told this facility houses mainly German art. Is that correct?"

"Yes, but about ten percent of the material belongs to countries other than Germany."

"Ten percent is no matter. Washington is not interested in those items."

Schwartz let the name hover in the air. Walter was adept at dealing with the army at battalion level, but Schwartz was insinuating levels of command far above his own rank of colonel. Walter felt the combined weight of Regiment, Division, Corps, and Army Group press down upon him. But Schwartz had added the vague and distant "Washington" to the pile, to intimidate Walter.

"Washington?" Walter asked.

"Yes. There is going to be an exhibition of German paintings in Washington."

"This is the first I have heard of any such exhibition."

"Well, I am now informing you of the exhibition."

"I don't see what this has to do with me."

"You are to choose a couple hundred of the best examples for shipment to the U.S."

"Shipment?" Walter asked, stunned.

"For the exhibition in Washington. German pictures are to be in that exposition, and they must be shipped from Germany. From here."

"But these are all the property of German museums."

"You will find the State Department does not share your opinion. You are in charge of the selection. We expect this order to be fulfilled in the coming month."

Schwartz was enjoying Walter's confusion and discomfort. He liked to drop the names of people he had never met and to forge connections to higher authority when dealing with subordinates. He had casually mentioned "State Department" to goad this little captain into action and to remind Walter that Schwartz was familiar with people in high places. Walter adamantly stated, "Mounting exhibitions is not the mission of this facility."

"This is a warehouse of confiscated material and you are in charge of this place," Schwartz said.

"I can't do that," Walter protested, "We are not organized to -"

"I act on the authority of the Civil Affairs Department," Schwartz interrupted, "and you will do this on my authority. With your orders you will receive a list of different kinds of art. All that is required of you is to find suitable items in your warehouse and crate them for delivery."

Walter stood speechless. Whatever Schwartz was now ordering went against Walter's duty as a soldier and his character as a man. Walter straightened his back and said, "It is impossible."

"Anything from higher authority is possible," Schwartz assured Walter. "What is impossible is to disobey those orders," he threatened.

"I have received no such orders," Walter affirmed.

"You will."

Schwartz had nothing left to say. He turned on his heel so Walter would be in no doubt the consultation was over. He strode toward the exit, and Bonner held the door open for him. Walter guided them back through the compound to the main gate.

Walter thought again of Mutt and Jeff because they looked so comical. Then he remembered the cartoon characters were also insane. Schwartz and Bonner could not be forgotten when you turned from the funny papers to the sports page.

They approached the main entrance just in time to see Murray's guards searching the staff car. Schwartz looked down at the gaping trunk, his rheumy eyes contracted in disdain, and quietly demanded, "What is the meaning of this?" Murray's tone was as even as a gun sight and he explained. "All vehicles leaving this facility are to be searched."

"And have you found any contraband?" Schwartz asked.

"Only a bag of golf clubs, which I presume are your personal property, Sir."

"You assumed these belong to me."

"This facility is not a golf course, Sir."

The men sniggered behind their rifles as Schwartz thrust himself into the back seat. Bonner sat nervously behind the steering wheel as he put the car in gear and drove through the gate. Walter did not dare to look at any of the guards, for the men were already calling the visitors "Stringbean and the Boner." Walter was both relieved and worried as he watched the staff car disappear into the morning fog.

Murray was offering him something brown, and Walter's fingers caressed a half full paper bag folded into a tight little package. It was a relief to deal with something tangible after all the hints and threats that had drooled out of Schwartz. Walter opened the bag to see the sparkling diamond dust of real sugar and had to ask Murray "Where did you get this?"

"It's only a half bag."

"Where's the other half?" Walter asked.

"Poured it into their gas tank."

Chapter 27

Grumble

Laughter greeted the end of Glenn's tale. He looked at Michael and saw that he was seething. "I really hate such people," Michael said. Judith was disgusted by the garritrooper officers and said, "I've seen that type in every job I've had." Michael was quick to agree. "Yeah. Give them a title and a mission statement and they become little kings." Glenn was surprised by their bitterness and wondered at their indignation .

Bobby was amused for he had learned to leave his resentments in the past. He had retired from the NYPD after twenty-five years and was very used to the garritrooper boss. His father had taught him to laugh at fools. When Bobby had come home in his first patrol car, Jimmy pointed to the sign painted on the car door, "Courtesy-Professionalism-Respect." Jimmy shook with laughter, and Bobby learned to be silently critical of authority. Whenever he received anything under an official letterhead, he always read between the lines. Bobby's pension was his liberation, and the rest of his working life was spent "doing the business" with his father. Jimmy had always treated him well and frequently warned Bobby, "expect to get the respect you give."

Bobby looked at Judith and Michael and explained, "I guess now you know a little bit better why Dad was always working for himself." But Bobby knew Jimmy in the taxis or Dad in the junkyard had always worked twelve-hour days for them.

Judith and Glenn shared their experiences of colleges, and Judith had a sharper tongue than Glenn wanted to acknowledge. When she spoke of lazy professors, she railed against their affectations of superiority. "You never learn anything from them and they're supposed to be so intelligent." Glenn understood her resentment and shared the disappointment. Glenn had half a century of anecdotes about PhDs whose degrees really meant

"Piled Higher and Deeper." He could have wasted the entire evening telling tales of college stupidity and insanity in the high places of institutions, but this night was for Michael and Judith, so he held his tongue and was glad of it.

Instead, Glenn told them about the man who invented blood banks, Charles Drew. Drew was a medical genius who devised the whole system of blood donation and plasma transportation. "He was so good at his research that he saved millions of lives, right on the front lines." Judith was enthralled by the tale of a man who had fought with his mind. "Drew was Black and he refused to segregate the blood, so they fired him from the Red Cross," Glenn said.

Michael hung on every contradiction. He grunted, "Typical," and Judith asked if Drew actually had resigned in protest. "I don't think so," Glenn replied, "because they said they just didn't need his services any more. Why anybody would throw away such talent and promise is beyond me." Michael was barely controlling his rage. "That's because the work doesn't mean a damn thing to them."

Glenn wanted to cut to the main point quickly, so he told them about the radio programs Drew broadcast after the war. "It was when there was a lot of talk about integration in the army that I really listened to him. Drew said the problem was 'small minds' and the bigger problem was when people were promoted, they took their 'small minds to high places.' That's what really pissed us off about Stringbean and the Boner. You couldn't argue with them because you couldn't reason with them."

Judith had been mulling the garritrooper mentality over in her mind, when Michael asked, "So what do you do when the boss is such an asshole?"

"Stand up to him." was Glenn's firm answer.

"Easier said than done." countered Michael.

Glenn saw that Judith was itching to something and nodded to her. "I think I know what you're talking about," she said. "I found a paper which looks like it was standing up to a bad thing."

"What paper?" asked Glenn.

She stood and strode over to the sideboard. Michael watched her open a drawer and pull out a new plastic file. She had the paper on the top, and Glenn saw she knew exactly where to find it. Bobby leaned forward from his chair and said, "Yeah, Glenn, I was wondering about that piece of paper." Judith was very confident handling the sheet. It seemed to him that she was familiar with whatever she was offering him, but perplexed by its significance. Bobby was more forthright. "I've read that thing five maybe even six times and I can't make hide nor hair of it."

Glenn stretched forth to receive the paper and read the date aloud, "November 7, 1945." He knew exactly what it was. "Where did you find this?" he asked Judith.

"In a cornflakes box," she simply said.

Glenn slumped back into the easy chair holding the paper firmly in his fingers. He looked into each of their expectant eyes and hung on Michael's gaze a little longer. He almost whispered to them all. "You want to know about standing up? This piece of paper is standing up to everything and for everything. This is the Manifesto."

Chapter 28

Manifesto

Wiesbaden, Germany,
MFAA Collecting Point
November 6 - 7, 1945

Walter held the piece of paper like a thing infected. The courier stood before him, watching Walter's face flush as he read the order. With each delivery, the courier had grown to like this fussy officer, who never treated him as an inferior. Today he regretted having to deliver this bad news, whatever it was. Walter peered through his glasses at the courier's grimy face and almost begged, "H.Q. wants me to sign for this?" The courier scraped his goggles over his helmet and fumbled in his dispatch bag for yet another piece of paper. His shoulders shrugged in apology as he said, "Yes, Sir. They were very clear that you must sign this receipt."

Walter scowled at the letter in his left hand and blinked at the receipt form. He went for his fountain pen as if he were pulling a pistol out of a shoulder holster. Over the past three months, he had routinely signed consignment orders for hundreds of crates of artwork worth millions of dollars, but he had never been ordered to sign an official receipt for a single piece of paper. This was a deliberate insult, which he suspected was added to some yet unknown injury. He signed, very deliberately and legibly, so as to contain his anger within his neat penmanship. The courier took the receipt along with Walter's smile, which said, "I don't shoot messengers." He saluted, turned on his heel, and hurried back to his motorcycle parked at the Guard House.

Walter felt the rage surging within him. He reminded himself that the courier "was only following orders, just like I am supposed to follow these infernal orders." He walked slowly past the three galleries and took comfort in the hum of honest work oozing from each room. He had to talk this over with Edith if he were not to explode.

Edith's eyebrows steepled into a question mark over her glasses as Walter offered her the paper. "Mutt and Jeff are no longer funny," he said. She sensed Walter's wrath and was both surprised and secretly delighted he could get rip-roaring mad. She scanned the document, immediately identified the source of the problem, and asked. "The Col. Schwartz, who signed this order, is the same buffoon who visited us two weeks ago?" Walter blurted, "Yes. And that other one, Bonner."

She read aloud in mock falsetto, "'From 7th US Army to Office Mil. Govt. for Stadtkreis Wiesbaden.' So this is an order from the Army but it is also a policy statement from the civilian government." Walter jumped to confirm her growing suspicion. "Yup. From both the military and civilian administrations." Edith mused while sucking the leg of her glasses.

Their minds searched for the meaning of the order, which Edith had dropped on her desk through fingers of contempt. "From war to peace via Mutt and Jeff," she giggled. Walter could only muster a wry smile, so Edith talked over his frustration. "Sergeant Murray and the boys were right about that pair, but this is much more serious than fire regulations and some officious non-entity looking for non-existent holes in the roof."

Out of habit, she began smoothing out the folds and creases of the order. She read aloud to Walter, "Higher headquarters 'desiges,' d-e-s-i-g-e-s, that immediate preparations be made for prompt shipment to UNITEK of a selection of at least two zero zero German works of art of greatest importance." She wrinkled her nose to say, "They can't even spell 'designs,' but they are very sure that we must make 'immediate preparations' and that we be 'prompt' about it. They want two hundred works of art."

"Not just anything we have lying around," said Walter, "but two zero zero of 'German' works of 'the greatest importance.'" Her white knuckles scraped out the paper's ridges from the center to the edges. Edith talked as her balled hand rubbed the letter, "Schwartz said he would send us a list." Walter snorted "They don't even know what they want." Edith held her anger, "So, we are to make the selection for them." With each stroke of her fist over the order, the seriousness of their situation became frighteningly clear. "This is no ordinary order."

"The first time I have ever seen such a thing," sighed Walter.

"But it won't be the last," Edith asserted. "This is just the beginning."

Edith became very sympathetic and looked at him with as much concern as comfort through her thick glasses. "You look like you're about to cry."

"It just seems to me that everything that we have done here to show the world the integrity of the United States will be discredited if this shipment takes place."

Edith had reached the same conclusion but thought, "Walter has to say this for Walter, but we all have to first understand what this means and then act." She took command, and Walter was happy to give her control of the situation, since he could barely control himself. "This is no time for weeping," she assured him.

"What will we do? What can we do? These are not suggestions or consultations. This is a military order."

"We have to have a pow-wow," she said with a mischievous glint in her glasses.

"When?" Walter asked.

"Tomorrow." Edith replied, with the confidence of the smartest girl in school.

Edith pulled open a squealing drawer and grabbed a sheaf of papers. "I created this little phonebook because I have to talk with the seekers in the field."

"The phone lines are not reliable," Walter said.

"It's all we have. With a little prodding, I have been able to make connections all over Germany, and even into darkest Belgium. We can contact as many field officers as possible and have most of them here in the morning."

They knew this order was not just the tip of the iceberg, but the tip of the spear, and it was pointed right at them. There were other things going on behind the scenes which they knew nothing about. There was talk in "high places" where they would never go, and that whispering of the powerful was behind this unmistakably clear order. Walter and Edith both knew how the system worked.

There would be casual talk over tall drinks and fat cigars, and somebody would come up with a "good idea." The idea would gain attention or respect for its originator and there was always government money to put the good idea into practice. The money cascaded through the chain of command until it became a policy. The casual suggestion in a smoke-filled room would slither down the ladder of ranks to become an order. Ignoring an order could ruin your career; challenging it could cost your life. Such pieces of paper were terrifying.

Walter's fear fought with his rage until he said, "You know what this means." Edith calmly replied, "Yes. It means a court martial in time of war." Walter whispered, "That means a firing squad."

They sat staring at the paper, almost begging it to disappear, but it refused to leave. Edith said, "We'll have to make all these calls today. Right now. The men will have to be informed today. If they are going to get here tomorrow, they must start their journeys today."

"There just isn't enough time or telephones," Walter protested.

"We have three telephones here. One in the guardhouse and another in the workshop."

"If they're working," Walter added. "Two of us can't man five phones, even if they are connected."

Edith looked almost coquettish as her eyebrows dragged narrowed eyes of defiance over her glasses, "Bring in Murray and his helpers."

Johnny sat with his hands behind his neck listening to Walter and Edith. They had worked themselves into a panic about "not enough telephones," and "time's running out," and "this is very important." Johnny was a thorough gentleman, so he wouldn't interrupt a lady, even if she was having an attack of verbal diarrhea. He couldn't find a hole through Edith's words and wondered how the woman could breathe and talk at the same time. He noticed Walter sweating, so whatever they wanted had to be serious. When he couldn't stand it any more, he leaned forward, framed his face in his hands and almost shouted, "What's the big problem?"

Walter explained they had to convene a meeting of all the Monuments Men for tomorrow. Since the surrender, more teams had been deployed, but they were scattered all over Germany, France, and Belgium. Johnny looked at Edith, who told him, "We don't have enough telephones to contact them all." His eyes darted between them and he said, "Then use the radio." Edith and Walter fell silent and their heads tilted at Johnny as if they were curious birds. "Those little things you carry around won't work. What are they called? Oh yes, the 'walkie and the talkie.'"

Johnny realized she didn't know the first thing about army communications and was gentle with his explanation. "A 'Walkie-Talkie' and a 'Handie-Talkie' are different radios." Edith was eager for more, "So, what's the difference?" Johnny was concise. "You carry the 'Walkie-Talkie' strapped to your back. The 'Handie-Talkie' is what we use on patrol in the compound."

"But those things can't talk all over Europe."

"Of course not. They have a range of three miles."

"Then they won't help us."

"But I know a man who can." Johnny assured them.

Edith and Walter sat enthralled, listening to Johnny explain the radio system. "From the tank turret, I can talk to a squadron of four tanks, but I have a commander's set, which will communicate with the company. From the company signals net, I can be connected to the regiments, and from regiment to division, and then all the way to anywhere in the Army."

Walter was aware they didn't have much time and said, "It will take too long to have each message delivered all the way up the chain of command and then down to the individual Monuments Man." Johnny smiled and enjoyed informing them of the relay system. "We set up the radios so the message is automatically relayed through the whole system. Click, click on the handset and the operator at division knows what we want to do."

"You mean you can talk to anybody from your tank?" Edith asked incredulously.

"Yup," Johnny assured her. "It's like a big beehive. We just jump from cell to cell until we get to the right bee. We got a friend at Division Signals who can get you to the local operator anywhere in the States for five dollars."

Edith grinned her relief to Johnny, and Walter asked, "How long will it take?" Johnny was not going to play games with their worries and rose from his chair, "Let's do it right now."

They followed him out of the building and gathered in a huddle with Jimmy and Glenn at the bow of Johnny's tank. He scootled up the hull and disappeared down the turret hatch. The driver's hatch creaked open in front of Edith's face, and she saw Johnny talking into a handset. "Yeah. Jake? Gotta get messages through to Corp and Army Group levels." Walter heard the distant squelching of Jake's voice and Johnny telling him, "No time to haggle. Gotta do it now." Johnny poked his head and shoulders through the hatch and told Jimmy and Glenn, "Fire up the sets. He's going to open the lines." They led Walter and Edith to two other tanks and repeated the process, until they were all able to talk with radio operators all over the American Zone.

Glenn and Jimmy told Edith they didn't like giving orders to officers, so Walter prepared a message for them to deliver and said, "This way, I'm giving the orders." Now that honor was served and asses were covered, Glenn, Jimmy, and Johnny made the radios crackle all over the zone and informed the teams, "You will report to Collecting Point, Wiesbaden, tomorrow, 11-07-45 at 0900 hours to discuss orders from Headquarters. By Command, W. I. Farmer, Captain."

Jimmy, Johnny, and Glenn knew that Edith and Walter were "stirring some shit," and were honored to help. Edith looked at each of the three tanks and said, "Knights in steel steeds riding to this lady's rescue." Walter knew those radio messages were crossing some line drawn in the sand. Edith's gaze followed the antenna swaying in the breeze above Johnny's turret and said, "We must have a chat with Jake." Walter turned to Edith and the determination in her narrowed eyes gave him confidence. He nodded gratefully and simply said, "Indeed."

That evening Edith strolled around the compound until she met Johnny. He liked the way she would bump into him and was always prepared to do her a favor. He was curious when she asked, "Can I make a private call?" He led her to the command tank, pulled a black overall out the driver's hatch, and said, "Put this on. You'll ruin your clothes with all the grease." Edith stepped into the legs, and Johnny pulled up the back for her to slide her arms into the sleeves. Edith had the odd sensation of a man dressing her. She liked it. He ran up the front of the tank, turned back, and bent over to stretch out his arm. He told her, "Put your right foot on the tread and give me your left hand." Edith raised her hand, and Johnny pulled her up. Johnny grabbed the base of the gun barrel and swung himself up to the turret. He knelt and Edith felt the power in his hand dragging her up.

They stood before the oily open circle of the turret hatch. Edith looked into it as if it were a wishing well and said, "It's rather roomy inside." Johnny pointed out the tank's features like a car salesman. She listened to Johnny talk of the bow, deck, turret, and stern. Then she remembered a tank had originally been called a "land battleship" and giggled like a girl. Johnny dropped himself through the hatch, and tuned the radio. He told Edith to "sit on the hatch cover." She sat with her rump on the open cover and her legs dangling into the turret. She could see Johnny holding an earphone and talking into a handset. He raised his head and asked, "What's the name?" Edith bent down, twisted her head under the armor-plated ceiling, and said, "Charles Parkhurst. He's a Navy Lieutenant at HQ in Berlin." Johnny's voice was quiet and strangely distant when she heard him say, "Yeah. It's Parkhurst. Navy Louie. First name Charles... Berlin." Johnny pulled off the earpiece and whispered up to Edith, "This may take a while."

Edith sat patiently on her steel cushion, happy for the silence, drinking in the November chills. The sky was cobalt blue, and she imagined the night weaving silver stars on a magic loom. She looked down at Johnny talking into the handset and for a moment she was a little girl again sitting on Telegraph Hill in Halifax when the night sky swirled around her. She heard Johnny's voice, gently haggling with Jake, and knew this was extra work he didn't need. He was so solicitous of her, and this call was just the latest in his string of little kindnesses. She appreciated him more than she could say.

Johnny pulled himself over Edith's knees and out of the hatch. He offered her the handset and gently placed the earphones around her head. Johnny heard Parkhurst's voice, "Hello?, Hello?... Is that you, Edith?" He stepped away from her to the side of the turret, turned to say, "I'll leave you to your call," and jumped off the side of the hull. Edith spoke into the handset, "Yes, Charles. I'm here." She was listening to Charles but watching Johnny walk out of range of hearing. He stopped about twenty yards away to light a cigarette, and she realized he was standing guard over her privacy. Parkhurst's voice, dripping with anger, called her back to business and she told him, "Yes. We got their order today."

The next morning a very unusual gathering of jeeps, motorcycles, civilian cars, and a reconditioned ambulance assembled at the Collecting Point. Johnny Murray had positioned his tank twenty yards into the courtyard to form an obstruction. Each vehicle was stopped by four particularly attentive guards before being moved forward to be halted by the gun on Johnny's tank. Johnny had called out the entire guard squad and drilled them into an impressive display of security. He flagged every other vehicle to the left or right where Glenn and Jimmy waited for the visitors.

When five officers were present, either Glenn or Jimmy would escort them into the building and guide them to Gallery A. Glenn and Jimmy were told to stagger their escorts, so Edith and Walter could greet each contingent as they arrived. From his turret-top perch, Johnny observed each "little gaggle of geniuses" and was satisfied the armament and I.D. checks had impressed them all with the seriousness of the situation.

Edith had organized this reception procedure because not everybody would arrive at the same time. This would give Walter the opportunity to introduce the reason for the meeting. The reception was like the start of an academic conference, where new friends and old enemies would socialize before they got down to business.

By 1000 hours, thirty-two Monuments Men were gathered and seated in a semicircle facing Edith and Walter. They came from all the collecting points, from Munich, Frankfort, and Offenbach, and from assignments much further afield. The radio net had gathered as many as could be reached. Gallery A was a din of gossipy guffaws punctuated by clattering coffee cups and gesticulating pipe stems. Johnny, Jimmy, and Glenn led the last group of officers to arrive into the room, and lingered at the back of the crowd to see what was going on. Walter was reminded of private exhibitions of new merchandise, but Jimmy could recall heavyweight prize fights which oozed the same atmosphere of uncertainty, expectation, and high stakes.

Johnny signaled to Jimmy and Glenn it was time for the enlisted men to leave the officers to whatever they were up to. Edith saw them heading for the door and knew they would know everything before the meeting ended. She commanded them to halt with her pleasant, "And just where do you think you're going?" Johnny indicated this was not the place for them, but Edith dismissed his etiquette. "Sit down and join us. It will save your back bending over the spyhole you carved through the rear wall." Johnny, Jimmy and Glenn smiled at Edith's invitation and obeyed her order to "sit" with the eagerness of puppies sensing it was time to play. They sat on the extreme right of the group and waited for the first bell.

Walter and Edith were the masters of this ceremony. He hammered on his cup with a pen. The tinkling soared over the chatter and brought all to attention. "We've called you here to discuss an order from H.Q.," Walter intoned. "Order" and "discuss" got their undivided attention. These two concepts didn't match. No one ever discussed orders.

Edith chimed in. "We have been ordered to select two hundred German paintings to be shipped to Washington."

"Ordered?" one incredulous officer asked suspiciously.

"Yes, ordered," Edith affirmed

"Have there been any explanations of this extraordinary order?"

"Orders are, as you well realize, orders," Walter said, "and our response, it seems, is not to reason why."

"There have been dark threats," Edith said.

"Oh, ours is but to do or die," laughed one feeble joker in the crowd.

The audience didn't laugh. They went very quiet as the enormity of what they were considering started to sink in. They breathed together like a leaky organ trying to belt out a delicate chord. A sigh escaped because they were too afraid to gasp.

Parkhurst stood up holding his hat in his hand. His voice was strong and seethed with outraged contempt. The naval uniform stood in sharp contrast to the green of his colleagues. Parkhurst was waving his arm, and his blue hat made stabbing gestures to emphasize his points. Walter was listening to Parkhurst's lecture but looked at the Navy cap-badge hovering in the air. He was watching the eagle spread its wings around the union shield and realized that it had recently been polished. It looked like the headlight of a locomotive. Parkhurst's voice rose out of the blur, said, "Something like that has been suggested. I was ordered to accompany the 'shipment' back to the States."

"And just who gave you these orders?" a voice called from the back.

"Schwartz, that political busybody from Civilian Affairs. You may not have heard, but he has been appointed to the board of the National Gallery in Washington."

"So what's he doing here?" A British voice demanded.

"Shopping," Parkhurst said.

"When do you leave?" asked a serious looking young man.

"I don't," Parkhurst said adamantly, "I told him to go to Hell. I refused to have anything to do with his smash and grab game."

"This Schwartz didn't clap you in irons?" asked a shocked voice.

"He wanted to, but as you see, I lived to tell about it," Parkhurst joked, but his smile disappeared when he said, "So must we."

The reflective silence was oppressive. Nobody spoke, and each digested the poison they had just heard. If they did as Parkhurst suggested, they could kiss their careers good bye. Nobody wanted to grasp the nettle. If they followed Parhurst's lead, they could lose everything. One croaky voice slipped out of the silence to say, "There will be consequences." Another voice bleated, "But this is an order and we must obey orders."

There was safety in obedience and relief in clearly stating that orders had to be obeyed. Captain Everett Lesley bellowed above the hubbub. He raised the debate to a higher plane than self interest and said, "This sounds much too familiar for comfort." A thoughtful silence blanketed the room.

Edith and Walter were champing at the bit to confirm just how "familiar" this order was. Walter clarified the problem, "We are being ordered to ship these paintings stateside." Edith caught the scent and added, "We are to do this for the 'safekeeping' of the art." She let her words seep through their silence and almost whispered, "The very word the Nazis used to justify their thefts."

Edith held back to let Walter take the lead, "That is what's so disgusting about this. We are ordered to do the very same thing the enemy did." Edith completed his thought, "And we are to do it on the orders of our superiors." Parkhurst could not contain his anger, "That's right. There's nothing superior about this. It's just a another form of grand theft." A voice from the group said, "The difference is that no one is going to shoot us." Parkhurst's face was stone when he replied, "I do not share your confidence," and silent panic froze Gallery A.

Johnny was straining every nerve to follow them. He was intelligent, but he had no experience of this sort of talk. The newness of these words was a big challenge to him, but he understood the ideas. Commanding a battle tank had made him accept the fog of war, but this talk of insubordination was creating a cloud in his head and he wanted to shake it. He pushed the side of his nose with his left hand to get more air into his head, and then he realized just how to keep up with what these men were saying. If he closed his eyes, he could listen to them as he had listened to radios in action. The disembodied voices screaming in his ears in a tank turret were the only way they could survive a battle in a steel box that could flame up like a Ronson lighter. This room was their battleground, and Johnny could listen as he would in a tank battle. His hand shoved his head to the right as he had so often commanded a driver "Traverse right," and he started tracking the conversation again.

Edith broke the silence, "I wouldn't jump to that conclusion or expect to find any comfort in the delusion." Johnny traversed his head to the left and heard an officer ask, "What are you talking about?" He cocked his ear to the left and heard, "You are asking me to betray my country." Johnny elevated his head as Parkhurst rose to his full stature to proclaim, "No, I'm telling you our country has betrayed us." The room erupted and the words exploded over Johnny's head like star-shells at night.

"It's not the country; it's just the government."

"The same government that we are sworn to serve."

As he would command the tank's gunner to "elevate," he raised his head to sniff the words, "It's not the same government. It's just a different regime and that's what really bothers me." Johnny depressed his face to rest his chin on his chest and listened to the worry and hurt in the voices he would not see. He kept his eyes closed tight and followed to the voices running around inside his skull. "Me too. If this order is any indication of things to come, then I am worried for what's next." The one word "betrayal" screamed through the fog like an armor-piercing shell.

Johnny worked his nose to sniff the air, and Glenn and Jimmy nodded and blinked back at him. Jimmy and Glenn and Johnny could smell it. Their nostrils flared to catch the scent of fear. Any combat soldier could recognize that aroma coming over the hill. Rookies' noses were not so keen, but anybody who had survived one battle had his ears and his nostrils honed into a fine instrument. The odor of sweat and "swamp ass" lingered in the room and rose with the officers' indignation. Jimmy knew fear was nothing to be ashamed of. They all knew there was no courage without fear, without risks to face and to overcome. The fragrance wafted from speaker to speaker and grew with every word spoken. Jimmy and Glenn suddenly knew that the geniuses were facing their moment of combat.

There was no fumbled slotting of bullets into magazines, no greasing of rifles or sharpening of bayonets, for they were going to fight with their words and their defiance. Jimmy watched the determined way they unscrewed caps from fountain pens and he thought of canvas covers ripped from machine guns. Here they were fighting with notes scribbled in field message books. Debate was strategy and "Honor" their battle cry. This was Glenn's fight too. He felt a sense of belonging because Edith had invited them into the fray. Jimmy was happy to sit and listen, even if he could understand just one word in ten, because he shared their knowledge of the need to stand and fight. Parkhurst's rage snapped their minds back to attention. "That fool, Schwartz, reminded me I have a wife and two children. I reminded myself of the shame I would bring upon them, if I carried out this order. There are some things more important than the Army brass."

"There is the Commander-in-Chief. The President," a voice said, and another replied, "There are also some things more important than some jumped up haberdasher in the White House." "Such as?" queried another. The reply came clear from Parkhurst, "Such as the honor of the country."

Glenn scribbled the words into his notebook. He understood this was important and was desperate to keep the words. His pencil was running over the pages leaving a trail of sentences like paw prints in snow.

"This is all very high minded."

"What else is our mission? We came here to destroy the Nazis and now our own government is acting just like them with this order. "

"I work at G-5 Headquarters and know this Schwartz. That great streak of stupidity is claiming the only 'safe' place for these works of art is in the United States. It's as though we can't even keep the rain off the *Mona Lisa*."

"That's absurd."

"It's insulting."

"Of course it is. That's just the pretext. But the more ridiculous the excuse is, the more people are supposed to accept it."

"And this particular absurdity came down the chain of command."

"That's right. It's really an order for grand theft. But we are not to question it because that would be insubordination in time of war. We all know what that means."

"He's not being melodramatic or even hyperbolic. I saw a clipping about a Marine in the Pacific. He was shot for not following orders."

"But the fighting's finished. The Germans surrendered."

"But the Japs are still in play, and as long as they are, we are at war and subject to the Military Code of Justice."

"Which can be swift."

To Johnny's left sat a young officer with a shirt too big for his body. The man was intent on the proceedings and was copying notes into his field book. His uniform was rumpled serge. His shoes were well worn but cleaned down to the welts. He had fingers as long as his nose, which flared when Edith said something of interest. The nose seemed to be connected to his fingers because he would bow periodically to the message book and write in tiny letters, which he then surrounded by little boxes. Johnny was fascinated and kept stealing glances over his shoulder to look at the pages filling with little squares, little building blocks of whatever Edith was talking about. Johnny liked the man's fastidious attention to detail and wondered who he was.

The officer wore gold cuff links on his field-worn shirt. Johnny's attention was captured by the links. They bounced up and down as he was writing, and Johnny's eyes followed the golden trail to the bright yellow tip of the officer's fountain pen. The squares were marching down the page in column of route. Inside each square was a neat little dash, so that each box was a perfect reproduction in miniature of everything Edith was saying.

The left cuff link sailed into the air, and Johnny listened to the officer throw a question at Edith with the raised hand of an enthusiastic schoolboy. "Wouldn't this situation interest Janet Flanner?" he asked. Johnny heard Edith give a low squeal of delight. "This would be meat on the table for Flanner. Excellent contribution, Lieutenant Kissel."

Kissel quietly returned to his lettered squares. Johnny whispered into his ear conspiratorially, "Who's Flanner?" Kissel looked intently at Johnny and replied with a twinkle in his eye, "She's a journalist for *Stars and Stripes*." Johnny took a step back in his mind. This officer with the quiet way and the cuff links was more than your average Venus Fixer. He had a sense of stirring it up. Just the mention of this Flanner broad said he knew about this way of fighting with words and was not afraid. Johnny judged Kissel "OK for the Fray," which was about the highest compliment a dogface could pay to any officer.

Jimmy could just about follow the debate, but this was the first time he had been in a room filled with so many ideas and he was getting a headache. He leaned over to Johnny and asked, "What the hell's going on?" Johnny whispered the one word that made them all sit up, "Mutiny." Johnny raised the heel of his hand for a nervous rub of his nose, and Glenn stopped writing. Jimmy's eyes narrowed to "alert" and flashed in admiration of the Venus Fixers. He held back the tears that one weeps for the brave.

Jimmy heard Edith calling his name and jerked to attention. "I think you have something to contribute to our discussion, Sergeant Mulvaney," she said directly to him. Jimmy stood and mumbled through his shyness, "It looks to me like we did so much for the stuff that we got a problem with what the stuff's going to do to us."

Roars and guffaws rippled through the hall, and Edith saw the embarrassment glowing through Jimmy's face. He quickly sat down and hunched his shoulders beneath their laughter. Her eyes narrowed on the mockers through her glasses like a sniper winking through the scope, and said "Sergeant Mulvaney has succinctly stated our problem." Her head traversed over the audience as if she were searching for targets. "It seems I have to remind our colleagues of the basic conventions of rhetoric. Sergeant Mulvaney has admirably encapsulated our conundrum in a simple antimetabole."

This was too much for Johnny, who leaned into Kissel's ear to whisper, "What?" and heard Kissel's almost silent but perfectly articulated response. "You say something twice. The second time you say it, you say it backwards." Johnny caught hold of the tail of the idea, but it was wriggling in his mind.

Edith mercilessly pulled rank and learning on the men and gave a little lecturette on the conventions of 17th century rhetoric. The more quizzical the expressions of the men, the more she poured it on. She found the chink in their pretensions and was twisting the knife as only a lady can.

“Those of you who are not completely culturally illiterate will remember that an antimetabole reverses, in the second clause of a sentence, the grammatical construction of the first clause of the sentence. Sgt. Mulvaney’s theorem is that ‘we did so much for the stuff’ that we are now facing an unintended consequence in ‘what the stuff’s going to do to us.’ We have recovered all of this art so that, sadly, it is in a position to be stolen once again.”

Her eyes scanned the group and landed on the officer who had laughed the loudest at Jimmy. Glenn saw that she was counting to ten. He knew her trick of making people squirm and smiled to see the officer doing just that. No one dared chuckle as Edith intoned, “I also must add that the Sergeant’s grammatical tenses are perfect. He put our wartime mission in the past tense, while the mission of the peace is in the future tense. We are not here to review that past but to decide the future.”

Jimmy was lost. He whispered to Glenn, “What’s she doing?” and Glenn answered, “She ripping the shit outta them.”

“Do you know what she’s talking about?”

“Kinda.”

Glenn was falling in love with Edith who was full of character and brains and just plain good sense. She wasn’t going to sit back and let them lord it over Jimmy. She was going to show them Jimmy had their predicament just right, even if he didn’t have their fancy words. She could give them all more words than they knew, and that was her gift. Glenn saw that she was like Stout, a person of knowledge and understanding, but also one of strength. She was not going to just let things happen. She was fighting with her words, just as he had fought with a rifle. She was amazing.

Edith called for Jimmy to stand up. He brought himself to a relaxed attention and looked into the faces of all those intelligent eyes staring back at him. There was no laughter. There was only the readiness to listen, now that Edith had well and truly wrapped her ruler over their fingers. They dared not laugh, and their smirks retreated behind their shame. Jimmy stood before them.

"Well, you guys have been the experts and we've been the drivers and the guards. We all did our bit for the stuff, and that is what has made it all so valuable. Now we got orders from the American government to do with the German stuff what the Nazis did with everybody else's stuff. That's what's getting my goat. I ain't going to obey no American order that turns me into a Nazi. No way."

Johnny stood up beside Jimmy to second the motion, "We lost too many people to do this. If we follow this order, there'll be rumbling graves from here all the way back Stateside." Glenn saw Kissel's eyes looking straight ahead. Kissel had his own thousand-yard stare, and Glenn knew he was peering into the heart of the matter. As Glenn rose, the feet of his chair gouged a shivering shriek from the floor. "I didn't come here a hero. I'm not going home a coward."

The officers sat nodding their heads in approval of these sergeants three. Edith had hit them in their education, but Johnny hit them in their very manliness. Some of these officers had spent Christmas in London making lists of looted artwork. Jimmy's Christmas had been in Bastogne, and he had decorated a tree with tin foil and hand grenades. The officers were humbled by the dangerous service of these three simple men. Until now, they had risked only their reputations and not their lives. Jimmy, Glenn, and Johnny were surviving proof of the cost of what they were doing. From the hands of those who had laughed the loudest came the first applause. Jimmy, Glenn, and Johnny were confused and quietly sat down as the accolade rippled and rose to a climax.

Walter capped the longest, and Edith beamed approval of them all. Walter asked Everett Lesley to speak. Johnny knew Captain Lesley as just plain Bill. He was one of those feisty professors, and the men loved him because he could hold a Thompson in one hand and a fountain pen in the other. Bill was in such a foul mood that Johnny didn't want to get on the wrong side of either his gun or his pen. The air was full of the aroma of Lucky Strike cigarettes and Players pipe tobacco, but the veterans only smelled combat. Lesley took command and said he was going to "write up something," so they all got up for the Seventh Inning Stretch.

Johnny, Jimmy, and Glenn went to the guard house for some lunch. They explained to the guards it sounded like the officers were going to defy the government for the sake of the art. The guard burst forth, "You don't say," "Shit," "That takes guts," and "Well, someone had to do it!" They were as one with the officers in the gallery. Glenn could almost see the principles they had discussed walk out of the main building and saunter past the guardhouse window. He started to think that maybe words can jump from person to person, dragging the ideas with them. Here were the men understanding what was happening among the geniuses, and really there was no difference. They all agreed on the necessity, indeed the duty, to defy the order. It was clear enough. Jimmy didn't give a rat's ass about abstractions. It was the action that he understood - the doing of right was what made it right. Jimmy believed doing nothing was just a wish, just a hope, like a letter or a present or a package left unopened and unwrapped and forever forgotten.

Johnny was anxious to get back to the meeting. He wanted to hear what Lesley would make out of that room full of indignant rage. "Come on," he ordered, and they followed his lead in lock step to find out what Lesley had written up. They arrived just in time to hear his address. They huddled at the door and heard every word booming through their determination.

"Ladies and Gentlemen, we have composed a statement which expresses our objections to this order. There is no need for further debate. The document will be placed on this desk for one hour. That is time enough for all of us to decide whether or not to sign this record of our views. I will read it, and there shall be neither interruptions for clarification nor points of order."

There was not a movement throughout the room during the entire recitation of Lesley's words.

U.S. Forces,
European Theater
Germany
7 November 1945

1.

We, the undersigned, Monuments, Fine Arts and Archives Specialist Officers of the Armed Forces of the United States, wish to make known our convictions regarding the transportation to the United States of works of art, the property of German institutions or Nationals, for purposes of protective custody.

2a.

We are unanimously agreed that the transportation of these works of art, undertaken by the United States Army, upon the direction from the highest national authority, establishes a precedent which is neither morally tenable nor trustworthy.

2b.

Since the beginning of United States participation in the war, it has been the declared policy of the Allied Forces, so far as military necessity would permit, to protect and preserve from deterioration consequent upon the processes of war, all monuments, documents or other objects of historic, artistic, cultural or archaeological value. The war is at an end, and no doctrine of "military necessity," can now be invoked for the further protection of the objects to be moved, for the reason that depots and personnel, both fully competent for their protection, have been inaugurated and are functioning.

2c.

The Allied Nations are at present preparing to prosecute individuals for the crime of sequestering, under pretext of "protective custody" the cultural treasures of German-occupied countries. A major part of the indictment follows upon the reasoning that, even though these individuals were acting under military orders, the dictates of a higher ethical law made it incumbent upon them to refuse to take part in, or countenance, the fulfillment of these orders. We, the undersigned, feel it is our duty to point out that, though as members of the Armed Forces we will carry out the orders we receive, we are thus put before any candid eyes as no less culpable than those whose prosecution we effect to sanction.

3.

We wish to state that from our own knowledge, no historical grievance will rankle so long, or be the cause of so much justified bitterness, as the removal, for any reason, of a part of the heritage of any nation, even if that heritage may be interpreted as a prize of war. And though this removal may be done with every intention of altruism, we are none the less convinced that it is our duty, individually and collectively, to protest against it, and that though our obligations are to the nation to which we owe allegiance, there are yet further obligations to common justice, decency and the establishment of the power of right, not of expediency or might, among civilized nations.

Lesley stopped reading, and everybody stopped breathing.

Johnny and Jimmy and Glenn moved into the room and made their way through the babble of officers milling around the table. They knew that signing Lesley's letter was dangerous, but they were going to do it anyway.

Edith turned away from one animated conversation and strode back to the table. Johnny asked her, "Got a pen, Ma'am?" Walter saw what was happening and joined them. "We want to sign this," Glenn said. Walter turned to Edith for advice and she spread her hands before her. "I will not allow you to sign this document," she said. Glenn was hurt and demanded to know why. Edith raised her finger, and Jimmy noticed that it was shaking. He smiled to see her wagging that finger at them, but listened to her reasons. "Officers can resign their commissions. Enlisted men get shot." Walter was quick to add, "That's a very real consideration."

Now they understood. She was not excluding them. She was pulling rank to protect them. They nodded their acceptance, along with their respect for "Battle-Ax Edith" and "Fussy Farmer." They walked out of the room as quietly as they could and tiptoed down the corridor as if escaping a birth or a funeral.

They spent the next hour in the guard house, watching the parade of officers leave the compound. Glenn saw that some were glum and others elated, but each had a different walk going out than he had coming in. Johnny listened to the different rhythms of their boots as they left. He remembered everything from the staccato of steel heels on infantry boots sparking over the cobbles to the muffled drumming of rubber soles. His ear was as attuned to the noises of frightened men as his nose to the aroma of fear, and he was hearing a new song. Glenn caught the postures of the officers as they drove by the guard house window. Some were hunched over the steering wheels as if trying to peer through dirty windshields. Other shoulders arched back over the tops of their seats, but each man's pose revealed his decision and his character. Jimmy could smell the difference as their pride wafted by him. His nostrils flared and he wondered why he could also smell steamy soap.

Chapter 29

Portrait of a Young Man

Glenn held the piece of paper like a thing resurrected. His old hand grasped the Manifesto with the reverence of remembered triumphs. More than degrees and certificates, more than awards and commendations of service, this piece of paper held what had made him a man. He looked longingly at the faded type. "So Jimmy even managed to scrounge this."

They all laughed in chorus, remembering the man who could liberate anything and make a life from what other people had thrown away. Judith was curious and said, "This looks like one of those old-fashioned copies." Glenn examined the paper and explained, "When it was typed up, they had five sheets of paper with carbon paper between them. The typewriter sounded like a steam hammer."

Bobby sat beside Judith clasping his hands. His eyes were moist with pride. "I never knew Dad was such a hero. He never told me anything about this."

"That's the way it is with the real ones. The phony heroes are the ones who brag."

Glenn passed the paper for each to see and to lock into their memories. Judith wanted to know about the copy. "I noticed that his signature was much brighter than the typewriting. It looks like he signed it years after he got it."

"He would have had to wait," said Glenn, "As I said, enlisted men weren't allowed to sign it."

Michael understood that Walter and Edith were actually saving the lives of the three sergeants. Something else also became clear. All day his grandfather had been sharing these memories, and the one thing they had in common was just how easy it would have been for Anda to be killed. He could have been impaled in Bastogne, crushed in Merkers, or shot by a firing squad. There were just so many ways he could have died. If any one of those things had happened, Michael wouldn't even be here.

They sat with the last of the day slanting through the windows. The mellowness spreading through the living room was matched by the softened hearts and ripened admiration for a person they had known all their lives but only partly understood. Jimmy was sitting with them as much as if he had not passed away two years before. Glenn sang his praises of the young man who had shared the war road with him. Bobby was the child of the man's maturity and would forever see his father as he had been at forty-five. Judith communed with the old man in whose arms she slept when her grandmother drove them both home from a day at Coney Island. Michael simply nodded to Judith when she said, "Granddad was a very special man."

Michael recalled the last two days and saw the thread running through Anda's tales. There was value in the selling of an old painting at the auction, but each story was the worth of the men who had saved an entire civilization. The Wiseman tribe, old photos stashed in the hall closet, even the golden giants on the library door, all proclaimed people who had known the worth of their lives. These Monuments Men had known the true worth of what they had accomplished, but they had never trumpeted their triumphs. Even that modesty showed them to be bigger people than their enemies. Anda had given Michael the truth of Anda's life. It was a challenge, and Michael knew it.

Judith and Bobby treasured their Jimmy from youth to age and to his death. Sergeant James Mulvaney was all of the Jimmys of their lives, and Judith and Bobby were pleased to have met all of those men who made up one person. Michael was jolted from his séance when Glenn said, "We still have some business to do tonight."

Bobby stood and left the room. Judith sat with her elbows on her knees passing one palm lightly over the other, lost in her thoughts where the others would not intrude. Glenn looked at Michael, "This will concern you," and there was no doubting the command in his tone. Michael was prepared for anything now, for the day had ganged up on him and he had neither objections nor fight left in him. He was prepared to accept whatever would happen.

Bobby returned carrying a picture and held it in front of Michael. “Isn’t that the painting you were telling me about?” asked Michael.

“Which painting? I’ve told you about so many,” Glenn said.

“The one from Merkers Mine. The one Jimmy took home.”

Glenn beamed praise at Michael, “The very one.”

Glenn and Bobby waited for Michael and Judith to drink in the canvas. Michael looked over the buildings, so clearly outlined against the blue sky that was holding Judith’s attention. Together their eyes travelled the road between the farm buildings to the pastures in the middle distance, where the cows grazed and a farmer sat on a fence smoking his pipe. It was a tranquil scene and nothing special. Judith thought she had seen the same thing in Woolworth’s Five and Dime when she was a kid.

Michael looked at the figures in the painting, like when Anda had opened the big picture books in his childhood. He always searched for the people and once even asked of a Pissarro country lane, “Anda, where have all the people gone?” Anda had spun a yarn about everybody having gone to market, except Jack, who was really stupid and came home with some magic beans and received a good spanking from his mother because he’d been a real jerk.

Bobby asked Glenn, “Will you show him or will I?” Michael’s attention snapped back from the beanstalk to the painting. Bobby waited a moment until Glenn said, “No, you show him.” Bobby turned the painting backwards, and the eyes of a young man peered out to Michael. The young man was wearing the clothes of five hundred years ago. A white ruffled shirt peeked from behind the fur cloak draped over his left shoulder. His head was turned sideways and his gaze stared straight out of the painting from beneath penciled brows. Michael thought he was a delicate-looking creature with gentle fingers. The young man looked like he was wearing lipstick.

Glenn sat still, watching Michael's reaction. Michael knew he was approaching some test but could not sniff out what it would be.

Glenn broke the silence and suggested, "Let's play a little game." He stood up and took the picture from Bobby. Glenn placed one corner of the frame on the carpet so that it was standing before Michael at a forty-five degree angle. He held the opposite corner in the palm of his left hand. "You have to decide which picture is 'nice' and which is truly 'magnificent.'" Judith and Bobby placed themselves on each side of Michael and waited for Glenn to start the game.

With his right hand he offered them the farm scene. Judith was the first to yell, "Nice!" and Michael followed her lead. Glenn's right hand slowly turned the canvas so that the young man looked back at them. Together they whispered, "Magnificent." Glenn's right hand repeated the game three times, and they all could tell the difference between nice and magnificent. With every rotation of the frame, Glenn pulled them from nice to magnificent and then let them rest. The beauty of the young man was staring them square in the face, even if he was a bit cock-eyed. They all looked at the young man, pulling in every detail of his face and his clothing.

Glenn now told them to "look through the window over his shoulder." They followed his command, and their eyes wandered to the window behind the young man. They saw faraway mountains and a town in the middle distance. It was the type of detail that would have been missed when looking into the young man's face. Glenn swung the painting back to the farm scene on the reverse. Bobby was the first to make the connection. "The same scene is in this picture as what's on the back." As soon as he said it, Judith and Michael saw the barnyard in a completely different light. At the top of the canvas behind the barn, far beyond the grazing cattle, was the same mountain range and the same town as in the picture of the young man. They waited for Glenn's revelation.

"This is the most amazing hiding place for an Old Master's work. Instead of concealing the painting in an attic, someone hid it behind another painting. Someone removed the portrait of the young man and put it behind the farm scene. Then they nailed both pictures to the original frame. Nobody ever looks behind a painting in a frame. Jimmy took both canvases home rolled up in his socks. He made a frame out of an old table and nailed both canvases back-to-back to the frame."

Glenn swung the painting for Michael and Judith to see the distant scene beyond the barnyard. When he turned the canvas again, they peered over the young man's shoulder at the same distant hills. They looked into the figure's eyes. Judith said, "I thought he was a girl at first." Glenn grinned, "That's Raphael's little joke. You can't tell if this is a man or a woman."

"So what is it?" Michael demanded.

"The experts call it Raphael's *Portrait of a Young Man*," Glenn answered, "but that's because they are just as confused about who this is. It could be anybody of noble bearing. There is nothing in the painting to say whether this is a baron or a model from the streets. All we really know is, whoever he or she is, this person beams self-confidence. I like to think this is Raphael's depiction of character itself and character is something for both men and women."

Michael's eyes delved deeply into the painting and saw the portrait of a young girl. Light shone from her head and drew him into the rectangle of her world. She sat straight in a chair. Her shoulders were relaxed, and her right elbow rested on a table. Her right hand dangled loosely straight down, the fingers slackened. He sensed all of the tension of her body dripping from those fingers as she held herself in perfect balance. He was bathed in the girl's serenity and her eyes gazed directly at Michael. She seemed to be piercing him with soft waves of challenge and those eyes demanded, "What will you do?"

Glenn saw the painting capture Michael, and it was a triumph. He had always known there was a connection between Jimmy and Michael because when they got it, they really got it. He held Raphael's portrait before them and the beauty filled the room.

Glenn did not have to say it, for they all thought of Edith and Walter and all the rest of those monumental people who had made their protest, risking all because they knew "there are yet further obligations to common justice, decency and the establishment of the power of right." The sun dipped low over Raphael's wondrous face and brought them all within its smile.

Chapter 30

The Judgement of Paris

Michael sat at the kitchen table, watching Glenn prepare the coffee. He looked down the hall and the apartment seemed different. That morning, he had expected to be on the road to Pennsylvania, but Glenn had hijacked him to Jersey. He smiled to think how strange had been this day. Sunday with Bobby and Judith had even more surprises than Saturday at Sotheby's. The Raphael lay on the table with young eyes looking up at him.

Bobby had bragged, "Judith is great with the computers," and insisted that she show them her system. Glenn and Michael watched Judith fill the computer screen with hundreds of files and pictures. She had scanned all of the documents in the cornflakes boxes and even created little cartoon icons for each file. When she opened a slideshow of images, some of the photos from Anda's album flashed before Michael's eyes. Glenn saw a picture of traffic barriers on the Queens Expressway and exchanged a quick glance with Bobby. He knew Judith had saved everything on her wonder-machine. She brought up the PDF of the Manifesto, and Michael asked, "Could I have a copy?" Judith happily obliged, tapped her mouse, and the paper rose from the printer like Venus on the half-shell.

Bobby and Judith had made arrangements to visit them next weekend to decide what to do with the painting. Michael was uncertain about what they could do, but welcomed this chance for all four of them to conspire. The adventure was growing and the possibilities appealed to him. Judith had found something called The Commission on Restitution. Bobby explained that it was "some organization that took care of art looted during the war." Glenn played devil's advocate and stated, "We should give it to that commission you were talking about." Judith and Michael exploded into objections. Glenn was pleased that he had provoked them. He grasped his renewed faith in their good judgement.

With his experience of official organizations, Bobby kept his mouth shut and his ears open to the opinions of the young ones. Judith was adamant that “those politicians on those Commissions were just one law removed from jail themselves.” Michael added, “If that Commission is anything like a city hall, we better keep very quiet.” Bobby agreed with Michael, “I seen stuff in the police force.” Glenn was impressed with their skepticism.

They were agreed that the Raphael was too valuable to be entrusted to a bunch of high-class thieves, but Glenn sensed they were talking about more than money. Michael admitted, “It’s a miracle she made it this far,” and they all looked at the Raphael and wondered at its survival. Nobody suggested they take another trip to Sotheby’s. Judith peered curiously into the portrait and whispered what they were all thinking. “She looks like she wants to go home.” They agreed that money would be a roadblock for them finding a way to return the painting.

Bobby was clear that “even if it’s worth a hundred million bucks, selling stolen goods still adds up to zero.” Glenn asked, “So what’s the difference? You puffed the Van Meegeren yesterday.”

“The difference is that was junk people were willing to pay top dollar for,” Bobby said. “It was also your junk, and we were doing you a favor.”

Glenn was unconvinced and pressed Bobby, “So why do we sell one and give back the other?” Michael heard the words catch in Bobby’s throat, “That was just business. This is something else.”

“What’s the something?” Michael asked.

“It’s like the spare parts,” Bobby explained as much to himself as to Michael. “All the stuff in the warehouse is just junk, until someone wants it.”

Glenn and Michael followed Bobby’s idea, but the painting forced him to continue. “Look at it,” Bobby commanded, “This is quality stuff. We gotta do the right thing by it.” They agreed, but were confused as to what they could do.

The more they discussed what to do, the more objections the painting itself raised. If they sold it, they would be rich thieves. If they gave it back, they might be suckers when the Commission claimed they couldn't find the owner and auctioned off the painting "for the public good." If they just kept it, Judith said there was no guarantee that some burglar wouldn't get to it, and Bobby added, "If the house burns down, the insurance will never pay up." Their decisions twisted and turned as had the painting when Glenn spun the frame on the rug. It was getting late and the road back to Brooklyn wasn't getting any shorter, so they agreed to think about it and decide together later. In the meantime, Glenn would keep Raphael's confusing lass or lad. Glenn told them, "I can pull out the Hide-a-Bed for her," and then gently placed the portrait on the back seat of Michael's car.

Glenn had been silent for most of the way home because Michael couldn't stop talking. All the stories had percolated through his brain and now the dam had broken. Glenn answered his questions about Jimmy, Posey, and Stout more to keep Michael going than to add anything in particular. Nothing more was necessary now that Michael was hooked. Michael had all the bare facts Glenn had needed to share and the answer was sitting in the back seat.

When Michael mentioned the painting, he'd jerk his head to the back as if he were asking the image for directions. He bubbled more about Edith and Farmer because their stories raised such perplexing questions. Why had they been so quick to make their protest? Surely they knew they were skating on thin ice just by organizing that meeting.

Glenn said, "There was an even bigger risk, if we didn't speak out boldly." They could not live with themselves, if they just stood around and complained about Schwartz and his order. "They risked their careers. That was enough, but Edith wouldn't let us risk our lives." Michael's head nodded almost to the steering wheel, "That was damned fine of her." Glenn gazed through the misting windshield and said, "Farmer knew all about military justice and just how unjust it could be. He told us of executions for insubordination; all enlisted men." Farmer would do nothing that would put someone else's back against the wall. That was the measure of the man. Glenn capped his opinion with, "He was very much like Edith." Michael turned on the windshield defroster and saw the road clear ahead.

Glenn remained silent on the last leg of the journey home as Michael turned from talking to thinking. The road was glistening, but Michael knew the ice crews had already been at work. He enjoyed the smooth glide all the way over the bridges and through town. The traffic was light and the occasional slow spots were more of a rest than an annoyance, so he sped along happy that the wheels were turning in the right direction as Glenn snuggled into the warmth of the heater. Glenn liked the cocooned feeling of the car at night. Michael was careful with most things, but his car was his treasure. He would spend an entire Saturday washing, waxing, shining, and detailing everything he drove. It was like the way he hung up his clothes without being nagged to do it. Glenn took comfort in the gleaming paintwork, for it was proof that Michael cherished the things which were closest to him. Hope shone off the hood.

The night somehow felt special beyond the surprises at the Mulvaneys' home. There was even a free parking space right in front of Glenn's apartment. Michael backed into it with two swirls of the steering wheel and was glad they were home. They walked up to the front door with Michael carrying the painting. Glenn drew his keys and twisted open the lock with a jerk of his wrist. When they thumped the snow from their boots, Glenn guided Michael into the kitchen and told him, "It's getting late. You should call Anne and tell her you're staying another night."

His eyes bored into Michael's like a challenge. The command to call Anne fit another little piece into the puzzle scattered through Michael's mind. There was a hint of resolution in his voice when he told Glenn, "It's only ten thirty. I can be home by one." The news Michael was going home lifted Glenn's spirits to get to the big question. Glenn had to know what Michael was going to do about "Hello Hello" but it was one of those questions that would cause more problems, simply in the asking. Glenn was completely stumped about what to do and what to say. "I might just be an old man sticking his nose in where it doesn't belong," he tried to reassure himself. "Then again, if Michael doesn't cut this piece of stuff off, the whole family could be destroyed. Ask and thou shalt receive more grief than you imagined."

"Are you sure you want to get back?" he asked more for himself than for Michael.

"I'm sure," Michael said. "Just wait 'til I tell Anne about all that's happened."

"She doesn't know about the sale?" Glenn asked.

"No, I haven't talked to her."

The fact stood boldly between them. Michael had not phoned home, and now they both knew it. Without their saying another word, the problem was out in the open. Each knew that the other knew what neither wished to admit.

"I'll make you a thermos of coffee." Glenn turned his back on Michael to fuss with pots and the stove, and he spent more time than he needed searching in the cabinets for the travel jug, which was right in front of his face. Michael turned the *Portrait of a Young Man* back and forth in his hands and then placed it face up on the kitchen table. He opened his coat, shrugged it off his shoulders, and sat facing the painting. Glenn could hardly hear Michael's low tone when he said, "Anne and I have a lot to talk about." It sounded like a confession dragged out of indecision and Glenn held to it like an anchor. "Are you sure about that?" he gently prodded. Glenn didn't want to turn and look at Michael; his eyes might light a destructive rage and Glenn could not live with that, not tonight.

Michael sat at the table approaching a moment he wanted desperately to evade, but he could not move. Judith had put the copy of the Manifesto in a little plastic sleeve. Michael extracted the paper from his coat pocket and laid it on the table to the left of the painting.

All the men in all the stories seemed to jump out of the translucent envelope and the old album to gather in a chatty circle on the table. Those men had done so much more than he could have imagined. Edith's courage was not unusual in such fine company. They had noble visions in their heads and that quiet valor which goes unsung. He had never heard of the Monuments Men before Glenn opened the album yesterday morning, but their stories echoed in his mind, calling him to a place he had never known. Their sepia shades seemed to merge with the flesh and fur of the painting. Michael's eyes let the colors flow together.

Glenn had to do something. Time was running out in more ways than he could tell Michael. He could not keep Michael over for another night of stories and photos. Glenn wished so much he could take his own years and experiences and all he had learned and just pour them into Michael. That was impossible. Michael had to do this for himself. If he could exchange souls with his beloved Michael, Glenn would gladly give up whatever was left of his life. It would be worth it, but it could not be done.

His right eye caught the telephone table, and he grasped at the little device in desperate hope that he had not gone too far. Michael might run, and there would be nothing left. But courage always walks hand-in-hand with fear, Glenn reminded himself, and he reached beyond his grasp to pick up the phone. Glenn shivered and tussled with the buttons until he saw Hello Hello's phone number burn itself across the amber screen. He turned to Michael, shuffled through two terrified steps, and calmly placed the phone to the right of the *Portrait of a Young Man*.

Michael knew it all. The number said that Glenn knew it all. The portrait gently asked, "What will you do?" Michael felt Anda's eyes cutting into him. Glenn looked over Michael's shoulder to avoid his eyes and saw an old print of *The Judgement of Paris* hanging on the hallway wall. He had kept it there like an old raincoat he could grab at the last minute to take to a class that seemed ready for a story. Passing around the painting made the students look closely at it as he recounted the story of the Greek hero who had to decide which of three women was the most beautiful. Glenn would spike their interest by telling them, "Zeus was a very horny god" and then adding that he was also "a bit of a coward." Zeus had a mortal named Paris choose the winner for him, so that Zeus wouldn't "get in trouble with his girlfriends." Glenn looked down at Michael studying the portrait and remembered Judith's first opinion. Judith thought Raphael's young man was really a woman. If it were so, Glenn thought, "Michael has at least three women to think about, Anne, Hello Hello, and the young woman in the portrait."

Michael knew full well what faced him. In his mind's eye, he saw the Monuments Men from the photos. They shuffled and lounged on the table as if waiting. They were joined by Edith, Nanna, Anne, Sally, and Judith. They all seemed to follow the gaze of Raphael's woman and turned to look at him.

He now knew what this was all about. Anda came from a time when honor was important, but Michael's world had no time for such things. Michael had been born into the "Generation of Me," and his peers wore their selfishness as campaign medals. How could he explain to Anda that the woman on the other end of the number was actually no conquest but a trap? If he told Glenn the truth, it would sound like a lie. Anda would see the truth of that affair as an excuse and have nothing but contempt for Michael. There was no explanation that Anda could accept, let alone understand. That woman had started as an office flirtation and ended as a cage. She had the contracts for snow removal, and every four months she gave them to Michael and to others as she chose. Everything, the mortgage, the bills, even the food on the table depended on those contracts. Michael was completely trapped, but explaining this to Glenn was impossible. Glenn would have to jump into the twenty-first century, but his whole moral code was fifty years in the past. That was two generations, and Glenn was too old for such a leap.

Glenn stood with the coffee pot in one hand and the jug in the other, frozen before Michael. There was nothing to say. Something had to give, if they were not to remain there like pillars of salt. The fumes from the pot wafted up his nose, but Glenn ignored their siren scent and waited. This had to be Michael's time.

Michael's mind was trapped by the table. Decision faced up at him as he marched his eyes from the Manifesto to the portrait to the phone. The page, the canvas, and the amber rectangle leered at him. He felt all those letters, and paint, and numbers had ambushed him. There was no place to hide.

Glenn's fingers were starting to burn, but he did not feel any pain. He knew that *The Judgement of Paris* was as simple as choosing the Prom Queen in comparison with Michael's decision. All Paris had to do was pick the most beautiful woman and Paris had plenty of practice at that. Michael had no preparation for his own choice. Michael had to be the best a man could be, choosing a principle higher than a price.

Glenn neither could nor would help him. There would be no hand to hold him up on shaky skates, no training wheels on his bicycle. Michael would have to face this alone and with silent resolution. Glenn knew such are the moments which test men's souls, and if they don't have one, they always fail. Failure is always an option. Glenn willed Michael to step over that shadow-line separating the boy from the man.

Michael took one last look at the Manifesto and gazed deeply into Jimmy's signature. Michael nodded to the painting, picked up the phone, and pointed it at Glenn. Glenn stood frozen, holding steaming coffee as he watched Michael's thumb dance across the buttons. Glenn's eyes drooped to the phone and he read "Delete" blazoned across its amber shield. Michael's thumb firmly strangled a button and Glenn heard the phone asking, "Are you sure?" Michael pressed the button again, and the sound of the electric rattle gurgling from the phone was like morning bells in Glenn's ears. Michael knew there had to be more certainty for Anda, for his grandfather was never satisfied with a single answer. Everything had to be repeated and reinforced. Michael stood up tall and assured, and the chair made a metallic screech behind him. He pulled his cell phone from the little holster on his belt, and Glenn watched Michael slide open a little door to reveal even more buttons. Michael found the number and selected "Edit." He held the phone open and close to Glenn's face, so that Anda would be reassured when Michael pressed "Delete" for the second and last time. Michael snapped shut the cover and returned the phone to his belt.

They stood looking into each other's eyes. Glenn put the coffee pot on the table, Michael immediately snatched it up. "You don't want to spill any on the picture." Glenn watched Michael place the pot safely in the sink and reminded him what Stout had said, "The Old Masters are tough; that's why they've survived so long."

Glenn offered Michael the thermos and asked again if he wanted to stay the night. Michael was clear that he really did want to get home and that was enough for Glenn. He walked Michael down the hall. Michael held the thermos with a casual "thanks" and told Glenn, "I'll call you next week, and we can talk about what to do." Glenn told Michael to be sure to "give hugs to everybody" and closed the front door.

Glenn went back into the kitchen and saw there were just enough dregs left in the pot for half a cup. He poured what remained into a mug, juggled his ashtray in the other hand, and went to the window to say his "good night." He sat for an hour recounting all the adventures of the day to Ellen and telling her how Michael got the shock of his life when he saw Judith in the driveway. She laughed at this because it had been her idea all along. As the kaleidoscope of lights outside resolved itself into green, Glenn communed with his love in the joy that knows no distance and refuses to accept limits. He blew a smoke ring at the frozen window and raised his mug to say, "Our Little Boy is going to be Okay."

Chapter 31

Old Friends

Michael and Anne walked arm-in-arm out of the shadow of the tunnel and into Spring. The first warm breezes were nuzzling Winter, and it was the time of open collars and slack scarves. They watched Frankie and Teddy squealing twenty feet in front of them. This was to be a special day out, a trip to the city with a big list of longed-for adventures. The boys were ruthlessly taking advantage of everything, along with their parents. They had already been to the big toy store and gotten so many goodies that Michael had to drag all the loot to the car. But that was for later, when they got home. Now was the time for brother to beat up brother, and Momma didn't seem to mind when Frankie forced a handful of snow down Teddy's neck. Teddy was running ahead planning a revenge ambush from behind a frozen tree. Daddy would make sure the games didn't end with stitches in the emergency room. Michael needed no directions to tread through the old paths of Central Park.

There had been decision, but no confession. He didn't have to confess to someone who really loved him. She'd already known enough and didn't need the added pain. After the fifth outraged and threatening voicemail from Goodbye Goodbye, Michael had deleted more than numbers. He had reached the point where the whole thing made him laugh. What amused Michael most was that he had liberated himself from her contract trap just when he could most afford it. When he had stood up to erase her number before Glenn, he had completely forgotten about the money from the sale of the *Head of Christ*. When he was sitting at the kitchen table, it had slipped Michael's mind that he was now a millionaire. Michael had shown courage when he thought he had the most to lose. Now, it was the riches at home he valued the most.

Glenn had chuckled to the living-room window that they had made three point seven million dollars on a real fake, when all the time the real masterpiece was hiding behind a fake. It was a good joke, and they all shared it at Dora's Cafe.

They still had to decide what to do with the Raphael. Glenn was sure they did not have the resources to trace the owner, so they all knew they had to contact the Commission on Restitution. That was the first big problem. None of them trusted any government agency, especially when it came to a work of art worth millions. They all shared a long dinner of boiled beef and latkes, with Solly adding pithy comments, in unrepeatable language, about the government these days.

Bobby was sure those Commission people would "have their very own shysters who would make everything so complicated that the painting would just disappear." Glenn was just as sure the money would magically appear in the bank accounts of the lawyers and the commissioners they represented. Judith had trusted Anne from their first greeting and loved to whisper confidences in her ear as the men argued over the obvious. She turned to Anne and said, "Half the stuff in Granddad's junkyard he bought at government auctions. It's all stamped 'Condemned,' and it's all brand new." Anne nodded knowingly, for she had come to appreciate that Judith always had proof of her opinions. Judith turned back to the men and summed up the inevitable decision. "So, we gotta do a good thing by using bad people."

At their first meal together at Dora's, Solly kept staring at Bobby. He'd never seen anybody eat so much at one sitting. He was proud that his cooking was so appreciated but also worried that, "This guy will eat the whole fridge." Somewhere between the endless trays of pastries, they had decided first of all to have the painting secured. "It's just been dumb luck that it hung on the office wall safely all those years," observed Bobby. The next week, Glenn and Michael rented a safety deposit box at one of the more expensive private banks on Wall Street. It was nice to get the millionaire treatment with free coffee from very polite fat men in expensive suits. They giggled like naughty schoolboys when they placed the Raphael into its tidy little apartment and collected the matching set of keys. Michael quipped as they walked out of the bank, "So that's how the other half of one percent live."

Over the weeks, they had met at Dora's regularly and developed their strategy. Now that the painting was physically safe, they had to figure out a way of keeping it safe. They had endless discussions about approaching the Commission, and Glenn kept drawing circles in his little notebook because that was where all their talk kept going.

The frustration was mounting when Michael suddenly mentioned that officer with the gold cufflinks. They all stared at him as if he were crazy. "Cufflinks?" Bobby queried. Anne didn't know about this part of the story, so Michael dredged up all he could remember from Glenn's tale and said, "That man in the cuff links. He told Edith about some journalist." Glenn reminded them of Janet Flanner and how she had written articles about the 200 paintings sent to Washington after the war. "That officer was on to something when he brought her up," Glenn said. He grinned around the table, "Michael has made the jump from the cuff links to publicity." That was the real break through their maze. They agreed they would have to make the painting public before they went to the Commission. If they could make enough stink about finding the picture and how important it was, they could have many eyes watching over it. The publicity would be like a guard.

Glenn sat back as the others bubbled in excitement. Bobby jumped at the idea because "even those hoodlums can't steal something like this in broad daylight." Glenn saw the sense in this and said he knew three art journalists. "This would be meat to them." He savored the lovely symmetry of Michael's suggestion. Stout had made the connection between the art and the gold in the Merkers mine, and the gold had kept the art safe from looting. Michael had made the connection between the gold cufflinks and the publicity, and the publicity would keep the Raphael safe from backroom deals. Stout had played checkers in Merkers; art jumped from gold to safety. Michael was jolted out of his daydream when he heard Judith ask, "Do you think we could get on Oprah?"

The next problem was establishing the recent provenance of the painting. Glenn explained to Bobby that this meant "the paper trail of the ownership" and that it would complicate the situation to have to explain how Jimmy really came to "own" the painting. Judith perked up at this challenge and devised a lovely solution.

In the drawers of Jimmy's old roll-top desk at the junkyard, she found blank receipt books. There were three different tablets for old stores, but "Melvin's Pawn and Auctions" looked most promising. The store had been bulldozed in 1962 to make room for yet another expressway. She double-checked the city's Register of Deaths and discovered that Mr. Al Melvin had died of natural causes on April 9, 1996. It didn't take her long to rustle up an old Remington typewriter, and after four attempts, she got just the right combination of faint typewriter ribbons and spelling mistakes to produce documents which proved the fact of an "old painting of a woman soled" to "Mr. James Mulvaney on Tuesday, September 4, 1950." Anne signed Mr. Melvin's name and complimented Judith on her forgery. Judith lowered her eyes, and Anne knew that there were more connections between Glenn and Bobby and Judith than she had realized. Al Melvin's receipt was a perfect map to a dead end.

Glenn had contacted the journalists, who jumped at the human-interest story of "Old Master Discovered in Junk Yard." They all had a good cackle about it around the table at Dora's. Anne searched the internet until she found an organization of veterans with an interest in repatriating looted art. Bobby phoned the number Anne gave him, and the man on the other end seemed suspicious when Bobby told him, "Yeah. I got sumfin yous might like to know about." He gave the phone to Judith and the sweetness of her voice melted the skepticism. The veterans' group knew what to do and contacted the Commission. Now there were too many people in the know for the painting to fall through the cracks.

But to Michael, what mattered was the treasure at his elbow and the joy they were having in Central Park. Anne had glowed more from week to week from being included in the little square of conspirators around the table. Judith had noticed Anne and Michael holding hands under the table and was glad for them. But today, the ice was crunchy and shattering into crystal mosaics under their feet. Anne and Michael let the boys run free and watched them plough through the snow. Teddy came racing up to them around the corner. He pointed back and yelled, "There's a big dog over there." Anne took his mittened hand in hers, and Michael said, "That's who we're going to see. He's an old friend."

Teddy was the more sensitive of the two and huddled close to his parents as they all rounded the bend. Frankie was already climbing up the base of the statue. Michael ordered him back to the path, and Frankie immediately jumped down with a great show of bravado. Frankie was clutching the quarter he'd pried out of a frozen fountain. Anne looked at the coin stuck to his mitten and remembered when the Santa in the toy store had asked him what he wanted for Christmas, Frankie simply demanded "cold hard cash."

Michael made Frankie and Teddy look up at the statue and slowly began telling the story of a dog everybody thought was stupid, but turned out to be a real hero. Teddy was especially enthralled by the drama of the sled race and the mission to deliver the medicine. Frankie exclaimed that Balto must have had "awesome legs."

Michael guided them closer to the statue from the path, and Anne watched them crawl up the mound to Balto's back. Michael and Anne were filled with the pride that only comes to fathers and mothers. Frankie was riding Balto's back like a bronco breaker. Teddy grabbed hold of Balto's legs and edged himself along the concrete ledge closer to Balto's face. Michael thought of that dog's magnificent determination all those decades ago and of the people in Anda's life. He remembered Edith Standen and said to himself, "Sometimes courage wears a skirt and wags a finger, and sometimes it wears fur and wags a tail." He hoped he could number himself in such a company.

Michael watched Teddy hold Balto's ear with one hand and gingerly inch his feet along the base of the statue. Michael could not hold back his tears as he watched his son stretch forth his hand to touch Balto's nose.

Acknowledgments

So many people have contributed to the writing of *Balto's Nose* that it is impossible to thank them all.

The first sentence was written while I was discussing Art History with a student, Amanda Ely. Amanda's lovely curiosity sparked the first glimmers of Balto's story.

The first chapters were written at the Wildacres Retreat in North Carolina, when we were the guests of Philip and Amy Blumenthal. Their kindness is reflected in the peace they provided during a turbulent time.

Sean Murray of Dublin, Ireland, read the first chapters and told me to "just get into the middle of the story" which was his way of demanding *in medias res*. Sean's phenomenal command of languages is only matched by his critical insight.

Stephen Preston of London, England, helped form the final draft. His encyclopedic knowledge of Baroque music and Classical literature brought his wonderful ear to the reading and the writing.

Adam Kissel, of Philadelphia, is responsible for the developmental editing. Adam's amazing eye for detail and his magnificent sense of aesthetic proportion kept Balto in the race.

George and Jennifer Matty, of Dover, New Jersey, read and re-read all the mistakes which I made after Adam's editing and made sure that we did justice to the wonderful personalities who people this story.

Anna Thibeault is the source of all inspiration and perspiration in writing *Balto's Nose*. Without her love and belief, this would have been impossible.

Thomas Thibeault

Born in Canada, raised in Ireland, lives in the United States, Thomas has retired from a thirty year teaching career which has taken him to Europe, Russia, the Middle East, and the Far East.

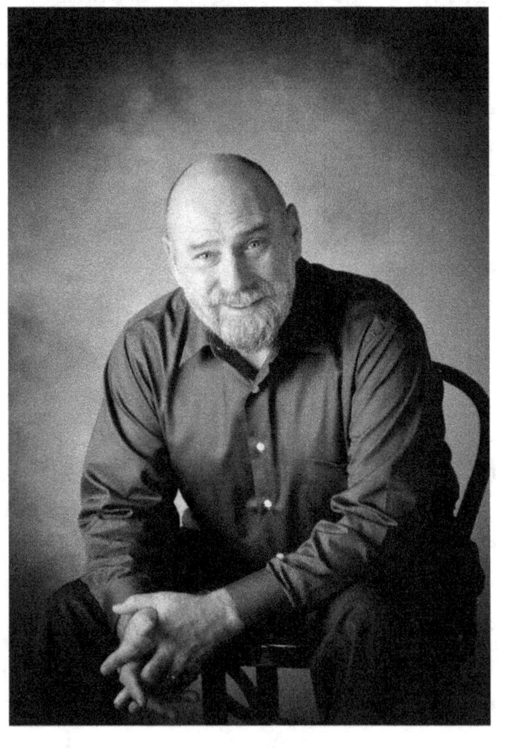

Half a century of wide reading, wider traveling, and concentrated thinking have provoked Thomas into writing.

Those travels involved working as a deck hand, soldier, truck driver in Africa, art model in Ireland, train brakeman in Canada, and a tour guide at the pyramids.

Thomas brings a wealth of experience to writing which expresses our primal experiences. He lives in Georgia with his wife, Anna, and their fifteen cats.

photo: Mark Williams Studio

www.ingramcontent.com/pod-product-compliance
Lightning Source LLC
LaVergne TN
LVHW010601100826
845148LV00014B/2804